PILGRIMS ALL

PILGRIMS ALL

Collected by MARY McKENNA CURTIN,
Formerly of the Department of English, University of Pittsburgh

THE BRUCE PUBLISHING COMPANY
MILWAUKEE

SHORT STORIES BY
CONTEMPORARY CATHOLIC WRITERS

At night was come in-to that hostelrye
Wel nyne and twenty in a companye,
Of sondry folk, by adventure y-falle
In felawshipe, and pilgrims were they alle. . . .
    Chaucer — Prologue to *The Canterbury Tales*

To
MOTHER AND FATHER

Acknowledgments

FOR their kindness in making available the materials from which these stories have been collected, I am indebted to Reverend Valentine J. Koehler, O.S.B., and Reverend Fintan R. Shoniker, O.S.B., of St. Vincent College, Latrobe, Pennsylvania; to Sister M. Hieronyme McCaffrey, R.S.M., and Miss Genevieve Warnock of Mount Mercy College, Pittsburgh; and to Miss Lorena A. Garloch of the University of Pittsburgh. Many of my friends have also been extremely helpful, partly through their suggestions of stories and authors but even more because of their continued interest in the project. I should like to thank especially my former colleagues in the English Department at the University of Pittsburgh; Mr. Robert C. Broderick; Miss Margaret Connolly of Sarasota, Florida; and, most of all, my husband, Dr. Frank Daniel Curtin of the English Department, St. Lawrence University.

Contents

Introduction

I N THE history of the Catholic Literary Revival, no one
fact has disturbed readers and critics more than the lack of
distinguished fiction, written by Catholics from a Catholic
point of view. For almost a century now, since the Oxford Movement first occasioned a revival of letters within the Church, Catholic writers have been producing notable work in poetry and satire,
in history and biography, but not until recently in fiction. Curiously, during this same century the short story developed from an
uncertain, indefinite, almost suspect literary hybrid into a popular
and distinguished art form. Yet only within the past twenty years
have Catholic writers paid appreciable attention to that form.
Only within the past twenty years have they written stories that
compare in literary excellence with those of their non-Catholic
colleagues. Even today in many circles the short story is little
recognized as a significant contribution to Catholic literature. In
1935 Calvert Alexander, S.J., wrote an excellent *History of the
Catholic Literary Revival,* in which he discussed Catholic nov-
elists but made no mention of short-story writers. In 1939 Sister
Mary Louise, S.L., edited a comprehensive *Anthology of Modern
Catholic Literature,* in which appeared selections of poetry, biography, history, essays, and satire, but no short stories. These omis-
sions may be attributed partly to the long neglect of short-story
writing by Catholic authors and partly to the fact that recent
work in the field has been too scattered for adequate evaluation.
Catholic writers may have been slow in discovering the possibilities of the short story, but in recent years they have achieved
more success than has been accredited to them. As the stories in
this volume will show, their accomplishment has been worthy of
note and is today one of the most promising elements in the
Catholic Literary Revival.

The purpose here has been to indicate by examples the work

of Catholic short-story writers within the past two decades. It might be well to say immediately that the Catholic short story has no identity as a separate literary *genre*. Religion, if it enters fiction at all, does so obliquely and not directly; it has no bearing upon literary qualities and form. The assumption here has been that a modern Catholic short story should first of all be a good story; and, since this book has been limited to the contemporary period, an attempt has been made to select only those narratives which conform to present-day standards of good story writing. Those standards vary and fluctuate under analysis, as all artistic standards do. Defining the limits of any art form is always hazardous; yet, when the form is popular, numerous attempts at definition will be made. So it has been with the short story. Ever since Poe first formulated a principle for short-story writing, critics and writers, recognizing the form as a distinct literary type, have been perceiving new patterns and phrasing new definitions for the modern short story. Poe, with his insistence upon "a certain unique or single effect" in a prose tale, first established the distinction between the short story and the novel, a distinction which is qualitative rather than quantitative; and this distinction has been consistently maintained by later writers. In 1885 Brander Matthews elaborated upon the difference between the two forms, pointing out that a short story was not so called only because of its brevity. "A true short story," he wrote, "is something more than a mere story which is short. A true short story differs from the novel chiefly in its essential unity of impression. . . . A short story deals with a single character, a single event, a single emotion, or the series of emotions called forth by a single situation." Later, in 1914, Ethan Allen Cross made a similar distinction. "The novel," he pointed out, "is complex, composed of many experiences, usually of a number of people, pieced together into unity. It is a broad cross section of life; broad enough to cut through many experiences of many people, but still showing them as a unified part of life. The short story is a cross section of life, too, but of a single life or at most a thread of life where it crosses and becomes entangled with one or two other subordinated threads — a section through a knot."

Like the novel the short story depends for its effectiveness upon three elements: the characters, the plot, and the setting; but, because of its narrower scope, it will frequently emphasize one of these elements more than the other two. It is possible, therefore, to classify short stories in three main groups: those which achieve their effect through reality of character, those which possess little characterization but which have strong plot interest, and those which base their effectiveness upon "local color" or setting. In our own day, under the impetus furnished by psychologists, the character story has become the type most favored by writers and critics. In a sense it may be called typical of the twentieth-century short story at its artistic best. Yet, since innumerable stories continue to be written with plot or setting as the predominant interest, it would not be wise to limit any contemporary definition to one particular type. The short story is as varied in form and in content as the novel, and for that reason, if for no other, the most elastic definition will be best. As Bliss Perry points out in *A Study of Prose Fiction*, the short story may be "the merest sketch of a face, a comic attitude, a tragic incident; it may be a lovely dream, a horrid nightmare, or a page of words that haunt us like music."

Although further possibilities present themselves for classifying short stories according to material and form, only one other categorical division need be commented upon here, a division based chiefly upon the manner in which the author handles his idea or theme. Contemporary stories may thus be divided into two main types: the thesis or purpose story and the artistic story. The exact point at which the two kinds diverge is sometimes difficult to define. The difference is mainly one of emphasis and of effect. The thesis story may be said to exist for the sake of explaining an idea. It is didactic rather than artistic and, in its most obvious form, is called propaganda. Although propaganda stories have varying degrees of literary merit, good propaganda often approaching good art, most critics agree that the twain do not meet. In the thesis story, reality of character and of situation are subordinated to the moral or doctrine which the narrative is intended to illustrate. In the artistic story, char-

acter and situation have equal importance with theme. The three
are blended organically, integrated as it were, so that the theme
grows out of the character or out of the situation. Frequently the
importance of plot is diminished and stress is placed upon mental
attitudes of the characters rather than upon physical action. This
latter type of narrative has been often and variously defined. One
of the best recent definitions is that of Professor James W. Linn of
the University of Chicago. According to Professor Linn, the modern short story is "the presentation in a brief, dramatic form of a
turning point in the life of a single character." In this type of
story the theme may occur simply as the meaning of the story
as a whole, as the significance to be drawn from the narrative.
The revelation of character alone may become a commentary on
human nature, and usually does; or the idea may be implied in
the author's attitude toward the behavior of the characters. In
any event, all short stories worthy of serious consideration contain some significant idea, whether implied or expressed, and this
idea may be called the theme. Also, the skill with which a theme
is embodied in a characterization or suggested by a situation
determines the classification of a modern short story as thesis or
artistic fiction.

In Catholic literature the thesis story preceded the artistic. It
did so naturally. The thesis story lends itself easily to any cause,
whether of religion, of philosophy, or of sociology; and in the
early years of this century, ever since the Meynells opened their
drawing room to the *litterati* of the 1890's, in fact, Catholic writers
have been consciously serving a cause: attacking the forces of
materialism, defending belief in God against agnosticism, restoring
spiritual values to a world lost in the mazes of the physical
sciences. Almost inevitably it followed that such writers had little
time for cultivating the art of fiction. Instead, they spent their
talents chiefly on exposition and polemics, with some few carrying
on the poetic tradition of Patmore, Hopkins, and Thompson. Occasionally an essayist or a biographer diverted his attention briefly
toward the short story or the novel and then hurried back to his
own hearth. Occasionally a poet wrote a parable or a prose sketch
which approximated the short story. But these men did not regard

fiction seriously. They used it for variety, as a new means of conveying their ideas, or as a brief form of satire. The result was that for many years Catholic short stories remained almost entirely in the category of thesis fiction.

The best of this type may be sampled in the work of G. K. Chesterton and Hilaire Belloc, both of whom are essentially expository rather than narrative artists. Because they had profound things to say, and because they wrote brilliantly, their stories not only contribute much to the cause of Christianity but also rank with the best of English thesis fiction.

To the writers who have abjured the obvious in favor of the artistic, however, we must look for the kind of short-story writing that contributes most to modern Catholic literature and which holds the greatest promise for the future. For this reason, although a few thesis stories have been included, the emphasis here has been placed upon the artistic type of narrative, where we find a more mature adaptation of the Catholic philosophy in fiction and a more lasting effectiveness. One more phrase requires explanation. Catholic philosophy, as here used, is synonymous with Christian philosophy. In fiction, as in poetry, it is seldom possible to differentiate between what is singularly Catholic and what might be more inclusively called Christian. Indeed, it is doubtful that such a distinction should be made. The short-story writer is not concerned with defining theological differences. His purpose is to interpret in the light of his own philosophical and religious beliefs the nature and behavior of human beings: their joys and their sorrows, their accomplishments and their failures, their loves and hates and ambitions and confusions. In so doing, a Catholic writer will reveal a Catholic attitude toward his material; but, since the Catholic writer is also a Christian, his attitude, more often than not, will be indistinguishable from that of other Christian writers.

The Christian attitude, however, is a matter of paramount importance and one which has been largely neglected in modern fiction. When it has not been ignored or repudiated entirely, it has found, on the whole, a limited expression. Emphasis has been placed on the humanistic aspects of Christianity rather than upon the complete concept, which unites the human and the divine. The result has been a narrow, pessimistic view of mankind. When the spiritual side of man's nature is ignored, the Christian virtues lose their meaning; divorced from their divine source, they cannot have significance, and human existence becomes, at best, a futile effort to retain the effects of the religion without adequate cause. The genuine Christian attitude, while it encompasses all of man's sorrows and weaknesses, offers still a constructive, optimistic philosophy of life. Its center is God, its circumference, eternity. It recognizes in man a spiritual as well as a physical being. It acknowledges conscience and the individual's responsibility for good deeds and evil. It is thwarted not by mystery nor intimidated by fact. It is supplementary rather than contradictory to psychology and the other sciences. It is a philosophy of life based on faith beyond, and only beyond, the limits of human knowledge and reason and understanding.

This is the philosophy which writers of the Catholic Revival have been asserting and clarifying, writers like Jacques Maritain and Eric Gill, Bernard Wall and D. B. Wyndham Lewis, Ross Hoffman and Christopher Dawson. Upon these scholars has rested much of the burden of clarifying and interpreting the truths of Catholicism in relation to contemporary moral and spiritual problems. Part of this task, a small but important part, the short-story writer may assume. His function is to interpret for his readers the meanings and values of ordinary human experience. He writes neither for the mystic nor for the scholar but for the more numerous men and women whose philosophy of life depends upon scattered fragments of the truth gleaned from simplified representations of a greater whole. Fiction writers usually reveal the influence of some school of philosophical thought. It is but natural then that Catholic writers today should reflect in their stories the philosophy of other writers of the Revival. This philosophy may reveal itself not only in the theme or significance of the story, but also in the author's treatment of character and of background.

A short story, first of all, involves a "turning point in the life of a single character," a conflict of some sort: between man and man, between man and nature, between man and his environment, or between man and his God. Now, whether the conflict be completely resolved at the end of the story or be left hanging in mid-air, the author cannot escape, either by direct expression or by implication, some judgment of his character's behavior. Merely by making his readers sympathetic to a character, the writer implies a judgment. Thus, by associating with a certain code of conduct a character whom he makes appealing to the reader, the writer enlists the reader's sympathy for the code as well as for the character. Conversely, the characters whom the reader learns to dislike or disapprove of are those who behave according to a code which the writer rejects, and which he wants the reader to reject as well. In a Catholic story, therefore, we may expect to find the author sanctioning only such behavior as conforms to the Christian moral law, particularly as that law is defined by the Catholic Church.

In treatment of background a Catholic writer need not differ from other writers. He may, but he need not. He is under the same compulsion as they to write honestly and sincerely of what he sees and knows in life. One advantage he has. The Catholic scene has not been adequately dealt with in American and British fiction, so that a comparatively new field presents itself. Paradoxically, it has been best portrayed, and most sympathetically, by a writer who is not a Catholic, the eminent American novelist Willa Cather. In other instances, the Catholic environment has been presented unfavorably usually for the purpose of exposing the hypocrisies and the ignorance, if not the evils, of certain Catholics. Such books have been challenged by Catholic critics, sometimes unjustly. One of the services of fiction is to make readers aware of the ills of society, so that they may be corrected; and no honest Catholic denies that his religion suffers from the conduct of some of its votaries. Nor need he fear the truth in any part, so long as it is not misrepresented as the whole. On the other hand, all Catholics have a right to resent a book which portrays their religion as a stifling influence upon the moral and intellectual advancement of the individual. Such a view indicates not only a complete misunderstanding of the religion but also an extremely limited knowledge of Catholic life. The Catholic writer can correct such an impression, not by contradiction but by counteraction. He can write about people who suffer the same sorrows, the same doubts, the same temptations as other men, but whose religion acts as a vital force for good in their lives, a sustaining power as real as the bread they eat. He can and must be honest and frank. He need not sacrifice the realism which modern writers cherish. Although he may condemn it, he need not gloss over sin when he sees it. His obligation is to know his scene well and to treat it justly.

Before he can achieve anything at all through fiction, however, the Catholic writer must cultivate his art. He must learn the technique of good storytelling. He must become skillful in presenting a character, dramatically and convincingly, in a critical situation. He must learn how to create suspense and avoid the obvious. And he must realize that the short story is no longer a medium for religious teaching as it was in the Middle Ages. The modern story is secular rather than religious. If the writer's convictions are strong, they will be reflected in his work, but no amount of conviction and zeal compensates for literary mediocrity. If a story is not well written, it had better not be published. It will fail to achieve the effect desired by the writer and may prejudice the reader against the material or the ideas which the author is attempting to express.

The stories in this volume do not all possess the same degree of literary excellence, as they do not all deal with equally significant ideas; but the group as a whole represents a substantial amount of good story writing, certainly enough to allay for some time the complaints of the readers and critics who believe that expert Catholic writers do not write fiction. In another way these stories have importance. Since its origin in the days of Defoe and Addison, the modern short story has never before been so lacking in positive values as it has been in the twentieth century. The supposed threat of science to religion started a decline of idealism in fiction, and the first World War completed it. By 1918 the writers of England especially and of America also were suffering from acute disillusionment, caused partly by war and partly by disappointment in the omnipotent promises of the natural sciences. In the English short story this frustration manifested itself in a negative, cynical philosophy of life. In the American, it found some outlet in the cause of social reform. But, by and large, modern short-story writers have appeared, to their readers at least, a doubting and an unhappy lot. At the same time, the fact must be recognized that they have been writing not only for but about a skeptical and an unhappy age. Whatever of despair and cynicism are to be found in modern fiction may be attributed to the society from which it springs. Yet one also looks to the writers for the first signs of change. In a sense fiction writers serve a dual purpose: they reflect the ideas and morals of the society in which they live, while they simultaneously contribute some influence toward the change of those same ideas and morals. The concrete expression of Christian ideas and ideals to be found in these stories, therefore, may be taken not only as the promise of a salutary effect upon the minds of readers but also as an indication that the Catholic Revival has become stronger and its influence more widespread.

To The Mountains

PAUL HORGAN

i

JULIO lay as quietly as he could. Only his eyes kept moving,
turning toward the open door that led into the other room,
as if by looking there he could hear better what the women
were saying. His brother Luis was asleep beside him. The same
blanket of catskins covered them both. Luis could sleep no matter
what happened. The firelight on the walls and the ceiling was
enough to keep Julio awake, even if his mother were not weeping
in the next room. It was a silent night outside; like all the other
nights in this place of home.

"When the fire goes out I will go to sleep," thought Julio; his
legs ached from holding them still. Four nights ago his mother
had given birth to a baby girl. Josefina Martinez came nine miles
from Bernalillo to assist. The father was in Mexico on a wagon
train. The trade in the summer and autumn of 1800 was promising, and the weather very fortunate. Rosa's baby came with no
one there but her two sons and Josefina the midwife. They made
a huge fire in the front room and left the door open so that the
heat would wave silently through. The boys stayed outdoors and
shuddered like horses under the November moon. From within
came the wafting firelight and the nimble sounds of repeated
sufferings.

Each boy felt like the deputy of his father. Luis was sixteen
and Julio was thirteen. Luis was a stout boy — legs and arms like
cottonwood branch, round and wieldy. Julio was slender and
something like a half-grown cat in his physical ways. He was

From *Figures in a Landscape* by Paul Horgan. Published by Harper and
Brothers. Copyright, 1937, by Paul Horgan.

wary and respectful of life's dangers. He had grown with caution, because fear slowly told him more as he grew up. Everything Luis did easily, because he was older, Julio had to learn to do because he was younger, and thus everything was harder for him. The boys had no one but each other for companions, mostly; for they lived in the Rio Grande Valley a way out from the village of Bernalillo. They sometimes went there on horseback, when their father could spare the animals from work in the fields. Once, riding to town, Julio's horse had stamped and run wild, because a hunter in the tall saplings by the field near the river had shot his musket at a rising goose. Julio often dreamed of it, and the triumph of regaining the horse's head.

The brothers slept and the firelight faded down.

In the back room, Rosa presently slept too, and Josefina sat watching her and the new baby.

Josefina was greatly girthed, with two circles of fat at her middle. She was heavy-faced and her eyes were kind, even when her tongue was sharp and filthy. Thus her character: good heart, from instinct; wicked mind, from dealings in the hard world.

The baby lay by its mother's side.

"The face of a *piñón*," thought Josefina, staring at the tiny brown head and the little open mouth that breathed so roundly.

The house was thick as a fortress, with adobe walls. It stood on a little green flat of land above the fields, beyond which lay the Rio Grande. Over it went two mighty cottonwoods, planted by the grandfather of this house a long time ago, who himself had left the service of the Governor of New Spain to scratch his own land and yield it to his own sons. To the east the fields faded into mesa country, rising face of gravelly sand that held dusty bushes. The mesa rolled away and lifted hills where little pine trees grew. In morning, distant under the early sun, the pine trees seemed to exhale a blue air; and from the blue air rose the mountains, whose mighty trees looked, far away, like scratches upon the face of blue rock.

The mountains were miles away from the house of the family, and sometimes they were altogether hidden by weather: cloud, or rain, or wind alive with dust. At other times the mountains were momentously close, as if moved in golden light by the hand of God, and every cañon, every wind course and water hollow in the rock, stood clear to the eyes of the wondering brothers. Hardly a day of their lives failed to be somehow influenced by the mountains off there to the east.

Josefina came into the front room to kick some more wood on the dying fire; for cold was quick to get through her petulant flesh.

She woke Julio; but he lay with his eyes shut, identifying the noises she made, and the profane rumble of her musing. When she went back, he heard his mother speak sleepily; then the baby squeaked and began to cry, what sounded to him like a mortal utterance and farewell of that alien little life in his mother's bed.

"Yes, if you all four of you get through the winter, that will be one of God's little jokes," said Josefina, slapping her hands on her cold belly. "This house never gets warm; and nothing to cover with, those boys out there, freezing on the dirt floor with a dirty old catskin . . ."

"My husband will bring back plenty of money and furs and clothes from Mexico," said Rosa. But she began to cry again, and mumble little sad doubts against the baby's hot temple.

"So, I will stay as long as I can," said Josefina. "But you know that can't be forever. — Be quiet now. You will choke the baby. Here, I'll take her, though God knows she may freeze to death. Get back to sleep. I will warm her."

Josefina took the baby.

Julio leaned and crouched from his bed to see what they did. There was a coldly steady candle burning by the wooden saint in the corner of the bedroom. Josefina held the baby with one arm . . . at her warmest and most copious being, she laid the baby . . . and drew her dress together and held her arms like a cradle. Her cheeks quivered at the striving touch of the baby; some pleasure deepened in her being; and for no reason that she could recognize, out of her assortment of past events — midwife, servant, thief, and harlot — she began to blush.

Her eyes watered and she smiled and sighed.

Julio backed into his bed again. His brother Luis flinched and jerked like a dog that is tickled when it dozes. Julio held his breath for fear he would wake Luis. Yet he wanted to talk to him. He wanted to stir his brother into a fury of doing; to save this family; to prove that it was not a world for women — that it was their own little tiny sister who so blindly threatened their mother's life and will, and who opened the disgusting bosom of a fat witch to lie there for warmth!

So his thoughts were confused and furious.

The fire was alive again in little flames like autumn leaves. He could not sleep. He could not forget. He hated his fears. They were with him, vaguely enlivened by Josefina's talk.

It was not long before winter.

In the broken darkness of firelight, Julio lay awake and prayed until he was answered by the same thing that always answered prayers, the earliest voice he had been taught to recognize, which no one else had to hear — the voice of God Himself in his own heart. Father Antonio made him know when he was a very little boy that the stronger a man was, the more he needed the guidance of God. So when he felt afraid and feeble alongside his mild strong brother, he had only to pray, and shut his eyes, and remember Jesus, who would presently come to him and say, "I see you, Julio Garcia; it is all right. What is it?"

"The mountains, to the mountains," thought Julio in answer to his own prayer.

"Blessed is the fruit of thy womb: Jesus . . ."

"What is in the mountains?"

". . . now and at the hour of our death."

"There is much that my brother and I can do in the mountains, and as soon as he awakens I will tell him; we will take my father's musket and go hunting; we will bring home skins to keep our little sister warm, and show our mother that this is a house of men, who do what is right, no matter how hard it is to do."

"Amen."

ii

Against the mica panes of the small deep window the early daylight showed like fog, silvery and chill. Luis jumped alive from sleep and went like a pale shadow to the dead fireplace, where he blew ashes off a few remote coals and, shivering in his bare skin, coaxed a fire alive. Then he found his clothes and got into them. He began to laugh at Julio, curled like a cat under the mountain-cat skins, waiting for warmth in the room. Then he thought with pleasure of the work to be done outside, in the marching dawn; cold mist over the river; the horses stirring; animals to feed and release. He went out, already owner of the day.

Julio was awake all that time; and he squinted at the fire, judging nicely just when it would need more wood, lest it go out; and just when the room would be comfortable. He was soon up, listening for sounds in the other room. Presently Josefina came to make breakfast. She felt tragic in the cold morning, and her face drooped with pity for her heart which was abused.

"I am going home," said she.

"No, you can't do that," said the boy.

She looked at him with sad delight in his concern.

"Why can't I? What do I get around here for my pains? I was freezing all night."

"When my father comes home he will pay you plenty. Luis and I can — we will bring you a glorious piece of fur."

"Oh, indeed; and where from?"

"We are going to the mountains."

"A pair of fool children like you? Another thing for your poor mama to worry about! If she lives through the winter it will be very surprising."

"What do you mean?"

She had nothing to mean, and so she made it more impressive by quivering her great throat, a ridiculous gesture of melancholy.

Julio ran outside and found his brother. They did not greet each other, but fell into tasks together.

The sky was coming pale blue over the river, and pale gold edges of light began to show around the far mountain rims. The house looked like a lovely toy in the defining light, its edges gilded, its shadows dancing.

"Luis."

"What?"

"I have an idea."

"Well?"

"Did you feel cold all night?"

"No, but you would not lie still."

"I am sorry. I heard Josefina talking to Mama."

"The poor old cow."

"Do you realize that we are so poor that we haven't got enough things to keep us warm, especially with the new baby here? And an extra woman in the house? — She ought to stay with us until Mama is well again."

"What are you going to do about it?"

"You and I should take the musket and go to hunt cats in the mountains, and bring home enough furs to satisfy everybody."

"Yes," said Luis, without surprise, "I have thought of that, too."

"Then I can go?"

"I suppose so — if you behave yourself. It's no child's errand, you know."

"Of course not. Then will you tell Mama?"

"All right."

Now the smoke was thick and sweet above the house.

The light spread grandly over the whole valley.

Luis went to his mother's bedside and leaned down. The baby was awake and obscurely busy against her mother's side.

"Mama."

"My little Luis."

"Julio and I are going to the mountains for a few days, to get some furs."

"No, no, you are both too young! That little Julio is just a baby. Now, Luis, don't break my heart with any more troubles!"

"What troubles? We have no troubles!"

"Your father is gone, we have no money, my children shiver all night long, that Josefina is a fat crow, Father Antonio hasn't been near us since the baby was born."

She wept easily and weakly. Luis was full of guilt, and ideas of flight. He leaned and kissed her cool forehead and laughed like a big man.

"You'll see. We will come back like merchant princes."

"Then you are going?"

"Yes, Mummie, we'll go."

She stared at him in a religious indignation. This was her son! So even sons grew up and went away and did what they wanted to do, in spite of all the things women could think of to keep them back!

Later Julio came to say good-by, and she shamelessly wooed him to stay, with the name of God, and her love, and his pure dearness, and various coquetries. He felt a lump in his throat, so he shrugged, like his father, and went to the other room, where he paused and said, "Thank you, Josefina, for staying until my brother and I get back."

"The devil takes many odd forms," said Josefina with a pout.

They had two horses and the musket which their father had left at home upon his last departure for Mexico. They had a rawhide pouch containing things to eat, loaves and chilies and dried meat. As soon as they were free of the little fields of home, Julio began to gallop; and Luis overtook him and, saying nothing, reached out for the halter and brought him down to a walk. Julio felt very much rebuked; he sat erect on his horse and squinted his eyes at the mountain rising so far ahead of them, and thought of himself as a relentless hunter.

The boys toiled over the land all morning.

They paused and looked back several times, touched by the change in the look of their farm, which lay now like a box or two on the floor of the valley; and they thought respectively, "When I have my farm, I shall want to be on higher ground," and "What if something dreadful has happened since we left home! If the baby choked to death, or a robber came, I should never forgive myself."

The mountains looked strangely smaller as they advanced. The foothills raised the riders up, and from various slopes the mountain crowns seemed to lean back and diminish. The blue air in cañons and on the far faces of rock slides and broken mighty shoulders was like a breath of mystery over the familiar facts of memory.

"Let me carry the musket now for a while."

"No, we might as well decide that now. I am to have it all the time."

"Why, that isn't right!"

"No, I have had more experience with it. It is our only arm. Now be sensible."

"Just because I am the younger, you always do this way. I tell you, I am an excellent shot."

"You may be. But I am nearly four years older, and — I just think it better this way."

"I wish I'd known before we started."

"Why don't you go back, then?"

"I will."

But they rode on together. Easily triumphant, Luis could afford to be indulgent; later on he rode close to Julio and knocked him on the back and winked.

"You think I am not as much of a man as you are," said Julio bitterly.

"Well, you're not."

"You'll see! I can show you!"

The brothers' love for each other was equally warm, but derived from different wells of feeling. Sometimes they felt only the love; at other times, only the difference.

Now in afternoon, riding on the windy November plain, and knowing that before nightfall they would be in the very shadow of the nearest mountain reach, they felt their littleness on that world. The air was lighter so high up above the river valley. They looked back: an empire of sand-colored earth, and there, in the far light, the river herself, furred with trees. They looked ahead, but in doing that had to look up.

It was a crazy giant land; a rock that looked like a pebble from here was higher than a tree when they got to it.

"We must find a place to leave the horses."

"What?"

"You idiot, we can't expect horses to climb straight up cliffs like that over there!"

"Sure, we'll find a place to leave them."

"It must be nearly too late to go into the mountains tonight."

"We'll make a fire here."

"If it is clear enough tonight, they could see our fire from home."

"They could?"

The thought made Julio shiver. But then it was already getting chilly. The sun was going down.

iii

They awoke the next morning under the cold mountains, and in their rested souls there was a mood of gods. They caught their horses and rode along the last little flat before the great rise, and before the sun was up over the rocky shoulder they had found a little box cañon where there was a growth of straw-colored grass, and through which there washed a small creek. Leading the horses, they walked far into the narrow shadowy cañon and at last Luis said, "There!"

"What?"

"Here is the place to leave the animals. We can make a little fence down here, and then be safe when we go off to hunt."

"What will you build your fence with?"

"Some big rocks and then a lot of branches that will seem high to the horses."

"Where does that river come from, do you suppose?"

"If you'll stop talking long enough to get to work, we'll go and find out."

The light of builders came into their eyes, measuring, devising; after a few trials they had a system for their work; they moved harmoniously. Given need, materials, and imagination, nothing wanted. They grew warm, and threw down their coats. The sun quivered in watery brilliance high beyond the rocky crown.

When they were done, they untethered the horses and took up the food, the musket, the powder, balls, their knives, their tinder, and went up the cañon, following the creek. It led them into shadow; they had to wade; the rocks widened — sunlight ahead; then a miniature marsh with moss and creatures' tracks; then a little waterfall, which they heard, a whisper in diamond sunlight, before they saw it; and under it a black pool plumbed by the sun to its still, sandy floor.

The fall came down from a rocky ledge halfway up the face of a gray stone cliff.

The forest shadows beyond it, which they saw looking up, were hazy with sunlight and noon blue.

"We'll swim!"

The boys took off their clothes and fell into the water; for a moment they hated the cold shock, and then they were happily claimed by the animal world. They were away from everything. They were let to their senses. They dived and splashed and bellowed, awakening the silences to echo, which only tempest and beast had awakened before them. This was a bath of a superman; not the idle, slow, muddy, warm current of the Rio Grande, which suggested cows and babies paddling and hot mud drugging boys who swam in summer.

They came out into the warmer air and slapped until they were dry; then they dressed.

"Up there — we've got to get up there someway."

Luis pointed up to the higher world beyond the fall. There were gigantic pines standing in light-failing ranks; and behind them a great plane of rock shaggy with its own breakage.

So they retreated from the waterfall and went around it, climbing and clawing until they had gained the upper level. They stood to listen. Enormous and pressing, the quiet of the mountains surrounded them. Their eyes, so long limited to a tame river world, hunted ahead. They were explorers, so far as they knew. What no man has ever seen before! There was a mysterious sense of awe in the first eye that owned it.

As they passed in and out of shadow they felt alternately cold and warm.

As they went, they were often forced by the huge silence to stop and let their own sounds die away.

They would laugh at each other at such moments, then go on.

In midafternoon they thought they must plan to go back, since it took them so long to come. The horses would need company and perhaps protection against beasts.

The sun was yellower and cooler.

The way they had come no longer looked the same; coming, they had watched another face of it; now, retreating, they had to look back often to recognize their course. They lost it, or thought they had, when they came to a bench of gray stone in a spill of light through branches. They then looked aside, and saw the ledge curve and vanish in a stout hillside, and emerge a little farther on and there become the rocky shelf over which rustled their waterfall of the sunny noon.

"It is made by Heaven for our purposes!" said Luis.

"Yes, it certainly is. — How do you mean?"

"Well, the cats probably come and drink and lie here, and other animals. We could be here on this shelf, you see."

"And fire down on them?"

"Sure. Come on."

They started along the ledge and then shagged back and nearly fell down to the cañon floor below when a boom of air and shock arose and smote them from a few feet ahead. It was the thunder of a great bald eagle who beat his way off the rocks and straight up over them, his claws hanging down, his hot red eyes sparkling for one tiny second in the light of the sky. Then he wheeled and raised his claws and extended his head and drifted off in a long slanting line like the descent of the mountain edge over which he vanished.

The boys were breathless.

It scared them.

It also hushed them — the grandeur of that heavy bird leaving earth for air.

"How I should love to get a bird like that!"

"To kill him?"

"Or at least get some of his feathers."

"Maybe he dropped some."

Julio moved forward and then crouched and called for his brother.

"Luis, look! Hurry! Here is what he had!"

They were looking at a partially picked mountain-lion cub, off which the eagle had been feeding.

"Julio, you see, now? Here is where the big cats will come. They will roam until they find it, and they will watch. The eagle carried off the baby cat. He'll come back, too!"

Julio acted like a very small boy. He kicked the carcass of the cub off the ledge into the shaly slide below.

"What did you do that for?"

"I don't know."

"It was wonderful bait! Now it's gone!"

"Well . . ."

"Oh, come on!"

The godlike temper and power of the day were gone for them both — Luis exasperated, Julio tired and guilty.

As they went down to the cañon where the waterfall seemed to stand, not fall, in a mist of blue shadow now that the sun was sinking, they looked up, and saw the eagle so high that he seemed like a spiraling leaf, and Luis shrugged and said, "Oh, cheer up! I suppose he would have come back anyway and carried his supper off!"

But Luis, though he was again friendly, could not offset the chilling of the whole day; and the rocky clear cold cupping of night in those walled places closed over Julio and confirmed his hunger, his bitterness, his youthful rue at the turn of happiness into misery, like the turn of day into dusk.

All right, if everybody was older than he was, let them parade and give orders. If Luis felt so superior, Julio would show him some day.

They scampered down the cañon as fast as they could, for where they had left the horses was a station of home to them.

When it was dark enough, they looked for stars, and saw some, but clouds had come, and a damp, warmish wind, and the cañon talked in wind, trees keening, and now and then an almost silent thunder of a wind-blow when it met a distant high rock mountain-face.

By the last light of their fire, Luis examined his musket, to see that the day's toil over hard ground hadn't damaged it any.

"Let me see it," said Julio.

"What for?"

"Oh, can't I just *see* it?"

Luis handed it over.

Julio sighted along the barrel.

"She's a lovely one," he murmured. Then he gave it back, ready to go to sleep, chuckling with affection for Luis, who would be so surprised.

iv

Dawn came with a ghostly diffusion of misty light — the slow march of shapes.

Julio was ready.

He rolled with almost infinite slowness to the ground, free of the blankets, and left Luis slumbering like a mummy who knew the cold of centuries.

He crouched and slowly went around the other side of the bed, and took up the musket and ammunition from the side of his brother.

He sniffed the air and it was bitter sweet with cold and some drifting new flavor.

He didn't know, in his excitement and caution, that it was the presage of snow.

He went up the cañon chewing on a hank of jerked meat from his pocket. He was abroad in his own wilderness, with his own gun; in effect, with his own destiny. He remembered yesterday's trail very well, and he toiled while the light grew; yet, there being no sun, everything had a new look, though he had seen it before. He came after a long time to the pool and the waterfall. There he stopped and looked back. Now he realized how far it was; how many hours divided him from Luis, who must have been awake and wondering hours ago.

What would Luis do?

Would he kick the hard ground in fury, and halloo for him? Or would he set out in pursuit?

But which way would Luis decide to go?

Or perhaps he was weeping at the conviction that his beautiful young brother Julio had been carried off in the night by beasts of prey.

Then the image of a devouring lion shouldering a musket was too odd, and Julio laughed; then he smartly turned to see where another's laugh came from; then he laughed again, at his echo in the rocky room with the sky roof.

The waterfall was like a wraith made of heavier air than the gray essence that filled the intimate little cañon.

"The cats will come to the ledge," thought Julio, faithful to his brother's wisdom, even though he outraged it.

He went around the long way, slowly going across the fat roll of the rocky hillside, and found himself then in the tall forest up there. He knew that a hunter must wait; so he settled himself to do so on a tiled shelf of moss, between two big boulders, lacy with fern and dark with shadow.

His stomach was clutched by doubts and partly whetted hunger. Hardest of all was to keep the silence of the mountains, lest he startle his game.

Many times he was ready to get up, relieve the ache of his set legs, go back to Luis and pretend that he had only wandered a few feet away from camp.

But he was afraid now. He was afraid of the way the sky looked, dark and soft, and wind very high up which pulled the clouds past the peaks as if tearing gray cloth on the sharp edges.

He was lost, really.

The musket was a heavy sin across his lap. It was loaded. Perhaps he should unload it and scamper back.

But then, if a mountain cat came to the ledge, he would be helpless.

Then he remembered for the first time that he might be in danger from the animals. It sent blood back through him, and he grew angry at such menace.

"If they think they can hurt me, they are crazy, those wildcats!"

So he spent the early day and noon in thoughts of himself and his furies, while the peace of the forest was held, and the sky now came down in darkness and again blew upward in windy lets of silvery light.

And he stayed, watching.

He was so alone and silent that the first touch on his cheek out of the air startled him, and he turned his head quickly to look; but what had touched his cheek was the snow, shortly after noon.

It came down, dandled by the odd currents of airy wind in the irregular mountains, like white dust sifting through the ancient stand of trees up the mountainside.

Julio blinked at the spotty snow falling before his eyes, and he licked the delicious flakes that starred his lips.

The rocks were beginning to look white. The air was white, and the distance was white.

The distance was reduced. When he tried to peer as far as he would, his sight seemed to go so far and then turn black.

All suddenly, a most childish wave of lonesomeness broke over him, and he knew how far away he was, and how solitary; how subject to the mountains.

He got up.

Something else moved, too, in the whitening world.

He saw it, obscurely dark against the white stone shelf below him in line of sight. It was a mountain lion coming down the ledge with beautiful stillness and almost the touch of snow in its own paws.

Its heart-shaped nose was along the ground, smelling the fresh snow and whatever it covered.

Julio lifted the gun, which was as light as he wanted it in this moment, and watched, and licked the snow off his upper lip. Then, with his eyes wide open and his cheeks blown up, he fired.

He couldn't hear the lion cry, or the echo of the amazing blast through the cañons and the aisles. He was deaf from it. But he sat down behind his rock and watched while he reloaded, and saw the cat spilling its blood on the snow; and then gradually he could hear it moaning as his head cleared. Then it suddenly died. The snow continued on it passively, cooling the blood, and making it pale, and finally thickening over it entirely.

After a long time Julio came down from his rock and touched his game.

He glanced around to see if any more cats happened to be there. There were none. He was exalted and indifferent. He rolled the heavy lion off the ledge down to the sloping hillside below it.

There the snow was thinner. There he set to work to skin the cat, as he had watched his father skin animals at home, for leather, for fur, for rawhide.

v

His knife was so wet and cold that it tried to stick to his hands. He was late in finishing. He felt proud.

Maybe Luis would be annoyed, but not for long. To bring home the first fur? He had a loving warm tender heart for all animals, now that he had conquered one of the greatest. He felt that animals must love men in return, and serve them humbly.

Done, then, he returned to thoughts of others, and then he could have groaned aloud when he really imagined what Luis might feel.

"Do you suppose my brother is in danger because I took away his gun? What if he has been attacked? What if I had not had the gun when the lion came? It would be the same with him, without any protection! Oh, my Jesus and my God, help me to get back in a hurry, and have him safe when I get there!"

Now, with heavying snow and night beginning to fall, the hunter could not scramble fast enough to undo what his day had done.

He shouldered his new skin, which was freezing and heavy, and his gun and his supplies, and went down off the shaly hill. In the bottom of the chasm, where the waterfall entered the stream, it was dark. The black water of the creek alone was clearly visible. He stopped and called out, then turned to listen, but the spiraling flaky darkness was vastly quiet.

He hurried on and sobbed a few times, but he said to himself that it was simply that he was cold, not that he was sorely afraid and sorry.

"Certainly I can see!"

But he paid for this lie when he struck a rock that cut his cheek and threw him down to the ground, where the soft copious snowfall went on secretly to change the mountains, to enrich stony hollows with soft concavities, to stand the bare ridges barer above snowy articulations.

He struggled to make a small fire, scratching twigs and needles and branches from the lee side of rocks, having to feel for his wants. At last he produced a flame, and his heart leaped up, the firelight on the snow was so lovely. In the light he saw where he was, and collected more branches, building craftily to bring up his flames, until the cañon was roaring with light and heat at that spot.

He sat, then lay on his new fur, with the raw side down.

The snowflakes made a tiny, fascinating little hiss of death when they fell into the fire.

"Luis will be all right. I will get to him early in the morning; as soon as it is light I shall start out."

He dozed and awoke, at last to see his fire gone. Then he knew he must stay awake.

What he knew next was so strange that he felt humble. In spite of trying not to, he had fallen asleep, and was then awakened afterward by wave after wave of sound, through the falling, falling snow which hushed everything but this clamor that had awakened him, the ringing of a bell. The bell clanged and stammered and changed with the wind; like the bell of the church at home, miles up the valley on a still hot summer Sunday morning.

"But this is not — there can be no church in these mountains!" he said in the blackest density of the snowfall that night. And he listened again, but now heard nothing — nothing beyond the faint sense of hushing in the air made by the falling snow.

The bell was gone; it had served to awaken him; somewhere beyond this cold separating fall, it had rung out for him — true, even if it came to him as a dream of security. He did not lie down again; but sat, marveling, and sick for home.

vi

The snow continued with daybreak.

He set out again as soon as he could see a few feet in front of him. As the light grew, so did his sense of folly. It was as if he had dreamed of the things that might happen to his brother Luis.

All his greatness of accomplishment disappeared. What good

was this smelling and frozen catskin now? He threw it down by an icy rock and found that he could now run, trotting, without the awkward burden of the cat hide, which was stiff and slippery — with its frozen leggings of fur which stuck out, ragged and indignant, the congealed ghost of the cat.

The snow died away as Julio hurried. The wind became capricious and bitter. It scratched in long sweeps down the cañon and bore out over the open plains, which Julio could begin to see as the day grew and he toiled farther down the shadowy chasm.

He kept staring ahead for sight of the spare pines which stood by their camp. He remembered seeing the pines against open sky the first night there — which meant that they were nearly out of the mountain's fold.

He thought he saw the sentinel trees once; broke into a hard run; and then stopped, panting, when he saw that the gray light on a wall of rock had looked for a moment like a misty sky out there over the plain.

The musket was heavy and cold in his grasp. He had it still loaded. Perhaps he ought to shoot it off, a signal for his brother? But he would call first.

He cried out, and stood to listen, his whole body turned sideways to hear an answer.

There was none.

Now he knew that the bell he had heard last night, waking him up during the snowstorm, was a miracle, sent to keep him from freezing to death in his sleep.

So he began to run again, and his heart nearly burst. He thought perhaps there would be another miracle, to keep Luis safe and bring Julio back to him right away.

The boy crawled over the rocks that seemed cold enough to crack in the weather; he waded where he had to in the glazed creek. Suddenly it was lighter; the sky lay before him as well as above him; and at last he looked down on the miniature meadow of the cañon mouth where the horses were fenced. There! Yes, there were the guardian pine trees.

"Luis, Luis, I am back!" he cried, but he choked and made only a sobbing sound. There was no fire burning at the camp, and Julio was thumped in the breast by fear again, as if Luis had gone back home with the two horses and left him as he deserved to be left, alone in the mountains.

He hurried and then saw the horses, far down the way.

Then he heard a voice, talking to him from a distance; no words; level, careful sounds; it sounded like Luis.

"Luis, where are you?"

Julio came down farther.

He squinted around, and then upward.

"I am glad to see you back. Stop where you are!"

"Luis!"

"Be careful."

At the same moment, Julio heard how Luis spoke from the tree where he was hanging and he saw the wolf at the base of the tree, which sat staring upward, perfectly quiet and ready.

The wolf was huge and looked like a dog, except that he was gray, the color of rock — which was why Julio didn't see him for the first little while.

The wolf must have heard him, for his ears were standing up and the fur on his spine was silvery and alive. Julio stood shocking-still and was perfectly sure that the wolf's eyes were straining toward him as far as they could without the turn of the head; and the animal was ready to turn and attack him if necessary.

So there was a grotesque interval of calm and silence in the cañon.

Luis was hanging to the pine tree, which had a few tough fragments of branch about sixteen feet above the ground.

The sun tried to shine through the bitter and cloudy day.

Luis looked white and sick, half-frozen; his eyes were burning black in new hollow shadows.

"Julio," said Luis, as lightly as possible, never taking his eyes off the wolf; indeed, as if he were addressing the wolf.

"Yes, Luis," whispered Julio.

"You have the gun there with you, haven't you?" asked the older brother, in an ingratiating and mollifying tone, to keep the wolf below him still intent upon his first design.

"Yes, Luis."

"Well, Julio," said his brother with desperate charm, velvet-voiced and easy, "see if you can load it without making much disturbance, will you?"

"It is loaded, Luis."

"Oh, that is fine. Then, Julio, pray Jesus you can manage to shoot the wolf. Julio, be easy and steady now . . . don't — move — fast — or — make — any — noise — Julio — for — the — love — of — God."

To Julio it was like coming back to the reward of his folly. He held his breath, to be quiet.

He thought Luis was going to fall from the tree — his face was so white and starving, his hands so bony and desperate where they clutched.

"Why, of course I can shoot the terrible wolf," said Julio to himself; slowly, slowly bringing the musket around to the aim.

Luis, from his tree against the gray pale sky, went on talking in tones of enchantment and courtesy to the wolf, to keep alive the concentration, until Julio fancied the wolf might answer, as animals did in the tales of early childhood.

"We shall see, my dear friend wolf, just sit there — one — more — minute — if you please — until — my — brother gets the thing ready. . . . Are — you — ready — Julio . . ."

The answer was the shot.

The wolf lashed his hindquarters around so that he faced Julio, whence the sound had come. \

He roared and spat; but he could not move. His back was broken. He sat and barked and snapped his teeth.

Julio ran a little way forward, then was cautious. He stopped and began to reload.

Luis fell to the ground. He had his knife ready.

But he could not move as quickly as he would. He was cold and stiff and cramped. He hacked his knife into the animal's breast, but the stab was shy and glancing. The wolf made a crying effort and scrabbled its shattered body forward and took Luis by the leg.

"Now, Julio! Your knife!"

Julio dropped the musket and came down to them.

"Where, Luis?"

"Under his left forearm!"

"Wolf!" said Julio, and drove his knife.

vii

For a moment they all stayed where they were — the brothers panting; the animal dead, and slowly relaxing thus. The brothers sweated and couldn't speak, but hung their heads and spat dry spit and coughed and panted.

"Did he bite you bad?" asked Julio.

"No, he couldn't bite very hard, not even like a dog — he was too hurt."

"Let me see."

They peeled the cloth away from the leg just above the knee. The teeth had torn the cloth and the flesh. It did not hurt. It was numb. It bled very little. The skin was blue.

There was nothing to do to the leg except cover it again. They took as long as possible at it, but they had presently to come to the story of the young brother's folly, and as soon as that was done they felt elated — the one penitent and grave, the other pardoning and aware that the terrors of the experience were more useful to his young brother than any words of rebuke.

". . . And I know right where I left the lion skin; we'll get it later! We can get many more!"

Julio was ballooning with relief, now that it was all over and done with. He felt as he always felt after confession in church — airy and tall.

The physical misery in snow and wind and rocky mountain temper — this was their outer penalty. But the boys knew an inner joy at the further range of their doing. Simply being where they were, at odds with what menaced them — this was achievement; it was man's doing done.

Late that day the sun did break through and a little while of golden light seemed to relieve the cold. It didn't snow again that night. They kept their fire high. Luis was, oddly, too lame to walk. But he was glad to lie and watch the flames, and smile at

Julio's serious bearing, full of thoughtful play in his face which meant plans and intentions.

viii

The day after the snowstorm the valley itself came back in a kind of golden resurge of autumn. The house at the little farm was soaked with melting snow; running lines of dark muddy thaw streaked from the round-worn edges of the roof to the walls and the ground.

The temper of the river was warmer than the mountain weather. The willows and cottonwoods lost their snow by noon. The mountains were visible again, after the day of the blind white blowing curtain over the plain.

Not many travelers were abroad; but Father Antonio came down the road shortly after noon, and Josefina saw him, his fat white mare, his robe tucked above his waist, his wool-colored homespun trousers, and his Mexican boots. She went to tell Rosa that the priest was coming at last, and to stop crying, if that was all she was crying for.

The priest dismounted in the yard and let his horse move.

Josefina tidied herself in honor of the visit, and he came in, catching her at wetting her eyebrows. She immediately felt like a fool, from the way he looked at her; and she bowed for his blessing, furious at his kind of power over and against women.

"I didn't get your message about the baby until two days ago, and then I said nothing could keep me from coming as soon as I could. Isn't it fine! Where is he? Or is it a girl? I hope you have a girl. Already those bad boys of yours — where are they?"

Rosa felt as if authority had walked into her house and that she need have no further fear.

Father Antonio was a tall, very spare, bony man nearly fifty, with straw-colored hair, a pale wind-pinked face, and little blue eyes that shone speculatively as he gazed. He was awkward; he couldn't talk without slowly waving his great-knuckled hands in illustration of his mood; and he loved to talk, putting into words the great interest of his days. Everything suggested something else to him; he debated with himself as if he were two Jesuits, they said in Santa Fe, where he was not popular with the clergy because he preferred working in the open land among the scattered families of the river basin.

"Where are the boys?" he asked.

Rosa was at peace. Her cheeks dried and her heart seemed to grow strong. She felt a spell of calm strong breath in her breast. She was proud.

"They have gone hunting. They have been gone several days now. In the mountains."

Josefina lingered on the outside of a kind of sanctuary which the priest and the mother made, a spiritual confine which she could not enter, a profane and resentful woman. But she could toss her opinions into it.

"They are little fools, a pair of chicken-boned infants, crazy, going to the mountains! It snowed there for two days. They will never come back."

Rosa watched the priest's face, ready to be frightened or not, by his expression.

He glanced at Josefina, a mild blue fire.

"They are probably all right."

Josefina mumbled.

"How will a man ever know what goes on," asked Father Antonio, "unless he goes out and looks at it?"

"How long can you stay, Father?" asked Rosa.

"Till we christen the baby."

"But —"

"I'll wait till the brothers come back, so the baby will have a godfather."

"I — godmother," simpered Josefina on the outskirts, making a fat and radiant gesture of coquetry.

"Why not?" said the priest mildly, taking the sting out of her scandalous contempt.

It sobered her. She blushed.

"When your husband comes back in the spring with the wagon train," said Father Antonio, "you can send some money to my church."

"Gladly," said Rosa.

"Those must be big boys by now. I haven't seen them for months. Luis? Julio? That's right. When I was a boy I had all the desires to go and look at what was over the mountains. Then when I was away, there, in Mexico, at the seminary, the world on this side of the mountains was just as inviting and mysterious. Eh? When I came back to go to work, everybody bowed to me, and behaved properly as to a priest. But I always felt a little guilty for that, and went fishing or hunting. The animals had no respect for me, which was a relief, for they knew not of God, whose weight is something to carry, I can tell you!"

This was strange talk to the women.

"Next to catching a sinner and taking away his sin, I like best to fetch a trout, or play a long game of war with a beaver in the river pools. So now I know why your two big brown babies went off to the mountains."

"Oh," thought the women. "That explains it."

ix

Father Antonio stayed over a week. The boys were missing. The priest would go and look at the mountains in all times of day, to see if he could see anything, even in his mind, which might be played with as news for the distracted mother.

But all he saw were the momentous faces of the mountains; light or the absence of light; at dawn, a chalky black atmosphere quivering with quiet air; at noon, silvered by the sun, the great rock wrinkles shining and constant; at evening, the glow of rose, as if there were furnaces within the tumbled stone which heated the surface, until it came to glow for a few moments, then cooling to ashy black from the base upward until it joined the darkening sky like a low heavy cloud.

"I have promised to stay for them, and I will," said the priest.

He spent the days making Rosa agree to get strong; until she finally arose from her bed and ordered her house again. He did the tasks of the outdoors. There was no need for Josefina to stay now; but stay she did, touched in her vanity by the godmother-hood which had been mentioned once.

She came in one day, still holding her arm over her eyes, as if staring into the distance, the golden chill of the open winter.

"I think I see them coming!" she cried.

They all went outdoors.

"You are crazy," said the priest.

They looked and looked.

The plain and the slow rise into the mountain-lift were swimming with sunlight. They searched with long looks until they had to blink for vision.

"See! Like a couple of sheep, just barely moving?" insisted Josefina, pointing vaguely at the mountains.

"Where?"

"Yes, I do see! She is right! She must have Indian blood."

The mother was the last to see and agree.

There was an infinitesimal movement far on the plain, hardly perceptible as movement; some energy of presence, a fall of light and cast of shadow, just alive enough to be convincing. It was the hunters, coming on their horses on the second day's journey out of the mountains.

Late in the afternoon they arrived.

The marks of their toil were all over them.

To go and come back! This being the common mystery of all journeying, the mother could hardly wait for them to speak; to tell her everything.

She brought the baby and the boys kissed the tiny furred head.

The priest gave them his blessing and they bent their shaggy necks under it.

Josefina stared and then squinted at them, whispering something.

"Luis, you are hurt!"

"Not any more."

"But you *were!*"

"I will tell you sometime."

"Now, now!"

"How long have we been away?"

"Ten days!"

The boys talked, confirming each other with looks.

Luis and the wolf; the bite; the fever; the body as the residence of the devil, and the raving nights. Julio and his amazing skill as a marksman; his reckless courage; the two of them together after Luis' recovery; shagging up and down rocky barriers, mountain sprites, and their bag of skins.

"Look at that!"

They got up and opened out their two packs of furs, and there were cats, the wolf, a little deer, and a middle-sized brown bear.

"Who got the bear?"

"Luis! It was wonderful! The bear was in a tree, watching us, and what made him nobody knows, but Luis looked up, and *whang!* and *boo!* Down fell the bear, and all it took was the one shot!"

"But you should have seen Julio the time he saved my life, when the wolf was waiting for me to fall down, I was so cold and weak! Up in my tree!"

The silence was full of worried love: what had they not done! But safe. Yes, but — what if — !

The brothers looked at each other.

Nothing would ever be said about the other thing. Nobody ever managed to grow up without being foolish at some time or other.

The priest thought, "The boy Julio looks taller. I suppose it is only natural; last time I was here he was — "

Luis took the baby sister to hold.

There was plenty of fur to keep her warm.

Julio sighed. It was a curiously contented and old man's comment.

Father Antonio felt like laughing; but there was some nobility of bearing in Julio's little mighty shoulders that did not deserve genial patronizing.

The priest glanced at Josefina. He knew his materials like a craftsman. He thought, "Josefina sees — she even smells as a female — what has taken place in Julio. She stares at him and then squints and whispers to herself. How little is secret! How much makes a life!"

The mother's arms were free of her infant. She went and hugged

Julio, because, though she hardly thought it so clearly, she knew that he had gone and conquered the wilderness which was his brother's by birth. She knew that — and what lay behind it — as only a child's mother could know it; with defensive and pitying and pardoning love, so long as it might be needed.

x

"I wish I could write, now," said Luis.

"Why?"

"Then I would write to my father about it."

"But he could not read it."

"No, but he could get somebody to read it to him."

"Should I write and tell him about it for you?" asked Father Antonio.

"Oh, if you would, Father!"

"I'll be glad to — the minute I get back to my house where I have pens and paper. You have told me the whole adventure."

But when the priest did return home, and sit down to keep his promise to the delighted brothers, what they had told him seemed to him man's story, and all he finally wrote was: —

DEAR GARCIA,

Your wife has had a dear baby girl, and both are well and happy, with God's grace. Your two sons are proud of their family, and when you return, before hearing from their lips anything of their adventures during your absence, you will see that they are already proper men, for which God be praised in the perfection of His design for our mortal life.

The Farewell Party

ALBERT EISELE

M R. HENRY VOLLMER had sung in the choir for more than thirty years and it was only natural that now, with the Vollmers moving away, the choir members should give him a surprise party.

And this was the night. Mr. Vollmer stood at a window and watched a long line of cars approach along the curving road that led to the farmplace, the cars following one another closely and studding the road with their lights. A lump came into Mr. Vollmer's throat.

"Emma," he said in an unsteady voice. "I'm just afraid that when these good people go home tonight I'll break down and cry like a baby! I always do. Such things get me."

"Well, that's the way the Lord made you, Henry, and you can't help it. And besides, tain't no disgrace for a man to cry."

The choir was composed of eight men. All had brought their wives or sweethearts, and so the Vollmer house was filled. Decks of cards were tossed on tables, and soon everybody was playing progressive five hundred.

"Now, then!" said Mr. Gassonade, the choirmaster, as he seated himself for the second game. He raked in the scattered cards, herded them together and deposited the pack in front of the lady to his right, Mrs. Keene. "Visiting lady deals!" he said politely.

"Oh, dear me!" exclaimed Mrs. Keene, "must I deal?" Her shoulders shuttled and her head wagged.

She dealt the cards gingerly, pausing at intervals to check up and assure herself that all was well. "Have you too many cards?"

From *The Catholic World*, April, 1938. By permission.

— "Oh, what have I done!" She looked to Mr. Vollmer, her partner, for advice and comfort.

And when finally she had decided to play a card she would pass it slowly to the center of the table, hesitate another moment, relinquish her hold on the card and then look at Mr. Vollmer and say, "Oh, I never should have played that!" Mr. Gassonade seldom engaged in side talk while at cards, but during this game he suddenly looked up at Mr. Vollmer and said, "I see by the paper where beer has come back to Kansas after being gone fifty-six years."

"It was gone long enough," said Mr. Vollmer solemnly.

Mr. Vollmer lost this second game, as also he had lost the first. "Oh, you couldn't expect to win, with me for partner!" purled Mrs. Keene in agitation. Her head bobbed and wagged in little bows of apology and regret.

Mr. Gassonade and his partner, victorious, moved on to the next table, Mr. Vollmer remaining but shifting to another seat.

He lost the third game, and also the fourth and fifth. His luck began to draw attention; players at other tables were saying, "Mr. Vollmer hasn't won a game yet!" His fame spread.

He went around and around the table like a horse around an old-fashioned feed grinder. He tried to take his fortunes philosophically; but something, it seemed, had settled in his breast and was beginning to ferment. He tried to console himself with the feeling that he was permanently staged at a fixed point of vantage from where, like the person who stands on a street corner, he could get a good view of things.

Everyone, it seemed, passed before him. There was Mr. Kosmoski, a tenor. Mr. Kosmoski had a fine-timbred voice, very effective on the lower ranges, but inclined to thin out on the upper. Mr. Kosmoski, as an aid, ate peppermint candy — he always had a fresh supply of it, and would pass the bag around and then place it on the organ, where it was open to general foraging.

Opposed to Mr. Kosmoski and his theories was Mr. Hermann, a basso. Mr. Hermann bolstered up his voice with elderberry wine. He carried a bottle with him, and would usually take the necessary swig while ascending the dark stairway that led to the loft. "Nothing tunes up a man's sounding-board like a good drink of elderberry wine," he was fond of saying. Mr. Kosmoski, however, stood his ground, and Sunday after Sunday publicly passed around his peppermints, a tactic which was somehow closed to Mr. Hermann and his bottle.

Mr. Vollmer, in the meantime, had lost the sixth, seventh, and eighth games. His face was red, his mustache bristled, and he was now definitely angry.

And there was Leo Fleming, who had brought his girl with him. The two billed and cooed and tickled each other under the chin. Mr. Vollmer glared at them.

And tenor Philip Kesseling, a good singer and a demon at cards. He played to win; and it was ironical that the two ladies of that ninth game were Mrs. Kosmoski and Mrs. Wetternich, the two most lackadaisical players of the entire gathering. Mrs. Kosmoski played a card and then addressed Mrs. Wetternich: "Did you hear that Lincoln program over the radio the other night?" "No," said Mrs. Wetternich, "I didn't hear it." "It sure was good," Mrs. Kosmoski continued; "it gave everything from the time he was born till he was shot." "Well, for goodness' sakes!" Mrs. Wetternich exclaimed; "and did he live long after he was shot?" "I really couldn't say," replied Mrs. Kosmoski; "there was a lot of music in between, and talking. Is it my play now?"

And Mr. Schmidt, a tenor. Mr. Schmidt was getting old and shaky. He sang by ear, and held a score in his hands merely for the looks of things. It took him a long time to learn his part, but once he learned it he had it. As a card player he was fumbling and inept, the cards falling continually to the table, to his lap, and to the floor. In some strange way he acquired, as the evening wore on, an aura similar to that of the magician who makes cards tumble from armpits and other unseemly places.

It was Mr. Keene, a basso, who opposed Mr. Vollmer at the eleventh game. Mr. Keene was an inveterate latecomer at Mass, and for that matter the choirmaster never bothered much about teaching him the *Kyrie* or even the *Gloria.* But Mr. Keene could play cards, and he gave Mr. Vollmer a fearful walloping. It was Mr. Vollmer's eleventh straight defeat, and he was now boiling inside like a threshing engine.

Then came the twelfth game, the last of the evening. "Everybody keep their seats after this game!" someone announced, this being a promise of sandwiches and coffee.

Mr. Vollmer's partner for this final game was Mrs. Schmidt, and his opponents Mr. Wetternich and Mrs. Hermann. Mrs. Schmidt was a very preoccupied sort of person. She wore strong glasses, which gave her deep-set eyes an oscillating appearance, but her gaze at the same time was fixed and staring. She went seemingly into trances, and when in this condition there was nothing for the other players to do but wait till she came back.

"I have always maintained," she addressed Mr. Vollmer in her slow and measured speech, "that the Catholic Church should make better provisions for its young people to meet one another and become acquainted. A mixed marriage is nothing but a joy and a delight to the devil. The devil is as much a partner to a mixed marriage as is the bridegroom." Her eyes, made manifold by the strong lenses, were on Mr. Vollmer like those of a myriad-orbed apparition.

"A mixed marriage," she went on, lost to the card game, "begins its journey without the blessing of God. There is no Nuptial Mass, and any marriage that is contracted without the blessings of a Nuptial Mass is not a marriage at all, but merely a farce." She moved her head slightly and for a moment her eyes came into focus: they were steady and unblinking like those of an owl. "What we Catholics need are gathering places for our young — study clubs, recreation halls, basket socials, and, under the proper supervision, of course, dances."

All of which was a perennial subject with Mrs. Schmidt. The woman had three unmarried daughters at home, and none of them had a husband in sight. Several desirable young men of the parish had in recent years been married out of the Church, and the villainous injustice of all this loomed so mountainously to the mother that she could hardly understand why public demonstrations did not manifest themselves — she felt that there should be uprisings of the populace; revolution; bloodshed. She brooded intensely over the matter.

She came out of her trance and played her cards. She and Mr. Vollmer won the deal. Mr. Wetternich dealt afresh; the cards shot out from under his hands like grain from an end-gate seeder. Mr. Wetternich was an insurance man, a vapid and blustery fellow who played cards with a vast enthusiasm. He strove always for a noisy table. "You do the playing and I'll run the rake!" he would shout whenever his partner took a trick; and when the opposition won he would exclaim in tones of surprise and dismay, "Oh, oh! Oh, oh! Oh, oh!"

"You got the jump on us," he addressed Mr. Vollmer, "but things'll look different after this next deal. You watch us go! — Oh, boy!" He gathered the cards together and slapped them loudly on the table in front of Mr. Vollmer. "Your deal!" he said, "shoot 'em around!" Mr. Vollmer shuffled the cards and then presented them to Mr. Wetternich to cut; Mr. Wetternich removed the top half of the pack and slapped it to the table with another resounding clap. "Just right!" he beamed; "cut just the way I want 'em! Ha, ha, ha! Now watch my hand! Attaboy!"

He did draw a good hand, and the score was evened. The score then seesawed until the time for the bell drew near. Mr. Vollmer, in what was undoubtedly the final hand of the game, drew a strong run in hearts: he bid eight in the suit, and was not overbid. He had the cards to win, and now if the play could be completed before the bell rang, he would have won a game.

Mr. Vollmer suddenly perked up. For the last hour or two he had been sullenly and bitterly resigned to the bludgeonings of vile fate, but now with the smell of victory in his nostrils he was a new man. He would yet win a game.

But the bell was imminent, and so it was strategy for Mr. Vollmer to rush the playing. He quickly threw away his discards and led. Mrs. Hermann, to his right, played promptly in turn. But Mrs. Schmidt had her gaze on Mr. Vollmer, and she was talking. "We hear so much nowadays as to what is wrong with the world," she said, "but how seldom do people put their finger on the real cause. It is in the mixed marriage that all evil has its root." Her hands were resting on the table, and the cards in them were pushed together in compact form.

"If you will play your cards quickly, Mrs. Schmidt," said Mr. Vollmer, "I think we can still win this game."

"We must bring our young men and our young women together," said Mrs. Schmidt firmly, " — we must take steps in these days and times which it was not necessary to take years ago. It behooves us — "

But here the bell rang, at which Mr. Wetternich bellowed, "We win!" and reaching across the table shook hands violently with his partner, while Mrs. Schmidt turned her head and stared long and studiously in the direction of the ringing, as though she had heard something suspicious.

Refreshments were served, but Mr. Vollmer merely nibbled at his food.

And then came the booby prize — a little fuzzy rabbit that jumped and squeaked when one pressed a rubber bulb attached. Mr. Wetternich, the insurance man, slapped Mr. Vollmer on the back: "We beat him twelve straight! — it shouldn't have been a rabbit at all, but a skunk!"

And presently everybody went home. Mr. Vollmer stood at a window and glared at the disappearing headlights.

"Oh, Henry," spoke Mrs. Vollmer softly, as she laid a hand on her husband's shoulder, "I'm so glad that you didn't break down and cry tonight when the people left!"

The Hammer of God

G. K. CHESTERTON

THE little village of Bohun Beacon was perched on a hill so steep that the tall spire of its church seemed only like the peak of a small mountain. At the foot of the church stood a smithy, generally red with fires and always littered with hammers and scraps of iron; opposite to this, over a rude cross of cobbled paths, was "The Blue Boar," the only inn of the place. It was upon this crossway, in the lifting of a leaden and silver daybreak, that two brothers met in the street and spoke; though one was beginning the day and the other finishing it. The Rev. and Hon. Wilfred Bohun was very devout, and was making his way to some austere exercises of prayer or contemplation at dawn. Colonel the Hon. Norman Bohun, his elder brother, was by no means devout, and was sitting in evening dress on the bench outside "The Blue Boar," drinking what the philosophic observer was free to regard either as his last glass on Tuesday or his first on Wednesday. The colonel was not particular.

The Bohuns were one of the very few aristocratic families really dating from the Middle Ages, and their pennon had actually seen Palestine. But it is a great mistake to suppose that such houses stand high in chivalric tradition. Few except the poor preserve traditions. Aristocrats live not in traditions but in fashions. The Bohuns had been Mohocks under Queen Anne and Mashers under Queen Victoria. But like more than one of the really ancient houses, they had rotted in the past two centuries into mere drunkards and dandy degenerates, till there had even come a

From *The Innocence of Father Brown*, by G. K. Chesterton. Copyright, 1911, by Dodd, Mead & Co. By permission.

whisper of insanity. Certainly there was something hardly human about the colonel's wolfish pursuit of pleasure, and his chronic resolution not to go home till morning had a touch of the hideous clarity of insomnia. He was a tall, fine animal, elderly, but with hair still startlingly yellow. He would have looked merely blond and leonine, but his blue eyes were sunk so deep in his face that they looked black. They were a little too close together. He had very long yellow mustaches; on each side of them a fold or furrow from nostril to jaw, so that a sneer seemed cut into his face. Over his evening clothes he wore a curious pale-yellow coat that looked more like a very light dressing gown than an overcoat, and on the back of his head was stuck an extraordinary broad-brimmed hat of a bright green color, evidently some oriental curiosity caught up at random. He was proud of appearing in such incongruous attires — proud of the fact that he always made them look congruous.

His brother the curate had also the yellow hair and the elegance, but he was buttoned up to the chin in black, and his face was clean shaven, cultivated, and a little nervous. He seemed to live for nothing but his religion; but there were some who said (notably the blacksmith, who was a Presbyterian) that it was a love of Gothic architecture rather than of God, and that his haunting of the church like a ghost was only another and purer turn of the almost morbid thirst for beauty which sent his brother raging after women and wine. This charge was doubtful, while the man's practical piety was indubitable. Indeed, the charge was mostly an ignorant misunderstanding of the love of solitude and secret prayer, and was founded on his being often found kneeling, not before the altar, but in peculiar places, in the crypts or gallery, or even in the belfry. He was at the moment about to enter the church through the yard of the smithy, but stopped and frowned a little as he saw his brother's cavernous eyes staring in the same direction. On the hypothesis that the colonel was interested in the church he did not waste any speculations. There only remained the blacksmith's shop, and though the blacksmith was a Puritan and none of his people, Wilfred Bohun had heard some scandals about a beautiful and rather celebrated wife. He flung a suspicious look across the shed, and the colonel stood up laughing to speak to him.

"Good morning, Wilfred," he said. "Like a good landlord I am watching sleeplessly over my people. I am going to call on the blacksmith."

Wilfred looked at the ground, and said: "The blacksmith is out. He is over at Greenford."

"I know," answered the other with silent laughter; "that is why I am calling on him."

"Norman," said the cleric, with his eye on a pebble in the road, "are you ever afraid of thunderbolts?"

"What do you mean?" asked the colonel. "Is your hobby meteorology?"

"I mean," said Wilfred, without looking up, "do you ever think that God might strike you in the street?"

"I beg your pardon," said the colonel; "I see your hobby is folklore."

"I know your hobby is blasphemy," retorted the religious man, stung in the one live place of his nature. "But if you do not fear God, you have good reason to fear man."

The elder raised his eyebrows politely. "Fear man?" he said.

"Barnes the blacksmith is the biggest and strongest man for forty miles round," said the clergyman sternly. "I know you are no coward or weakling, but he could throw you over the wall."

This struck home, being true, and the lowering line by mouth and nostril darkened and deepened. For a moment he stood with the heavy sneer on his face. But in an instant Colonel Bohun had recovered his own cruel good humor and laughed, showing two doglike front teeth under his yellow moustache. "In that case, my dear Wilfred," he said quite carelessly, "it was wise for the last of the Bohuns to come out partially in armor."

And he took off the queer round hat covered with green, showing that it was lined within with steel. Wilfred recognized it indeed as a light Japanese or Chinese helmet torn down from a trophy that hung in the old family hall.

"It was the first hat to hand," explained his brother airily; "always the nearest hat — and the nearest woman."

"The blacksmith is away at Greenford," said Wilfred quietly; "the time of his return is unsettled."

And with that he turned and went into the church with bowed head, crossing himself like one who wishes to be quit of an unclean spirit. He was anxious to forget such grossness in the cool twilight of his tall Gothic cloisters; but on that morning it was fated that his still round of religious exercises should be everywhere arrested by small shocks. As he entered the church, hitherto always empty at that hour, a kneeling figure rose hastily to its feet and came toward the full daylight of the doorway. When the curate saw it he stood still with surprise. For the early worshiper was none other than the village idiot, a nephew of the blacksmith, one who neither would nor could care for the church or for anything else. He was always called "Mad Joe," and seemed to have no other name; he was a dark, strong, slouching lad, with a heavy white face, dark straight hair, and a mouth always open. As he passed the priest, his moon-calf countenance gave no hint of what he had been doing or thinking of. He had never been known to pray before. What sort of prayers was he saying now? Extraordinary prayers surely.

Wilfred Bohun stood rooted to the spot long enough to see the idiot go out into the sunshine, and even to see his dissolute brother hail him with a sort of avuncular jocularity. The last thing he saw was the colonel throwing pennies at the open mouth of Joe, with the serious appearance of trying to hit it.

This ugly sunlight picture of the stupidity and cruelty of the earth sent the ascetic finally to his prayers for purification and new thoughts. He went up to a pew in the gallery, which brought him under a colored window which he loved and always quieted his spirit; a blue window with an angel carrying lilies. There he began to think less about the half-wit, with his livid face and mouth like a fish. He began to think less of his evil brother, pacing like a lean lion in his horrible hunger. He sank deeper and deeper into those cold and sweet colors of silver blossoms and sapphire sky.

In this place half an hour afterwards he was found by Gibbs, the village cobbler, who had been sent for him in some haste. He got to his feet with promptitude, for he knew that no small matter would have brought Gibbs into such a place at all. The cobbler was, as in many villages, an atheist, and his appearance in church was a shade more extraordinary than Mad Joe's. It was a morning of theological enigmas.

"What is it?" asked Wilfred Bohun rather stiffly, but putting out a trembling hand for his hat.

The atheist spoke in a tone that, coming from him, was quite startlingly respectful, and even, as it were, huskily sympathetic.

"You must excuse me, sir," he said in a hoarse whisper, "but we didn't think it right not to let you know at once. I'm afraid a rather dreadful thing has happened, sir. I'm afraid your brother — "

Wilfred clenched his frail hands. "What deviltry has he done now?" he cried in involuntary passion.

"Why, sir," said the cobbler, coughing, "I'm afraid he's done nothing, and won't do anything. I'm afraid he's done for. You had really better come down, sir."

The curate followed the cobbler down a short winding stair, which brought them out at an entrance rather higher than the street. Bohun saw the tragedy in one glance, flat underneath him like a plan. In the yard of the smithy were standing five or six men mostly in black, one in an inspector's uniform. They included the doctor, the Presbyterian minister, and the priest from the Roman Catholic chapel, to which the blacksmith's wife belonged. The latter was speaking to her, indeed, very rapidly, in an undertone, as she, a magnificent woman with red-gold hair, was sobbing blindly on a bench. Between these two groups, and just clear of the main heap of hammers, lay a man in evening dress, spread-eagled and flat on his face. From the height above Wilfred could have sworn to every item of his costume and appearance, down to the Bohun rings upon his fingers; but the skull was only a hideous splash, like a star of blackness and blood.

Wilfred Bohun gave but one glance, and ran down the steps into the yard. The doctor, who was the family physician, saluted him, but he scarcely took any notice. He could only stammer out: "My brother is dead. What does it mean? What is this horrible mystery?" There was an unhappy silence; and then the cobbler, the most outspoken man present, answered: "Plenty of horror, sir," he said, "but not much mystery."

"What do you mean?" asked Wilfred, with a white face.

"It's plain enough," answered Gibbs. "There is only one man for forty miles round that could have struck such a blow as that, and he's the man that had most reason to."

"We must not prejudge anything," put in the doctor, a tall, black-bearded man, rather nervously; "but it is competent for me to corroborate what Mr. Gibbs says about the nature of the blow, sir; it is an incredible blow. Mr. Gibbs says that only one man in this district could have done it. I should have said myself that nobody could have done it."

A shudder of superstition went through the slight figure of the curate. "I can hardly understand," he said.

"Mr. Bohun," said the doctor in a low voice, "metaphors literally fail me. It is inadequate to say that the skull was smashed to bits like an eggshell. Fragments of bone were driven into the body and the ground like bullets into a mud wall. It was the hand of a giant."

He was silent a moment, looking grimly through his glasses; then he added: "The thing has one advantage — that it clears most people of suspicion at one stroke. If you or I or any normally made man in the country were accused of this crime, we should be acquitted as an infant would be acquitted of stealing the Nelson Column."

"That's what I say," repeated the cobbler obstinately; "there's only one man that could have done it, and he's the man that would have done it. Where's Simeon Barnes, the blacksmith?"

"He's over at Greenford," faltered the curate.

"More likely over in France," muttered the cobbler.

"No; he is in neither of those places," said a small and colorless voice, which came from the little Roman priest who had joined the group. "As a matter of fact, he is coming up the road at this moment."

The little priest was not an interesting man to look at, having stubbly brown hair and a round and stolid face. But if he had been as splendid as Apollo no one would have looked at him at that moment. Everyone turned round and peered at the pathway which wound across the plain below, along which was indeed walking, at his own huge stride and with a hammer on his shoulder, Simeon the smith. He was a bony and gigantic man, with deep, dark, sinister eyes and a dark chin beard. He was walking and talking quietly with two other men; and though he was never specially cheerful, he seemed quite at his ease.

"My God!" cried the atheistic cobbler, "and there's the hammer he did it with."

"No," said the inspector, a sensible-looking man with a sandy moustache, speaking for the first time. "There's the hammer he did it with over there by the church wall. We have left it and the body exactly as they are."

All glanced round, and the short priest went across and looked down in silence at the tool where it lay. It was one of the smallest and the lightest of the hammers, and would not have caught the eye among the rest; but on the iron edge of it were blood and yellow hair.

After a silence the short priest spoke without looking up, and there was a new note in his dull voice. "Mr. Gibbs was hardly right," he said, "in saying that there is no mystery. There is at least the mystery of why so big a man should attempt so big a blow with so little a hammer."

"Oh, never mind that," cried Gibbs, in a fever. "What are we to do with Simeon Barnes?"

"Leave him alone," said the priest quietly. "He is coming here of himself. I know those two men with him. They are very good fellows from Greenford, and they have come over about the Presbyterian chapel."

Even as he spoke the tall smith swung round the corner of the church, and strode into his own yard. Then he stood there quite still, and the hammer fell from his hand. The inspector, who had preserved impenetrable propriety, immediately went up to him.

"I don't ask you, Mr. Barnes," he said, "whether you know anything about what has happened here. You are not bound to say. I hope you don't know, and that you will be able to prove it.

But I must go through the form of arresting you in the King's name for the murder of Colonel Norman Bohun."

"You are not bound to say anything," said the cobbler in officious excitement. "They've got to prove everything. They haven't proved yet that it is Colonel Bohun, with the head all smashed up like that."

"That won't wash," said the doctor aside to the priest. "That's out of the detective stories. I was the colonel's medical man, and I knew his body better than he did. He had very fine hands but quite peculiar ones. The second and third fingers were the same in length. Oh, that's the colonel right enough."

As he glanced at the brained corpse upon the ground the iron eyes of the motionless blacksmith followed them and rested there also.

"Is Colonel Bohun dead?" said the smith quite calmly. "Then he's damned."

"Don't say anything! Oh, don't say anything," cried the atheist cobbler, dancing about in an ecstasy of admiration of the English legal system. For no man is such a legalist as the good Secularist.

The blacksmith turned on him over his shoulder the august face of a fanatic.

"It's well for you infidels to dodge like foxes because the world's law favors you," he said; "but God guards His own in His pocket, as you shall see this day."

Then he pointed to the colonel and said: "When did this dog die in his sins?"

"Moderate your language," said the doctor.

"Moderate the Bible's language, and I'll moderate mine. When did he die?"

"I saw him alive at six o'clock this morning," stammered Wilfred Bohun.

"God is good," said the smith. "Mr. Inspector, I have not the slightest objection to being arrested. It is you who may object to arresting me. I don't mind leaving the court without a stain on my character. You do mind perhaps leaving the court with a bad setback in your career."

The solid inspector for the first time looked at the blacksmith with a lively eye; as did everybody else, except the short, strange priest, who was still looking down at the little hammer that had dealt the dreadful blow.

"There are two men standing outside this shop," went on the blacksmith with ponderous lucidity, "good tradesmen in Greenford whom you all know, who will swear that they saw me from before midnight till daybreak and long after in the committee room of our Revival Mission, which sits all night, we save souls so fast. In Greenford itself twenty people could swear to me for all that time. If I were a heathen, Mr. Inspector, I would let you walk on to your downfall. But as a Christian man I feel bound to give you your chance, and ask you whether you will hear my alibi now or in court."

The Inspector seemed for the first time disturbed, and said, "Of course I should be glad to clear you altogether now."

The smith walked out of his yard with the same long and easy stride, and returned to his two friends from Greenford, who were indeed friends of nearly everyone present. Each of them said a few words which no one ever thought of disbelieving. When they had spoken, the innocence of Simeon stood up as solid as the great church above them.

One of those silences struck the group which are more strange and insufferable than any speech. Madly, in order to make conversation, the curate said to the Catholic priest:

"You seem very much interested in that hammer, Father Brown."

"Yes, I am," said Father Brown; "why is it such a small hammer?"

The doctor swung round on him.

"By George, that's true," he cried; "who would use a little hammer with ten larger hammers lying about?"

Then he lowered his voice in the curate's ear and said: "Only the kind of person that can't lift a large hammer. It is not a question of force or courage between the sexes. It's a question of lifting power in the shoulders. A bold woman could commit ten murders with a light hammer and never turn a hair. She could not kill a beetle with a heavy one."

Wilfred Bohun was staring at him with a sort of hypnotized horror, while Father Brown listened with his head a little on one side, really interested and attentive. The doctor went on with more hissing emphasis:

"Why do these idiots always assume that the only person who hates the wife's lover is the wife's husband? Nine times out of ten the person who most hates the wife's lover is the wife. Who knows what insolence or treachery he had shown her — look there?"

He made a momentary gesture toward the red-haired woman on the bench. She had lifted her head at last and the tears were drying on her splendid face. But the eyes were fixed on the corpse with an electric glare that had in it something of idiocy.

The Rev. Wilfred Bohun made a limp gesture as if waving away all desire to know; but Father Brown, dusting off his sleeve some ashes blown from the furnace, spoke in his indifferent way.

"You are like so many doctors," he said; "your mental science is really suggestive. It is your physical science that is utterly impossible. I agree that the woman wants to kill the co-respondent much more than the petitioner does. And I agree that a woman will always pick up a smaller hammer instead of a big one. But the difficulty here is one of physical impossibility. No woman ever born could have smashed a man's skull out flat like that." Then he added reflectively, after a pause: "These people haven't grasped the whole of it. The man was actually wearing an iron helmet, and the blow scattered it like broken glass. Look at that woman. Look at her arms."

Silence held them all up again, and then the doctor said rather sulkily: "Well, I may be wrong; there are objections to everything. But I stick to the main point. No man but an idiot would pick up that little hammer if he could use a big hammer."

With that the lean and quivering hands of Wilfred Bohun went up to his head and seemed to clutch his scanty yellow hair. After an instant they dropped, and he cried: "That was the word I wanted; you have said the word."

Then he continued, mastering his discomposure: "The words you said were, 'No man but an idiot would pick up the small hammer.'"

"Yes," said the doctor. "Well?"

"Well," said the curate, "no man but an idiot did." The rest stared at him with eyes arrested and riveted, and he went on in a febrile and feminine agitation.

"I am a priest," he cried unsteadily, "and a priest should be no shedder of blood. I — I mean that he should bring no one to the gallows. And I thank God that I see the criminal clearly now — because he is a criminal who cannot be brought to the gallows."

"You will not denounce him?" enquired the doctor.

"He would not be hanged if I did denounce him," answered Wilfred with a wild but curiously happy smile. "When I went into the church this morning I found a madman praying there — that poor Joe, who has been wrong all his life. God knows what he prayed; but with such strange folk it is not incredible to suppose that their prayers are all upside down. Very likely a lunatic would pray before killing a man. When I last saw poor Joe he was with my brother. My brother was mocking him."

"By Jove!" cried the doctor, "this is talking at last. But how do you explain — "

The Rev. Wilfred was almost trembling with the excitement of his own glimpse of the truth. "Don't you see; don't you see," he cried feverishly; "that is the only theory that covers both the queer things, that answers both the riddles. The two riddles are the little hammer and the big blow. The smith might have struck the big blow, but would not have chosen the little hammer. His wife would have chosen the little hammer, but she could not have struck the big blow. But the madman might have done both. As for the little hammer — why, he was mad and might have picked up anything. And for the big blow, have you never heard, doctor, that a maniac in his paroxysm may have the strength of ten men?"

The doctor drew a deep breath and then said, "By golly, I believe you've got it."

Father Brown had fixed his eyes on the speaker so long and steadily as to prove that his large gray, oxlike eyes were not quite so insignificant as the rest of his face. When silence had fallen he said with marked respect: "Mr. Bohun, yours is the only theory yet propounded which holds water every way and is essentially unassailable. I think, therefore, that you deserve to be told, on my positive knowledge, that it is not the true one." And with that the old little man walked away and stared again at the hammer.

"That fellow seems to know more than he ought to," whispered the doctor peevishly to Wilfred. "Those popish priests are deucedly sly."

"No, no," said Bohun, with a sort of wild fatigue. "It was the lunatic. It was the lunatic."

The group of the two clerics and the doctor had fallen away from the more official group containing the inspector and the man he had arrested. Now, however, that their own party had broken up, they heard voices from the others. The priest looked up quietly and then looked down again as he heard the blacksmith say in a loud voice:

"I hope I've convinced you, Mr. Inspector. I'm a strong man, as you say, but I couldn't have flung my hammer bang here from Greenford. My hammer hasn't got wings that it should come flying half a mile over hedges and fields."

The inspector laughed amicably and said: "No, I think you can be considered out of it, though it's one of the rummiest coincidences I ever saw. I can only ask you to give us all the assistance you can in finding a man as big and strong as yourself. By George! you might be useful, if only to hold him! I suppose you yourself have no guess at the man?"

"I may have a guess," said the pale smith, "but it is not a man." Then, seeing the scared eyes turn toward his wife on the bench, he put his huge hand on her shoulder and said: "Nor a woman either."

"What do you mean?" asked the inspector jocularly. "You don't think cows use hammers, do you?"

"I think no thing of flesh held that hammer," said the black-smith in a stifled voice; "mortally speaking, I think the man died alone."

Wilfred made a sudden forward movement and peered at him with burning eyes.

"Do you mean to say, Barnes," came the sharp voice of the

cobbler, "that the hammer jumped up of itself and knocked the man down?"

"Oh, you gentlemen may stare and snigger," cried Simeon; "you clergymen who tell us on Sunday in what a stillness the Lord smote Sennacherib. I believe that One who walks invisible in every house defended the honor of mine, and laid the defiler dead before the door of it. I believe the force in that blow was just the force there is in earthquakes, and no force less."

Wilfred said, with a voice utterly undescribable: "I told Norman myself to beware of the thunderbolt."

"That agent is outside my jurisdiction," said the inspector with a slight smile.

"You are not outside His," answered the smith; "see you to it," and, turning his broad back, he went into the house.

The shaken Wilfred was led away by Father Brown, who had an easy and friendly way with him. "Let us get out of this horrid place, Mr. Bohun," he said. "May I look inside your church? I hear it's one of the oldest in England. We take some interest, you know," he added with a comical grimace, "in old English churches."

Wilfred Bohun did not smile, for humor was never his strong point. But he nodded rather eagerly, being only too ready to explain the Gothic splendors to someone more likely to be sympathetic than the Presbyterian blacksmith or the atheist cobbler.

"By all means," he said; "let us go in at this side." And he led the way into the high side entrance at the top of the flight of steps. Father Brown was mounting the first step to follow him when he felt a hand on his shoulder, and turned to behold the dark, thin figure of the doctor, his face darker yet with suspicion.

"Sir," said the physician harshly, "you appear to know some secrets in this black business. May I ask if you are going to keep them to yourself?"

"Why, doctor," answered the priest, smiling quite pleasantly, "there is one very good reason why a man of my trade should keep things to himself when he is not sure of them, and that is that it is so constantly his duty to keep them to himself when he is sure of them. But if you think I have been discourteously reticent with you or anyone, I will go to the extreme limit of my custom. I will give you two very large hints."

"Well, sir?" said the doctor gloomily.

"First," said Father Brown quietly, "the thing is quite in your own province. It is a matter of physical science. The blacksmith is mistaken, not perhaps in saying that the blow was divine, but certainly in saying that it came by miracle. It was no miracle, doctor, except in so far as man is himself a miracle, with strange and wicked and yet half-heroic heart. The force that smashed that skull was a force well known to scientists — one of the most frequently debated of the laws of nature."

The doctor, who was looking at him with frowning intentness, only said: "And the other hint?"

"The other hint is this," said the priest. "Do you remember the blacksmith, though he believes in miracles, talking scornfully of the impossible fairy tale that his hammer had wings and flew half a mile across country?"

"Yes," said the doctor, "I remember that."

"Well," added Father Brown, with a broad smile, "that fairy tale was the nearest thing to the real truth that has been said today." And with that he turned his back and stumped up the steps after the curate.

The Reverend Wilfred, who had been waiting for him, pale and impatient, as if this little delay were the last straw for his nerves, led him immediately to his favorite corner of the church, that part of the gallery closest to the carved roof and lit by the wonderful window with the angel. The little Latin priest explored and admired everything exhaustively, talking cheerfully but in a low voice all the time. When in the course of his investigation he found the side exit and the winding stair down which Wilfred had rushed to find his brother dead, Father Brown ran not down but up, with the agility of a monkey, and his clear voice came from an outer platform above.

"Come up here, Mr. Bohun," he called. "The air will do you good."

Bohun followed him, and came out on a kind of stone gallery or balcony outside the building, from which one could see the illimitable plain in which their small hill stood, wooded away to the purple horizon and dotted with villages and farms. Clear and square, but quite small beneath them, was the blacksmith's yard, where the inspector still stood taking notes and the corpse still lay like a smashed fly.

"Might be the map of the world, mightn't it?" said Father Brown.

"Yes," said Bohun very gravely, and nodded his head.

Immediately beneath and about them the lines of the Gothic building plunged outwards into the void with a sickening swiftness akin to suicide. There is that element of Titan energy in the architecture of the Middle Ages that, from whatever aspect it be seen, it always seems to be rushing away, like the strong back of some maddened horse. This church was hewn out of ancient and silent stone, bearded with old fungoids and stained with the nests of birds. And yet, when they saw it from below, it sprang like a fountain at the stars; and when they saw it, as now, from above, it poured like a cataract into a voiceless pit. For these two men on the tower were left alone with the most terrible aspect of the Gothic; the monstrous foreshortening and disproportion, the dizzy perspectives, the glimpses of great things small and small things great; a topsy-turvydom of stone in the mid-air. Details of stone, enormous by their proximity, were relieved against a pattern of fields and farms, pygmy in their distance. A carved bird or beast at a corner seemed like some vast walking or flying dragon wasting the pastures and villages below. The whole atmosphere was dizzy and dangerous, as if men were upheld in air amid the gyrating wings of colossal genii; and the whole of that old church, as tall and rich as a cathedral, seemed to sit upon the sunlit country like a cloudburst.

"I think there is something rather dangerous about standing on these high places even to pray," said Father Brown. "Heights were made to be looked at, not to be looked from."

"Do you mean that one may fall over," asked Wilfred.

"I mean that one's soul may fall if one's body doesn't," said the other priest.

"I scarcely understand you," remarked Bohun indistinctly.

"Look at that blacksmith, for instance," went on Father Brown calmly; "a good man, but not a Christian — hard, imperious, unforgiving. Well, his Scotch religion was made up by men who prayed on hills and high crags, and learned to look down on the world more than to look up at heaven. Humility is the mother of giants. One sees great things from the valley; only small things from the peak."

"But he — he didn't do it," said Bohun tremulously.

"No," said the other in an odd voice; "we know he didn't do it."

After a moment he resumed, looking tranquilly out over the plain with his pale gray eyes. "I knew a man," he said, "who began by worshiping with others before the altar, but who grew fond of high and lonely places to pray from, corners or niches in the belfry or the spire. And once in one of those dizzy places, where the whole world seemed to turn under him like a wheel, his brain turned also, and he fancied he was God. So that though he was a good man, he committed a great crime."

Wilfred's face was turned away, but his bony hands turned blue and white as they tightened on the parapet of stone.

"He thought it was given to *him* to judge the world and strike down the sinner. He would never have had such a thought if he had been kneeling with other men upon a floor. But he saw all men walking about like insects. He saw one especially strutting just below him, insolent and evident by a bright green hat — a poisonous insect."

Rooks cawed round the corners of the belfry; but there was no other sound till Father Brown went on.

"This also tempted him, that he had in his hand one of the most awful engines of nature; I mean gravitation, that mad and quickening rush by which all earth's creatures fly back to her heart when released. See, the inspector is strutting just below us in the smithy. If I were to toss a pebble over this parapet it would be something like a bullet by the time it struck him. If I were to drop a hammer — even a small hammer — "

Wilfred Bohun threw one leg over the parapet, and Father Brown had him in a minute by the collar.

"Not by that door," he said quite gently; "that door leads to hell."

Bohun staggered back against the wall, and stared at him with frightful eyes.

"How do you know all this?" he cried. "Are you a devil?"

"I am a man," answered Father Brown gravely; "and therefore have all devils in my heart. Listen to me," he said after a short pause. "I know what you did — at least, I can guess the great part of it. When you left your brother you were racked with no unrighteous rage to the extent even that you snatched up a small hammer, half inclined to kill him with his foulness on his mouth. Recoiling, you thrust it under your buttoned coat instead, and rushed into the church. You pray wildly in many places, under the angel window, upon the platform above, and on a higher platform still, from which you could see the colonel's Eastern hat like the back of a green beetle crawling about. Then something snapped in your soul, and you let God's thunderbolt fall."

Wilfred put a weak hand to his head, and asked in a low voice: "How did you know that his hat looked like a green beetle?"

"Oh, that," said the other with the shadow of a smile, "that was common sense. But hear me further. I say I know all this; but no one else shall know it. The next step is for you; I shall take no more steps; I will seal this with the seal of confession. If you ask me why, there are many reasons, and only one that concerns you. I leave things to you because you have not yet gone very far wrong, as assassins go. You did not help to fix the crime on the smith when it was easy; or on his wife, when that was easy. You tried to fix it on the imbecile because you knew that he could not suffer. That was one of the gleams that it is my business to find in assassins. And now come down into the village, and go your own way as free as the wind; for I have said my last word."

They went down the winding stairs in utter silence, and came out into the sunlight by the smithy. Wilfred Bohun carefully unlatched the wooden gate of the yard, and going up to the inspector, said: "I wish to give myself up; I have killed my brother."

Black Bread

TERESA BROM

YEARS ago Karel lived in a little village in Moravia with his mother and his younger brothers and sisters. One fall when Karel was nine years old his mother said, "Karel, you are old enough to go to school now. Tomorrow morning you will walk out to Farmer Havel's house near the school. You will work for him mornings and evenings, and go to school in the afternoons. In the spring you will come home again."

Karel cried, for although he was already nine, he did not wish to leave his mother and brothers and sisters and his good friend, Mr. Janek, the button maker, who always let him assort the buttons he had made and tie them into little yellow sacks.

"But you will like it at Farmer Havel's," Karel's mother said. "He is rich."

"I don't care. I want to stay here. Why do I have to go?"

Karel's mother sat down beside him on the doorstep. She put her hand on the brown, straight hair and said, "Karel, we are very poor, you know. If you go to school and work you will be helping me take care of Jan and Jakub and Eva."

But Karel still cried.

"And, little one," his mother said, "do you want to know something else? At Farmer Havel's they eat white bread every day, and not black bread as we do."

Karel stopped crying. "White bread every day — and not just once a year at Christmas time?"

"Every day, Karel, every day." His mother dried Karel's eyes with a fold of her gray dress. "And now go to sleep, for you have a long way to walk tomorrow."

From *The Sign*, September, 1936. By permission.

Karel lay down in the bed beside his two brothers, but he could not sleep for a long time. He could not stop thinking of what his mother had said about the white bread at Farmer Havel's. He had never before heard of anyone who ate white bread every day.

The next morning when it was just light enough to see, Karel and his mother walked out of the village and down the road. When they came to the place where the big wooden cross was, they stopped.

"Be a good boy, Karel," she said. "You know where to go — straight down the road until you come to the white church. You'll get there by this evening." She handed Karel a bag of apples and a bundle containing a few pieces of clothing.

Karel looked up at his mother. She was very pretty in the early morning light. She didn't look tired. "Good-by, mother," he said as he took the parcels.

"And on Easter night I'll be waiting right here for you."

Karel began to cry again. "I wish I could stay here," he said.

"Karel, be quiet. Remember how good you will have it — white bread every day."

"That's right." He smiled, and turned to go. "Good-by, Mother." He walked down the middle of the road, the bundle of clothes in one hand and the bag of apples in the other. Once he turned around and waved the apples at his mother, who still was watching him. One of the apples rolled out, and Karel ran after it and picked it up and put it back into the sack. When he looked around again, his mother was no longer there.

Karel enjoyed walking in the early morning. He had never been away from home alone before. He imagined he was a soldier marching to a battlefield; then he pretended he was a horse, and ran down the road, raising clouds of dust. Once he sat down on the side of the road and ate an apple. There was a worm in the apple; he carefully pulled the worm out and laid it on a leaf in the shade. He walked on again. Now a few carts and wagons passed him. Once in a while the men on the carts and wagons waved to him. One old man with a reddish beard and a big black hat stopped the wagon he was driving and asked Karel if he wanted a ride. Karel climbed up.

"Where are you going this morning?" the old man asked.

"Oh, I'm going to work and to school, too," he said.

"Do you think you'll like it?"

Karel laughed. "Oh yes. I'm going to be with rich people. I'm going to have white bread every day. And maybe sweet things too."

"No," the old man said, surprised.

"And maybe a new suit for Christmas. Or else a calf for my very own."

They drove on. Then the man said, "I don't go any farther." Karel jumped down from the wagon.

"Good-by — and thanks for the ride."

It was not so pleasant walking in the afternoon. It was hot and dusty. The dust was thick on everything — it lay on the red grapes growing along the roadside, on the fallen leaves, and on the fence rails. Even the black crows, hopping around the fields, looked gray from the dust. Karel was very tired. The dust bit into his eyes and made a funny taste in his mouth. He was hungry, too, but he knew he would get white bread when he came to the farm.

Just as it grew dark that evening he came to the white church. Right next to it was a large farmhouse. Karel walked to the back door and knocked. A little girl opened it. "I'm Karel Prokhup, the boy who is to help here."

"Who is it?" a voice asked. A big man with black hair stamped up to the door. "Oh, yes — yes — Karel. Come in."

Karel went in. The kitchen was well lighted. There was a big table in the middle of the room, all covered with food. And sure enough, in the middle of the table was a big plate full of thick slices of white bread. It was all true, what Mother had said.

"I suppose you want something to eat first," the farmer said. "Here, Ani, give this boy something."

A big girl came out of a small room next to the kitchen. "Come with me," she said to Karel. Karel followed her into the little room. She motioned that he should sit down by a small table. "Here, I'll get you something to eat."

"But — but I thought they were eating out there," Karel said.

"Of course, but you don't think Farmer Havel wants his hired help eating with him, do you?"

The big girl brought a bowl of thick cabbage soup, potatoes and a plate of bread. Karel looked at the bread first. It was black bread — just the kind he had at home every day.

"What's the matter?" the girl asked. "Why don't you eat?"

Karel began to cry. "Please, I'd like to go to bed — I'm tired."

"Of course you are." The big girl smiled at him. She took his hand and they went up a narrow stairs to a little room. There was a bed with a straw mattress on it and a chair without a back. But there was a red cover on the bed, Karel noticed.

"There you are. Farmer Havel will wake you in the morning and tell you what you'll have to do. Good night."

Karel undressed and lay down in the bed and cried. Soon everything was quiet downstairs. Karel stopped crying and listened. A branch from a tree hit against a small window of the room every time the wind blew. He wondered if people always were disappointed about things, and if they always cried. He wished he were home now, with his brothers and sisters and Mr. Janek, the button maker. Well, maybe it wouldn't take very long until Easter, and then he could go home again and tell his mother that the hired help at Farmer Havel's didn't get white bread, but black. And his Mother would be waiting for him there on the road beside the wooden cross.

Karel worked for Farmer Havel for many years. It was always hard work. At first, Karel fed the pigs and chickens and cows in the morning and helped Farmer Havel's wife with the housework. In the afternoon he went to school. At night he fed the animals again and cleaned the barns and chopped wood. Later, when he didn't go to school any more, he worked in the fields. But every Easter he would go home, and always his mother would be waiting for him at the same place on the road.

When Karel was nineteen he fell in love with Berta. Berta was a girl who lived on the next farm. She was the only girl Karel had ever seen who had small hands. She always wore pretty dresses — red and blue — and she had shining, brown hair. They often went on long walks together in the fields, after Karel was through with his work. He loved her very much, and she said that she loved him too. One night he asked her if she would marry him when he had saved enough money. She said she would. Karel was happy then.

Before, the thought of going home at Easter had been the one thing that he had lived and worked for. Now it was the hope of marrying Berta. He worked harder than ever and saved everything he could. Finally, when Karel was twenty-three, he had saved enough money to get married. His cousin, who had just bought a delicatessen store in Prague, had promised he would let Karel work for him. In the fall they made plans for their marriage. Karel was to meet Berta just outside the entrance to her father's farm. From here they would walk to the next town and take a train to Prague where they would be married. On the day on which they had planned to leave, Karel went into the woods back of the fields and picked a big sack of blueberries and two large bunches of red grapes. These he put into a small basket. When he returned to the farm, he bought a loaf of white bread from Farmer Havel's wife and put it into the basket with the fruit. They would eat it on the train. Karel laughed to himself. It would be a kind of wedding feast — before the wedding.

At six o'clock that evening Karel took the basket of food and a small carpetbag containing his clothes, said good-by to Farmer Havel and went down the road to meet Berta.

Karel saw her from a distance — standing beside the brown fence, her dress blowing in the wind. He walked faster when he saw her.

"Berta," he said when he reached her. "At last I am to be really happy!" He set the basket and the carpetbag on the roadside and put his arms around her. He kissed her. Then she pulled away.

"Karel," she said, "I'm not going with you."

He laughed and kissed her again. When he held her close in his arms like that he could not imagine her being away from him.

"You silly Berta," he said. "Of course you're going with me. How could you stay home now — after all we have planned?" She moved away from him, and walked down the road a little way.

"I didn't know until today how hard it would be to leave

Mother and Father — and my two new white kittens. Maybe I'd never see them again," she said as she turned and looked at him.

He went up to her and tried to take her in his arms again and kiss her. She turned her face away, and touched his bright green tie. He looked at her for a few moments. Karel knew now that she would never come with him, no matter what he said.

"It is too bad — that I have to go on — alone," he said.

He picked up the carpetbag. The heavy loaf of bread had crushed the blueberries, and there were dark blue stains spreading on the outside of the basket at his feet.

"Good-by, Berta," he said.

"Good-by. Oh, Karel — I'm so sorry. But I can't go — I can't. You wouldn't want me to be unhappy, would you?"

Karel turned quickly and walked down the road. He was glad that it was growing dark, so that the men passing by in the carts couldn't see that he was crying. It was always the same, he thought — one could never be really happy — one was always disappointed. He would have to buy a little piece of black bread at some farmer's house on the way to the station, because he would have nothing to eat until he reached Prague in the morning. The white bread was back there in the stained basket on the roadside beside Berta, who was still watching him, her red dress blowing about in the wind.

Karel went on alone to Prague. He worked in his cousin's delicatessen store for many years. When he was thirty he bought the store. Soon after he married a girl who lived across the street. They had one daughter — Helena. But Karel's wife died before Helena was a year old. Karel was very sad. He hired a housekeeper to take care of the little girl in the three rooms upstairs while he worked downstairs in the delicatessen store. He wanted to do everything to make his daughter happy. He loved her and worked for her; and she was now the one thing in life that he cared about. He worked in the delicatessen store every day, among the pickles and spiced sausages and sticky cakes; and every time that he sold anything it made him very happy, because it was all for Helena. He saw to it that Helena always had white bread.

Helena learned to play the violin. When she was twelve, Karel sent her to a music school in Vienna. When she was eighteen, he sent her away to a German university. He was very lonely during all the time that she was gone, but he knew that when she had finished at the university she would come back to him. She would show him how to enjoy the city, which in all the years he had never learned to love. They would be companions.

Helena was to come home the next day. Friends were bringing her home in a car, she had written. Karel watched the door of the delicatessen store all day. Every time a customer opened the door, Karel's heart beat faster, and he leaned far over the counter to see if it was Helena. Finally, a little before suppertime, she came. There was a man with her, but Karel didn't look at him; he looked only at Helena, for now she was home to stay.

"Helena," he said, as she kissed him, "I'm so glad you're home. I waited for you all day. Come upstairs — I know you are hungry."

"But we've eaten, Father. And look, I want you to meet Peter."

Karel looked at the man beside Helena then. He had a mustache, and wasn't very tall.

"This is Peter Krety, Father," she said. "We were married this morning."

"Married!" Karel didn't know what else to say.

"You see," Helena went on, "I really wanted to wait until you had seen Peter first; but he has to go on to Vienna for three months to finish his study. And he wanted me to be with him."

"Of course — of course — " Karel said.

"And you wouldn't want us to be unhappy, would you?"

Three more months away from him. But then they would be back again. And perhaps the three of them could enjoy the city together —

"But come upstairs," he said.

"We can't — we have to go now. Our train leaves in twenty minutes."

They would write, they said. And after three months they would come and stay with him for ten whole days. Then he could really get acquainted with his new son-in-law. And she would tell him everything — and how happy she and Peter would be living in the country where Peter could practice his farming. Hadn't she told him? Peter was studying experimental farming.

"I've never liked the city," she said. "It will be so wonderful getting away alone with Peter, where we can live simply as people should. Oh, and I'm going to do all sorts of things — things I've never done before — plant a garden, and cook. I'm even going to learn how to bake black bread — you know, the kind they have in the country."

Karel said of course he knew, and of course she was right. And he hoped she would be happy. Yes, he would write. And he would see them in three months — for about ten days.

When they had gone, Karel stood for a while, moving the long fork in the pickle barrel back and forth. He would have to hurry to get out the two special orders before seven o'clock. Perhaps he would let them go. What did it matter if he lost two customers now?

Mrs. Andres, his housekeeper, opened the back door of the store. "What do you want for supper tonight?" she called. "You forgot to tell me."

He looked at her a moment. "Black bread," he said. "Black bread — you know — the kind they have in the country —."

The Mockbeggar

SHEILA KAYE-SMITH

M R. AND Mrs. Reginald Dalrymple were walking along the highroad that leads from Iden to Wittersham across the Isle of Oxney. They were very particular about being given their full name of "Reginald" Dalrymple to distinguish them from Mr. and Mrs. Charley Dalrymple, who were in Northampton workhouse; from the Peter Dalrymples, who tramped in Wales; from the Stanley Dalrymples, who were in prison; and from Serena Dalrymple, who had put herself outside the pale of decent society on the roads by marrying a "nigger."

Mr. Reginald Dalrymple was about sixty-five years old and his back was bent. Otherwise he looked hale enough, and his face, at least as much as could be seen of it through a thatch of brown whiskers, was red as an autumn pear. He wore a frock coat, gray-flannel trousers, a pair of brown beach shoes with rather inadequate uppers, and a bowler hat.

Mrs. Reginald Dalrymple was about three years younger than her husband and inclined to stoutness, though she looked an able-bodied woman. She wore a very handsome cape trimmed with jet, a woolen muffler that might have been gray, but to which she referred as "me white scarf," and a man's cap set at a rakish angle. She wheeled a perambulator, which did not, however, contain a baby, but the Reginald Dalrymple's luggage — indeed it may be said, their complete household equipment, which at first glance would appear to consist entirely of old rags. However, a more sympathetic inspection would reveal a really excellent kettle (the leak was only just below the spout), a suspicious-looking rug,

From *Joanna Godden Married and Other Stories,* by Sheila Kaye-Smith, published by Harper and Brothers, New York, 1926.

an assortment of cups, a tin plate, a screw driver, an ancient copy of *Tit-Bits*, a photograph of a robust young woman with a hat full of feathers, and another photograph of a sailor.

"I'm beginning to feel me feet," said Mrs. Reginald Dalrymple to her husband.

"And I'm thinking it's coming on to rain," said he, with a look up at the lowering sky.

It was autumn, and the red leaves were shaking against soft clouds of October gray which the wind brought down from Benenden in the west.

"Where's our next chance of a doss?" asked Mrs. Dalrymple.

"There's the Throws up at Potman's Heath," replied her husband, "but I reckon they'll be — damp tonight."

"Reg! Don't use such words," said Mrs. Dalrymple, with dignity. "You forget my mother was a Stanley."

"I'm never likely to forget it, the way you goes on about it. Anyone 'u'd think she'd been Queen Victoria on her throne, to hear you talk! But what I say is, it's coming on to rain and there ain't no union within fifteen miles. Besides, you're feeling your feet," he added, kindly.

"I've walked twelve miles since dinner, Reg," said Mrs. Dalrymple, with a little plaintive sigh.

"Hook on, then," said he, extending a ragged elbow.

She hooked, and for some moments they walked in silence. Then he said:

"It'll be awkward for you pushing the pram with one hand," and took it from her — though Mr. Reginald Dalrymple had often boasted that he had never come down to wheeling a perambulator, and never would.

"I've been thinking," said she, a few minutes later, by which time the rain was spattering freely in the dust — "I've been thinking we must have come near that mockbeggar place by the Stocks. The house was standing there five years ago when we was on the roads with Sue and her lot, and if it hasn't tumbled down since there's one good room in it, anyway, with the ceiling tight, and there's water in the well at the bottom of the yard."

Mr. Dalrymple reflected. "You're right, Hannah! — I believe

you're right this once. We should be coming to that mockbeggar in half an hour. It'll be raining the —— skies down by that time, so we might go in and light a fire and not trouble about getting farther tonight. It's a good way from the nearest place and we're not like to be meddled with."

Mrs. Dalrymple was feeling her feet more and more, in spite of the supporting elbow and the removal of the pram. She was also beginning to get wet, though this did not worry her, being of custom. She was far more preoccupied with the thought that she could not walk a twelve-mile stretch without getting tired — and she'd been able to walk twice that as a girl, when she and Reginald had tramped all round the country by Chichester. She had had the children then, as well — one slung at her breast and the other hanging on her skirt when his dad did not carry him. She was glad when she saw three sharp gables suddenly draw themselves against the sky, which sagged low over the fields, squirting rain.

"That's it," she said; "that's the mockbeggar. I knew it was somewhere in these parts, though we haven't been here since Sue was on the roads with her man. D'you remember that time we dossed under the stack at Wassall?"

Mr. Dalrymple grunted. He was looking for a gap in the hedge, for it struck him that it would be best to go straight across the fields to shelter instead of walking round by the road. He soon found what he thought was a proper opening, and proceeded to enlarge it to meet the ample requirements of his wife by pushing the perambulator through. He then gallantly offered a hand to Mrs. Dalrymple, and after much gasping and effort and crackling of twigs she was at his side in the paddock which belonged to the mockbeggar.

A "mockbeggar house" in Kent is any large-sized house which stands empty close to a highroad, and seems to mock the beggar who plods along, thinking he will find charity at those doors which, on his close arrival, are found to be either swinging on their hinges or barred on emptiness. The mockbeggar at Wittersham was an especially large house, which, owing to want of repairs, a poor landlord, and a defective water supply, had stood empty for some time. It was probably about fifty years old and was built in comfortable Victorian style, but neglect and the misty weather of the Isle of Oxney — that cone round which steam all the mists of the Rother levels and Shirley brooks — had eaten holes in its solid fabric of roof and wall and made its shelter doubtful even to the Reginald Dalrymples, to whom uncracked walls and fair slated roofs were only the occasional experience of the workhouse.

"A downstairs room 'u'd be best," said Mrs. Reginald.

They went into one next the passage on the ground floor. It was full of dead leaves and bits of glass from a broken window, but there was grate in it where a fire might possibly burn, and the rain was confined to a small pool under the window sill.

"You unpack here, Hannah, and I'll go and get some water for the kettle."

Mrs. Dalrymple extracted the kettle from the pram, carefully wrapped in a piece of newspaper, and while her husband went off she proceeded to arrange her various belongings. The sinister-looking rug she put in the corner with a nice comfortable bit of sacking; that was the bedroom. The cups, the plate, and a broken knife she put on the remains of a shelf; that was the kitchen. While the two photographs she set proudly among the dust and cobwebs on the mantlepiece; that was the parlor. She was then, according to custom, going on to make herself comfortable by taking off her shoes, when she was startled by a thudding noise overhead.

An empty house is full of noises, and Mrs. Dalrymple had a wide experience of empty houses. Mere scuttlings of rats or hoot-ings of owls or rustlings of crickets or howlings of wind in chim-neys could not alarm her, but this sound she knew at once was none of these. It was a footstep, a human footstep, which moved in the room overhead, and she held her breath to listen. The next minute she heard more and worse — the murmur coming to her through the boards was a human voice. She stuck her head out of the window (no need to open it first) and made a sign to Reginald, who was coming up the yard with the kettle. The sign urged both silence and attention, also haste. His response was immediate; they had often been together in these emergencies, demanding a quick stealth. He did not speak a word till he was back beside her in the room.

"It's people!" said Mrs. Dalrymple, in a hoarse whisper; "there's people here!"

"How d'you know? Where are they?"

"They're up above. I heard 'em talking. Listen!"

They both listened. The sounds in the upper room continued — voices and footsteps.

"There's two," said Mr. Dalrymple. "I can tell by the feet. Who can it be? It's road people like ourselves, most like; no one else 'u'd ever come here."

"I wonder if it's anyone we know. It might be the Lovells — you know Lance and Aurelia Lovell are walking in Kent."

"I hope it ain't folk in the house after repairs," said Mr. Dalrymple, struck by a sudden thought. "You never know your luck, and someone may have bought the place."

"I hope it's not that stuck-up Eleanor Ripley and her husband," said Mrs. Dalrymple. "We had enough of their airs when we met them at Maidstone. She's got saucers to all her cups."

"Well, I'd sooner it was her than gaujos," returned Mr. Dalrymple; "it 'u'd never do for us to get found here, and it 'u'd mean a-spoiling of the place for visitors."

"You go and have a look," suggested his wife. "Take off your shoes."

Mr. Dalrymple shuffled them off without undoing the laces, and left the room with extreme caution. His progress upstairs and along the passage was as silent as only his kind know how to make it.

Mrs. Dalrymple strained her ears, which were as quick as they were when she was seventeen. The voices continued, but she detected more than conversation — she thought she heard a sound of sobbing. Time went on. Reginald was evidently maneuvering with his usual discretion, for the flow of talk above remained uninterrupted. Indeed, so velvet-footed was he that he was back at her side before she expected him, and, old stager though she was, nearly made her jump.

"It's gaujos," he said, in a low voice. "There's two of 'em, mighty queer . . ."

"How queer?"

"Oh, the girl's got short hair like a boy, and the boy he's soft-looking. They're only a boy and girl. Maybe we could scare 'em out."

"I don't want to scare them," said Mrs. Dalrymple. "The night ain't fit for a dog and I'd be sorry to turn 'em out in it. But if they ain't road people, what are they doing here?"

"They're quarreling," said Mr. Dalrymple — "quarreling and crying."

"I thought I heard crying."

"It's the girl's crying, into a handkerchief. She's got a white handkerchief with a blue border."

"Are they gentry?"

"Fine gentry, I should say, by their clothes, but I don't think they're after repairs or taking the house or anything."

"What are they doing, then?"

"Sheltering from the rain, like us, and I don't think they've got much money, for they're talking a lot of words about the price of a ticket to London."

"Is that what the trouble's about?"

"No, I don't know as it is. I can't make out a lot of their foolish words, but it seems as either he wants to marry her and she won't, or else as they are married and she wants to get shut of him and he won't have it."

"I should think not!" said Mrs. Dalrymple. "I'm for sticking to your lawful certificated husband, and that's why I'd never go to the workhouse except just now and again for a rest. You know that Eleanor she says a woman should be able to get rid of her husband if she wants to, and take a new one, which you can't do in a workhouse, but I was always brought up to strict notions as to marriage. My mother was a married woman, and so is my daughter after me."

"Well, maybe they ain't married. I don't rightly know. They had too many words for me to be able to make out the lot of them. But hold your tongue, Hannah; they're coming down."

Steps sounded on the rickety stairs of the mockbeggar — unskill-ful, gaujo steps that made every stair creak.

Mrs. Dalrymple made a hasty movement as if to gather up her possessions and thrust them back under the rags in the peram-bulator, stirred, perhaps, by some dim instinct of far-off ancestors who must not let the stranger look upon their household goods.

Her husband laid hold of her arm. "Don't be scared; they're nothing — hardly cut their teeth yet!"

At the same moment a young man appeared in the doorway. He was tall and loosely knit, with a heavy coltishness about him, as of one not yet full grown. Behind him a girl's face stood out of the shadows, framed in a queer little stiff mane of cropped hair. Her eyes were bright and resolute, but at the same time frightened.

"Hullo!" said the youth, truculently, to Mr. Dalrymple. "What are you doing here?"

Mr. Dalrymple looked the aggressor up and down. "This place belongs to us as much as you."

"*More* than you," said Mrs. Dalrymple, "seeing as we're road people and you're house people who have no business here!"

"Well, I might ask what your business is."

"Our business is to have supper and a doss on a wet night, and if you keeps clear and don't come round talking foolishness we won't meddle with you, and there's room enough for the lot of us."

"It's all right, Bob," said the girl. "Let's go back." Her face was flushed, and her eyes were a little swollen under the straight line of her fringe.

Mrs. Dalrymple suddenly became professional.

"I'm not the one to interfere with a real lady and gentleman," she whined, putting on the manner which she kept for well-dressed strangers. "I'm sure you're a real fine lady and gentleman, and if the lady will only cross my hand with silver I'll tell her some gorgeous things about herself, and maybe about the gentle-man, too. I can see a lot of money coming to you, lady — even more than the price of a ticket to London!"

The girl darted a surprised look at her companion.

"Come, lady," wheedled Mrs. Dalrymple, "I'll tell you a high-class tale about husbands."

The girl turned away with a heightening of her flush. "I can't bear this nonsense," she said, in a low voice to the young man. "These people needn't interfere with us, nor we with them. Let's go upstairs."

The youth looked sulky. "It's all very well," he said, "but they've got the only decent room; the rain's coming through all the ceilings above."

"You should have put your traps in here," said Mr. Dalrymple, "then we should have kept out of it; but as we're here we mean to stick. My old woman's wet through, and she's going to have a dry doss, I'm blowed if she ain't."

"Oh, well, come on," said the young man. "It may clear up before night, and then we'll start again."

He turned away, following the girl upstairs, and the Reginald Dalrymples were left in peace.

"There's queer things you meets on the roads," said Mrs. Dalrymple, "and it isn't so much the people you meet as the places where you meets 'em. What are those two doing here? I'm beat."

"You're curious," retorted Mr. Dalrymple, "fair eat up with curiosity, because you're a woman. Now I don't think twice about 'em as long as they leaves me alone, and nor won't you, Hannah, if you've got sense. Here, let's have a fire and get ourselves dry."

He turned to the all-providing pram and from its depths drew forth its last treasures — some blocks of wood and a bundle of sticks. The Dalrymples always carried a supply of dry firewood about with them, for they were getting old and considered themselves entitled to a certain amount of luxury in their old age.

A fire was soon lit and the kettle put on to boil; once it was blazing, the addition of a few damp sticks gathered outside no longer mattered. The room grew warm and Mrs. Dalrymple's clothes began to steam. Her husband took off his coat and put it over her shoulders.

"There you are, Hannah," he said. "I don't want it. This weather makes me sweat, but you've got to take care of your bones."

They made tea, which they drank in great comfort, with half a stale loaf and a lump of lard. Outside, the rain was hissing down, while the wind howled in the chimney.

"It'll be wet upstairs," said Mrs. Dalrymple, pleasantly.

The fire was beginning to die down, and Mr. Dalrymple did not fancy going outside to get in more sticks.

"I'll go and have a look at the banisters," he said, "and maybe there's a bit of a cupboard door."

The banisters looked satisfactory as fuel, and he was in the act of wrenching a couple of them out when he saw the young man on the staircase above him.

"Hi!" said the latter, dejectedly, "we're half flooded out upstairs. I was going to suggest that we come in with you till it stops raining. We'll clear out as soon as the weather lets us."

"We're poor people," said Mr. Dalrymple — "Mrs. Reginald Dalrymple and I are poor people, and we can't afford to take lodgers at our fire without a bit of silver."

"We aren't asking you to take us as lodgers, damn it! I'm just asking you to let the young lady come and sit in a dry place. It's what you wouldn't refuse a dog."

"I would certainly refuse a dog," returned Mr. Dalrymple, with dignity. "My wife and I never allows no dogs to sit with us, it being well known dogs have fleas and my wife being a lady as 'll have nothing to do with fleas!"

The young man surveyed Mr. Dalrymple as if he himself belonged to that species.

"Well, if you want money," he said, "I suppose you must have it. Will a shilling do you?"

"A shilling will do me very well," said Mr. Dalrymple, loftily, "and it includes the fire. We have a very excellent fire!"

"So I gather," said the young man as he coughed in the smoke that was eddying upstairs.

But even the Dalrymple quarters, full of smoke and the smell of ancient rags, were better than the leaking, dripping rooms where he and Meave Anstey had been struggling in vain to keep warm and dry. Meave was shivering now, and her face was no longer flushed, but blue, as she sat down gingerly beside Mrs. Dalrymple's fire.

"Cross my hand with silver, lady," said that good woman, returning unabashed to the attack, "and I'll tell you the prettiest fortune that ever was spoke."

"I don't want your lies," said the girl, angrily, with a sudden gulp.

"Lies, lady! I never tells lies! May I be struck dead if I does."

"My wife is well known as a truth-telling woman," said Mr. Dalrymple, "and I'll thank you not to miscall her!"

For some reason Meave felt rebuked, though she believed neither of them.

"I'm sorry," she said. "Well, you may tell my fortune if you like, but I've only got sixpence."

"Thank you, lady. Thank you kindly, lady. Sixpence will buy me a packet of tea at the next village, lady. And I'll drink your very good health in it, for I never drinks nothing stronger than tea, which is well known."

Meave held out a soft, artistic-looking hand, which was by this time more than a little grimy.

"I likes dirt on the hand," remarked Mrs. Dalrymple; "it helps me to see the lines better. Now what I see is this: I see a railway line, with a train on it going to London, and you and a gentleman are in that train, and when you get to London I sees a church, and a priest, and a great crowd of people, and rice, and slippers. I see all that, and you in the middle of it, beautiful as an angel, and beside you a tall, handsome young gentleman with light hair and brown eyes."

The girl angrily pulled her hand away. "Don't talk such nonsense, please! I can't stand it."

"You don't want to get married?"

"No, I don't. As if I'd — Rice! . . . Slippers! . . . White veil . . .!" The scorn grew in her voice.

"There's a wedding cake," encouraged Mrs. Dalrymple, "with sugar all over it!"

"I don't want to hear any more. Look here, you're a fortune-teller, aren't you? I suppose I'm the first girl you've ever met who hasn't wanted to hear about marriage?"

"You would be the first if I believed you," said Mrs. Dalrymple, who had dropped her company manner in the familiarity of the scene.

"Well, you can believe it. I don't want to get married — I don't believe in marriage," and she threw a defiant glance not at Mrs. Dalrymple, but at the young man.

"But a girl can't never live by herself. It ain't natural."

"And it ain't safe," said Mr. Dalrymple. "I've known more than one time when my wife here might have got copped if it hadn't been for having me handy to show her the right trick."

"I don't mean to be alone," said the girl. "I don't believe in that, either. What I hate is the hypocrisy and the slavery of marriage." Her voice rose and warmed; she became a little lecturer. "It's the idea of losing my freedom which I can't bear. If women hadn't been slaves for centuries none of them could bear it. When I choose my mate we shall both of us be free — free to love and free to part. There shall be no keeping of the outer husk when the kernel has rotted."

Mr. and Mrs. Dalrymple stared silently with their mouths open, and the young man looked uneasy.

"You see me and my friend here, now," continued Meave, "and even you, a woman outside the ordinary conventions of society, immediately form the idea that we're going to be married. I tell you you're utterly wrong. If we were going to be married we shouldn't be running away; we should be sitting at home, unpacking wedding presents. We are going to join our lives together, but in freedom, not in bondage. We shall be free to part whenever we choose, free to work, free to go our own ways . . ." She had almost forgotten that she had not got her debating society before her.

"Well," said Mrs. Dalrymple, "I don't want to part and I don't want to work and I don't want to go any different ways from Mr. Dalrymple, so I can't see the sense of what you're saying. Mr. Dalrymple and me has been married close on forty years, and we've got a daughter Sue who's been married twenty years to a fine feller in the osier trade. She has a caravan with brass rods on the door and lace curtains in the windows, and five of the dearest little children you could think of; leastways, the eldest's nearly grown up now. And we've got a son Jerome who's a sailor and has had two wives one after the other. The wife he's got now lives in a house and has a china tea service. We're proud of our children, but they've gone away from us now and I don't know what we'd do if we hadn't got each other."

"She's uncommon set on her children," said Mr. Dalrymple. "That's their likenesses up there on the shelf, what we carries about with us everywhere. My daughter Sue 'u'd have us stay with her, and once we went and stopped with my son and daughter at Portsmouth and slept in a bed. But we'd just as soon be along of each other here."

"Reckon you wants your husband more when you're old than when you're young," said Mrs. Dalrymple. "I'm getting too old to do most of the things I used, and I don't know what I'd do if it wasn't for Mr. Dalrymple, who does them for me. Our idea is to keep on the roads till we're old enough to go into the married quarters at the workhouse. It 'u'd break our hearts if we was to be separated after all this time. . . . I don't hold with being parted from your certificated husband."

"You gets used to each other like," said Mr. Dalrymple. "If I was to go on the roads with anyone else I'd be so bothered and vexed I shouldn't know what to do."

"If I was ever to see you on the roads with anyone else . . ." said Mrs. Dalrymple, menacingly.

"Not likely, old lady," said he, pushing her cap over one eye in playful affection.

"Now, now," said she, "none of your larks." But she looked pleased and a little proud of him.

The rain had become a storm, with a rush of wind in the chimneys of the mockbeggar. Dead leaves flew rustling round the yard, and the pool under the window was a little lake. But beside the fire it was warm and dry, though the smoke, as it eddied and waved under the low ceiling, made Meave choke a little, and strange tears come into her eyes — of course that was the smoke. She felt proud and happy. She had broken free at last . . . and she was saving Bob, who otherwise would have become a slave, having all the instincts of one. . . .

"Ooo — ooo . . . yah!" A loud yawn from Mr. Dalrymple made her start. "I'm —— sleepy," he added, conversationally.

"Now don't you start using words again," said his wife. "I'm not accustomed to them, being a Stanley, and I reckon the young lady ain't, either, for all her uncertificated ideas. If you wants to go to sleep — go."

"I'm going," said Mr. Dalrymple.

"Then take back your coat. I've dried under it nicely."

"I don't want any coat. I'm warm as a bug."

"You want it, and you'll take it. Here now."

An amiable tussle followed, which ended in Mr. Dalrymple putting on his coat, while his wife had the piece of sacking in addition to her share of the rug. They took no more notice of Meave Anstey and Bob Pettigrew, but were soon asleep, with the queer, stiff, silent sleep of animals who rest among foes.

"Rum old pair," said Bob, under his breath. "I'm sorry you've been let in for this, Meave, but it's better than being swamped up stairs."

"Oh, they're all right! I rather like them, though of course they're frauds. They're decent to each other, which is odd. I rather thought that type of man always bullied his wife."

"Men aren't quite such rotters as you think — even tramps."

He spoke irritably, for the sordid side of the adventure was unpleasantly obvious on this night of wind and rain without, and stuffiness and teasing smoke within. To his surprise, she did not take up his challenge. She sat watching the old couple as they lay huddled in the corner, a confused blot of rags and shadows.

"It's love that holds them together," she said, in her debating-society voice, hushed down to a whisper, "not the mere fact of marriage."

"I dunno," said he, truculently. "I don't believe they'd be together now if they weren't married — anyhow, not together like this."

"Why not? Why shouldn't lovers be faithful?"

"It's different, as I've told you a hundred times. Especially when you're old. I'd think nothing of it if they were young or middle-aged. But they're old, and there must have been lots of times when they were tired of loving and tired of life, and 'u'd never have gone on if they hadn't belonged to each other."

"That's just it — they were tied."

"And the tie kept them together over the bad places. It's like being roped on a climb; when one or another of them went down, there was always the rope, and as soon as they were on their legs again they didn't notice it. I believe people who aren't married — no matter how they love each other — somehow they're hardly ever in together at the finish. . . . You generally find that if the going's rough they drift apart. Why, you, yourself, say you'd hate to belong to a man all your life; you want the one great Moment, and then not to spoil it by going on together. I think there's a good deal to be said for that, though, as I've told you dozens of times, I want to marry you."

He looked very young as he sat there beside her in the dying firelight. He was only a boy or he wouldn't have come with her — he wouldn't have let her force her adventure on him like that. He was very young — but he would grow old, like Mr. Dalrymple. That soft brown lick of hair on his forehead would be gray — his face a little worn, perhaps. Should she see it then, or would they have gone their separate ways? She wondered what he would look like when he was old — what he would be like — kind, protective, unselfish, like Mr. Dalrymple — a strong arm to lean on when she needed it most? . . . Growing old together . . . together not only at the start, but at the journey's end . . . but tied . . . as Mr. and Mrs. Dalrymple were tied . . . by the memories of struggles and toils together, by adventures and hardships shared, by long years of companionship in wayfaring, by the love of their children. . . .

She bowed her head suddenly over her lap and tears fell into her hands.

"Meave — darling — what is it? Tell me."

His arm was round her, his shoulder under her cheek.

"Bob . . . Bob . . . will you always love me — when we're old?"

"Of course I shall always love you."

"As much as that?" and she waved her hand toward the indefinite mass of Mr. and Mrs. Dalrymple.

"I should hope so," with a little contempt.

"Then . . . Bob . . . let's go back."

"Go back where?"

"Home. I want us to get married."

"My little Meave! . . . But you said — "

"It's seeing them. They're so happy — they're so true. They're dirty, terrible, shameless old things, but they're happy; they've got something that we haven't got — that we can't ever have, unless we're married."

He had wisdom to be silent, hugging her without a word.

"Let's go back home. It's not ten o'clock yet, and we can tell mother we were caught in the rain and waited to see if it would stop. She need never know."

"And we'll get married?"

"Yes, though you know she'll make us go in for everything — bridesmaids and rice and church bells and all that."

"Never mind; it'll make Mrs. Dalrymple's fortune come true."

They both laughed a little.

"When shall we start?" he asked her.

"Oh, soon — now."

"But it's coming down in buckets."

"Never mind; we're only an hour from home. We haven't got to face all that walk into Rye and then the further journey to London."

She shivered a little, and he drew her close in sudden, fierce protection.

"I shouldn't have let you come. I've been a fool about all this. I didn't believe in it, and yet I gave way because I was afraid of losing you. I should have had sense enough for both of us, and made you go my way instead of yours."

"Is that what you're going to do in the future?"

"Yes — when you're a silly little thing."

She laughed, and their lips came together.

It was he who remembered the need for quick action.

"Come, we must be getting off, or we sha'n't be home till it's too late to explain. Are you ready?"

"Quite. I'm glad we didn't bring any luggage, except in our

ulster pockets. It would have been difficult to explain why we'd gone for a walk with two suitcases."

They giggled lightheartedly, and went out on tiptoe.

They were off. But just as they were leaving the mockbeggar she remembered something that had been left undone.

"Bob, we ought to tell them. I want them to know."

"For heaven's sake don't go back and wake them up! What d'you want them to know?"

"That we're going to be married."

"What on earth has that got to do with them?"

"Oh, nothing, of course . . . but I thought. . . . Give me a leaf out of your pocketbook, there's a darling."

He gave it, and she scribbled on it, "We are going to be married," and, creeping back into the room, put it on the mantelpiece beside the pictures of the blowsy girl and the sailor.

"And look here" she added, "as we're not going to London, we might just leave the price of our tickets with them. It may help them a lot."

"They'll probably spend it on drink."

"Well, let them. I don't care. I can't bear to think of people without proper boots on their feet."

The firelight was playing reproachfully on the toe of Mr. Dalrymple's shoe.

"Nor can I. Well, here's the money. It'll be a surprise for them when they wake up."

He put it beside the paper on the mantelpiece, and they went out.

It was daylight when Mr. and Mrs. Dalrymple woke. The storm had ceased.

"Hullo! They've gone," said he.

"Not taken any of our things with them, have they, Reg?" asked his wife, looking anxiously round.

"Not they. They're gentry. Gentry don't take poor people's things without a lawyer."

"You never know. Besides, they was queer gentry. All that talk

she had about marriage . . . it was shocking. If I'd ever heard my
Sue using such words I'd have — "

"Wot's this?"

Her husband had found the treasure on the mantelpiece.

"I'm blowed if they haven't left their money behind 'em! Ten
bob if it's a tanner! Well, I'm blowed!"

"That's luck for us, anyway, if it ain't exactly luck for them."

"Oh, I reckon they done it on purpose. They'd never have put
their dough just there by our Jack's likeness. It's Christian charity,
that's what it is."

"I don't believe it's Christian charity — that 'u'd be tuppence.
Ten bob's nothing but an accident. Howsumever, it makes no
difference to me what it is so long as it's there. I could do with a
plate o' ham."

"A plate o' ham and a cup o' coffee, and a bottle o' whisky to
come along with us to Tonbridge."

"That's it. But look there, Reg — there's writing on the paper."

"So there is. Pity we ain't scollards."

"Maybe it's a word for us."

"That's what it is, I reckon."

She picked up the paper and inspected it solemnly, then passed
it on to her husband, who did the same.

"Pity we never got no school learning, Reg."

"I've never felt the want."

"But I'd like to be able to read the word they've left us."

"That's because you're a woman and made of curiosity. I, being
a man, says let's take the money and be thankful. And now, old
lady, pack up your traps, for, thanks to this bit of luck, we'll have
our breakfast at the Blue Boar."

A Little Beaded Bag

MORLEY CALLAGHAN

WHEN young Mrs. Evans came in at dinnertime and noticed that the little white beaded bag she had tossed on the chair in the bedroom that afternoon was gone, she was sure Eva, the maid, had taken it. The girl had been helping her clean out the chest of drawers in the bedroom, and they had found the bag that had been put aside a year ago because the little white beads had come loose around the metal clasp. Mrs. Evans had looked at it and hesitated, remembering the first night she had carried it to the party her friends gave for her and her husband when they returned from Europe, and then she sighed, knowing she would never get it fixed, and tossed it at the pile of rubbish on the paper they had spread out on the floor.

"My, it's pretty, isn't it?" Eva said brightly as she picked it up. Mrs. Evans took it from her, looked at it and hesitated again, wondering if she ought to keep it after all, and undecided, tossed it onto the bedroom chair.

When her husband who was a young lawyer came home she might never have mentioned the bag to him at all, if he hadn't tossed his brief case on the sofa and sat down sullenly and refused to speak to her. They had quarreled the night before. They had been married only a year, but in the last few months there seemed to be some tension and strain between them that puzzled her and made them sometimes want to hurt each other terribly. And when she saw him hiding gloomily behind the newspaper, she was touched and regretted the quarrel: she wanted to tell him that he was wrong about last night, that he was crazy if he thought she really expected him to drop all his old friends, and that she under-

From *Harper's Bazaar* (N. Y.), September, 1937. Printed by permission of the author and of *Harper's Bazaar*.

stood that he could still be in love with her and yet want to have some freedom of his own.

"David," she said, a little timidly, "David, I was thinking — "

"I'm tired," he said in a surly voice, and when he didn't even look at her, she suddenly remembered that he liked Eva and used to ask her questions about her people on the farm, so she said, casually, "You may be interested to know Eva stole that beaded bag of mine."

"What's that? What bag?" he exclaimed.

"You know the one, the one I had a year ago."

"Why, the kid wouldn't touch it," he said sharply. "You know that as well as I do. She's a fine kid. You've been trying for weeks to find some little flaw in her, and you've had to admit, yourself, you couldn't. Don't start picking away at her."

It seemed so unjust that he should challenge her like this. As they faced each other, she said bitterly, "I'm not picking at her or you. I'm telling you a fact. The bag was there this morning and it's gone."

"I don't think she's taken it, that's all," he said.

"We can soon find out if you doubt it," she said quickly.

"Well, I certainly doubt it."

"Of course, you do," she replied, "of course you do. You mean you doubt my judgment about everything. Well, I'll show you," she said, and she smiled very brightly at him.

She went into the kitchen where Eva was getting the dinner ready. She sat down and watched the girl's soft hair, and her plump young shape as she moved around. The girl grew nervous and began to smooth her apron and look very scared. Mrs. Evans kept watching her steadily, never smiling, never speaking, and when Eva reddened and half turned, she offered no explanation. And it got so that Eva could no longer stand the shrewd, calm, knowing expression in Mrs. Evans's eyes, and she turned nervously. "Is there anything wrong, ma'am?" she asked.

"Do you remember that purse this morning?"

"Yes, ma'am. Weren't you going to throw it out?"

"You know I wasn't throwing it out, Eva."

"Well — "

"Somebody took it."

"Maybe I threw it out in the trash barrel," she said, and she looked at Mrs. Evans, as if pleading with her to make some friendly little remark about it being unimportant anyway and that she was sure the bag would turn up.

But Mrs. Evans, seeing how disturbed the girl was, said easily, "Eva, would you run down to the drugstore and get me some cigarettes?" and she smiled.

"Right now?" the girl asked, reluctantly.

"Yes, right now, please."

Eva was frightened and sullen, and she was trying to make some kind of plan as she stood there. Then she turned to go back to her room, but Mrs. Evans called sharply, "You don't need your coat, Eva. Just go as you are." They faced each other, and all the independence that must at one time have been in the girl's people gave her strength for just a moment to resist an antagonism that she did not understand. In the last month she had hardly spoken to either Mr. or Mrs. Evans. When she heard them quarreling at night she was afraid they would call her to bring them a drink and her hand would tremble and Mrs. Evans would be impatient, and then Eva would hear Mr. Evans defending her goodnaturedly. But now she nodded obediently and went out in a wild rush, for she was scared of losing her job.

Mrs. Evans went straight to the girl's bedroom and David followed, scowling at her. She trembled with excitement going through Eva's dresser drawer, pushing aside little boxes of cheap powder, an old photograph of Eva's father, who was a big, poorly dressed man, a few letters which she held in her hand wondering if Eva had talked about her; and then with her heart pounding with excitement as she listened for the sound of the girl's footsteps, and feeling strangely like a thief herself, she went to the cupboard and pulled out the girl's club bag and fished through the nightdress, the old tattered prayer book, the love-story magazine. At the bottom was the damaged white beaded bag. She held it up in her hand, her face serious; and then she stood up triumphantly and smiled at her husband who turned away as if he was sick. As she followed him into the living room the door slammed and the girl came rushing in, flushed, her eyes full of apprehension, and she handed Mrs. Evans the cigarettes.

"Thanks, Eva," she said, a little coldly, and the girl reddened and wheeled around and went into her bedroom.

"Well, now, was I right? Am I right about something?" she said to David.

"No, you weren't right," he said quietly.

"It was in her bag, you saw it yourself," she said excitedly. "Don't you believe your own eyes?" But it bothered her terribly that he only stared at her. She whispered, "Haven't I got a perfect right to find out if I've got a thief in the house? What are you staring at me for, wasn't I right?" But he sat there as if she were a stranger and she puzzled him.

Then they heard Eva calling, "Mrs. Evans, could I speak to you a moment, please?" and she came in, holding out the dainty little white purse, trying to smile innocently. But her eyes showed how completely helpless she felt with the little white purse, as if it had been something bright and elusive that had betrayed her.

"You found it," Mrs. Evans said uneasily.

"Yes, I found it, don't you see," she whispered, nodding her head eagerly, begging Mrs. Evans to say just something simple like, "That's fine," begging her with her flushed face just to take the purse and not to use the complete power she had over her to make her a liar. As they looked at each other steadily they were both distressed.

"Where did you find it?" Mrs. Evans asked.

"In the trash barrel," Eva said rapidly, never taking her eyes off Mrs. Evans's face. "I must have picked it up with some papers and things. I remembered I put all those things you wanted thrown out in one pile, and I thought I might have picked it up, too, and I went and looked. I'm very sorry, Mrs. Evans."

"Why, thanks, Eva, thanks," Mrs. Evans said, hesitatingly, and when the girl hesitated, too, and then went, she hoped it was all over, but when she turned to David he was looking more distressed than ever. She grew ashamed, yet she fought against this shame and she said, indignantly, "What's the matter with you? She took it and she knows I caught her."

"Maybe you're satisfied," he whispered.

"I don't know what you mean," she said.

"You know she didn't intend to take it. You know you made her a thief. You humiliated the kid, you took away her self-respect," he said, coming close to her as if he was going to shake her. "My Lord, if you know what you looked like going through the kid's things."

"I didn't, I didn't," she whispered.

"You're ruthless when you get started — just like I told you last night, utterly ruthless."

"It's got nothing to do with us," she said angrily.

"Yes, it has. You're still at me, and it doesn't matter about the kid," he said. "Keep it up, keep getting everything tighter till it snaps and then we'll hate each other."

He looked so utterly heartbroken that she put out her hand and touched him on the arm, trying to plead with him. "I didn't mean it like that. I knew I was right, that's all."

"Sure, you were right. You're right about so many things," but he was shaken a little because she looked so frightened, and he muttered, "I don't know what's the matter with you," and he swung away from her and she heard him going out.

She sat down slowly with her hands up to her face, crying out within herself, "I was right," and then, "Oh, no, I know I was wrong. But I just want him to be close to me always. Why can't he see it?" and as she looked down at the little beaded bag in her hand which was so small and unimportant, it seemed to her that day after day with her doubts and discontent and suspicion she did a whole succession of little things which were right but which cheapened her life and David's as she had just cheapened Eva's.

And she got up quickly and hurried to Eva's bedroom and called anxiously, "Eva, may I come in?"

Eva was sitting on the bed, sullen and waiting fearfully.

"Eva — this purse," Mrs. Evans said, holding it up and trying to smile. She was so apologetic that Eva looked away, her face red. "I only wanted to see if it could be fixed," Mrs. Evans said. "There are a few beads loose. You're good with a needle, aren't you? Couldn't you fix it up for yourself?"

"I don't know. It's awfully pretty, isn't it?" Eva said, taking it in her two hands and fingering it shyly. "It's terribly pretty."

"Take it, please take it," Mrs. Evans whispered, and Eva looked up astonished because Mrs. Evans had one hand up to her lips and though her voice was so eager her eyes were brimming with tears as if she was begging her to help her.

The Peacemaker

ENID DINNIS

ALL the countries in the north were preparing for war; and all the countries in the south, or the east and west, for matter of that, were in the same bad way. And the little countries in between were looking on and wondering. And all the holy people in those same countries were praying for peace.

War was a terrible thing, for already mighty engines of destruction had been invented by means of which not merely belligerent armies might be annihilated but the cities and homes of civilian folk as well. Little children became the rank and file in the battle line when "Civilization" got into the head of man and the cup of Knowledge sent him reeling into the temple of Moloch instead of his own front door.

In the religious houses, for many still existed, prayers were being put up for peace, for statesmen whose names thundered through a world afflicted with the wireless were busy plucking a crow with one another, and wise folk said that it was a carrion crow.

At any moment news of an outbreak of hostilities might be expected. The world, so to speak, held its breath.

In the little priory which hid itself away in the hills in one of the small countries, the community had been bidden to pray its hardest. Dictators were sitting at round tables, and those to whom they dictated — millions of them — were standing in the munition factories and the places where they make airplanes preparing for war, since the "square deal" was but faintly to be hoped for from

From *The Magnificat*, May, 1938. By permission.

a round table. The community consisted of men of prayer who said their daily Office and many other prayers as well. The holy Father Prior exhorted them to prayer over and above the normal.

The order went forth. Everything that could possibly be put aside was to be left so that the monks might add special hours of prayer to the prescribed number.

Now, Brother Odo was a mighty man of prayer. His prayer had reached great heights, so it was said. It was real, solid prayer, with none of the fanciful distractions that Brother John, for instance, could seldom avoid when he sat thinking of the mysteries of religion. Neither did he fall asleep like Brother Joseph.

Brother Odo knelt in the chapel and prayed for peace.

He was in the midst of his prayer when Brother Tarcisius came up to him and tapped him on the shoulder. Brother Tarcisius spoke in a loud whisper.

"It will be your turn to go and answer the doorbell," he hissed in the brother's ear. "Brother Ostiarius is sick and we are taking turns at the door."

"Why my turn?" Brother Odo asked. "Is it Father Prior's order?"

"Well, no," Brother Tarcisius said, forgetting this time to whisper, "but the others have all taken their turn."

Brother Odo considered the matter. He had been brought to earth with something of a crash and it was rather nerve shattering.

His tone was just a little sharp.

"Who's on the door now?" he asked.

"Brother Leo," the other replied.

"Well then, why can't Brother Leo go on doing it? Prayer is of the first importance."

Brother Odo did not add that he was providing prayer of the first quality. The inference was in better taste.

Brother Tarcisius explained patiently.

"Brother Leo has to go to the kitchen to help to peel the potatoes," he said.

Brother Odo became definitely vexed. The Prior had told them this very morning to set to and pray their hardest for peace. "Men of peace," he had said, "are the warriors who attack the men of war and scatter them." Noble words they had been; and here was he — Odo — being interrupted in the midst of his prayer and asked to go and listen to the doorbell!

"Well, if Brother Leo can't do it," he said, "how about Brother John?" (Brother John's feather brain was far more suited to applying itself to potato-peeling than to prayer.)

"It's Brother John's time for saying his prayers," Tarcisius said. "He's been minding the door already during his free time — his usual time for private prayer."

Brother Odo rose from his knees. It was preposterous! — that a religious community could not eat potatoes in their jackets for once in a way when men were praying to avert the greatest calamity in human history.

"I will go and speak to the cook," he said, with quiet dignity.

Meanwhile Brother Leo was pacing to and fro in the porter's lodge.

He was in the last stage of permissible impatience. He caught sight of Brother Odo crossing the hall. He stepped out and accosted him.

Brother Odo eyed the porter's *locum tenens* coldly. It was but a step-brotherly affection which existed between them, for they had been reared in different provinces and water is thinner than blood. The two did not hit it off too well, at the best.

"Well, now," Brother Leo burst forth, "here am I due in the kitchen a good seven minutes ago. Do you suppose that potatoes peel themselves?"

Brother Odo mounted his dignity, if indeed he was not already on it; he seldom descended to *terra firma*.

"I am not proposing to relieve you," he replied. "I am on my way to the kitchen to tell Brother Econome that I consider it disgraceful for a mere potato to come in between the brethren and the high task that Father Prior has laid on them."

"You mean that I had better go into the chapel and say prayers instead of peeling potatoes?" Brother Leo said.

"Not at all," Brother Odo replied. "I mean that you should have gone on minding the door, and that I should not have been interrupted."

Brother Leo appeared to be at a loss how to express himself. A monk is not allowed the vocabulary of a politician, even when the latter is in print. Brother Odo's naïve point of view was not unlike that of the greater nations pointing out their duty to each other. He contented himself with remarking:

"Well, if that doesn't beat everything I've heard from you, Brother!" His face had waxed ruddy with suppressed convictions. "Well," he concluded, "I'm off, anyway."

"And I don't propose to stay here," Brother Odo retorted. "It is no part of the duty laid upon me by holy obedience to supply for Brother Ostiarius. It has been done by those who volunteered. I do not feel myself in a position to volunteer. There is a principle involved — the eating of a potato with or without its skin in given circumstances."

Brother Tarcisius had by this time arrived on the scene. He was just about at the end of his tether. He was appreciating the holy Rule which gave every brother his own task. Volunteering didn't seem to work at all.

"I'd best go up and lay the matter before Father Prior," he said.

It was just at that juncture that Brother John appeared round the corner. He was hastening to the chapel to get in some prayers. He had been detained in the infirmary looking after the comfort of the sick brother.

Brother John glanced interrogatively at the little group. Their voices were raised above the monastic norm. It must mean that some grave news had come through — that war had been declared. The young brother felt justified in breaking the silence himself.

"War?" Brother Tarcisius answered, tartly. "Go along! It's only a question of who is going to mind the door for the next hour. I'm just going up to ask Father Prior to come and settle it."

Brother John opened his eyes wide.

"But Father Prior is much too busy to be worried about who keeps the door," he said. Then he added: "I can stay here and mind the door if Brother Odo doesn't want to. I can say my prayers and keep one ear on the bell."

Brother Odo gave the proposal his prompt attention. "I don't see why you shouldn't," he said. "After all, it is important that we give the best that we have. As you say, you would pray here as well as anywhere else."

The tone was condescending, and the accent on the "you" was not complimentary. It did not, however, appear to offend the young brother. The latter had a great esteem for Brother Odo. He was a mighty man of prayer, although a little difficult at times.

"Well," Brother Leo observed, rather drily, "at any rate *my* business is in the kitchen. I take it that a monk accepts his task whatever it may be. We leave it to the pious folk in the world to pick and choose."

Brother John scented trouble. He butted in, hastily.

"Well, I'm here, so there is nothing to trouble about," he said. "I'll mind the door or peel the potatoes, whichever you like. I can say my prayers whilst I peel a potato all right."

Peace was restored. Brother Odo returned to the chapel. Brother Leo went to the kitchen and peeled potatoes to the greater glory of God, and Brother John established himself in the porter's lodge, whilst Father Prior remained unmolested in his cell coping with an intricate plan of the Priory drainage which was under repair, a letter from the Ordinary which required a circumspect answer, and a complaint from a neighbor *re* straying cattle.

It proved to be a busy hour for the doorkeeper. The world and his wife seemed to be requiring alms, or speech with Father Prior. The workmen engaged on the drainpipes were also in and out. It would seem that the interruptions were but punctuated by the occasional upliftings of Brother John's heart and mind to God. He smiled a wry smile in that direction and murmured, "Give peace in our time, O Lord!"

Brother John had made his sacrifice of the delightful hour in the chapel with the courtesy that minimizes the cost, but the cost had been considerable. Prayer time was very joyous to Brother John. He loved the special time in the chapel when, in the stillness, thoughts came into his mind that were very delectable. Of course they were not the deep thoughts that emanated from the mind of Brother Odo in the books that bore his name on the title-page — they were only just fancies, almost distractions, if one had rigid ideas as to how prayer should be made. But the recurring workmen and beggars kept them at bay.

How lucky it was that he had chanced to come along at that moment, Brother John thought to himself. The idea of Brother Odo being expected to act as doorkeeper when he might be praying for peace! It was lucky too, that he had been able to smooth down Brother Leo. "Give peace in our time, O Lord!" Brother John ejaculated, as he dragged his mind back from the distracting thoughts. It was not so easy knocking at the door of heaven and listening to the knocks on the door here below. One ear open to the bell, one to the Voice of which Samuel of old had invited speech.

"Give peace in our time, O Lord!" Brother John repeated.

There was a momentary lull in the business of the porter's lodge. Thoughts in the form of pictures floated across the consciousness of the man who was minding the door. He seemed to see a dark group of airplanes hovering up in the sky. They were evil, and their purpose was sinister. Below was another group of planes, white and shadowy. Brother John gathered that they were in opposition to those above. He sat there with closed eyes and watched the issue.

Suddenly a single plane shot up from the group below. Straight and sure it shot up — far beyond the attacking group, but as it passed beyond them — through their midst, as it were — the engines of the black monsters suddenly appeared to have become powerless. Their flight was checked. They became stationary. The airman of the upflying plane possessed a secret, an antiaircraft secret, which must make the country which he represented supremely immune from air attack.

Brother John opened his eyes. A brother was asking him if he had a piece of string to tie up a parcel.

"Sorry, Brother," he said. "I believe I was asleep and dreaming."

The brother took the string and made off. Brother John pulled himself together. "Give peace in our time, O Lord!" he said.

The great news reached the priory on the following day. The prayers of the Church had been answered. The menace of war had been removed in a manner almost miraculous. The nations might rest for a while, at any rate.

Father Prior addressed his community eloquently on the subject of the great preservation. He pointed out how there is no limit to the power of the prayer of a just man — a man who is humble of heart and a lover of peace. He was proud to think that the priory had taken its part in the united prayer of the Christian nations.

And Brother John chanting his Office in Choir thanked God with a full heart that He had made mighty men of prayer like Brother Odo, and that He had given them the fitting opportunity to wrest from heaven the great thing for which they prayed.

And to think that they had expected Brother Odo to mind the door!

The Man Who Lashed Out

HILAIRE BELLOC

HIS LORDSHIP the Mayor of Bilgeton had broken with his rule not to appear in party politics during his year of office. He had consented to preside over the vast meeting gathered in the Jubilee Hall to welcome Mr. Michael Firley; for the occasion was a very grave one, a farewell honor to the great public man who was their Member of Parliament, and who was now retiring after an honorable and unbroken service of twenty-two years in the Commons.

His Lordship the Lord Mayor of Bilgeton introduced the speaker of the evening in a few well-chosen words, which I will summarize in *oratio obliqua.*

They were gathered there tonight, not as Liberals or Conservatives, still less as supporters of the Labor Party (laughter), but as Englishmen, to welcome one of the greatest Englishmen of our time, and one who had honored — he thought he might say honored — the city of Bilgeton by accepting its freedom upon a recent occasion (applause). He did not believe in long speeches from the chairman upon such an occasion as this (cries of "Go on!"), but he would be lacking in respect to the etc., etc., etc., if he did not, etc., etc., etc. The career of Mr. Firley — if he were still plain Mr. Firley he was sure that was through his own choice (cheers) — was a household word throughout the Empire and wherever the English language, etc., etc., etc. He could not forbear, etc., etc., etc., from, etc., etc., etc., and, etc., etc., etc., such as has made us what we are (loud cheers).

His Lordship then called upon Mr. Firley, a tall, lanky man, scholarly, a gentleman, only gray, yet over sixty; spare — already

From *A Conversation With An Angel and Other Essays,* by Hilaire Belloc, published by Harper and Brothers, New York, 1929. By permission.

weary of this world; but in whose eyes might be perceived this evening a strange gleam.

Upon the rising of their Member the vast audience heaved to its myriad feet and sang "For He's a Jolly Good Fellow" to the tune of "Malbrook," and in all the keys adapted to the great variety of voices present. They concluded with three loud cheers, under each of which Mr. Firley raised one eyebrow and depressed the other in a quick, nervous movement, of which he was not the master.

When stuffy silence had fallen, the man whose career was ending coughed slightly, balanced his eyeglass on his left forefinger, and delivered himself of the following words:

"Men of Bilgeton, when I see you here before me in such numbers, and consider to what ages you have succeeded, what a story there lies behind that generation of which you are the ephemeral members, of what centuries you are the latest crown (cheers), I am moved to regard you, not without a certain awe, not without a certain pity, but also with a picture in my mind of very different things, very different places, very different men. Those of whom you are the sons and (little as you know it) the heirs, crowd before me. I recall what heritage of beauty lay to your hands as to those of all our race, what wealth of wisdom, what established laughter, what consolation in tears. It was for you the Charioteer came out of Asia driving the panther team, and for you that the Paphian broke into her youngest smiles. It was for you, and to bring you forth, the latest fruit of time, that the gods on their cloudy summits to the North conceived the mighty parents of the world. O, harvest of what unnumbered aeons! O, heirs of what an inheritance! (Loud cheers.)

"I know not how it is, but in the contemplation of your economy (when my mind dwells on it from within), in the contemplation of your dwellings, of what were once, I suppose (and perhaps still are), your places of worship, of the ornaments you are pleased to use for the variety of your dress, when my corporeal eyes dwell upon these externals of your lives, I muse! I find something inexplicable. Am I in a bewilderment for things, lost? Am I gazing across too wide a gulf of years? Or do I dwell in a

world that is other than the world we seem to see? I know not.
. . . But I am in an admiration of what time can effect (applause).

"It was but some few days ago that I filled a leisured evening
— the day had been fine, the air in the declining light was still,
the prospect clear — that I filled an evening, I say, with gazing
from the heights of the moor above down into your busy valley.
I saw rising from lowering belts of coal smoke (cheers) the tall
chimneys of Messrs. Haileybury's Limited (loud and prolonged
cheers), the considerable expanse of the railway station roof,
sub-fusc — nay, 'grisatre.' I caught a glimpse of the narrow river
confined between brick walls of now respectable antiquity
(cheers), but the distance was too great to allow me to perceive
the details of what objects might be floating upon that historic
stream. From the general hum of the great hive there came occasionally sharp sounds detached — the clang of an electric tram,
and, at their appointed hour, the indiscriminate hooting of many
sirens (laughter and cheers). I could also faintly catch the peculiar shrill cry of newsvendors, and at irregular but frequent
intervals there pierced through, in vivid stabs, the warning
whistles of locomotives.

"But all this I saw and heard as upon a background of other
things: first, the valley itself contained no more than a few
thatched homes of yeomen; the river turned one mill, and that
for corn; there were sheep upon the higher pastures. Far away, in
some fashion general, as it were, and sustaining it all, was a bound-
ary of mighty and beneficent sea waters informed with the Medi-
terranean air. Great roads had impressed upon a wide landscape
the spirit of a mighty soldiery, and Authority brooded over the
whole. Authority it was, Authority which gave regularity to every
shrine and every habitation, every domestic custom, every law:
to the plains, to the mountains, to the souls of men. I saw all this
first dimly guarded by beneficent powers not of this world, which
later changed to have evil faces, but fled at last before the strong,
dim forms of the saints (cheers). I heard the clash of armies,
but they were the armies of Christian men, and I saw fantastic
loveliness arise in garment and in brick and in wood and in
stone.

"All these things I saw as a man may see a vision; I looked for its fruits — but the vision faded. There lay before me — Bilgeton (loud and prolonged cheers).

"I have nothing more to say. Nor would I have spoken as I have — I trust that I have not wearied you by any obscurity or by allusions that might be unfamiliar to you (cries of 'No, no!') — had I not determined to put a term to the career of one whom you have fondly believed (cheers) to be your representative (loud cheers). Or rather, had not such an occasion been provided for me by others.

"My Lord Mayor (turning to that official) was good enough to remark that I was plain Mr. Firley. I can no longer conceal from you that the necessity of finding a seat of the safest kind for the nephew of Lady Cumbledown (loud cheers) has — by I know not what association of ideas — suggested to his Majesty the conferring upon me of a peerage under the style and title which has graciously been granted me of Bilgeton (loud and prolonged cheers, during which the vast audience again heaved to its myriad feet and attempted in some confusion to renew the former chorus, while Mr. Firley wearily waved them down with his hand and at last obtained a hearing). Nay, fellow citizens, if I may so call you (cheers). Men, Bilgetonians, do not be too eager to congratulate me on what will be but the last phase of an exhausted life. (No! No!) For I make no pretense to that concealment of age which is the vulgar fashion of our day. I go to a peerage, due to I know not what, but you to the daily life of Bilgeton, and, as Socrates has said through the mouth of Plato (or Plato through the mouth of Socrates), who can tell which fate is the better? In the greater leisure that is now before me (I have not hesitated to accumulate out of politics what I thought necessary for the security of my later years) I shall return to communion with the classics, to the occasional enjoyment of a picture or a statue, to the rarer consolation of reasonable converse — perhaps, who knows (it would be good fortune indeed) — with a true human friend. What will follow after, I know not, neither do any of you; for the things beyond this world the gods have hidden from human eyes!" (Tempest of cheers.)

The right honorable gentleman abruptly sat down, after having spoken for seventeen minutes and thirty-five seconds.

His Lordship the Mayor said, when the thunder of cheering had gradually died down (I again use the *oratio obliqua*), that they had all enjoyed an intellectual treat. They could not all be scholars like Mr. Firley (cheers); they could not all — least of all he himself (cries of "No, no!") — claim to express themselves with the same facility, etc., etc., etc., when their children and their children's children, etc., etc., etc., of this great Empire (more and still louder cheers, at the conclusion of which the vast audience heaved for a third time to its feet and for the third time intoned their familiar choral salutation, to which Mr. Firley listened with a look of patient agony and acknowledged with a slight apathetic bow from his stooping figure).

One Night

ELIZABETH JORDAN

EXACTLY how it had happened Paul Kelly himself did not know. One minute he had been staring through a red haze of fury at his young partner's grinning face. Donahue had a nasty grin — superior and rather taunting. It had annoyed Kelly even in their school days of close friendship — that friendship which had led to their partnership when they left school and opened a small garage "on a shoe string" as both admitted. The grin had frequently annoyed Kelly during the two years that had passed since then.

Donahue was by way of being a mechanical genius. He could lift the hood of any disabled car, cast a seemingly casual glance at its insides, and diagnose its trouble as a skillful physician diagnoses that of a patient. Also, he could cure the trouble. He was arrogant about it. Arrogance was Donahue's note. His, he frequently remarked, was the master mind of the garage. Kelly, he added, had the gift of gab and a certain flair for business if he did not push it too far. He had no idea of Kelly's intelligence, and admitted it freely and to others besides Kelly. He also admitted, rather patronizingly and when he was in an especially good humor, that Kelly was good at "contacts" — that Kelly made friends and brought in business.

All Kelly remembered now was that Donahue had got off a few caustic comments tonight and that they had precipitated a fight — the first actual fight in which the partners had ever engaged. At that, it could not be called a fight. Fights were not

From *Extension Magazine,* October, 1934. By permission of the magazine and author.

Donahue's strong suit. His strength, he frequently pointed out to Kelly, lay in brains, not brawn. He was a delicate chap, with a tricky heart, a heart that periodically missed a beat. The doctor said it was not a serious condition and that Donahue would get over it in time. Kelly, who was a big chap and an ex-football player, had kept his hands off Donahue.

"I'd no more strike you than I'd strike a woman," he had once said contemptuously, and had seen his partner's face whiten with anger under the words. Kelly had never repeated them since, but he was convinced that Donahue had traded on that knowledge, and had again and again goaded Kelly to the limit of his quick temper, knowing he was physically safe in doing it.

Tonight he had gone too far, had said too much. For days the partners had been on the edge of their nerves, at the limit of their patience with business conditions and with each other. Kelly remembered that red haze, remembered Donahue's taunting grin and words, remembered the sudden fury that rose in his heart. Incredibly, he had struck out blindly, furiously, and Donahue, with an odd little grunt and a look of utter stupefaction, had reeled backward, toppled over, and crashed on the garage floor. Kelly had experienced a moment of dazed incredulity. He *couldn't* have struck Donahue. Or had he? Evidently he had.

He looked at Donahue with a grimace of scorn. It was like the fellow to drop like a wooden soldier under a little jolt. He stood waiting for Donahue to raise his head, to struggle up. He'd give him a hand and — well, yes, he'd admit that he regretted striking that blow. He did regret it. It wasn't a sporting thing to do to a chap like Donahue. It was like striking at the face of a man who wore eyeglasses. But when he had admitted his fault he'd tell Donahue that the end of their partnership had come. No use going on like this. Cat and dog life — that's what it was. They'd part friends though — no hard feelings or anything of that sort.

He bent to give Donahue a hand up, and was struck by the odd look of the huddled motionless figure on the floor. The eyes were open, staring up at him. He felt for the heart. It was still. An icy chill slithered down his spine. The next instant he was clutching, almost clawing at his partner, shaking the limp body, calling to deaf ears. An instant later he had dropped the body on the floor again and was over at the garage door, fumbling frantically at the catch, while he stared back at the abandoned figure. He heard his own breath escaping in quick gasps.

"God!" he gasped. "Oh, my God!"

He opened the door, slammed it behind him, and plunged into the wet blackness of a driving rain. Then he turned back, re-entered the garage, turned out the electric lights there, left the garage again.

He was running now, along the soaked country road — running as frantically as if the dead man were padding after him, noise-lessly and with those staring gray eyes boring into the back of Kelly's neck. His condition was one of sheer blind panic. He had no idea of which way he had turned, or of where he was going. He could not think. The noise of his panting breath seemed a sound from behind him.

He did not know how long he ran, but at last he stumbled, uttered a cry and went down. Almost he felt another body flop down on his — a light body, a body with thin, powerful, skillful hands, reaching from behind for his throat. He cried out again, struggled to his feet, and with a mighty effort turned at bay. Nothing was near him but the wet road, the pounding rain that had soaked his clothing, and the line of trees close to the road on either side, which stood watching him like black shadows. He caught his breath in a quick gasp and with it caught wildly at returning sanity. No light anywhere. He had no idea where he was, or of how long he had been running. He tried to pierce the blackness around him. Fields beyond those trees, no doubt, but if there were any houses they were dark and silent. Vague thoughts struggled to the surface of his mind like timid fish in a pool. The folks on those farms, if there were folks and farms near him, must be asleep in their beds. It had been half-past eleven when he and Jim Donahue had begun their row. He had just come back to the garage, soaked through after a two-mile walk from Damascus. Yes, his cap was still on his head. He had not lost it, nor his wet overcoat, in his crazy flight.

His crazy flight. Why had he made it and to what had it led

him? To this nightmare setting of darkness and storm — fit environment for an escaping murderer.

His brain grew clearer. He realized that he was standing still, and he began to walk. He was a murderer then — an unintentional one, as God was his witness. But who would believe that? Father O'Malley would, but no one else he could think of. Everyone knew that he and Jim had not been getting along well, had been on each other's nerves. Still, one doesn't kill a man simply because he gets on one's nerves. Doesn't one? He himself had done exactly that. Having done it, what should he have done next? Now that he was past his first mad horror and terror he might be able to think things out. He'd see Father O'Malley early in the morning, confess everything, get his advice.

He straightened, swung back his shoulders, and hurried onward, keeping to the middle of the road to avoid the puddles in the ruts at the sides. He'd come to some light or landmark soon and know where he was. In what direction had he turned when he came out of the garage? He couldn't remember that. The garage stood at two crossroads. He might be on his way to the small town of Damascus two miles from the garage — the town from which he had returned that night after an errand there. Had walked, too, in that downpour, and had felt injured. It was one of the things that had made his temper flare up when Jim turned — Jim, warm and comfortable in his snug workshop, while Kelly pelted on foot through the flood. Couldn't get a car at any price because there was a dance going on in the darned town and every fellow in it was taking his girl.

If he had turned to the right he ought to be back in Damascus by this time. If he had turned left in his panic he'd have five miles to go to Janesville Junction. He could get a train there toward morning — but did he want to? Hadn't he made a big mistake in this getaway? The thing he should have done — he saw it clearly now — was to telephone to a doctor he knew in Damascus and get him out there on the double quick. He could have told the doctor Jim simply toppled over. Everyone knew Jim had a rotten pump. There wouldn't be any marks of the blow – or would there? He wasn't sure — but probably not, from a soft tap like that. Must have hit Jim in what they call the solar plexus. If he stuck to the story that Jim simply collapsed he'd have been all right now. Perhaps he'd be all right anyway. Was it too late to go back, ring up the doctor and start the yarn now? But in which direction was the garage? He was plunging along, still unconsciously avoiding the rain-filled ruts at the sides of the road. If he could light a match and look at his watch —

His eyes widened. There were lights not far away — lots of lights. The lights of a town — just come into view around a curve in the road. Damascus, of course. There was no other big town near. His heart leaped, then stopped. Was this a good break or a bad one? He stopped, too, to answer the question. If he went back to Damascus he'd have to pretend he hadn't left there — that he hadn't returned to the garage at all. He'd have to stay there all night — because he couldn't get a car — yes, that was the dope — and go out early in the morning to discover Jim's body — or find someone else had discovered it. He must decide quickly. It was a help now to have decisions to make, to have hard thinking to do. Anything was better than that black panic in which he had been a murderer, flying from the law, with a dead man at his heels. He began to run again. Damascus was unusually lit up. He remembered why. The dance, of course. That dance at Flaherty's to which he had been tempted to go. He stumbled onward, reaching the town limits, and hurriedly turned into a side street. He must be careful. Mustn't be seen re-entering the place. He skirted Main Street and entered it from the other end.

The windows of a hospitable bar winked at him. He knew the place and the bartender. Thankfully he entered it. He needed a drink badly. The bartender, a fellow named Simpson, was alone in the old taproom of the inn. He nodded to Kelly without interest. He had been dozing, and he looked sleepy and ill-used. Kelly ordered whisky and when it came took it over to a chair near the open fire, removed his overcoat, put his wet feet on a fender, and drank the whisky slowly and thankfully. Before he did so he glanced at his watch. Five minutes of twelve. He restored the watch to his pocket stealthily but the bartender had observed the action and lounged across the room.

"What time is it?" he yawned.

"A little after eleven."

"Is that all? Gee!" The room had no clock and if Simpson had a watch he did not take the trouble to look at it.

"Is that all?" he repeated. "I must of been asleep."

He yawned again and Kelly saw that he had been drinking heavily. Simpson, in his opinion, was a souse at all times. Tonight's lack of business had given him an opportunity to break his own record. This was a break!

"Have a highball?" he suggested.

"Don't care if I do. Can't shut up the place till twelve. Takin' another yourself, Kelly?"

"Yes — a straight one. Bring two for yourself while you're about it. That'll even us up."

"Sure."

The barkeeper brought the drinks, settled into a chair beside his generous patron, and stared at him drowsily over the rim of his glass.

"You're wet," he observed solemnly.

"Why wouldn't I be? I've been all over this infernal town trying to get a car to take me out to my garage. No luck. All at the dance."

The bartender nodded like a wise child.

"All at the dance," he echoed, and added without rancor, "blast 'em. I wanted to go myself, but the boss thought they'd be business tonight. So they would of been if it hadn't rained."

He took a long swallow of his highball and sank into silence, blinking drowsily at the flames. He dozed off a moment, caught himself, and opened his eyes wide.

"Get dry here," he invited hospitably.

"Sure. Don't mind me, Jerry. You know me. Take a nap if you like and I'll rest and get dry. I s'pose I'll end by putting in the night here, but I won't be ready for bed till twelve. I'll call you then."

Jerry nodded. He was drinking his second highball and was past the desire for talk. His eyes closed. They opened occasionally under a lingering instinct of caution, but the big young fellow that owned half the Crossroads Garage was right there drying his feet and drinking his whisky.

Jerry dropped into oblivion.

At half-past twelve the big young fellow got up, looked appreciatively at his drying shoes, carefully wiped the mud off them with a newspaper, and burned the newspaper, put on his dry overcoat and walked to Main Street and the dance hall. He'd get some other alibis while he was about it. He paid for his ticket at the door, left his coat and cap in the men's room, and wandered in among the dancers. Almost at once he ran into an old acquaintance — a chatty lad named Chapelle, who was day clerk of the leading Damascus hotel.

"Hello, Kelly," he said hospitably. "How long have you been here?"

"An hour or so. Have some beer?"

Chapelle was ready for some beer, served in an annex pavilion next to the dance hall. The two chatted a few minutes, then separated. Kelly, about to return to the dancers, saw a girl sitting alone at a table, companioned by an empty beer bottle. He approached her, grinning mechanically. His panic was returning. He had to do something to get his thoughts off that limp figure on the garage floor.

"That's a sad sight, sister," he observed. "Want a fresh bottle?"

The girl looked at him remotely. She didn't seem to know him and he didn't remember her name, but he was sure he had met her somewhere.

"No thanks, Freshie," she said. "I drink only with my friends."

"I'm going to be one of 'em soon," Kelly predicted. "Why not now?" Jazz music drifted from the dance hall. His nightmare had lifted a trifle. In this atmosphere of light and melody he felt more normal. He now told himself he had been having a bad dream. That was all. But a chill swept over him at the memory of the dream. However, for the moment luck was with him. He

set his jaw. The girl was watching him. Her face was thin, sophisti-
cated, rouged, and not bad to look at.

"Get outta here," she said. "I don't want any hot air from you."

"Had a row with your boy friend?"

"Yep. What's that to you?"

"Not a thing. It usually comes on 'bout half past eleven, after
the boy friend has had a few drinks." He was standing beside
her, smiling stiffly down at her, repeating, parrotlike, his usual
formula on these occasions. He had almost convinced himself
that his recent experience had been a bad dream. Anything to
persuade himself he had been dreaming.

"You know a lot, don't you?" the girl said scornfully. "Well, we
had our row on the way here."

"You and I won't let anything like that happen on the way
home," Kelly predicted. "Wanta dance?" But when she frowned
and shook her head and turned a remote shoulder toward him
he drifted away without regret. Better go back to the inn, he
decided, and get a few hours of sleep. He felt queer and numb
and unreal, like one walking about in a dream. The whisky perhaps — or —

He got back to the inn at half-past one and found the old taproom still open, and still empty save for the barkeeper. Simpson
was asleep before the fire. Kelly did not wake him. He took off
his coat and shoes, put a few logs on the dying embers, and tried
to go to sleep. But his brain continued hectically active. Pictures
of the garage danced before his eyes. He saw again Jim's sardonic
grin, heard his jeering laugh, heard the impact of his own blow,
saw Jim go down, saw the motionless figure on the floor. . . . The
clearness with which memory produced these images was terrible.
He could not get away from them. Again and again they presented
themselves. Singly or in confused but recognizable masses they
swung before him. He turned in his chair and groaned, opening
his eyes to look around him. The fire had died down. He must
have caught a few winks of sleep then, after all, but with returning consciousness he saw the dim interior of the garage and Jim's
staring eyes. . . .

He wanted to stir up the barkeeper and make him talk. He wanted another drink — a big one, straight. But he dared not take it. He was going back to the garage at sunrise, rain or shine, to meet what he had to meet there. Yes, he must do it, all right. The breaks were with him. He had three witnesses to testify that he had been in Damascus all night, grumbling because he couldn't get a car to the garage, drinking at the inn, chatting with a friend and with the girl in red. He remembered now who the girl was — a stenographer at the hotel and a familiar figure at town dances. Her first name was Belle. He could not recall the last name but Belle was enough. Belle's acquaintance in town was wide. At sunrise he'd wake the barkeeper, see that he was sober enough to realize the hour and the fact that the guest was departing and that he had been there all night from eleven on. Then he'd drink a cup of coffee and be on his way.

The hours crawled like torpid snakes. The rain stopped, and at last a sickly light filtered through the room's two windows. Kelly got up, dropped a log with a clatter, was regretful when the barkeeper was aroused, but by consulting his watch and indicating the daylight, impressed the hour and his departure on the man. He also gave him fifty cents and paid twenty cents more for the two cups of bad coffee Simpson sleepily prepared.

When he went out into the street he took the pale sunshine of the early morning as a good omen. More breaks! But his legs sagged under him and his throat had contracted till he could hardly swallow. He straightened his big body, forced it to his will, and started out of town at a brisk pace. He could get a taxi now, perhaps, but he made no effort to do so. He told himself he needed the walk, the air, the time to think and plan. But all he really wanted was delay.

As he went he rehearsed his coming action — the telephoning, the interview with the doctor, the producing of Jim's heart drops, which Jim kept in a drawer of the garage desk. If he seemed rattled and dazed it would all be natural enough. Suddenly his heart began to pound. He found himself running again, then resolutely checked himself, and went on at a fast walk. If he were seen running. . . . He walked at his best pace. No one could criticize that. He was going to work, after being awake all night, and at a dance part of the time. God, where had he learned all this stuff that murderers plan and think? From books probably, and motion pictures. Besides, he wasn't a murderer. Or was he, in the eyes of the law? He didn't know, and didn't intend to find out. Even yet, he realized, there was time to make a clean breast of the whole thing — but who would believe him? What would Father O'Malley order him to do? He knew all too well. And what would the public think of a lad that killed his partner and pal, even by accident, and then went to a dance and a hotel bar? No, he'd stick to his plan.

He was running again, and again he checked himself. Easy was the word. He was almost there now. He'd stroll in — what was that word — nonchalantly. He checked again to a swift walk, moderated the pace as he reached the garage, listened at the door a minute with a pounding heart, then walked in.

Yes, it was still there — Jim's body on the floor. Wildly he had hoped that it might not be — that in some way he'd wake up from the nightmare. But there it was! His lips parted to cry out, but he retained his presence of mind. He closed the door behind him, leaving it unlocked, crept across the room, and bent over the still body.

But — God — *was* it still? No, he had been right in that first appalling impression. It was moving slightly and Jim's eyes, still open, looked up at him with life in their depths.

The next instant Kelly had shot across the floor, pulled a bottle from the desk, shot back, and was trying to force a thin stream of whisky past his partner's lips. Donahue gulped and choked. Kelly raised the man's head, supported it against an arm, more calmly now, put the bottle to his partner's lips again.

"Drink this," he ordered. His own lips were stiff, and the words were a croak, but Donahue understood them. He drank dazedly. Then, assisted by Kelly's supporting arm, he sat up and looked around him.

"What's the big idea?" he asked weakly.

Life surged back into Kelly. His blood leaped in his veins and his voice was almost natural.

"Oh, I suppose you must have passed out for a while after I left you," he said easily. "That pump of yours isn't much good, you know."

"But — weren't we fighting?" Donahue was staring at him.

"You bet we were. Yelling our heads off. That's why I got out."

"Didn't you hit me? I seem to have a memory of going down — but nothing clear — "

"Sure you went down, or you wouldn't be where you are. Must have gone down with a crack, too, and hit the back of your head in the bargain. Probably that's why you didn't come to sooner."

"Do you mean to say that I — Here, give me another drink of that!"

Kelly put the bottle to his lips again and Donahue drank deeply. Then he stared around him and for the first time realized that the sun was shining.

"My God, it's daylight!" he gasped. "D'you mean to say that I've been lying here all night?"

"Looks that way," Kelly said cheerfully. His heart was dancing in his breast. He could have danced himself and shouted. "But you're all right now," he added robustly. "The owl wagon down the road was opening up as I came along. I'll trot down there and get you some hot coffee and eggs. They'll fix you up. But I'd better get you a chair first."

He lifted Donahue's light body, feeling a wild impulse to hug it as its weight lay in his arms, and bore it toward a chair. "No, I guess the bench will be better," he muttered. "Better lie flat a while longer." Changing his direction he laid his friend on the broad workbench, and started for the door. Donahue stared after him.

"I seem to remember — " he repeated.

"Better hold your remembering till you've got something in your stomach," Kelly sang out, and disappeared. He didn't care much now whether Jim remembered that blow. It would make things easier between them if he didn't, but he was all right. That was all that mattered. He was back in an amazingly short time with eggs and coffee and rolls. He had brought a double supply, and after serving Jim with neatness and dispatch he drew another chair and worktable close to the bench and ate his own breakfast with a wolfish appetite. God, what a glorious world it was! But he mustn't seem excited — he realized that.

"I can't get this thing clear," Donahue muttered over his second cup of coffee. "Still, Doctor Walsh did warn me that something of the kind might happen if I overworked or got too much excited — "

"You were excited last night all right," Kelly agreed. He nodded at his friend. "Let this be a lesson to you," he said benignantly, and added over a mouthful of egg, "I made that deal with Ramsey yesterday."

"You did?" Donahue was excited again. They had been working over the Ramsey deal for weeks. "Why the deuce didn't you tell me so?"

Kelly grinned largely.

"You didn't give me much chance to tell you anything," he reminded his partner. "You were red hot because I didn't get back at eight o'clock to talk turkey with your friend Morse about that trucking proposition. But I was talking my head off with Ramsey at eight, and that — " he ended complacently, "means about a thousand a year to us. We can use the money."

"You bet we can," Donahue agreed. He added suddenly and abruptly: "I've got a devil of a temper, old man."

"So have I," Kelly assured him with another grin.

"Mine's worse." Donahue seemed to be thinking it out. He was sitting up now, finishing his second cup of coffee. "Yours is a flash and over. Look at you this morning."

"I'd rather look at you this morning," Kelly said robustly.

"You're a good egg, old man." Donahue was staring at him thoughtfully. Then he sheered away from sentiment. "Better than the eggs we've just been eating," he grinned. "But they didn't taste bad at that. What did you do last night after you left?"

"Went back to Damascus and dropped in at the dance," answered Kelly.

Donahue grinned. The last flickering point of suspicion died in him. He didn't know just what had happened and probably he never would, but old Kelly was all right. He stood up and tried a few rather wobbly steps.

"Guess I'll take things easy today," he said.

Kelly nodded.

"Good idea," he agreed. "Go home and let Mrs. Watson baby you. I'll run the garage. I didn't get much sleep last night, but I never felt better in my life than I do today."

The Threshing Ring

LEO L. WARD

L ARRY MARTIN, the station agent at Flora, stood with a hand shading his eyes in the door of the little dull green station. Scattered in little groups along the platform were the blue shirts and wide straw hats of many farmers. The men were gazing into the distance where they could see nothing except the glint and quiver of the two rails which joined and disappeared just before they reached the cleft in the bluish line of woods a half mile away on the prairie.

"Forty-eight just left Shelby," the agent was saying in a loud, hearty voice meant for everybody on the platform. "Ought to be comin' any minute now. Phelps over at Shelby said she pulled out of there already." There was a short silence; then a murmur of eager talk swept along the station platform. "Yeah, yeah, there she is! Smoke up there in the woods now. And she's coalin' hard, looks like. I tell you, boys, haulin' threshing machines, takes coal for that." Larry Martin's loose blue shirt quivered as he chuckled and looked at three or four farmers standing near him on the platform. All the squinted faces in front of the station suddenly broke into pleased grins.

"About the first threshin' rig you ever unloaded, ain't it, Larry?" It was Jay Westwright who spoke in an even, controlled tone from where he stood beside the station agent. Westwright was a tall, straight man, with a strip of grayish hair showing beneath his wide hat on either side of his long, thin face.

"Yeah, first threshing rig we ever put down here. What is it? Red River, didn't you say?"

"Yeah, Red River Special. Farmer's Friend, they call it." Jay's long face turned to gaze proudly up the track again.

A short distance up the platform and out at the very curb stood a little man with a slight bump high on his back. This was Burl Teeters, and he was gazing very fixedly and very thoughtfully up the track, his sweat-stained straw hat tilted far back on his little bald head and his hands shoved deeply into his belt. Beside him were the two Hamel boys, both also looking into the distance. Burl seemed to pay no attention to the excited talk going on all about him, except to throw an occasional scowl over his shoulder when Jay Westwright was talking. From time to time Lar and Zeb Hamel turned bearded faces to listen to what the station agent was saying.

"Where you goin' to set her down, Larry?" Jay Westwright asked. "Marley Simms over at the elevator said we could get all the water we wanted right here at the engine room. Wonder if we could set her down over there beside the engine room."

"Sure, Jay. We'll set that rig down just anywhere you boys want."

"Think that would give us room, Mr. Kenyon? Right in there between the grain office and the engine room?" It was in a quiet, respectful tone that Westwright asked the question of a youngish but serious-looking man who stood beside him. The youngish man wore a pair of neat blue overalls, above the bib of which a white collar and a narrow dark tie showed. He was Mr. Kenyon, the expert who had arrived yesterday from the factory.

"Yes, that will be all right. That will give us plenty of room." Kenyon spoke in a firm, quiet voice, and with a thin, quick smile.

"It's a pretty big machine though, ain't it?" asked Larry Martin. Everybody turned again at the sound of the agent's loud voice — everybody except Burl Teeters, who had now moved a few steps farther up the platform.

"Yeah, it's a forty-five inch rig," Jay said. "Thirty, forty-five, of course. Had to be that big for a ring our size."

"Well now, if that ain't enough room . . ."

"Oh, yes, that will be plenty of room, boys — plenty." The

youngish man in the neat blue overalls shook his head decisively.

Inside the station a thin insistent ringing suddenly drowned the monotonous chatter of the telegraph, and the agent, as he turned to the door with a wave of his black satin half-sleeve, shouted back to everyone on the platform, "Well, there she is, boys. She's comin' right in."

The wild, prolonged shrill of a whistle came from up the tracks. Little clusters of men edged farther out on the platform, and there was a murmur of subdued talk. Piggy Bailey jumped down from his perch beside a striped canvas mailbag on the station truck and pushed the truck out to the low curb of the platform, where he stood with one arm resting jauntily on the mailbag as the tall black bulk of the engine came rolling and grinding toward the station. The little clusters of men suddenly shrank back closer to the station as the engine came nearer.

Piggy Bailey was shouting at the engineer. "Got any thrashin' machines on this here train? We don't want nothin' smaller than thrashin' machines in this man's town." The engineer merely waved a big glove genially as the engine went hissing and grinding past the station.

The crowd, which had become quite silent, was now watching the boxcars go swaying slowly past, one after another. At last a glint of shiny steel appeared above the red top of a boxcar. Then everybody suddenly saw the hood of a threshing blower, and a moment later the threshing machine loomed beside the station platform. As the cars moved slowly past, the threshing engine became sharp and black against the blue sky and the separator incredibly huge and shiny. The flatcar came slowly to a stop, blocking the street that ran past the station. Then the men — all except Westwright, Kenyon, the station agent, and Piggy Bailey — began pushing and pulling each other off the platform into the street. Soon a chorus of jumbled talk arose out around the flatcar.

A trainman came running along the tracks. Larry Martin was shouting to him to set the threshing machine over beside the elevator. In just a little while a series of clankings came along the cars, and the whole train seemed to shudder once or twice. Then the great black engine and the red, shiny separator moved slowly away from the station on the long flatcar.

It was only a short time, however, before the threshing machine came floating back on the side tracks with a brakeman riding in front of it. Then Burl Teeters went hopping across the two sets of tracks toward the engine room at the elevator where he began waving direction to the brakeman. With a shriek of brakes the long flatcar came to a stop just beyond the low red engine room.

A moment later Burl was clambering over the edge of the car. Though his hat fell backwards onto the tracks, he seemed not to notice it. Now he was up on the car. Without his big hat he looked ridiculously small beside the tall wheels of the threshing engine. He edged his way around one of the great wheels. Suddenly he reached up, grasped the flange of the big steel belt wheel and tugged at it violently once or twice. The wheel turned slightly, and Burl stood back looking at it quizzically as though only half satisfied. Then Piggy Bailey whistled shrilly through his teeth from the station platform. The whistle came clear and high above the mumble of talk from the crowd now gathered about the flatcar. "Hey there," Piggy was shouting. "Hey, Burl, you the engineer? Thought you were goin' to be blower man." Burl grinned, a bit sheepishly. The crowd laughed. Then Burl shouted back at Piggy, "No, sir, I'm the engineer on this rig. I'm not no blower man." He turned again to examine the engine. Then he climbed up to the high seat on the toolbox. With one hand on the steering wheel, he pushed a lever with the other. Now someone shouted at him again. "What do you think of her, Burl? Hey, Burl, think she'll run all right?" It was Ambrose Mull, a huge man with faded green suspenders curving tight over his blue stomach, who stood halfway across the tracks. Ambrose chuckled to himself and turned to grin at Jay Westwright back on the station platform. Burl seemed at first to pay no attention to the shouting, but finally he turned to yell over his shoulder, "Yeah, guess maybe she'll run all right." Then he started climbing down from the engine, but stopped to open the firebox and peer inside. When at last he was on the ground he turned to Bert Helker, a tall man with slouched shoulders, and one of the Hamels, who was standing very near the car, and pointed a crooked outstretched thumb up at the engine. He was telling them that the only trouble might be the boiler. It didn't seem built back over the firebox quite far enough. "But I reckon it'll work good enough. Work all right if you get the right feller firin' it."

Soon there were many men working busily about the flatcar. Kenyon, the expert, was over there now and he was explaining to the men how to brace some huge timbers against the car. But above all the other noises, the hammering and talking and laughing, came the shrill voice of Burl Teeters in almost constant questions and suggestions. He kept asking Kenyon particularly whether he thought the timbers were large enough for "an engine as big as that."

After a little while Jay Westwright and the station agent came slowly across the tracks from the platform, the agent carrying a piece of paper in his hand. Then Kenyon moved out from among the men, and the three stood talking together in the shade of a maple tree over beside the grain office, while the work went steadily on about the flatcar.

But Burl also left the car and went over to the three men standing beside the grain office. He faced Westwright. "Well," he said, "how about some coal, Mr. Jay? Ain't you supposed to be gettin' the coal. A man can't fire no engine on hot air."

"The coal'll be here in plenty of time. Don't you be worryin' about the coal, Teeters."

"Yeah! You think you're runnin' the whole works. Well, I'll tell you one thing you're not runnin'. An' that's the engine. I'm the one that's running that engine." Burl's voice, as always when he grew excited or angry, had risen so shrill and high that it was almost like a tinkle above the noises back around the flatcar.

Jay Westwright's thin face became still narrower and very hard, then slowly broke into a faint grin as he turned to continue talking to Kenyon. Burl wheeled about contemptuously and went back toward the other men.

The lifting and bracing and wedging of the great beams went steadily on, amidst the constant loud talk and the shouted laughter of the men. But it was almost two hours later before the threshing outfit, by means of several heavy ropes and pulleys, was finally got off the flatcar.

And it was now standing out in the street, directly in front of the grain office. Wisps of steam were playing about the clean new cylinders, and black smoke was tumbling up lazily from the wide funnel of the engine over the street and across the roof of the grain office. Kenyon, the expert, stood between the engine and the separator, with one foot resting on the big red separator tongue, while he talked briskly with Jay Westwright and Bert Helker. He was asking about Teeters, whether they were going to let him try to run the engine, and Jay was saying that Burl could probably learn to run it all right, if Mr. Kenyon would just keep a close watch on him for a while. It would be easier than trying to stop him from going on the engine, once he got it in his head this way. Bert Helker's wide hat rim flapped agreement with Jay. But already Burl was up on the high platform of the engine, bent forward examining the water gauge. By this time a large group of men had gathered on the sidewalk in front of the grain office, and on both sides of the street little clusters of women and clerks in aprons stood watching the threshing machine.

Suddenly the brass whistle on the engine spurted steam. There was a deafening blast. With Kenyon standing just behind him on the engine platform, Burl Teeters slowly pulled a lever and the big belt began to race idly. A moment later the engine moved forward with a great clank. The separator lurched once or twice. And then the threshing machine was going up the street under a cone of dense black smoke. Burl Teeters kept turning the steering wheel, now one way, now the other. The low, wide wheels of the separator wandered slightly to the right, then back to the middle of the street again, and as the great machine moved on, the lugs of the engine wheels left a waving track behind them. From the door of the butcher shop Hunk Keller in his splotched white apron shouted to Burl above the puffing of the engine and the rumble of the separator. "Hold her down there, Burl. You better watch the speed limit." Farther up the street Joe Neff, standing on the curb in front of the poolroom, lifted his shrill, whining voice to ask, "Where's your firin' cap, Burl? An' say, you ought to wear gloves for that. Where's your gloves, Burl?" Burl Teeters seemed hardly to hear the shouting, but only turned from time to time to say something to Kenyon, whose eyes never left the engine all the way up the street.

The threshing machine had soon passed from between the two rows of little wooden store buildings and had entered the lane of dense maple trees beyond. Through the trees the smoke floated upward, fading into the clear blue sky above Flora. At last it was becoming smaller and smaller out at the end of the street, and then on the road that led away from the town. But some of the men in front of the stores kept watching the threshing machine until it was only a black dot out in the level haze of the wheatfields.

The threshing was beginning at Bert Helker's place, for Bert was at the north end of the ring and it was his turn this year. They had started in the afternoon when the grain would be quite dry, and by two o'clock they had already threshed off four loads of bundles.

Now two more wagons pulled in very close to the sides of the machine and the men began pitching the sheaves off their tall loads onto the conveyor, where the sheaves went leaping, one after another, into the dusty mouth of the separator, to be swallowed behind the flashing knives which fed the cylinder. In a little while three or four other loads came up, to await their turn back behind the engine. The drivers all climbed down from their wagons and gathered in the shade of one of the loads, where they watched the threshing with pleased grins on their faces.

Over beside the engine stood one of the Hamel boys, leaning on a pitchfork and talking to Burl Teeters, who sat, bent far forward, on the high box of the engine, directly behind the big belt wheel. Burl was wearing a little black cap with a celluloid bill. With one hand resting lightly on a tilted lever, he watched the separator closely, giving only occasional quick glances down at Hamel as he answered a question or asked the other man how he liked the "exack line on that belt there." Burl's eye followed the belt intently, where it dipped and twisted and came racing and flashing constantly back to the whirling drive wheel directly in front of him. Once he leaned far out and down toward Hamel, and with one hand pointing to the big belt wheel said, "See that belt there, Zeb — right in the same place on that wheel all the time. Tell you y' got to keep a good line on a belt for that." Then he quickly pulled himself up on his seat again, and the little black cap was craned far forward as before.

Up at the other end of the racing belt, the two men at the engine could see the big red separator only as a great blur of dust. Beyond that the flashing hood of the blower was belching forth its clotted stream of dust and straw in a slow semicircle. But high above the nearer blur of dust, three men stood together on top of the tall separator. They were Kenyon, the expert, Jay Westwright, and Bert Helker. They were gazing into the dust below them, at the wheels and belts, and the sheaves that kept leaping into the mouth of the separator. From time to time Kenyon and Westwright shouted to each other above the noise of the machine and Kenyon made frantic gestures, while Bert Helker listened curiously and nodded his straw hat until its wide brim would begin to flap. At last Kenyon leaned very close to the other two men and shouted above the roaring whir beneath him. Westwright's and Helker's straw hats were tossed upward as if in laughter, and Kenyon lifted his hand to slap Jay on the back. But suddenly Kenyon reeled violently backward. He saved himself from falling from the top of the separator by frantically grasping Westwright's arm with his uplifted hand. Westwright himself staggered, and Helker had fallen in a clump where he stood. The separator had suddenly lurched under them, had literally jumped and then fallen back under them with a dull, loud clank.

There was wild shouting everywhere. But the three men on the separator did not hear it. They heard only the great clank of the machine beneath them, and then a sharp snap, followed by a clap as of thunder very near them, just in front of the separator itself. At the same instant Kenyon saw what seemed to be the broken end of a belt flying through the sky above him; while Jay Westwright saw two wagons turning rapidly in sharp circles away from the machine. Now the moan and whir of the machine suddenly ceased, and the men on the separator again heard the wild shouting of other men all about them. Then Kenyon, the expert, and Jay Westwright, the shrewd leader of his neighbors, and Bert Helker, who was curious and indolent above most men in this world, saw an extremely strange and monstrous thing. They saw the great black nose of the threshing engine coming straight toward them. Close below them now, directly in front of the separator, they heard the quick panting of the engine. The next moment Kenyon, the expert, was only a blur of arms and legs waving and tossing through the air — he had jumped from the top of the separator. The tall form of Bert Helker had shrunk into a ball on the high back of the separator. And now Jay Westwright was stepping backward in stiff jerks until he almost fell over Helker crouching behind him. Jay stopped rigidly, legs braced wide, one long arm stretched out desperately as if to defend himself, his narrow face lengthened into a stricken stare. Then he heard again the quick, sharp pant of the engine. He saw black tumbling smoke. For an instant he smelt hot grease and steam. . . .

He remembered, an indefinite while later, having seen a sudden glint of something beside him, almost beneath him . . . like the shifting, shiny flash of a piston. . . And something huge and dark had passed by him. And nothing had hit the separator. There had been no terrific bump, no crashing of any kind. . . .

Suddenly he knew he could see more clearly. He turned his head slowly, tautly sidewise. What he saw was strangely real and clear. It was the threshing engine moving rapidly away, circling out from the separator. As it moved away he saw somebody running after it. And he heard someone shouting wildly. He heard many men shouting.

The engine was stopped now. It was stopped out there beyond the low yellow slope of the strawstack. And Kenyon, the expert,

was standing on the engine. One of Kenyon's hands was on a
lever and his head was turned sharply toward the small humped
figure of Burl Teeters on the platform beside him. But Burl's
arms were folded lightly and the shiny bill of his little black cap
was pushed carelessly up on his forehead as he stood there looking impertinently up into Kenyon's face. Neither of the two
men was speaking at all, but simply staring at the other, until
finally Kenyon turned abruptly to the levers and started the
engine. He was soon bringing the engine around in a wide burst
into a wild shrieking almost in his ear. Above the loud rumble
and pant of the engine there would occasionally rise a shrill
word or two . . . "belt loose . . . tighten it . . . push too far. . . ."
Though Kenyon hardly seemed to hear all this, when at last he
had brought the engine to a stop back near the separator Burl
was still yelling into his ear. He seemed to be saying something
about a "lever slippin'." Kenyon, apparently not listening at all,
looked critically down at the broken belt that lay twisted and
sprawling along the ground. Several other men came slowly up.
One after another they looked at the belt, then doubtfully up at
Kenyon, then back at the belt again. Then every face suddenly
turned again toward Burl Teeters, who was now leaning far out
over the engine's toolbox and shaking his short arm up at Jay Westwright, who still stood on top of the separator. Burl was all but
screaming at Westwright in a voice that sounded more than ever
like the wild tinkling of a little bell. "Now you're satisfied, eh?"
He kept repeating this almost in the same words.

Jay Westwright's head jerked backward. He looked at first
startled, then bewildered. But slowly his long face shortened in
a sneer, only to widen finally in a look of mingled contempt and
pity.

Then with a quick leap Burl was on the ground. He came
toward the separator in a half run and stopped just below the
end of the conveyer. The yelling began again. "What you have
to say about it? I'm just darin' you to say somethin'. I just dare
you."

Finally Jay started to answer, and Burl stopped abruptly in a
challenging silence. Jay's voice was strangely calm and steady.

"No, I ain't got nothin' to say, Burl. I ain't sayin' anything to you. You just be quiet, an' let's not have any trouble. 'Nough trouble, as it is."

Burl stepped back from the separator a pace or two, then burst into a thin, piercing laugh. The laughter continued, growing higher and more shrill until at last it suddenly dropped to a sort of jerky cackle. Then Burl's face became smaller and menacing as he said, "Yeah, you won't say anything! You don't dare, that's what you don't. You don't dare say anything about my runnin' that engine. It's your fault anyway, an' you know it. You bought that engine an' you got slippin' levers, that's what you did. That's what caused all this." Burl's short crooked arm straightened a little as it swept the belt lying on the ground. "I ain't goin' to have nothin' to do with it. It's your fault anyways, 'tain't mine. Buyin' that engine . . . it was all your doin's. Now just fix her up if you want to. That's what you can do."

Burl Teeters turned from the separator and started walking away in the direction of Bert Helker's barn up beyond the pasture. The slight bow in his legs seemed very wide as he went on with a kind of short stamping stride. Halfway to the barn he wheeled about and suddenly yelled back wildly at Jay Westwright, "If I hear of you sayin' anything . . ." His voice rose so shrill it became unintelligible. He turned again and went on toward the barn. And a little while later the men standing about the threshing machine saw Burl leave Bert Helker's farmyard in a buggy amidst a cloud of dust that kept following the buggy until it was beyond the hedge at the other side of the orchard.

That evening Jay Westwright, Kenyon, Ambrose Mull, and three or four other men who had come over to Bert's after their chores, sat smoking and talking around the feedway door of Bert's barn. Kenyon and Westwright were seated in the doorway. Bert Helker sat on a milk stool in front of them, and the others were squatting about on the ground amidst a litter of corncobs that had been thrown out from the feedboxes. Occasionally a glow would come to the end of Kenyon's cigar, and then the glow would drop to his knee. The lights from three or four pipes kept brightening now and again.

"So you don't think it'd do any good to splice it, Mr. Kenyon?" Bert Helker asked.

"No, wouldn't do a bit of good." There was a prolonged glow at the end of Kenyon's cigar. "Splicin' couldn't fix it. That belt was ripped, if you noticed. All along one side. And splicin' wouldn't do a ripped belt any good. Can't. Fabric's gone. Splicin' can't fix fabric like that."

"Looks like they ain't no way out of it. We'll just have to lay off a day." Jay Westwright spoke in a tone of reasoned finality.

"Yes. It'll take a day anyway to get a new belt in here. Even with telegraphing for it right off like I did there this afternoon."

"Funny, but I don't think I see yet just how he did it exactly, Mr. Kenyon." Bert Helker's head lolled slightly to one side as he looked at Kenyon and asked the question.

"Well, as I was tellin' you boys there this afternoon just after he stamped off like that . . ." Ambrose Mull, whose fat shoulders leaned back against the barn, started to laugh, and the others followed him. Even after the other men had stopped, Ambrose still chuckled gutturally to himself over beside the door. "As I was saying this afternoon, Teeters must have been monkeyin' with the levers. It's the only thing could have caused it. Of course you heard him tryin' to make out the lever slipped." Kenyon broke into a short, dry laugh, but none of the other men laughed now. They were all listening intently and silently, all except Ambrose Mull, who was still chuckling. "Why, a lever couldn't slip like that. No, sir, not on a Red River engine it couldn't."

"Yeah, I kind of think I see now," Bert Helker said slowly. "He just kind of pulled a lever, and then maybe pushed it too much. Got excited like when the belt broke. And as cons'quence . . ."

"Exactly. He was just itchin' around the levers there. Couldn't keep his hands off them. Pulled one ju-u-ust a little, you know. Course the engine started to backin', nacherly. Then the belt snapped, you see. And then — then he got good and scared and pushed the lever. Probably pushed it clear over. And then . . . well, the next thing we knew that engine was comin' straight for the separator. And, boys, how it ever missed that separator is more than I know. Some things are just queer, that's all — I've always said that. Simply no way of explainin' them. And it sure seems like that was one of them, right there this afternoon. . . ."

Kenyon was silent for a while, shaking his head solemnly while he looked down at the ground between his knees. Bert Helker on his milk stool pulled at his chin with a big hand. Ambrose Mull did not chuckle now, but only breathed laboriously over beside the door.

At last Kenyon's cigar glowed again, and he said, "Boys, I tell you if that engine had hit that separator . . ." He paused. "Well, it wouldn't just mean gettin' a new belt. Why, if you used it for kindlin' there wouldn't be enough of that separator left to start fire in the morning."

In the stillness that followed, the dusk seemed to become instantly darker. In the west, very low and far way, only a faint blush was left along the sky. The men sat for a while in silence, watching, watching this patch of light.

At last Kenyon stirred as if to get up from where he was sitting in the doorway, then with one hand grasping the jamb of the door he said in a matter of fact tone, "Well, I reckon we've lost an engineer anyway."

"No, sir." Bert Helker had spoken up impulsively. "He'll be right back here, Mr. Kenyon. You wait an' see if he ain't."

Ambrose Mull started sputtering and wheezing over beside the door. "Why, I'll bet ya he'll be right back here in the mornin' again, first thing. Sure as daylight he will. I tell ya, you don't know them Teeterses, Mr. Kenyon. Ya can't, unless you live right over there beside 'em like I do. Oh, I knows 'em, ever' last one of 'em. Knowed their dad afore 'em. An' they're all just the same. The whole lot of 'em always tryin' things they ain't got no business at. Messin' things all up ever' time. But you can't tell 'em nothin'. Can't never tell a Teeters nothin'. They're all half crazy, that's what they are. An' Burl, he's just about the worst of the whole keeboodle."

Another deep voice sounded, detached, as though the speaker was talking to himself, as it came out of the dusk before the barn. "Yeah, Teeters'll be back around that engine again. I just knows he will."

After a moment Kenyon spoke up again, speaking in a helpless, complaining tone. "But, boys, what we goin' to do? Can't have that fellow back on that engine again."

"Yes, but you'll never keep him off, Mr. Kenyon," said Jay Westwright. "He'll cause no end of rumpus to all the rest of the ring if we try it."

"Why, there ought to be some way of gettin' rid of him. We've just got to keep him away from that machine, boys."

"Can't never do it, Mr. Kenyon," Jay Westwright said, and Bert Helker repeated it.

"You never can," Bert said. "No use talkin'. You can't keep him away nohow. He's bound to be back."

"But couldn't you just kind of ease him out some way? Maybe get him out of the ring some way. Might buy up his share in the machine, boys. Couldn't you do that?"

"Oh, I don't know, Mr. Kenyon," said Jay. "I don't hardly think we'd ought to push him out of the ring that way. Don't see how we could do it very easy even if we wanted to. He wouldn't sell his share to none of us. Wouldn't sell it now anyways."

"No," Bert Helker said, "I don't see how we could do that, Mr. Kenyon. Don't think the boys'd want to put him out exactly."

Then Jay's voice came in slow, measured tones. "Fact, there's only one way I see of doin' it. I know it'll be mighty awkward, but the only way I see is for you to stay right around that engine. Just practically run it yourself, Mr. Kenyon. It's the only thing I see we can do."

"Well, you boys ought to know best, of course," said Kenyon. "It will make it kind of bad. I'd ought to be up around the separator most of the time. But if that's the way you boys look at it I suppose it's the only way. You know, I want to be accommodating. That's what I'm here for. I want you boys to be satisfied."

"That's about the only way we can do it, Mr. Kenyon — the way Jay said," said Bert Helker. "Fer he'll be right back here, wantin' to run that engine again, sure as shootin'. You can't stop Burl Teeters, onct he gets somethin' like that in his head. An' he won't ferget it either, like you might think after this afternoon. No way under blue heaven a gettin' it outa his head. He's a Teeters, that's all, just as Ambrose says."

There was absolute silence for a while. Then away on the prairie, from the direction of the patch of light at the edge of the sky, there arose a thin, distant calling. The voice seemed very far away, yet it came very clear through the damp dusk.

Ambrose Mull grunted. "There he is now. That's him, I heard him lots a times like that. It's just like him. That's a Teeters for you, callin' his hogs this time a night when ever'body else has his chorin' done an' forgot about it couple hours ago." Ambrose snorted and grunted a few times, and then was silent. Kenyon suddenly laughed, very briefly and as though to himself.

The thin distant calling continued, and now it seemed to be growing constantly clearer and stronger as it came out of the dusk. The men sat for a while, silently listening. Moment after moment the calling grew still clearer and louder. But it was shrill and thin, somehow like an impudent, insistent challenge too distant to be answered at all.

Suddenly Jay Westwright rose impatiently to his feet. The others were getting up now, one after another, Ambrose Mull puffing and wheezing as he did so. Ambrose's puffing was the only sound made by any of the men, except a scuffling of feet and a light rattle of corncobs here and there on the ground. The faint distant calling came again, more distinct than before. Then Jay Westwright's voice, lifted slightly as if with irritation, seemed to be saying something about a belt. Kenyon made some vague answer about "losing only a day or two." Other voices out in front of the barn were moving away slowly. But above the mutter and mumble of voices the thin calling continued to come, shrill and clear.

In a little while two or three buggies and one Ford were leaving Bert Helker's farmyard. The rattle of wheels and the quick fluttering purr of a small motor soon died away. Then the calling could be heard again, and it seemed even more distinct than it had yet been, a thin distant ringing that pierced the darkness which was settling everywhere over the prairie.

Meager Legend

MARY M. COLUM

HE WAS one of those whom things took hold of and ate into like acid on a plate: he knew that. If he had ever told Alice or even hinted at how he felt, it might have given his mind some outlet. He wondered if he ever had given her a hint. She had a habit, whenever he went to see them, of sitting beside him on the sofa and taking him by the arm, talking to him in her slightly foreign accent with her warm voice, looking at him all over as if she were trying to trace every line of him, hands, feet, face. Because she did that, he always refused the chair her husband offered, sitting instead on the sofa and waiting nervously for the moment when Alice, wriggling first in her chair, would finally come over and sit by him. Once when he came in, he had to accept a chair, as her husband was stretched out on the sofa reading a paper. Alice waited patiently for the moment when her husband dropped his paper and went out of the room to get something. Then, hastily, she took possession of the sofa, and after a while Mark got sitting beside her. That was all there ever had been between them — a few half-hours seated side by side under the eyes of her husband.

In his wanderings outside New York, playing with restaurant and club orchestras, it seemed to him, looking back, that he must have forgotten her for stretches at a time. No doubt if he married he would forget her altogether. He might have married that girl in Pittsburgh if he had had a steady job — if he had had some other kind of job — but music kept a man's emotions taut — even his sort of music — you had that sort of talent because you felt in that sort of way deep down, romantically, bitingly. It

From *Scribner's Magazine*, March, 1936. By permission.

was when he was playing in Cleveland, in a real orchestra, that Ted had written to tell him that Alice had a baby. They were so pleased that Ted felt he had to write to him. Mark remembered how he had written letter after letter in reply, tearing each one up as he finished it. Then the solution came: to send a telegram — he copied the wording of numbered sample messages that were on the counter.

Playing, that night, the refrain of something he had read somewhere in a newspaper ran through his head — a sentence from somebody who had written it all in a book, a sentence he had forgotten — but as he played, it rose up in his mind — "The children of Alice call Bartram father." If he could find that book it might tell him something, or help him, but he was no reader and he could not remember who wrote the book or what it was. Once, when he was playing in a little traveling orchestra in a strange city, he had asked the man who roomed beside him how long he thought love lasted, as over a drink he told him about Alice. The man did not seem to know what he was talking about. "Say, I never heard anybody talk like that before. Say, now, I think you ought to get psychoanalyzed."

Then when the orchestra broke up, as was the way of little orchestras in those years, he had driven in his old Ford to New York, something, as was usual when he had nothing to do, drawing him toward Alice and Ted. It was over two years since he had seen them; things had gone badly with them and he had some difficulty finding the apartment they had moved to. At first, coming in, he noticed nothing but Alice — he did not notice the change in her or her surroundings, but sat down beside her in illimitable content, feeling that a half of him which had been gone all the time he was away was restored to him, and that he was whole and entire again. Away from her, he functioned separately it was true, but when he saw her again he knew that in their separation he had been only half a man, and that to be completely himself he had to be near her. A small child was stumbling around on the floor dragging a toy — Ted's and Alice's child — a pale-faced little person with pale blue eyes. Then Mark noticed that the room was long and narrow and coldish, and that there was a smelly oil stove burning. Alice followed his eyes.

"We've no heat," she said. "It's one of those old unheated apartments. We had to get something cheap."

"Ted out of work?" Mark asked.

"Yes," she said. "Not exactly, and then — we — we — get something." Her voice stumbled over the words. "We get help. We get some help from the — from —"

"Yes," he said hastily. "Nearly everybody does. I'll have to get some myself. How do you set about it? I hear they come round and see where you're living . . . find out how much rent you pay, and all that."

"Yes, that's it. I rented one of the rooms — the front room — to a fellow who is an unemployed writer or dramatist or something. He gives me what they allow him for his room rent, but he's going when the weather gets colder . . . no heat, you see."

Mark saw the long, dingy, narrow room, the table, the couch bed, the few chairs, the long window looking out on the dingy yard. Off this there was a windowless room with a large bed in the middle and beyond that was the room he supposed was rented. Maybe he could get that room when the other fellow left — be near her all the time. She was tall and slender and very pale, and the child was pale, but it seemed to be able to run very quickly and to talk so that she understood. It was long since Mark had seen a small child and he was surprised.

"It never stops, does it? Never keeps at rest?"

She laughed. "He keeps going all the time. All children are like that — they go, go, all the time."

"What is its name?" Mark asked.

"Mark, you must not call him *it!* It's *he.*" Her eyes sparkled. "You are such a bachelor." She lifted the child and brought him near — a small, pale face that seemed a mixture of hers and Ted's was unwillingly pressed against his cheek. Mark had seen small children chiefly in parks, and this one did not seem an attractive member of the tribe, and he was relieved when Alice removed the sticky, sweety-smelling face from his.

"What is his name?" Mark repeated the question.

"Jonah," she answered.

"Why, what a name!" he exclaimed. Then suddenly he remembered that it was his own second name, an unused one he had dropped long ago. At first it used to be printed on programs — Violinists, Mark J. Steicher. Then the printers had dropped it, and he never used it again. His eyes met Alice's. She flushed. "That's strange," he said. "Did I ever tell you? Why, I must have told you."

"Yes, you told me once . . . you remember? Don't you remember when the names of the musicians were printed on the Lotos Night Club program? You said the initial J stood for Jonah — a name you used to have."

She came over to him and in her eagerness to explain she caught his wrist in an old gesture of hers. He had seen her do that to many people, even to other men, and suddenly, mechanically, he released his wrist, putting her arm down by her side. A quick flush passed over her face and bright drops stood behind her eyes which searched his. There was a noise of a key and a minute later Ted walked in, carrying his instrument in a case. They were all glad to see each other. All three stood together happy. Ted was making just a few dollars, he explained, playing twice a week in a cocktail lounge. He was not the same good-natured Ted at all, but a thin-faced, harassed man. Before they sat down to the meal Alice provided, of some salty meat, Mark went out and brought back a bottle of liquor which Ted eagerly mixed and drank with cheerfulness; he was glad to wipe out the cold room, the oil stove, and he held the child happily on his knee. Though he must have known that Mark knew better, he began to reminisce about the grand symphony orchestras he had played in and the celebrated conductors he had played under, and the fine money he had made. Leaving, Mark hilariously arranged with them to take the rented room, but awaking in the nighttime he suddenly knew that it would be all wrong — it could not be done — they could not all live together. "A mirage," he said, "an illusion." He remembered an old theater violinist who used to tell him that a man was drawn from one mirage to another in life until he became oldish, and then he saw no more mirages, but settled down to the idea that there had been some existence before he was born and that another would come after, and that the life he lived in between meant nothing — was just an error, a mistake of the Almighty's.

Mark had parked the old Ford in a garage and had a bed and a locker in a cubicle he had taken in a men's lodging house on the East Side, not so far from Ted and Alice. Thinking everything over as he drank his five-cent cup of coffee the next morning, it seemed to him that it would be foolish for him to stay — madness. Ted and Alice had their own life — he ought to go away — get any sort of work, do as other men did — get married, find a companion before the loneliness of middle age overtook him. On the subway journey uptown, however, he brought his bag; at the last moment he had climbed back up the three flights of iron stairs and taken it. What should he do — sell the Ford and stay — drive away and never see them again — not see them until he had a good job and was married? Coming out of the subway he saw a luncheon and beer shop sign down the street, and he walked toward it and then into it arguing to himself. The arguments on both sides seemed equally good — that had always been the way with him. He always found it hard to decide between things, but in the end whichever road he took seemed to be the right one. As he went up to the counter to pay, the barman addressed him cheerfully:

"Going traveling?" he said, looking at the bag. "Going to Europe?"

"No," said Mark. "Changing rooms."

There was a conversation about the price of rooms in the neighborhood, and Mark suddenly asked the barman to keep his bag for an hour or so till he looked around. The man placed the bag under the counter.

Walking up the worn brownstone steps and ringing the bell on the broken letter box, he struggled with himself, but as the rapid click came in answer, his mind suddenly soared into clarity. Alice and Ted were at breakfast, eating fried bread and coffee. One half of the table was spread with an old cloth, the oil burner was standing between their two chairs, the radio going, the child in pajamas and a little woolly wrapper walking, moving per-

petually, dragging the anonymous toy. Ted took the remains of
the bottle of gin of the night before and began mixing it.

"Here," said he, offering a glass to Mark. "Let's start the day
right."

Mark felt his spirits rise and resolution take hold of him as he
gulped down the liquor.

"Here's to me," he said gaily. "I've got a job down South, playing in one of those Florida cafés."

The remark made no impression on Ted, whose eyes began to
get the glazed dimness of drink.

"Won't you drink to me?" Mark said to Alice. Her eyes in her
white faced flamed with anger.

"I don't understand men who drink in the morning," she said.

"Ah, look here," said Ted thickly, "you don't understand men
at all."

"No, I don't," she said, looking fixedly at Mark. "I do not," she
repeated.

Mark poured himself another drink. "You seem to be proud
of that," he said truculently. "That's nothing to be proud of. Is
it, eh, Ted?"

"A man's better off like you, Mark, without any women around.
Look at this place! Look at that kid! If I was only by myself . . ."
A dozen swift emotions passed through Alice's eyes — fear, anger,
humiliation, hunger, cold, cruelty — there were so many all together that Mark was startled.

"When are you going?" she asked him.

"Do you mean when am I going out of here, or when am I going
down South?"

"I mean down South," she said gently.

"Oh, tomorrow," he answered, "tomorrow morning, in the Ford."

"Is it a good job?" she asked with an eagerness in her voice.

"Well, no. But there's sun down there and I won't have to
think of the cold. Then, I'll get my dinner in the restaurant and
maybe a drink thrown in." He stood up suddenly. "Well, good-by,
Ted; good-by, Alice. Good-by," he said to the child. "Good-by,
Jonah. You'll be bigger when I see you again." And he kissed
the sticky, sweetish face.

As he closed the door behind him he called good-by loudly once more, and ran swiftly, unsteadily down the worn steps. He walked toward the avenue, toward the beer shop, his mind half doped with the early morning drink. Suddenly he heard steps behind him, someone coming swiftly, breathlessly. "Mark, Mark!" called the voice. It was Alice. "Take me with you, Mark. Take me along." Turning round he saw her, and something inside him sank, a weight seemed to drag at him. Mechanically he took her by the arm. They stood staring at each other. "I want to go with you."

"I would take you," he said slowly and thickly, "but — but — "

Mingled emotions again swept her face — fear, longing, hunger, cold. "But not Jonah," she said. "Not Jonah — that's what you mean. I'd have to leave Jonah behind."

"That's it," he said, with difficulty finding his tongue. "I don't want another man's kid."

"I can't leave him — poor little Jonah," she sobbed slightly, without tears. "Ted is drinking. He wouldn't take care of him. He'd leave him in the cold. He'd leave him to starve. He'd go out to the club to play and Jonah would be there by himself in the cold."

She went on sobbing slightly, dryly, as she murmured each sentence in a far-off way. Mark turned away. She flung her arms around him, and gropingly her lips passed from his cheek to his mouth. A sudden flame ran through him and he turned and gripped her. "Ah, come along," he said. "Come on! Come with me! Leave the kid there. Come on!"

Her sobbing stopped, she drew back and took her arms away, glancing up and down the street as if she suddenly realized where they were. There seemed to be no one around. "No," she said, "no, no."

"Come on," he said, gripping her again by the arm. "My bag is all packed, all ready, there in the lunch room." He took her arm and pulled her forward. "Come on," he said, "till I get my bag." They moved slowly. Where the street met the avenue he could not remember whether the lunch room was to the right or to the left. Two lunch rooms exactly alike seemed to be staring at him, one on each block, undistinguishable. He walked toward one of them still half-dragging her by the arm. As they entered, he seemed to remember that the counter stood differently. "Ah, it's the other one," he said. "Just sit down and I'll be back in a minute." He ran back toward the other; he rushed in. The barman was serving some men with beer, cutting the froth off the glasses in a leisurely manner. "Did you get the room?" he asked Mark.

"Yes, give me the bag, please."

The barman started looking for the bag, which had been moved, and kept on talking about rooms, the drinking men joining in. When at length Mark got back to where he had left Alice she was no longer there — there was no trace of her. "Your lady gone up that street," jerked the man behind the counter. "She no wait."

Once more he handed over the bag for keeping and rushed out. Approaching the house where Alice lived he saw that she was standing at the head of the steps, her white face turned toward his running figure. She slipped into the hallway, and as he reached the steps, Mark saw, for a moment, Ted's face at the opened door. Then it closed behind them.

A Nun No More

JOHN FANTE

M Y MOTHER went to a high school which was run by the nuns. After she got through she wanted to be a nun too. My Grandma Toscana told me. But Grandma and the whole family didn't want her to become a nun. They told her it was all right for girls in other families to become nuns, but not their daughter. My mother's name was Regina Toscana and she was so holy the holiness lit up her eyes. She had a statue of St. Teresa in her room, and when they kicked about her becoming a nun she stayed in her room day and night praying to St. Teresa.

"Oh beloved St. Teresa!" she prayed. "Grant me the light to see the path thou hast made for me, that I might do thy holy bidding. Visit me with sanctifying grace in the name of our Blessed Mother and the Lord Jesus, amen!"

Some prayer. But it didn't do any good because Grandma Toscana still said nothing doing. She told my mother to cut out acting like a sick calf and get some sense. They all talked to her like that, Uncle Jim, Uncle Tony, and Grandma and Grandpa Toscana. They were Italian people and they didn't like the way she was acting, because Italians hate it when their women don't want to get married. They hate it and they think something is screwy somewhere. It is best for the Italian women to get married. Then the husband pays and the whole family saves money. And that was the way they talked to my mother.

Then my Uncle Tony got an idea. One night he brought a man

From *The Virginia Quarterly Review*, Autumn, 1940. Printed by permission of the author.

named Pasquale Martello to the house. Uncle Tony introduced him to my mother, and he had a hunch she would go for him and maybe marry him and forget about the nun business. My mother was a honey and I know it, because we have some pictures and I can prove it.

Pasquale Martello owned a grocery store and he was lousy with money, but otherwise he wasn't so hot for a girl like my mother. He sold fancy things in his store, like Parmesan cheese, salami, and a special kind of fancy garlic. He dressed real loud in green shirts with white stripes and red neckties. The only reason my mother went with him was on account of she was afraid of Uncle Tony, who raised hell if she didn't go out with him. Pretty soon Pasquale Martello got a crush on my mother and he tried to get her to marry him.

But he had so many bad habits that my mother got awfully tired of him pretty soon. For one thing, he ate too much fancy garlic and his breath was something fierce. He carried garlic around in a sack in his pockets and he used to toss it up in the air and catch it in his mouth the way you eat salted peanuts. He took my mother to different places, like Lakeside Park, and the dance, and to the movies. On account of that garlic you could smell him coming for miles. Every time they went to the movies people got up and found other seats. And my mother wanted to become a nun! It was very embarrassing for her. After the show they used to sit in front of the big stove in Grandma Toscana's parlor and talk. He was so dumb that my mother yawned right in his face and he never did catch on that she was hinting and wanted to go to bed. She had to tell him to go home or he would still be in that parlor, talking.

Every morning Uncle Tony asked the same question.

"Well, well! And when's the marriage going to be?"

"Never," my mother said. "There isn't going to be any marriage."

"Are you crazy?" Uncle Tony said. "That guy's got money!"

"I'm sorry," she said. "My life is in another direction."

"Meaning?"

"My life is dedicated to the service of our Blessed Lady."

"My God!" Uncle Tony said. "Did you hear that one! I give up!"

"I'm sorry," my mother said. "I'm really sorry."

"*Sangue de la Madonna!*" Uncle Tony said. "And after all I've done for her! There's gratitude for you."

My mother went up to her room and stayed there all day, until Pasquale came that night. He always brought my grandmother something from the store, cheese mostly, and sometimes tomato sauce in big cans, or Italian paste. Grandma Toscana liked him most on account of the Parmesan cheese, which was a dollar a pound in those days.

That night my mother told Pasquale it was too bad, but he would have to find another girl because she did not love him. He was crazy about her all right. He got down on his knees and kissed her hands, and he walked out of the house bawling. The next day he called Uncle Tony on the phone and told him my mother had given him the gate and wouldn't let him come around any more.

Uncle Tony got boiling mad. He ran home from work and raised hell with the whole family. When he came to my mother he shook his fist in her face and pushed her against the sideboard so hard it knocked the wind out of her.

"You crazy fool!" he hollered. "What good are you anyhow?"

"I'm sorry," she said.

"Good God!" he said. "Don't you know anything else but 'I'm sorry'?"

"I'm sorry," she said.

"Listen to her!" he yelled. "She's sorry!"

"But I am sorry," she said.

My Uncle Tony was in the grocery business too, but his store was a little one and he didn't sell Italian stuff, and he had it all figured out that when my mother and Pasquale got married he would merge his store with Pasquale's and they would all clean up. But Pasquale never came back to the house again. Before long he married a girl, and she wasn't an Italian either. She was an American and he didn't love her either. Grandma Toscana said it was a spite marriage. The Italians do that sometimes. A spite marriage is when you marry somebody else to get your real girl's goat and try to make her sorry she didn't marry you.

But my mother wasn't sorry at all. The whole thing tickled her pink.

In North Denver is the Church of St. Cecilia's. This was where my mother spent all of her time. It is across the street from the high school, an old red church without a lawn in front of it or anything, just the street, and not even a tree around. Once I went there for Christmas Mass with my mother. It was a long time after she got married. I mean, it had to be. The church is a big, sad church and the incense smells like my mother. It is a leery church. It scared me. I kept thinking I was not born and would never be born.

My mother knew all the nuns at St. Cecilia's. She used to bum around with them, and they put her in charge of the altars and she decorated them with flowers. She washed and ironed the altar linen and things like that. It was more fun than getting married. She was there all afternoon, so that Uncle Jim or Uncle Tony had to come for her at suppertime. Uncle Jim didn't mind because it was only a block away, but Uncle Tony raised hell. He thought church was a lot of boloney.

He said, "Instead of fooling around here all the time, why don't you stay home and help your mother?"

But my mother was a good worker and she told him to be careful what he said. She did all the washing and ironing around the house, and Grandma didn't have any kick coming, and once in a while she cooked the meals, but not often because she was not a good cook. She always did her work before she went to St. Cecilia's. Her garden was in Grandma's back yard, and she grew peonies and roses for the altars. Uncle Tony told her to cut out the church stuff or he would wreck her garden.

"You go to the dickens!" she said.

Oh, oh, that got him mad. Italian girls are not supposed to sass their big brothers. Uncle Tony wouldn't allow anything like that.

"By God, I'll show you!" he said.

He ran out to the coal shed and got the spade. Then he took off his sweater and spaded every flower in the garden to pieces.

It hurt my mother. She stood on the back porch and it hurt her. She was crazy about her garden, and when she saw him hacking it up she hung on the door and almost fainted. Then she ran out and screamed and screamed. She fell on the ground and kicked with her feet and hit with her hands. It scared Uncle Tony. He called Grandma. She kept screaming. He tried to lift her. She screamed and kicked him.

She was very sick. They carried her upstairs and put her to bed. The doctor came. He said she was a very sick woman. For a long time he came every day. They had to have a nurse. For a year she was sick and nervous. Everybody in the house had to be quiet and walk on tiptoe. It cost a lot of money for doctor bills. My mother cried and cried night and day. They couldn't stop her. Even the Sisters came, but they couldn't do anything. Finally Grandma Toscana called the priest. He gave her Holy Communion. Right away she felt better. Next day she was better than ever. Next day she was swell. Pretty soon she was able to get out of bed. Then she moved around more. All at once she was well again.

Grandma Toscana said it was a miracle. Uncle Tony felt like the devil. He told my mother how sorry he was, and he planted her a new garden. Everything was fine again. My mother liked the new garden better than ever, and Uncle Tony left her alone. Nobody bothered her any more.

She went on decorating the altars at St. Cecilia's. Also she taught school. She went on retreats. A retreat is when you pray and meditate for three days without talking to anybody. Once she went on a retreat for six weeks. Whatever the nuns did, she did. She was crazy about them. All they ever did was wash clothes, decorate altars, scrub floors, and teach kids.

Before long, sure enough Uncle Tony started kicking again, but not like before. He was afraid my mother would get sick again. He even brought more men to the house. He brought Jack Mondi, who was the biggest bootlegger in North Denver. He isn't any more because he got shot, but he was important when Uncle Tony brought him to meet my mother. He scared the whole family stiff. Before sitting down, he always put his gun on the table. Every few minutes he jumped up and peeked out the front window. He brought gangsters with him, and they waited for him on the front porch. Even Uncle Tony didn't know it was going to be that scary, so he tried to get rid of Jack Mondi, but he didn't try very hard. He was afraid he would get hurt.

Once Jack Mondi came to the house drunk and he bit my mother on the cheek. It was the first time anything like that ever happened to her, and she got mad and hauled off and slapped him. The whole family held their breaths and waited for Jack Mondi to shoot them down. Uncle Tony made a sign to my mother to go easy and not make Jack mad. But my mother didn't think he was so tough. She told him to get out of the house and never come back. He did it too. He stuck his gun in his pocket and walked right out without saying a word. For a long time they thought he would come back and shoot the whole family, but he never came back again. Uncle Tony was so scared he even went to church. But Jack Mondi never showed up again. After he got killed they read about it in the papers. My mother went to his funeral and prayed for the repose of his soul. She was the only woman in the church besides Jack Mondi's mother. Which proves my mother was a good sport.

Another guy with a crush on my mother was Alfredo di Posso. Uncle Tony brought him too. Whenever he found a guy he thought would make a good husband he brought him to dinner. There were others too, but I only know about Pasquale Martello, Jack Mondi, Alfredo di Posso, and a man named Murphy, but Murphy didn't cut much ice because he was Irish. Uncle Tony never did like the Irish.

Alfredo di Posso was a salesman for lima beans. Once in a while Alfredo comes to our town, so I know him. He doesn't sell beans in cans or anything like that. He sells them by the carload. When he comes to our town he stops to see my mother. He is a swell guy, always laughing. He gives me money, usually four bits. When my mother met him, he didn't have a religion. She made him join the Catholic Church, but he made fun of it; he made fun of everything. My mother got tired of it. She told him she could never marry him.

When my mother was twenty-one everybody in North Denver knew she was going to be a nun. Her favorite order was the Sisters of Charity. You have to take the train to their convent in Kentucky. For a long time you study stuff. Then you become a real nun. They cut off your hair and you wear black dresses, and you can't get married or have fun. Your husband is Jesus. Anyway, that's what Sister Delphine told me.

It was all set. My mother was ready to go. Uncle Tony hated it and so did the rest, but they couldn't do anything. Grandpa was disappointed. He had a shoe shop on Osage Street. He liked nuns. He thought they were swell people, he even did their shoe work for nothing, but he couldn't see why his own daughter had to get mixed up in it.

He promised to send my mother to Colorado U. if she would forget it. My mother wouldn't hear of it because she thought Colorado U. was an awful place. Right now my mother knows a Catholic who doesn't believe in God. He went to Colorado U. He was all right until then. Now the Catholics in our town are off him for life. They even kicked him out of the Knights of Columbus because he made smart cracks. So my mother wouldn't go to a school like Colorado U. It was Kentucky or nothing.

All day long Uncle Tony yelled at her, calling her a dumb cluck and a stupe. She almost had another nervous breakdown. He followed her around the house, yelling at her and trying to make her change her mind. Next door to Grandma Toscana's the Rocca people were building a new house. Uncle Tony had a big voice and he yelled so loud the bricklayers heard every word he hollered. They used to stop work on the scaffold and listen to him.

One morning two months before she was to leave for Kentucky my mother was eating breakfast, and Uncle Tony started right in on the same old argument. She didn't have any sense. Weren't they treating her all right at home? She wanted to bury herself in a hole and forget all the fine things her family did for her. Didn't she get enough to eat and plenty of clothes to wear? Then what more did she want? Why did she have to be so selfish? Think of her poor mother getting old without her around.

Why couldn't she think those things out and realize the mistake she was making?

My mother put her head down and started to cry.

One of the bricklayers was watching from the scaffold. He climbed down the ladder and walked over to the kitchen window. He was an Italian too, but not the ordinary kind. He had a red mustache for one thing, and red hair. He knocked on the screen and my mother looked up. Uncle Tony wanted to know what he wanted. The man had a trowel in his hand. He shook it in Uncle Tony's face.

"If you say another word to that girl I'll knock your head off!"

The minute my mother saw him something happened. Uncle Tony got so mad he went into the front room without speaking. My mother kept looking at the man with the trowel and the little red mustache. All at once they both started laughing. He went back to work, still laughing. At noon he sat on the scaffold looking down into the kitchen window. My mother could see him. He whistled. She laughed and came to the window. What he wanted was some salt for his sandwich. That was how it got started. The man was my father. Every day he laughed and asked for something. If it wasn't salt it was pepper, and my mother laughed and got it for him. Another time he asked for some fresh fruit to go with his lunch. One day he came to the window and laughed and asked if she had any wine. Then he wanted to know if she could cook. My mother laughed and laughed. Finally she told him not to bring his lunch any more but to come over and eat with her. He laughed and said sure. Two months later, instead of going to Kentucky, my mother came to our town and got married.

The Old Lady Takes A Hand

AUGUST DERLETH

THAT July evening, Bird Jenkins came over like a sudden wind from the north, his face as red as a turkey's, and his mild, sad eyes frustrated and angry. In one moment all the copper afterglow was lost to sight in Bird's mouth working helplessly at his drooping mustache, all the evensong of birds was gone before his baffled words.

"I tol' you we ain't oughta let old man Stulpy inta the Co-op!" he said belligerently, before he had thought to greet any one of us, before he had quite caught his breath.

My great-uncle, Ed Blake, descended laboriously from the top rail of the fence, his heavy bulk making this an onerous task. His face showed his displeasure, his mouth down-curved, his eyebrows drawn upon his eyes. On the back porch, my great-aunt raised her head to listen.

"He's got some fool scheme afoot," replied Bird. "I like t' died when I heard it in Badger Prairie this afternoon. He's got the chairman t' side in with him, and he's goin' t' put us t' shippin' hogs by truck 'stead a train. And his brother-in-law ownin' trucks. Hoh!"

My great-uncle was not disturbed. "Don't git het up; it don't look good in a little man like you," he said evenly. "He can't do it; it's a vi'lation of our contract with the railroad company."

Bird seemed to swell until the oversized clothes he wore looked momentarily as if they fit him. "Contrac'!" he shouted. "You know darn well that Stulpy ain't been stopped by any contrac' yet!"

Great-aunt Annie got up and came down the steps to stand within a few feet of where we were, her angular figure set

From *Extension*, October, 1941. By permission of the author and of *Extension*.

ominously against the dying afterglow in the west, her arms folded across her chest, her mouth forbiddingly tight, her eyes glinting above her spectacles as she looked over them at Bird and Great-uncle. For the time being, however, she held her peace.

"Anyway, he can't git the votes," continued my great-uncle. "There jest ain't that many farmers 'd have any trust in that old buzzard."

"There's some that has," replied Bird doggedly.

"But not enough," said Great-uncle with pat finality.

At this moment my great-aunt spoke with almost smug tartness. " 'Pears to me you two've plum forgot that last meetin'."

"I ain't," answered Bird, and at once the anger went out of his face: his eyes seemed to lose their brief fire, to grow melancholy and tired; his mouth sulked beneath the lugubrious half-moon of his yellow mustache.

For a moment my great-uncle did not understand; then his mouth opened ludicrously, but no sound came forth, and he stood staring sheepishly from Bird Jenkins to Great-aunt.

"Close that flytrap, Ed," said my great-aunt, with a weary smile. "You remember I told you two not to vote for that motion Stone put up; I seen right off that Stulpy was behind it — therefore, I said it. But you helped him vote it in. Now instead a havin' every member in this Co-operative have one vote, the way it's supposed to be, they got a vote for every share."

Great-uncle swallowed and pushed his lips outward as if he were about to make some announcement of importance, but all he said was, "Stulpy's got a hundred shares, and Stone's got fifty. With Bird's hundred, and my fifty, and your fifty, and Ed Burke's and Hank Bloom's twenty-five each, we got him beat already."

My great-aunt was unmoved. "And what about the rest?"

"Oh, I reckon they be knowin' how t' vote," said my great-uncle, a little more confidently.

"I ain't hopin'," replied Great-aunt shortly. "I know plegged well that Stulpy's a good talker — he'll talk a farmer into puttin' his name to a dotted line easier 'n fallin' off the fence. My soul and body! If you or Bird can hold a chance against Stulpy for talkin', I declare to goodness I don't know it."

My great-uncle turned abruptly to Bird. "How come we let Stulpy buy up them shares anyway? I be dogged if he's a farmer," he said violently, as if resenting this problem thrust upon him.

"Same's I asked you, Ed Blake, and you said he was a farmer since he took in that Largan place," replied Bird, faintly indignant.

Great-aunt made a sound like a snort of disgust. "A mortgage farmer!" she exclaimed. "He come along with some money in his fist and you couldn't hold back. My conscience! If that ain't just like a man!"

"Annie, you keep outa this," said Great-uncle heavily. " 'Tain't nothin' for no woman t' be mixed in."

"Ain't it?" she replied. "I didn't hear you tellin' me that when you let me pay that two hundred fifty."

Great-uncle affected not to hear. "You jest let me 'n' Bird handle it. We'll fix it," he said.

My great-aunt nodded vigorously. "If your luck holds out, you likely will. But more likely you'll just try to talk it to death, and I got a feelin' it ain't goin' to be talked to death!"

She turned then and walked back to the house, not entirely concealing the faint lines of worry on her forehead.

Great-uncle sighed and looked off into the darkening sky to where the evening star shone brightly forth. "Bird, I don't know how a man a my parts got mixed up with women," he said forlornly. "Not that she ain't the best there is — but a woman ain't like people."

Bird Jenkins had heard that so often before that he was no longer very sympathetic. It annoyed my great-uncle a little to see how hopefully Bird's eyes followed my great-aunt's figure toward the house.

The meeting was to be held on the first Tuesday in August, only ten days away, and almost every evening Bird and my great-uncle met to talk over the problem of saving the Co-operative Association from Stulpy's designs. Sometimes they were alone, sometimes joined by Hank Bloom and Ed Burke, and usually they met in my great-aunt's kitchen. As July drew toward its close, all four became more worried. The association had been formed by a group of farmers west of Badger Prairie; almost two hundred farmers had taken up one thousand shares at five dollars a share. As an organization, it had run smoothly enough under Chairman Stone, and the members had prospered modestly but to such an extent that they had become careless, and allowed themselves to be persuaded to change the voting method at the previous meeting.

My great-uncle's first bold suggestion that they withdraw if Stulpy gained control of the organization met with no favor, for the system of five per cent rebate on all purchases had worked to the profit of its members.

"I don't hold with drawin' out, Ed," said Bird. "Be dogged if I do."

"Nor I," said Hank Bloom.

Great-uncle withdrew his suggestion, grumbling. "Well, I reckon we c'n always take the floor t' oppose Stone and Stulpy," he said then. "But my old woman rightly says I ain't much of a talker."

"One thing's certain, and we're agreed on it," said Ed Burke. "Whatever happens, we're all votin' together against Stulpy. But I can see the trouble — all those with five and ten and twenty shares each'll be votin' with Stulpy, most likely."

"There's 'bout a hundred with a share apiece that'll be votin' against him," Bird put in hopefully. "Leastwise, they be divided and the chief part votin' our way."

"That's what we're hopin'," said Ed dryly.

My Great-aunt Annie stood it as long as she could. That was for three nights. After that, she left the house shortly after chores every night; sometimes she went out on foot; sometimes she took the horse and buggy; and once she had Barney drive her over to Betler's in the car. But most of the time she went alone, and left me to sit with the men. And before long I got out and sat on the porch or on the pasture gate to watch the stars roll over or listen to the lowing of cows in night pasture. The more they argued around in circles in the house, the farther away I went, until presently I had to get down into Whippoorwill Hollow and take my choice between being deafened by the hollering in the house and the whippoorwills' singing. I took the whippoorwills.

Great-aunt was that put out about it all that she took to going off in the afternoons as well. My great-uncle did not seem to notice, and as the time for the meeting drew near, he began to grow morose. After being once rebuffed, Great-aunt said tartly, "Let 'em stew. Leastwise, they're safe here." And one night she risked his anger by interrupting the hot argument in process by insisting that he sign a batch of checks that she pushed onto the table before him. He took the pen she handed him and scrawled his signature, glancing angrily at her and grumbling.

"Fine time t' be breakin' in on me; ain't the day long enough?"

"The first is tomorrow," she said. "And it's best to be businesslike."

"Businesslike!" he snorted. "Hoh!"

She only smiled at him mischievously and said dryly, "Hope still springin' eternal, Ed?"

Bird laughed until he caught Great-uncle's eye.

The meeting was attended by every member, and included even the wives of ten of them, apart from Great-aunt Annie. Stulpy had done his best to have the meeting fully attended, and now he was almost offensively in evidence: walking up and down the aisles with his hands clasped beneath his coattails, his foxlike eyes narrowed shrewdly behind his octagonal glasses, his white sideburns neatly groomed. His hard mouth was touched by a brief, distant smile, which became instantly ingratiating the moment any eye directly met his own. He was a good actor in his own narrow sphere, and for all the hatred and dislike he had stimulated while he was at the height of instigating foreclosures on mortgages he held, his smile and words had beguiled many a farmer into a feeling of sullen security. My great-aunt, however, because he had once tricked a relative of hers, saw no reason for overlooking his activities. "Any man who'd push a hard-hit farmer to the wall, the way he's done, is a low-down, ornery skunk," she said, and that settled Stulpy as far as she was concerned.

Chairman Stone occupied the rostrum, but within a few moments of opening the meeting, he relinquished the chair to Stulpy — "who has something to tell us."

Stulpy was at his best, smiling and bowing. He stood before

the meeting and began to explain, plausibly enough, his plan for shipment of stock by truck instead of by railroad. He edged around the contract with the railroad company with great care; by the words he used, he left the impression that there would be no violation of contract at all, but just a little permissible change, and in a few minutes he held the audience. He began to talk to them; he grew more confident, more convincing with every sentence. That his brother-in-law owned a fleet of trucks in which he himself had an interest he did not mention.

So he talked. All the time Stone, the innocent, easily led dupe, sat nodding and smiling. And when Stulpy had finished, he listened politely to everything my great-uncle and Bird Jenkins had to say; he had no trouble demolishing their contentions, and he made them look ridiculous without an unkind word. It was my great-uncle's chagrin to see even his wife's furtive grin, though he did not miss the suspicious glint in her eyes.

But Great-uncle did not begin actively to wonder until the ten farm women began to edge around toward my great-aunt. That was when Chairman Stone got up and called for a vote on the amendment Stulpy had proposed. His suspicions, however, were interrupted by Stone's calling upon Stulpy to tabulate the votes as they were cast.

"What you mean, tabulate votes?" demanded Great-uncle, rising.

"We want to come out in the open on this amendment, Mr. Blake," said Stulpy smoothly. "And in view of the fact that we are now voting by shares, it's virtually necessary to vote orally. We propose to call out the names of each member, from one-share members to those two holding the largest number of shares." He made a slight bow toward Bird Jenkins, smiling. "Perhaps we had better put that into a motion. Will somebody make it?"

"Yes, I make it," said Great-aunt suddenly.

My great-uncle was so astonished that he did not hear one of the women ranged like a phalanx behind his wife second her motion. He turned and looked at her as if she were out of order, his heavy jowls ponderously expressing his indignant disapproval.

Stulpy leaned over and whispered to Stone, whereupon the

chairman turned upon the woman who had seconded the motion.

"Mrs. Betler, are you a member of this organization?" he asked.

"Certainly," she replied.

"Since when?"

"Since I bought some shares last week."

Stone fingered his chin for an uncertain moment before he called for a vote on the motion. It was carried.

The voting on the amendment before the association began. Stone called off one name after another until he had completed the roster of the hundred one-share members. Great-aunt Annie had listened with growing satisfaction as the votes continued to be balanced, and even Bird smiled furtively once or twice. Thus far, Stulpy had gained no ground; but neither had he lost, for he remained undisturbed and confident.

Stone moved on to the group of fifty farmers with five shares each, but almost immediately Stulpy received a shock. The second name called was that of Fred Betler, a stocky, red-faced man.

"Three votes Aye," he replied.

Stone looked up quickly. "Splitting your votes, Betler?"

"No. That's all I got."

Stulpy flashed a glance at him, and then at Stone.

"You're registered at five," continued the chairman.

"I sold two."

"And I bought 'em," interrupted Mrs. Betler firmly.

Stone smiled dryly. "Very well. Mrs. Betler?"

"Two votes No," she said smartly.

Stulpy looked down again, but not before he had carefully counted the women present and flashed a glance of half-humorous appeal at the men now being called upon. He was not, in fact, nervous until he became aware that the majority of the fifty five-share members had but three shares each left, and that only ten women were present to account for twenty of the seventy shares sold. Then he looked long and carefully at Stone, pursing his lips and further narrowing his eyes; he was not entirely satisfied, but kept his eyes down to continue his tabulation. Stone, meanwhile, shot many a side-long glance at Stulpy, and, missing Stulpy's nervousness, seemed presently to have satisfied whatever doubts lingered in his mind. Thereafter his bearing became more aggressively confident, and Stulpy, noticing, regained his composure.

The ten-share members were next. The first member called upon voted No, at which Stulpy looked up with a faint frown. The second member was a man named Stossen.

"I ain't votin'," he replied. "I sold my shares."

Stulpy had opened his lips to protest when he saw the expression of satisfaction on Stone's face, and was misled. Disgruntled, he was still; he struck out Stossen's name, and so was prepared in a fashion for the withdrawal of three more members. The remaining five, however, voted Aye, in accordance with his hope; while he was somewhat soothed at this, he could not help showing faint doubts in his glances toward Chairman Stone, who remained serene.

The twenty-share members occasioned Stulpy some acute discomfort. He had not anticipated that half of them would vote in the negative, and that the remaining five members should have sold half their shares. The result of the voting was not in Stulpy's favor as it now stood; his amendment was being defeated, and Stulpy's glances at Stone were now openly suspicious.

Great-uncle Ed was delighted, but my great-aunt had a small contented smile that told more.

Ed Burke and Hank Bloom still further increased the opposition to Stulpy's amendment. So did the vote of my great-uncle. Stone's own vote was called next. At his registration of only fifty, Stulpy's expression of injured amazement would have shaken the chairman had he seen it. But he had not, for he went right on to call out my great-aunt's name.

By that time even my great-uncle had suspected that something was amiss, because the voting had not gone at all as he had feared it would. But he was not prepared for his wife's reply to the chairman.

"Biggest shareholders last, Mr. Stone," she said.

Stone looked at her coldly and said, "Mr. Stulpy and Mr. Jenkins are the biggest shareholders, Mrs. Blake."

"Not any more, they ain't," replied my great-aunt tartly. "But I'll vote if you're insistin' on it. And I'll vote my entire two hundred shares No."

Stulpy and Stone might not have heard, for all the immediate reaction: with one accord they turned and looked at each other — fixed, astonished, dismayed stares.

Great-aunt Annie smiled almost maliciously. "Yes, I figured that was the way it was between you," she said clearly. "I guessed each one of you thought the other one'd bought them missing shares."

The final vote was comfortably against Stulpy's amendment, and my great-uncle could hardly wait until we got out of the mill, where the meeting had taken place, before he began to ply Great-aunt with questions.

"Wasn't much to it," she replied shortly. "While you and Bird was a-settin' there figurin', I up and talked to some of them men until they saw it against Stulpy. And the women all had the sense to see what I seen right off."

"But them shares a your'n!" exclaimed Great-uncle. "Where'd you git all that money? Holy cow! Near a thousand dollars!"

Great-aunt stood and looked at him where he stood in the white wine of the moonlight, and for a moment there was stillness, so that we could hear in the quiet summer night the sound of Grell's falls at the foot of the millpond below the bluff. Then an expression of tenderness came into her face and she came over to him and took his arm gently.

"Why, Ed, that was your money," she said quietly.

"*My* money!" he hollered, staring at her in amazement.

"Why, yes," she said, smiling now. "You know that night you signed them checks? Most of them was blank. I just filled 'em out as I bought up them shares."

Angeline's Afternoon

RUTH KATHERINE BYRNS

NONE of us actually snubbed Angeline, but we acted cool to her for we resented her being at the July meeting of our club — not that we women who belong to Ye Goodly Companye are prejudiced against foreigners or anything like that but because the people of Fort Allen have never quite approved of Angeline's actions since she first came to our town as a war orphan. But Mrs. Bradley, the hostess (she that was an Adams girl), was always doing unheard-of things. Did you ever hear about the time she got that red-haired woman to come out from Chicago to read Irish poetry at the Benefit for the library? And as long as Mrs. Bradley had invited Angeline, the rest of us had to make the best of it.

Angeline certainly must have felt out of place there with her short, straight, yellow hair and her cross-stitched linen dress and all the rest of us women with our permanent waves or marcels, and wearing our best printed silks or blue crepes. But she didn't show it; not that young lady!

The meeting opened with the members responding to roll call by giving a patriotic quotation in honor of Independence Day. To be polite, Mrs. Ames, the secretary — she knows shorthand and used to work in the bank before she was married — called on Angeline last of all, and Angeline said, "Amen." None of us knew just what she meant as her "Amen" didn't sound exactly like a patriotic remark. That was the way Angeline had always been. Queer and beyond understanding.

Then the lesson began. Mrs. Martin, who used to be a Johnston girl (her mother was an Ames), was the leader and her very

From *The Catholic World*, July, 1933. By permission.

interesting paper was on "What July Fourth Means to America."
Mrs. Martin had a new navy georgette for the occasion and had
had her eyebrows plucked. All the Johnston girls had heavy eyebrows like their father. And she had her fingernails polished. It
was so hot that the georgette stuck to her skin above the under-
slip and along her arms.

Most of the women were fanning themselves with their hand-
kerchiefs or pieces of paper and I could feel that my clothes were
wet from sweat around my waist where the band of my petticoat
comes — I always wear a petticoat, usually a white nainsook one
as they boil out so nice and clean in the washing. But Angeline
looked cool and hard, like the pale topaz in old Mrs. Adams's
brooch.

Then I got to thinking about Angeline.

My mind went back to the time when the Clarks got Angeline
after their Marian died. They were always so close mouthed that
no one in town knew anything about their taking an orphan until
Angeline showed up at school one day. She had on a long black
coat with a little cape and all decorated with black silk braid.
Instead of buttonholes the coat had fancy loops of braid — "frogs"
I remember we called them. She had her hair hanging down
loose over her shoulders and not braided as all the rest of us
wore ours. That was in the winter when I was in the seventh
grade, the winter of 1915. I remember exactly because it was the
same year that we got our Encyclopedia.

Angeline would never tell us where she came from, except to
answer "Lithuania," and the Clarks, when you asked them, always
said, "She's a gift from heaven." But the Clarks never would tell
anything. Like the time they went to Chicago on the same train
with Mrs. Fred Henry when she was going down to buy her spring
stock of millinery. It's six hours to Chicago and Mrs. Henry tried
all the way to find out what they were going for. All the Clarks
would say was that they were taking Angeline to see an Opera.
As though we wouldn't all know that no one would go clear to
Chicago just to see an Opera when we have our lyceums and home
talent plays in Fort Allen every winter and the Chatauqua in the
summer.

Anyway, we decided that Angeline must be a war orphan, though she didn't look like the refugees we'd heard about. Remember how they told about the shiploads of orphans that were brought from Belgium to America and Canada? And how the Germans had cut off the right hand of every child? And, of course, we never heard the worst of it either. I was just a child but I shall never forget hearing those stories.

From the first we didn't take to Angeline because she didn't try a bit to be like the rest of us. She was smart enough in some ways though, and graduated from high school the same year I did, in 1920. That's how I know she must be at least twenty-nine even if she does look like an eighth grader. It's because of her short hair and her being so skinny. My husband always says he likes a woman to look like she had plenty to eat, though I do diet a bit on the sly.

We got used to Angeline and didn't pay much attention to her, but it seems as if there was always some story or other going around town about her.

There was all the fights she had with her music teachers. First she took lessons from Miss Jenson who is the organist at our church. But Miss Jenson couldn't do a thing with her. Angeline would play a piece the way she wanted to play it, adding notes and runs that weren't there at all and changing the time from fast to slow or slow to fast just as she felt like it, not keeping time with Miss Jenson's foot at all. Soon she had an awful fight with Miss Jenson that was the talk of the town, and began to take lessons from Lil Palmer. It was the same story over again and 'twas no time till she'd had trouble with every music teacher in Fort Allen. Then the Catholic priest heard about it. It was the same priest that is here yet, a queer foreign fellow himself, who'd rather walk three miles than ride in a sedan and who spends all his money on books instead of buying himself a car and joining the Golf Club. First thing we knew she was taking lessons from him. The Clarks didn't seem to mind a bit, which wasn't surprising as they didn't belong to any church themselves and when people don't belong to a church you can expect most anything from them.

The way she used to practice was a caution. Not nice tunes

with a swing to them but pieces without much sense — the same kind of music, if you could call it music, that the priest played. He ruined whatever bit of music she had picked up from the other teachers and in no time she was fighting with him too. One day they yelled at each other until you could hear them way over at the gravel pit. Him calling her a little fool and her calling him an old fool! But she stuck to him in spite of the fighting till she graduated from high school and then went away, quiet as you please.

No one could figure out where she went or what she was doing. The Clarks said she was in Chicago the first year and after that in New York and they said she was studying music. Music, mind you, when everyone in Fort Allen knew she couldn't play even a simple piece like anyone else. But I suppose they felt as though they had to give some excuse.

I remember the first time she came back after she'd gone away the Clarks had a party for her, the only party she'd ever had. But we showed them! Not a single one of us went except that young Dr. Powers — the one that was so peculiar he got no trade and had to leave Fort Allen. Good enough for the Clarks, I always thought, with their trying to act as though Angeline was one of us.

Then the Clarks both died and we thought sure we'd be rid of Angeline.

I'll never forget how surprised we all were the summer when she came back. And not alone either, but with a whole crowd of the queerest people Fort Allen has ever seen. A woman with short cut hair and who smoked right in plain daylight! A man who wore a little dark blue tam o'shanter and carried a cane though he wasn't lame at all! And another woman that we were sure was a Jew. And others just as bad. She stayed the whole month of July and nearly every day some new freak came to visit her and some of the others left. Mr. Robins, the depot agent, said that most of them bought tickets way to New York but some only went to Chicago when they left.

Of course we cut Angeline cold — just spoke when we met and that was all. Except for the peculiar priest. He still goes there nearly every day. It certainly looks bad to see him talking and laughing with those Jews and foreigners and folks from New York as though they were as good as Christians.

Angeline has come back every summer since then and always has a pack of company with her nearly all the while she's here. Birds of a feather do flock together, as Aunt Sarah always says. Often as not they stay up nearly all night at the Clark place and then the next day we don't see hide nor hair of them till noon. And the noise! Always banging the piano or sawing on a fiddle or singing, and never a note of good tuneful music. She hasn't even got a radio!

Mrs. Campbell, who delivered groceries from her husband's store when the delivery boy had his appendix out last summer, said you'd die if you saw the inside of the Clark place. All the oldest furniture from the attic brought down into the living room and Mr. Clark's mother's paisley shawl hanging on the wall in the parlor. And cigarettes and pipes and playing cards and magazines and books and pictures and sheets of music scattered over everything.

Then I got to thinking about the time, years ago, when Angeline laughed at poor old Mrs. Jackson's funeral when the minister got hiccoughs. And the time in high school history that she got up in class and argued with the teacher because he said Andrew Jackson was Stonewall Jackson — as though the history teacher wouldn't know better than a foreigner. And the time that she came to our church to prayer meeting and knelt down!

Hearty applause took my mind away from Angeline and made me realize that the Club lesson was over. I joined with the others in praising Mrs. Martin on her instructive and entertaining lesson. Only Angeline did not congratulate Mrs. Martin.

We were all quiet again as Mrs. Bradley passed around napkins and silver. Ice cream or lemonade would be welcome on that hot afternoon. I took advantage of the quiet to speak across the room to Angeline:

"You, being a foreigner, must appreciate the liberty of America, and the hospitality."

"I appreciate all the hospitality that the people of this town have ever given me," answered Angeline in a voice that was low but that seemed to linger after she had stopped talking. And for no reason at all we all kept still as though we were guilty of something. I don't know why, because there was Angeline herself admitting that she appreciated our having been decent to her.

Just then Mrs. Bradley and her sister-in-law brought in the refreshments and I must say that even though Mrs. Bradley is funny, like asking Angeline to her place, she is smart when it comes to planning cute refreshments. Slices of red, white, and blue brick ice cream bearing tall pieces of Lady Washington cake with flags stuck in each one. They looked for all the world like armories or submarines or something.

When everyone was served and we were about to begin to eat, Angeline put down her plate on top of the piano, sat down, and struck a cord and a few trills. Her thin fingers began to flash back and forth across the keys and we rose to our feet as we recognized the opening strains of "The Star Spangled Banner." Angeline played it through twice, with extra runs and chords in every measure and a lot of notes that spoiled both the swing of it and the tune. Then she switched to "America." The ice cream began to melt, but we, as befits patriots, kept our eyes on the piano and stood straight as though at attention. When she had played "America" through several times she began "America the Beautiful," and then "Columbia, the Gem of the Ocean." My cake tipped over as the ice cream melted from in under it, and the flag fell into the red, white, and blue soup; then the cake began to soak up the melted cream. It was the same with all the others.

As the last flag fell, Angeline struck a thundering chord and swung around on the piano stool.

"I knew such a patriotic group of patriotic women would enjoy some patriotic music," she said, and smiled. "I'm running along now, I don't care for any refreshments as I don't want to get fat."

Then Angeline went.

The Lady Who Was Always Right

PAUL CLAUDEL

A VERY clever and refined Lady saw herself in a dream as Hercules at a spot between two roads. It was like the entrance to a theater or music hall.

And, in fact, there were two ways.

The one at the left was a steep and narrow and rather dirty staircase lighted by raw and old-fashioned gas jets, no doubt leading to the cheap places in the Upper Circle, what they call in French the *Paradis*.

The one at the right was a wide and spacious and dignified porch, leading down in a gentle slope, and richly furnished with thick carpets, flowers, tapestries, gold-framed pictures, and graceful statuary.

All the well-dressed people, ladies and gentlemen, were going this way, laughing and chattering, all ready to enjoy the circumstance, and to have a good time.

The very clever and refined Lady had no hesitation whatever in going down the same way.

Sleek and oily ushers, all clad in smiles, went to meet all these charming people, and took their tickets with a smile. The refined Lady showed hers. It was not of the same color as the others, but no observation was made, and she was duly and respectfully introduced.

Well, after all, it was not a theater or music hall. It was more like a kind of enormous waiting room, or something in fact resembling a court of justice. Thousands and thousands of men and women were there, all silent or talking to one another.

From *America*, September 12, 1931. By permission.

The Refined Lady looked through her *face-a-main* and was very satisfied and comforted to see there all of her friends and acquaintances. But all of them looked rather subdued and did not answer or only in a very few strange mumbled words when she gaily talked to them.

Many also were there whom she had not seen for a very long time.

How jolly and pleasant!

But, no; after all it was not jolly and pleasant at all. Rather there was a sort of gloomy impression, growing every moment more gloomy and sinister.

On the other side of the room, as far as you could see, were all kinds of vulgar and impossible people.

The Refined Lady wondered how they could have received admittance, all making a rather sorry show and all bearing on their faces a mixed expression of bitterness and expectation.

On her own side all looked silent, stiff, sullen, subtly hurt, and congealed into a condition of vastly injured dignity.

The Refined Lady felt herself ill at ease and out of place. The more so because her ticket bore no readable number and she could not succeed in finding a seat.

At that same moment she heard an usher, like a page in the hall of a hotel, bawling her name through a megaphone.

"Here I am," she shouted. "Yes, I am Madame So-and-so."

The usher took her ticket and looked surprised.

"Well, Madame, I was just looking for you, but how are you standing here at the left of His Lordship, when you were expected at his right, as you may see by the color of your ticket?"

"I do not know who is this precious Lordship of whom you are speaking. I saw two openings at the entrance of that show, and, of course, I took the right one.

"I am accustomed all my life to do the right thing. I always was told that I should have no fear of being wrong if I was right, and that I should always be right if I did the right thing, if I took the right way, if I claimed the right place, if I insisted on my right, if I clung faithfully to what was written, meaning [concerning] Me, in the immortal Declaration of Rights."

And the usher said: "All right."

And the Refined Lady said: "If I am all right, where is my right and dutiful place in this show? For I cannot find it."

And the usher said: "My dear Lady, the fact is that by always doing in your life what seemed right to you, by always taking the right, by always clinging loyally and confidently to your own inner Declaration of Rights, the fact is that you have arrived, not at the right of His Lordship, but at his left.

"If you had looked properly at your ticket, you would have seen that at the entrance you should have taken not the right hand but the left, and so you would have arrived at the right of His Lordship, where a snug, cosy, little place was reserved for you."

"It does not matter," said the Refined Lady, "and it can very easily be remedied."

"I am sorry," said the usher, "but it is too late, and you must stay where you are until His Lordship cometh."

"And what will happen," said the Refined Lady, "when His Lordship, as you say, cometh?"

"You will see by yourself presently," said the usher. "All that I can say is that you will get the surprise of your life."

The Death of the Rich Man

PADRAIC COLUM

I T WAS a road as shelterless and as bare as any road in Connacht. On one side there was a far-reaching bog, on the other side little fields, cold with tracts of water. You faced the Connacht hills, bleak and treeless, with little streams across them like threads of steel. There was a solitary figure on the road — a woman with bare feet and ragged clothes. She was bent and used a stick; but she carried herself swiftly, and had something of a challenge in her face. Her toothless mouth was tightly closed, her chin protruded, wisps of hair fell about her distrustful eyes. She was an isolated individual, and it would be hard to communicate the sensations and facts that made up her life.

Irish speakers would call the woman a "shuler." The word is literally the same as "tramp," but it carries no anti-social suggestion. None of the lonely cabins about would refuse her hospitality; she would get shelter for the night in any one of them, the sack of chaff beside the smoldering fire, the share in the household bit. But though she slept by their fires and ate their potatoes and salt, this woman was apart from them, and apart from all those who lived in houses, who tilled their fields and reared up sons and daughters; she had been molded by unkind forces, the silence of the roads, the bitterness of the winds, the long hours of hunger. She moved swiftly along the shelterless roads muttering to herself, for the appetite was 'plaining within her. There, on her way, was a certain village, but before going through it she would give herself a while of contentment. She took a short pipe out of her pocket and sought the sheltered side of a bush. Then she drew her feet under her clothes and sucked in the satisfaction of tobacco.

From *The Commonweal*, May 16, 1928. By permission.

You may be sure the shuler saw through the village, though her gaze was across the road. Midway on the village street there was a great house; it was two stories above the cottages, and a story higher than the shops. It was set well above its neighbors, but to many its height represented effort, ability, discipline. It was the house of Michael Gilsenin, farmer, shopkeeper, local councilor. "Gilsenin, the Gombeen man," the shuler muttered, and she spat out. Now the phrase "Gombeen man" would signify a grasping peasant dealer who squeezed riches out of the poverty of his class, and few people spoke of Michael Gilsenin as a Gombeen man; but his townsmen and the peasants around will tell you that Michael Gilsenin had the open hand for the poor, and that he never denied them the bag of meal nor the sack of seed-potatoes; no, nor the few pounds that would bring a boy or girl the prosperity of America.

To the woman on the ditch Michael Gilsenin was the very embodiment of wordly prosperity. It was said that Michael's two daughters would receive dowries of 1000 pounds each. Michael had furnished the new chapel at a cost of 500 pounds; he had bought, recently, a great stock of horses and cattle; he had built sheds and stables behind his shop.

And Michael Gilsenin had created all his good fortune by his own effort. The shuler wondered what bad luck Eternal Justice would send on his household to balance this prosperity. And in her backward-reaching mind, the shuler could rake out only one thing to Michael's discredit. This was his treatment of Thady, his elder brother. It was Thady who had owned the cabin and the farm on which the Gilsenins had begun their lives. Michael had reduced his grasping and slow-witted brother to subordination, and he had used his brother's inheritance to forward himself. In forwarding himself Michael had forwarded the family, Thady included, and now, instead of life in a cabin, Thady had a place in a great house. Michael was old now, the shuler mused, he was nearly as old as herself. It was well for those who would come after him. His daughters had dowries that made them the talk of Connacht, and his son would succeed to stock, farms, and shop. The shuler stretched out her neck and looked down the road and into the village street. She saw the tall, gray building, the house of stone with the slated roof and the many windows. And she saw a man hobbling out of the village. He had two sticks under him for he was bent with the pains. The man was Thady Gilsenin.

Thady Gilsenin was grudging and hard-fisted to the beggars, but he always stayed to have speech with them. His affinities were with these people of the roads. By his hardness and meanness, by his isolation and his ailments, he was kin to the shuler and her like. She quenched the pipe, hid it under her clothes and waited for Thady Gilsenin.

He stood before her, a gray figure leaning on two sticks. His hands were swollen with the pains, their joints were raised and shining.

"Well, ma'am," said Thady, "you're round this way again, I see."

"My coming won't be any loss to you, Thady Gilsenin," the shuler returned. Thady turned round and looked back at the big house.

"And how is the decent man, your brother?" asked the shuler, "and how are his daughters, the fine, growing girls?"

"His fine daughters are well enough," said Thady, turning round.

"There will be a great marriage here some day," said the shuler, "I'm living on the thought of that marriage."

"It's not marriage that's on our minds," Thady said, in a resigned way. The shuler was quick to detect something in his tone.

"Is it death?" she asked.

"Ay, ma'am, death," said Thady. "Death comes to us all."

"And is it Michael that is likely to die?"

"Michael himself," said Thady.

This to the tramp was as news of revolution to men of desperate fortune. The death of Michael Gilsenin would be a revolution with spoils and without danger. She was thrilled with expectancy, and she said aloud: "O God, receive the prayers of the poor, and be merciful to Michael Gilsenin this day and this night. May angels watch over him. May he receive a portion of the bed of heaven through the gracious intercession of the blessed Mother of God. May he reign in splendor through eternity. Amen, amen, amen." And crying out this she rose to her feet.

"I'm going to his house," she said. "I'll go down on my two knees and I'll pray for the soul of Michael Gilsenin, the man who was good to the poor." She went toward the village striking her breast and muttering cries. Thady stood for a moment, looking after her; then he began to hobble forward on his two sticks. They were like a pair of old crows, hopping down the village.

She could never have imagined such comforts and conveniences as she saw now in the chamber of the dying man. There was the bed, large enough to hold three people, with its stiff hanging and its stiff counterpane, its fine sheets, its blankets and quilt, its heap of soft pillows. There was the carpet warm under her own feet, and then the curtains to the window that shut out the noise and the glare. A small table with fruit and wine was by the bed, and a red lamp burnt perpetually before the image of the Sacred Heart, and so the wasting body and the awakening soul had their comforts and their convenience. Michael's two daughters were in the room. They stood there broken and listless; they had just come out of the convent and this was their novitiate in grief. The shuler noted how rich was the stuff in their black dresses, and noted, too, their white hands, and the clever shape of their dresses. As for the dying man, she gave no heed to him after the first encounter. He was near his hour, and she had looked too often upon the coming of death.

They gave her a bed in the loft, and she lay that night above the stable that was back of the great house. She had warmed herself by the kitchen fire and had taken her fill of tea, and now she smoked and mused, well satisfied with herself.

"This night I'm better off than the man in the wide bed," she said to herself. "I'm better off than you this night, Michael Gilsenin, for all your lands and shops and well-dressed daughters. I'm better off than you this night, Michael Gilsenin, for all your stock and riches. Faith, I can hear your cattle stir in the sheds, and in a while you won't even hear the rain on the grass. You have children to come after you, Michael Gilsenin, but that's not much after all, for they'll forget you when they've come from the burial.

Ay, they will in troth. I've forgotten the man that lay beside me, and the child that I carried in my arms."

She pulled a sack over her feet and knees and up to the waist, and sleep came to her on the straw. But she was awake and felt the tremor through the house, when death came and took his dues. From that onward her sleep was broken, for people had come and horses were being brought out of the stable. Once old Thady came out, and the shuler heard him mutter about the loss in hay and oats.

When she came down to the yard she saw a well-dressed young man tending his horse. One of Michael's daughters came and stood with the young man, and the two talked earnestly together. The shuler knelt down on a flag and began sobbing and clapping her hands; she was working up to a paroxysm, but gradually, for she wanted to attract the attention of the pair without distressing them overmuch. The girl went indoors and the young man followed her. The shuler saw two empty bottles; they were worth a penny. She hid them under her dress and went into the house. She made her way to the front door, passing by many. People of importance were coming, and in such an assembly something surely would be gained. She stood by the street door and watched the great people come, priests, doctors, lawyers, shopkeepers and councilors. She stood there like an old carrion bird, her eyes were keen with greed and her outstretched hand was shaking. She heard old Thady saying:

"Now, thank God, we can be clear for the day of the fair. I was thinking that he would still be with us on the fair day, and we would have to close the shop, and that would be a great loss to us. Now we can have everything cleared off in time. God be good to Michael's soul."

The Woman Hanged Twice

J. A. HAMMETT

THE morning was cold, and dark with the promise of rain. Low-hanging clouds scudded rapidly across the sky like a flight of wild geese with the wind snapping at their tails. Far to the north a solitary star could be seen retreating on the wings of night, but almost at once it disappeared, its brilliance dimmed by the unseen sun mounting ever higher among the clouds. People were already astir, scurrying excitedly from door to door, their cloaks drawn close about them. About the market place a great crowd had gathered and still they came, pouring in from all sides, in all manner of conveyance. They swayed forward, fighting and clawing their way in an effort to secure positions of advantage, but those in front who had guarded their places since midnight were in ill-temper and rudely forced them back. There was something wild and uncontrollable in this great mob, something which seemed to pass from breast to breast like an all-consuming fire. They had come fierce and exultant, but as yet their madness smoldered, awaiting the kindling spark. The shadow of the gallows was upon them and they cowered at the sight of the hideous monster which flung its arms to heaven in a mad gesture of mockery.

Suddenly, in the distance, could be heard the low rumble of drums, echoing through the hushed streets like the monotonous gibbering of a madman. The people about the square listened. Then slowly their feet caught up the insistent tempo of the death beat until the air was filled with the frenzied roar of drums and beating feet. Nearer and nearer came the guards, the roll of their

From *The Catholic World*, August, 1933. By permission.

drums increasing with every step until, with a burst of brilliance, they rounded into view surrounding the little, wooden cart, lurching and bouncing all the way, in which rode the prisoner. Only a few cried out against her, for though they had come to jeer this daughter of a peasant, caught racing toward the sea with the body of a nobleman in her carriage, they were suddenly moved in some strange manner by the wondrous, almost virginal radiance of her face. They had come to see her crouched terror stricken in the corner of her cart, sobbing hysterically and screaming aloud her innocence. But instead they found her facing the multitude fearlessly, her head bent only toward the crucifix with which she rode to death. And those who had come protesting this injustice were moved and many of them wept, crying out to God for pardon.

Anastase turned for the last time to the grilled opening in the wall which served her narrow cell as a window. She, too, saw the dark, rain-charged clouds trying to outstrip each other in their race across the morning sky, but with the eyes of the spirit she saw beyond this. She saw the unseen sun and all the glories of silver-tipped dawn. She saw the long savannas of the blue, and beyond this the pearl-shelled shores of the sun-drenched Riviera where happiness had once been born. And for this all she shed not a tear, for there was even greater hope in the forgiveness which her confessor promised as the reward of penitence and faith.

A few moments passed and then Anastase, kissing the cold crucifix which hung above her bed, followed the guard down the empty corridor, down the stones worn thin by those who faltered as they walked to death, down the winding stairs that creaked and groaned at every step with the echo of some last word, down into the courtyard where the nuns stood weeping bitterly. For they had become attached to this strange young woman, so docile, so loving, so good, who yet had murdered as a fiend. They spoke no word, however, but observed the quiet for which she had asked. At last, she mounted the cart, the guard fell into formation, the drums thundered out their warning and the procession passed through the gates and down the cobbled way toward the square.

They moved steadily at first until the high road had been

gained. But as they approached the market place the crowds made it almost impossible to proceed. Yet, Anastase seemed unconscious of it all. She saw neither the faces distorted with mockery nor those swollen with weeping, but only the face of One whose brow was pierced with thorns, whose eyes were clouded with blood. He, too, had walked the way of death, but burdened with the sins of all mankind while she bore but her own. "Unworthy though I am," she whispered fervently, "direct, O Lord, my steps to Thee. . . ."

She raised her eyes for a moment and caught a gleam of laughter on the face of a child close by. How long ago it suddenly seemed since she had stood like that, clinging on tiptoe to her mother's dress, laughing innocently at the black cart of death. There had been no thought of sin in those days — only dreams of unending laughter. She thought of the days when she had gone to the convent school overlooking the Seine, and of the quiet hours spent in restful adoration in the faltering candlelight of the chapel. Above all she remembered the days of uncertainty, when she had prayed for strength to take the veil. But Philippe and Paris had come before God's word — poor Philippe, his lace flounce drenched with blood, his dead eyes staring into hers.

It had been a quiet life — too quiet for its tragic, violent ending. Yet she was not of the heart to complain. She had chosen freely, and now. . . . But she was not afraid. She faced the gallows courageously, only faltering once as she mounted the platform, shrinking from the noose and murmuring, "Oh, Philippe — if you had only known — you would not have wanted this . . . God knows you wouldn't, Philippe! God knows — and forgives you — as do I."

Josue drew his knees up close to his chest and buried his head in the bed clothes. The chill morning air made all thoughts of rising painful, yet Josue knew he must be up and about if he ever hoped to reach the market place in time for the execution. Already there would be a crowd surging about the gallows. That he knew for sure; he had heard them tramping through the streets in the night, and within an hour they would be leading the prisoner from the bastile. It had been a week since his last execution, and he smiled to himself to think of how he had trembled and grown sick on the morning of his first assignment. Fortunately, the prisoner at that time had been a ruthless murderer. He could never have swung the trap then had it been a young woman such as Anastase. She was so much like his own daughter — or rather, as he imagined his own daughter to be. Twelve years must have changed Lucie — it was such a long time.

As he made his way through the dimly lit streets to the bastile where he took his meals, his thoughts turned again to such a morning twelve years ago. His daughter had been only sixteen at the time — too young, as Josue said, for marriage. But Lucie was headstrong, hers was a love which could not wait, which could not be nurtured through the years, and so she had run off with the Captain of the Guards, leaving Josue alone with only a hastily scribbled farewell and a plea for forgiveness. He had been stern at first, refusing all offers to organize a search, mentally wording his terse, unrelenting answer to what he believed would be her inevitable cry for assistance. But as the years passed and he faced life with decreasing promises of happiness he had repented of his folly and sent messengers in all directions seeking news of Lucie. No expense was spared; his whole fortune had been placed at the hands of his solicitors until in the end, with still no trace of Lucie, he had been forced into penniless servitude. It was this which had forced him to accept the position of executioner, a position the very thought of which ever before had filled him with nausea and disgust.

He spent little time over his breakfast. It had already grown quite light and he knew that, unless he hurried, the procession which was then forming in the courtyard would reach the gallows before he had time to set the trap. Bolting down his last roll, he hurried into the street and set off again for the market place. Everywhere along the way there was excitement, and he shuddered to himself to think of the price one woman was to pay for the morning's entertainment. He was sure Anastase had never stood in that rabble, shouting and clamoring for the sight of some doomed sinner. He had talked to her but the day before in her cell, and in his heart he knew that of whatever sin she was guilty it paled when placed beside the sin of her lover. He had talked to too many murderers and criminals not to know that, and so it was that he tested the ropes and the trap with a prayer that the roll of drums would be silenced with a pardon. But even as he worked, loosening the trap, he heard the rhythmic beat of the muffled drums and the tramp of feet on the cobblestones. He listened quietly, fingering the black hood in his hands and suddenly his knees began to tremble and his whole being shuddered as the crowd turned exultantly toward the procession rounding the corner at the head of the street. He saw the multitude swarm about the guards and press closer to the little cart to catch a better glimpse of the fair prisoner. And even from a distance, he fancied he saw many of them stand awed and turn away with sorrow in their hearts. They had come to kill but their fierce cries were stilled with sadness. Slowly they drew nearer and at last he saw Anastase's face, and in that moment he knew that it was she with her high courage and faith who would give him the strength to do this deed. It was the face of one transfigured with hope, of one who sees beyond the things of this world to the shadowless infinities of the next.

The rain broke about noon and came down in torrents the rest of the day. Josue was thankful that it had held off until after the execution. It had been beastly enough as it was. He would never forget the look on that girl's face. She had been so brave, until the time came for the hood to be placed over her head. Then she had faltered, and such an agonizing look had passed over her face that he had been forced to turn away. But it had all passed in a moment. Clenching her hands, she had bowed her head whisper-'ing softly the prayer which died upon her lips: "Mother of God . . ."

There had been something haunting about her face, thought Josue, something which troubled him strangely. And about the way she had whispered that prayer . . . it was almost as if he had heard that voice before, as if what he had heard that day was but an echo from the past. She had been so like Lucie. Suddenly he started up — what, what if that had been Lucie? But no! He would have known her, she could not have changed so . . . she would have known him. Yet, Lucie had said that prayer. He remembered it all at once. He saw her with her hair streaming down her back, her eyes raised to heaven, her tiny hands clenched tightly before her. And then he heard again those words: "Mother of God . . ." so soft and fervent, so heart-rending in their devotion. It could not be! He was mad even to imagine such a thing. Was not Anastase the daughter of François, the cobbler? And had not François followed his daughter even to the gallows before fleeing in tears to the cathedral where the priests had found him prostrate before the altar hours afterward? No, it could not have been Lucie — but still, there were her eyes, and the prayer. . . . Suddenly he jumped from the table and poured himself a drink. It was madness, sheer madness, he cried to himself. He was growing old, getting sentimental, and abruptly he started to laugh. But almost at once the laughter died on his lips and the glass, slipping from his hand, crashed to the floor. She was there at the window!

Josue stood motionless staring into the eyes of the dead woman before him. For one awful minute he was too horrified to move, then suddenly snatching the bottle from the table he hurled it through the window. With a rush he crossed the room and flung open the door — but she had gone. Trembling and faint he returned to the house, fastened the shutters securely and hurried to his room. But he could not sleep. Everywhere those strange, sad eyes seemed to be staring at him, and once he fancied he even heard her voice. But as the night wore on and his nerves became quieted he slept from sheer exhaustion. And in the morning there were only the shattered glass and the broken window to tell of his strange vision.

It was well past noon, however, before he was able to leave the house. An unusual weakness had come over him and from time to time he imagined he heard voices and strange laughter, but there was no one. He told himself that it was all fancy; wild illusions springing from his overwrought condition, but no matter how often he argued in that direction he would always come back to the shattered glass and the broken window. He had not been drinking heavily. He knew it couldn't have been that. But he had seen them remove Anastase's lifeless body from the gallows. It couldn't have been she — unless. . . . But he dared not think of that! It was too ghastly. People didn't talk of such things — ghosts were only for children. . . .

But in the afternoon a strange thing happened. It was late, almost dusk, and Josue had been tramping though the streets for hours. Time and again he circled the square, stopping frequently to talk to the merchants, delaying, as long as possible, the time when he must return alone to the empty rooms which had suddenly become so frightening with their memories. Close to the cathedral he stopped to pay his compliments to the Bishop who sat reading beneath the lilacs in his garden. But even as he spoke a carriage rattled by and peering from among the curtains Josue saw the eyes of the dead woman!

Terror stricken he turned and fled, barricading himself in his rooms, with a roaring fire and blazing lamps to turn the shadowy darkness of the night into day. But she did not return that night nor the next. It was on the third day that the tragedy occurred. Trembling at every sound, imagining voices everywhere, and seeing those sad, strange eyes wherever he looked, Josue spent three days of horror. He slept not at all and ate but little. People began to whisper strange things about him but he spoke to no one. For hours he would stand staring blankly before him in the market place, muttering to himself, and once, at Mass, he screamed aloud when some child peered at him suddenly from around the confessional. And at night he was seen sitting before the fire, his back to the window, a candle in either hand. And it was here that he was sitting on the third night when suddenly he heard a step on the walk leading up to the house. Clenching the candles fiercely until the wax crumbled in his hands and the blood ran from his nails, he stared straight into the fire. He did not have to face about. He knew she was there, staring at him, whispering over again that quiet prayer. He felt her eyes like tiny bores upon his back, piercing him through and through, pleading with him, begging him for but a moment's time. And then suddenly he heard the latch slip, felt the cold air on his back and she was there!

Turning he saw her standing in the doorway, her eyes upon him, staring at him as in death. And then her lips moved, but before she could speak he was upon her, seizing her by the throat, dragging her after him out into the night. Catching her up in his arms he started to run madly toward the square. It had grown quite late, there was no one about, the market place was deserted, save for the shadowy monster that stood rearing its ugly head in the darkness.

Half dragging, half carrying the young woman up the steps, Josue climbed the gallows. The ropes were there, just as he had left them. It was but a matter of a few moments for him to set them straight. Then lifting the unconscious woman to his shoulders he fastened the noose about her neck. . . .

And there was only the moonlight to wash the blood from off her face and smooth the knotted hair that lay about her neck.

It was the Bishop who first sensed the double tragedy. Two old women, starting out for early Mass, found the body of the young woman swinging mysteriously from the gallows and fled in terror to the Bishop. Dispatching his servants at once to the scene of the crime, he had the body of the young woman brought to his house, and then it was that he saw the rusted key clenched tightly in her hand and the locket open at her neck. He sent for Josue immediately, but even before they returned to tell him that Josue had fled into the wood shouting like a madman, he knew. But he knew more than Josue. He had recognized Lucie!

A Chance For Mr. Lever

GRAHAM GREENE

MR. LEVER knocked his head against the ceiling and swore. Rice was stored above, and in the dark the rats began to move. Grains of rice fell between the slats onto his Revelation suitcase, his bald head, his cases of tinned food, the little square box in which he kept his medicines. His boy had already set up the camp bed and mosquito net, and, outside in the warm damp dark, his folding table and chair. The thatched pointed huts streamed away toward the forest and a woman went from hut to hut carrying fire. The glow lit her old face, her sagging breasts, her tattooed, diseased body.

It was incredible to Mr. Lever that five weeks ago he had been in London.

He couldn't stand upright; he went down on hands and knees in the dust and opened his suitcase. He took out his wife's photograph and stood it on the chop box; he took out a writing pad and an indelible pencil: the pencil had softened in the heat and left mauve stains on his pajamas. Then because the light of the hurricane lamp disclosed cockroaches the size of black beetles flattened against the mud wall, he carefully closed the suitcase. Already in ten days he had learned that they'd eat anything, socks, shirts, the laces out of your shoes.

Mr. Lever went outside; moths beat against his lamp; but there were no mosquitoes; he hadn't seen or heard one since he landed. He sat in a circle of light carefully observed. The blacks squatted outside their huts and watched him; they were friendly, interested, amused, but their strict attention irritated Mr. Lever. He

From *Story*, January, 1936.

could feel the small waves of interest washing around him, when he began to write, when he stopped writing, when he wiped his damp hands with a handkerchief. He couldn't touch his pocket without a craning of necks.

Dearest Emily, he wrote, I've really started now. I'll send this letter back with a carrier when I've located Davidson. I'm very well. Of course, everything's a bit strange. Look after yourself, my dear, and don't worry.

"Massa, buy chicken," his cook said, appearing suddenly between the huts. A small stringy fowl struggled in his hands.

"Well," Mr. Lever said, "I gave you a shilling, didn't I?"

"They no like," the cook said. "These low bush people."

"Why don't they like? It's good money."

"They want king's money," the cook said, handing back the Victorian shilling. Mr. Lever had to get up, go back in to his hut, grope for his money box, search through twenty pounds of small change: there was no peace.

He had learned that very quickly. He had to economize (the whole trip was a gamble which scared him); he couldn't afford hammock carriers. He would arrive, tired out after seven hours of walking, at a village of which he didn't know the name and not for a minute could he sit quietly and rest. He must shake hands with the chief, he must see about a hut, accept presents of palm wine he was afraid to drink, buy rice and palm oil for the carriers, give them salts and aspirin, paint their sores with iodine. They never left him alone for five minutes on end until he went to bed. And then the rats began, rushing down the walls like water when he put out the light, gamboling among his cases.

I'm too old, Mr. Lever told himself, I'm too old, writing damply, indelibly, I hope to find Davidson tomorrow. If I do, I may be back almost as soon as this letter. Don't economize on the stout and milk, dear, and call in the doctor if you feel bad. I've got a premonition this trip's going to turn out well. We'll take a holiday, you need a holiday, and staring ahead past the huts and the black faces and the banana trees toward the forest from which he would come, into which he would sink again next day, he thought, Eastbourne. Eastbourne would do her a world of good, and continued to write the only kind of lies he'd ever told Emily, the lies which comforted. I ought to draw at least three hundred in commission and my expenses. But it wasn't the sort of place he'd been accustomed to sell heavy machinery in; thirty years of it, up and down Europe and in the States, but never anything like this. He could hear his filter dripping in the hut, and somewhere somebody was playing something (he was so lost he hadn't got the simplest terms to his hand), something monotonous, melancholy, superficial, a twanging of palm fibers which seemed to convey that you weren't happy, but it didn't matter much, everything would always be the same.

Look after yourself, Emily, he repeated. It was almost the only thing he found himself capable of writing to her; he couldn't describe the narrow steep lost paths, the snakes sizzling away like flames, the rats, the dust, the naked, diseased bodies. He was unbearably tired of nakedness. Don't forget. . . . It was like living with a lot of cows.

"The chief," his boy whispered, and between the huts under a waving torch came an old stout man wearing a robe of native cloth and a battered bowler hat. Behind him his men carried six bowls of rice, a bowl of palm oil, two bowls of broken meat. "Chop for the laborers," the boy explained, and Mr. Lever had to get up and smile and nod and try to convey without words that he was pleased, that the chop was excellent, that the chief would get a good dash in the morning. At first the smell had been almost too much for Mr. Lever.

"Ask him," he said to his boy, "if he's seen a white man come through here lately. Ask him if a white man's been digging around here. Damn it," Mr. Lever burst out, the sweat breaking on the backs of his hands and on his bald head, "ask him if he's seen Davidson?"

"Davidson?"

"Oh hell," Mr. Lever said, "you know what I mean. The white man I'm looking for."

"White man?"

"What do you imagine I'm here for, eh? White man? Of course white man. I'm not here for my health." A cow coughed, rubbed

its horns against the hut, and two goats broke through between
the chief and him, upsetting the bowls of meat scraps; nobody
cared, they picked the meat out of the dust and dung.

Mr. Lever sat down and put his hands over his face, fat, white,
well-cared for hands with wrinkles of flesh over the rings: I'm too
old for this.

"Chief say no white man been here long time."

"How long?"

"Chief say not since he pay hut tax."

"How long's that?"

"Long, long time."

"Ask him how far is it to Greh tomorrow."

"Chief say too far."

"Nonsense," Mr. Lever said.

"Chief say too far. Better stay here. Fine town. No humbug."

Mr. Lever groaned. Every evening there was the same trouble.
The next town was always too far. They would invent any excuse
to delay him, to give themselves a rest.

"Ask the chief how many hours — ?"

"Plenty, plenty." They had no idea of time. "This fine chief.
Fine chop. Laborers tired. No humbug."

"We are going on," Mr. Lever said.

"This fine town. Chief say — "

He thought: if this wasn't the last chance, I'd give up. They
nagged him so, and suddenly he longed for another white man
(not Davidson, he daren't say anything to Davidson) to whom he
could explain the desperation of his lot. It wasn't fair, that a man
after thirty years' commercial traveling should need to go from
door to door asking for a job. He had been a good traveler, he had
made money for many people, his references were excellent, but
the world had moved on since his day. He wasn't streamlined; he
certainly wasn't streamlined. He had been ten years' retired when
he lost his money in the depression.

Mr. Lever walked up and down Victoria Street showing his
references. Many of the men knew him, gave him cigars, laughed
at him in a friendly way for wanting to take on a job at his age
("I can't somehow settle at home. The old warhorse you

know . . ."), cracked a joke or two in the passage, went back that night to Maidenhead silent in the first class carriage, shut in with age and ruin and how bad things were and poor devil his wife's probably sick.

It was in the rather shabby little office off Leadenhall Street that Mr. Lever met his chance. It called itself an engineering firm, but there were only two rooms, a typewriter, a girl with gold teeth, and Mr. Lucas, a thin narrow man with a tic in one eyelid. All through the interview the eyelid flickered at Mr. Lever. Mr. Lever had never before fallen so low as this.

But Mr. Lucas struck him as reasonably honest. He put "all his cards on the table." He hadn't got any money, but he had expectations, he had the handling of a patent. It was a new crusher. There was money in it. But you couldn't expect the big trusts to change over their machinery now. Things were too bad. You'd got to get in at the start, and that was where — why, that was where this chief, the bowls of chop, the nagging and the rats and the heat, came in. They called themselves a republic, Mr. Lucas said, he didn't know anything about that, they were not as black as they were painted, he supposed (ha ha, nervously, ha ha); anyway this company had slipped agents over the border and grabbed a concession: gold and diamonds. He could tell Mr. Lever in confidence that the trust was frightened of what they'd found. Now an enterprising man could just slip across (Mr. Lucas liked the word slip, it made everything sound easy and secret) and introduce this new crusher to them: it would save them thousands when they started work, there'd be a fat commission, and afterward, with the start. . . . There was a fortune for them all.

"But can't you fix it up in Europe?"

Tic, tic, went Mr. Lucas's eyelid. "A lot of Belgians; they are leaving all decisions to the man on the spot. An Englishman called Davidson."

"How about expenses?"

"That's the trouble," Mr. Lucas said. "We are only beginning. What we want is a partner. We can't afford to send a man. But if you like a gamble . . . 20 per cent commission."

"Chief say excuse him." The carriers squatted round the basins and scooped up the rice in their left hands. "Of course. Of course," Mr. Lever said absent-mindedly. "Very kind, I'm sure." He was back out of the dust and dark, away from the stink of goats and palm oil and whelping bitches, back among the Rotarians and lunch at Stone's, "the pint of old," and the trade papers; he was a good fellow again finding his way back to Golders Green just a little lit; his masonic emblem rattled on his watch chain; and he bore with him from the tube station to his house in Finchley Road a sense of companionship, of broad stories and belches, a sense of bravery.

He needed all his bravery now; the last of his savings had gone into the trip. After thirty years he knew a good thing when he saw it, and he had no doubts about the new crusher. What he doubted was his ability to find Davidson. For one thing there weren't any maps; the way you traveled in the Republic was to write down a list of names and trust that someone in the villages you passed would understand and know the route. But they always said "Too far." Good fellowship wilted before the phrase.

"Quinine," Mr. Lever said. "Where's my quinine?" His boy never remembered a thing; they just didn't care what happened to you; their smiles meant nothing, and Mr. Lever, who knew better than anyone the value of a meaningless smile in business, resented their heartlessness, turned toward the dilatory boy an expression of disappointment and dislike.

"Chief say white man in bush five hours away."

"That's better," Mr. Lever said. "It must be Davidson. He's digging for gold?"

"Ya. White man dig for gold in bush."

"We'll be off early tomorrow," Mr. Lever said.

"Chief say better stop this town. Fever humbug white man."

"Too bad," Mr. Lever said, and he thought with pleasure: my luck's changed. He'll want help. He won't refuse me a thing. A friend in need is a friend indeed, and his heart warmed toward Davidson, seeing himself arrive like an answer to prayer out of the forest, feeling quite biblical and *vox humana*. He thought: Prayer. I'll pray tonight, that's the kind of thing a fellow gives up, but it pays, there's something in it, remembering the long agonizing prayer on his knees, by the sideboard, under the decanters, when Emily went to hospital.

"Chief say white man dead."

Mr. Lever turned his back on them and went into his hut. His sleeve nearly overturned the hurricane lamp. He undressed quickly, stuffing his clothes into a suitcase away from the cockroaches. He wouldn't believe what he had been told; it wouldn't pay him to believe. If Davidson was dead, there was nothing he could do but return; he had spent more than he could afford; he would be a ruined man. He supposed that Emily might find a home with her brother, but he could hardly expect her brother — He began to cry, but you couldn't have told in the shadowy hut the difference between sweat and tears. He knelt down beside his campbed and mosquito net and prayed on the dust of the earth floor. Up till now he had always been careful never to touch a floor with his naked feet for fear of jiggers; there were jiggers everywhere, they only waited an opportunity to dig themselves in under the toenails, lay their eggs, and multiply.

"O God," Mr. Lever prayed, "don't let Davidson be dead; let him be just sick and glad to see me." He couldn't bear the idea that he might not any longer be able to support Emily. "O God, there's nothing I wouldn't do." But that was still an empty phrase; he had no real notion yet of what he would do for Emily. They had been happy together for thirty-five years; he had never been more than momentarily unfaithful to her when he was lit after a Rotarian dinner and egged on by the boys; whatever skirt he'd been with in his time he had never for a moment imagined that he could be happy married to anyone else. It wasn't fair if, just when you were old and needed each other most, you lost your money and couldn't keep together.

But, of course, Davidson wasn't dead. What would he have died of? The blacks were friendly. People said the country was unhealthy, but he hadn't so much as heard a mosquito. Besides you didn't die of malaria; you just lay between the blankets and took quinine and felt like death and sweated it out of you. There was dysentery, but Davidson was an old campaigner; you were safe if you boiled and filtered the water. The water was poison even to the touch; it was unsafe to wet your feet because of guinea worm, but you didn't die of guinea worm.

Mr. Lever lay in bed and his thoughts went round and round and he couldn't sleep. He thought: you don't die of a thing like guinea worm. It makes a sore on your foot, and if you put your foot in water you can see the eggs dropping out. You have to find the end of the worm, like a thread of cotton, and wind it round a match and wind it out of your leg without breaking; it stretches as high as the knee. I'm too old for this country, Mr. Lever thought.

Then his boy was beside him again. He whispered urgently to Mr. Lever through the mosquito net, "Massa, the laborers say they go home."

"Go home?" Mr. Lever said wearily; he had heard it so often before. "Why do they want to go home? What is it now?" but he didn't really want to hear the latest squabble: that the Bande men were never sent to carry water because the headman was a Bande, that someone had stolen an empty treacle tin and sold it in the village, that someone wasn't made to carry a proper load, that the next day's journey was "too far." He said, "Tell 'em they can go home. I'll pay them off in the morning. But they won't get any dash. They'd have got a good dash if they'd stayed." He was certain it was just another try-on; he wasn't as green as all that.

"Yes, massa. They no want dash."

"What's that?"

'They frightened fever humbug them like white man."

"I'll get carriers in the village. They can go home."

"Me too, massa."

"Get out," Mr. Lever said; it was the last straw; "get out and let me sleep." The boy went at once, obedient even if he was a deserter, and Mr. Lever thought: sleep, what a hope. He lifted the net and got out of bed (barefooted again: he didn't care a damn about the jiggers) and searched for his medicine box. It was locked, of course, and he had to open his suitcase and find the key in a trouser pocket. His nerves were more on edge than ever by the time he found the sleeping tablets and he took three of them. That made him sleep, heavily and dreamlessly, though when he woke he found that something had made him fling out his arm and open the net. If there had been a single mosquito in the place, he'd have been bitten, but, of course, there wasn't one.

He could tell at once that the trouble hadn't blown over. The village — he didn't know its name — was perched on a hilltop; east and west the forest flowed out beneath the little plateau: to the west it was a dark unfeatured mass like water, but in the east you could already discern the unevennesses, the great gray cotton trees lifted above the palms. Mr. Lever was always called before dawn, but no one had called him. A few of his carriers sat outside a hut sullenly talking; his boy was with them. Mr. Lever went back inside and dressed; he thought all the time, I must be firm, but he was scared, scared of being deserted, scared of being made to return.

When he came outside again the village was awake: the women were going down the hill to fetch water, winding silently past the carriers, past the flat stones where the chiefs were buried, the little grove of trees where the rice birds, like green and yellow canaries, nested. Mr. Lever sat down on his folding chair among the chickens and whelping bitches and cow dung and called his boy. He took "a strong line"; but he didn't know what was going to happen. "Tell the chief I want to speak to him," he said.

There was some delay; the chief wasn't up yet, but presently he appeared in his blue and white robe, setting his bowler hat straight. "Tell him," Mr. Lever said, "I want carriers to take me to the white man and back. Two days."

"Chief no agree," the boy said.

Mr. Lever said furiously, "Damn it, if he doesn't agree, he won't get any dash from me, not a penny." It occurred to him immediately afterward how hopelessly dependent he was on these people's honesty. There in the hut for all to see was his money box; they had only to take it. This wasn't a British or French colony; the blacks on the coast wouldn't bother, could do nothing if they did bother, because a stray Englishman had been robbed in the interior.

"Chief say how many?"

"It's only for two days," Mr. Lever said. "I can do with six."

"Chief say how much?"

"Sixpence a day and chop."

"Chief no agree."

"Ninepence a day then."

"Chief say too far. A shilling."

"All right, all right," Mr. Lever said, "a shilling then. You others can go home if you want to. I'll pay you off now, but you won't get any dash, not a penny."

He had never really expected to be left, and it gave him a sad feeling of loneliness to watch them move sullenly away (they were ashamed of themselves) down the hill to the west. They hadn't any loads, but they weren't singing; they dropped silently out of sight, his boy with them, and he was alone with his pile of boxes and the chief who couldn't talk a word of English. Mr. Lever smiled tremulously.

It was ten o'clock before his new carriers were chosen; he could tell that none of them wanted to go; and they would have to walk through the heat of the middle day if they were to find Davidson before it was dark. He hoped the chief had explained properly where they were going; he couldn't tell; he was completely shut off from them, and when they started down the eastward slope, he might just as well have been alone.

They were immediately caught up in the forest. Forest conveys a sense of wildness and beauty, of an active natural force, but this Liberian forest was simply a dull green wilderness. You passed, on a path a foot or so wide, through an endless back garden of tangled weeds; it didn't seem to be growing round you, so much as dying. There was no life at all, except for a few large birds whose wings creaked overhead through the invisible sky like an unoiled door. There was no view, no way out for the eyes, no change of scene. It wasn't the heat that tired so much as the boredom; you had to think of things to think about; but even Emily failed to fill the mind for more than three minutes at a time. It was a relief, a distraction, when the path was flooded and Mr. Lever had to be carried on a man's back. At first he had disliked the strong bitter smell (it reminded him of a breakfast food he was made to eat as a child), but he soon got over that. Now he was unaware that they smelt at all; any more than he was aware that the great swallow-tailed butterflies, which clustered at the water's edge and rose in green clouds round his waist, were beautiful. His senses were dulled and registered very little except his boredom.

But they did register a distinct feeling of relief when his leading carrier pointed to a rectangular hole dug just off the path. Mr. Lever understood. Davidson had come this way. He stopped and looked at it. It was like a grave dug for a small man, but it went down deeper than graves usually do. About twelve feet below there was black water, and a few wooden props which held the sides from slipping were beginning to rot; the hole must have been dug since the rains. It didn't seem enough, that hole, to have brought out Mr. Lever with his plans and estimates for a new crusher. He was used to big industrial concerns, the sight of pit heads, the smoke of chimneys, the dingy rows of cottages back to back, the leather armchair in the office, the good cigar, the masonic handgrips, and again it seemed to him, as it had seemed in Mr. Lucas's office, that he had fallen very low. It was as if he was expected to do business beside a hole a child had dug in an overgrown and abandoned back garden; percentages wilted in the hot damp air. He shook his head; he mustn't be discouraged; this was an old hole. Davidson had probably done better since. It was only common sense to suppose that the gold rift which was mined at one end in Nigeria, at the other in Sierra Leone, should pass though the republic. Even the biggest mines had to begin with a hole in the ground. The company, he had talked to the directors in Brussels, were quite confident: all they wanted was the approval of the man on the spot that the crusher was suitable for local conditions. A signature, that was all he had to get, he told himself, staring down into the puddle of black water.

Five hours, the chief had said, but after six hours they were still walking. Mr. Lever had eaten nothing, he wanted to get to Davidson first. All through the heat of the day he walked. The forest protected him from the direct sun, but it shut out the air, and the occasional clearings, shriveled though they were in the vertical glare, seemed cooler than the shade because there was a little

more air to breathe. At four o'clock the heat diminished, but he
began to fear they wouldn't reach Davidson before dark. His foot
pained him; he had caught a jigger the night before; it was as if
someone held a lighted match to his toe. Then at five they came
on a dead black.

Another rectangular hole in a small cleared space among the
dusty greenery caught Mr. Lever's eye. He peered down and was
shocked to see a face return his stare, white eyeballs like
phosphorus in the black water. The black had been bent almost
double to fit him in; the hole was really too small to be a grave,
and he had swollen. His flesh was like a blister you could prick
with a needle. Mr. Lever felt sick and tired; he might have been
tempted to return if he could have reached the village before
dark; but now there was nothing to do but go on; the carriers
luckily hadn't seen the body. He waved them forward and
stumbled after among the roots, fighting his nausea. He fanned
himself with his sun helmet; his wide fat face was damp and
pale. He had never seen an uncared-for body before; his parents
he had seen carefully laid out with closed eyes and washed faces;
they "fell asleep" quite in accordance with their epitaphs, but
you couldn't think of sleep in connection with the white eyeballs
and the swollen face. Mr. Lever would have liked very much to
say a prayer, but prayers were out of place in the dead drab
forest; they simply didn't "come."

With the dusk a little life did waken: something lived in the
dry weeds and brittle trees, if only monkeys. They chattered and
screamed all round you, but it was too dark to see them; you were
like a blind man in the center of a frightened crowd who wouldn't
say what scared them. The carriers, too, were frightened. They ran
under their fifty-pound loads behind the dipping light of the hurricane lamp, their huge flat carriers' feet flapping in the dust like
empty gloves. Mr. Lever listened nervously for mosquitoes; you
would have expected them to be out by now, but he didn't hear
one.

Then at the top of a rise above a small stream they came on
Davidson. The ground had been cleared in a square of twelve feet
and a small tent pitched; he had dug another hole; the scene came

dimly into view as they climbed the path: the chop boxes piled outside the tent, the syphon of soda water, the filter, an enamel basin. But there wasn't a light, there wasn't a sound, the flaps of the tent were not closed, and Mr. Lever had to face the possibility that after all the chief might have told the truth.

Mr. Lever took the lamp and stooped inside the tent. There was a body on the bed. At first Mr. Lever thought Davidson was covered with blood, but then he realized it was a black vomit which stained his shirts and khaki shorts, the fair stubble on his chin. He put out a hand and touched Davidson's face, and if he hadn't felt a slight breath on his palm he would have taken him for dead; his skin was so cold. He moved the lamp closer, and now the lemon-yellow face told him all he wanted to know: he hadn't thought of that when his boy said fever. It was quite true that a man didn't die of malaria, but an old piece of news read in New York in '98 came back to mind: there had been an outbreak in Rio and 94 per cent of the cases had been fatal. It hadn't meant anything to him then, but it did now. As he watched, Davidson was sick, quite effortlessly; he was like a tap out of which something flowed.

It seemed at first to Mr. Lever to be the end of everything, of his journey, his hopes, his life with Emily. There was nothing he could do for Davidson, the man was unconscious, there were times when his pulse was so low and irregular that Mr. Lever thought that he was dead until another black stream spread from his mouth; it was no use even cleaning him. Mr. Lever laid his own blankets over the bed on top of Davidson's because he was so cold to the touch, but he had no idea whether he was doing the right, or even the fatally wrong, thing. The chance of survival, if there was any chance at all, depended on neither of them. Outside his carriers had built a fire and were cooking the rice they had brought with them. Mr. Lever opened his folding chair and sat by the bed. He wanted to keep awake: it seemed right to keep awake; he opened his case and found his unfinished letter to Emily. He sat by Davidson's side and tried to write, but he could think of nothing but what he had already written too often: Look after yourself; don't forget the stout and milk.

He fell asleep over his pad and woke at two and thought that
Davidson was dead. But he was wrong again. He was very thirsty
and missed his boy. Always the first thing his boy did at the end
of a march was to light a fire and put on a kettle; after that, by the
time his table and chair were set up, there was water ready for
the filter. Mr. Lever found half a cup of soda water left in Davidson's syphon; if it had been only his health at stake he would have
gone down to the stream and drunk, but he had Emily to
remember.

There was a typewriter by the bed and it occurred to Mr. Lever
that he might just as well begin to write his report of failure now;
it might keep him awake; it seemed disrespectful to the dying man
to sleep. He found paper under some letters which had been
typed and signed but not sealed. Davidson must have been taken
ill very suddenly; Mr. Lever wondered whether it was he who had
crammed the black into the hole; his boy perhaps, for there was
no sign of a servant. He balanced the typewriter on his knee and
headed the letter, In Camp near Greh.

It seemed to him unfair that he should have come so far, spent
so much money, worn out a rather old body to meet his inevitable
ruin in a dark tent beside a dying man when he could have met it
just as well at home with Emily in the plush parlor. The thought
of the prayers he had uselessly uttered on his knees by the campbed among the jiggers, the rats, and the cockroaches made him
rebellious. A mosquito, the first he had heard, went humming
round the tent. He slashed at it savagely; he wouldn't have recognized himself among the Rotarians. He was lost and he was set
free. Moralities were what enabled a man to live happily and
successfully with his fellows, but Mr. Lever wasn't happy and he
wasn't successful, and his only fellow in the little stuffy tent
wouldn't be troubled by Untruth in Advertising or by Mr. Lever
coveting his neighbor's oxen. You couldn't keep your ideas intact
when you discovered their geographical nature. The Solemnity of
Death: death wasn't solemn; it was a lemon-yellow skin and a
black vomit. Honesty is the Best Policy: that he saw quite suddenly was palpably false. It was an anarchist who sat happily
over the typewriter, an anarchist who recognized nothing but one

personal relationship, his affection for Emily, Mr. Lever began to type: I have examined the plans and estimates of the new Lucas crusher. . . .

Mr. Lever thought with savage happiness: I win. This letter would be the last the company would hear from Davidson. The junior partner would open it in the dapper Brussels office; he would tap his false teeth with a Waterman pen and go in to talk to M. Golz. Taking all these factors into consideration I recommend acceptance. . . . They would telegraph to Lucas. As for Davidson, that trusted agent of the company would have died of yellow fever at some never accurately determined date. Another agent would come out, and the crusher. . . . Mr. Lever carefully copied Davidson's signature on a spare sheet of paper. He wasn't satisfied. He turned the original upside down and copied it that way, so as not to be confused by his own idea of how a letter should be formed. That was better, but it didn't satisfy him. He searched until he found Davidson's own pen and began to copy and copy the signature. He fell asleep copying it and woke again an hour later to find the lamp was out; it had burned up all the oil. He sat there beside Davidson's bed till daylight; once he was bitten by a mosquito in the ankle and clapped his hand to the place too late: the brute went humming out. With the light Mr. Lever saw that Davidson was dead. "Dear dear," he said. "Poor fellow." He spat out with the words, quite delicately in a corner, the bad morning taste in his mouth. It was like a little sediment of conventionality.

Mr. Lever got two of his carriers to cram Davidson tidily in his hole. He was no longer afraid, of them or of failure or of separation. He tore up his letter to Emily. It no longer represented his mood in its timidity, its secret fear, its gentle fussing phrases, "Don't forget the stout," "Look after yourself." He would be home as soon as the letter, and they were going to do things together now they'd never dreamed of doing. The money for the crusher was only the beginning. His ideas stretched further now than Eastbourne, they stretched as far as Switzerland; he had a feeling that if he really let himself go, they'd stretch as far as the Riviera. How happy he was on what he thought of as "the trip home." He was freed from what had held him back through a long pedantic career, the fear of some conscious fate that notes the dishonesty, notes the skirt in Piccadilly, notes the glass and too many of Stone's special. Now he had said Boo to that goose.

But you on the other hand who are reading this, who know so much more than Mr. Lever, who can follow the mosquito's progress from the dead swollen black to Davidson's tent, to Mr. Lever's ankle, you, I say, may possibly believe in fate, a kindly fate tender toward human frailty, ready to give Mr. Lever three days of happiness, three days off the galling chain, as he carried back through the forest his amateurish forgeries and the infection of yellow fever in the blood. The story may very well confirm your faith in that loving merciful omniscience if it has not been shaken by personal knowledge of the drab empty forest through which Mr. Lever now went so merrily, where it is impossible to believe in any spiritual life, in anything outside the nature dying round you, the shriveling of the weeds. There are two opinions about everything; it was Mr. Lever's favorite expression, drinking beer in the Ruhr, Pernod in Lorraine, selling heavy machinery.

The Return

MICHAEL McLAVERTY

THE people were leaving Inishleen. All week boats laden
with sheep, hens, and sticks of furniture sailed for the mainland where the government had granted new houses to the
islanders. And now the Conneelys, with their final cargo, were leaving. They were the last.

Sitting on a stone in front of his whitewashed cabin old Martin
Conneely watched sadly his married son and daughter-in-law busy
with the flitting. Chairs, stools, a wooden chest, and a brick-red
crock with partly blackened sides lay on the wet cobbles. Slowly
the house was emptying and Martin's heart was emptying with it.
His bony hands grasped more tightly the stick that lay between
his legs and he tapped it nervously on the stone flags. His watery
blue eyes traveled down the stone-fenced path in front of him,
out to the rocky quay with its wriggling boat, and then out across
the sea to the dim hills of the mainland. A moist wind filled with
the acrid smell of rotting seaweed blew wetly against his bronzed
face and short gray beard. He rested his eyes on the shore in
front watching the waves throwing white coiling ropes of water
on the black rocks. But always he was conscious of his son moving past him, adding to the pile, and clearing out the house that
had reared him and his for years, for years beyond memory.

He could bear no more. He sighed deeply as he rose to his feet
and leaning heavily on his stick he hobbled down the path. His son
Dermot appeared in the doorway with the sleeves of his blue
jersey rolled up. "Let you not be long, Father; we'll soon be goin',"
he shouted.

From *The Catholic World*, March, 1935. By permission.

The old man stopped, and keeping his legs in the same position, he turned his body slowly round.

"I'll be back in me own time," he replied in a broken voice. " 'Tis little time any of us has left now and I'll make the best of it."

"God help him, 'tis taking it hard he is surely," said the young wife.

" 'Tis the weight of sorrow is on him," replied her husband as they went on with the clearing.

Martin turned to the right and struck the hedgeless road that fringed a small semicircular bay. The road was made of white pebbles and sand. In stormy weather the waves crashed over it, the sea-drift falling like hail on the scraggy potato patches that sloped down to it. He walked along, but his feet crunching in the deep pebbles soon tired him.

He stopped, and leaning his two hands on his stick he looked at the ten little houses that were the island. Behind them rose Cnámh Mór, its gray toes sticking in the bog, and a baby cloud nestling against its cold breast. No smoke came from the chimneys; no hens scratched in the dungheaps; no children played. All was lifeless. Everything was gone, and on the white gable-ends were dark green triangular patches where the turf had lain. Shaking his head hopelessly and muttering in Gaelic he trudged on.

He was dressed in an old pair of trousers, patched with various garments and sewn by himself with white twine. His dark coat lay loose on him like the coat on an old scarecrow. He had no collar and his gray shirt was closed at the neck by a frayed linen-covered button. An old hat, much too small for him, was kept on his head by a piece of rag twisted ropewise, passing under his chin and round the crown. Below the hat at the forehead hung hair as white and fine as bog cotton. But Martin didn't seem to mind his tattered appearance as he walked to the graveyard which lay near the sea.

A mizzle of rain fell continuously, lying on the grass like a light frost, and filling with its dust spider's hammocks that swung on the loose stones of the graveyard wall. Over the wet-polished slabs of the stile the old man clambered.

Grassy mounds lay around him, their moss-covered headstones
tilted in all directions as if the dead had turned and shouldered
the burdens to the side. Martin, holding his hat in one hand, trod
through nettles and docks to where a fuchsia bush dangled its red
and purple bells above his dead — his wife and his people. An
unengraved slate stone, streaked white with bird-droppings, was
propped stolidly at the head of the grave. The old man knelt in
the rain-soaked grass and prayed in silence, the fuchsia leaves
whispering with light rain. Then he burst out: "There's no life in
me now nor nothin': I'm as hollow as the house we're leavin'; it's
lonely you'll all be now with no one comin' of a Sunday and all
of us gone. May God have mercy on your souls and the souls of
all the dead."

Slowly he rose, black flakes of wet showing on his knees. He
looked dejectedly at the slab of slate, the point of his stick
scratching the moss from the rough-edged top. Then prizing his
finger into a crevice, he flaked off a piece, the action disturbing a
host of tiny pink spiders. He put it into his pocket and turned
away. At the top of the stile he took a last look round, at the dark
tracks in the moist grass leading to the grave, and in the corner
the crumbling walls of the ancient church with the path around
it worn black by the feet of countless pilgrims. Martin yielded to a
deep sigh, and without turning around he walked back the road
again.

They were waiting for him in the boat. He stepped in and sat
in the stern, wiping the sweat off his brow with the sleeve of his
coat. No one said a word. Dermot took the oars and rowed out
until he passed through a narrow channel lying between two
spears of rock. Then he shipped the dripping oars and unloosed
the ropes from around the little brown sail. The sails flapped; the
boat shivered, and with a slap and a crunch of water, her bow was
turned to the mainland.

Dermot, at the tiller, sat beside his father, their backs to the
island. Mairéad sat on the wooden chest, her legs dangling beneath a navy blue skirt revealing her thick black stockings and
heavily-nailed boots besmeared with clabber. Her face was

flushed with youth. A black shawl was round her shoulders, V-shaped at the neck, showing her white throat. Occasionally her hand brushed a strand of black hair from her brown eyes, as she looked at the boiling stir of water in the boat's wake, at the island houses getting smaller, scattered like a handful of thrown pebbles. To her left were the cliffs of the island, a cold gray, their tops thatched with clouds, and white gulls screaming and flying from their crevices.

The drizzle blew to heavy rain and it fell with a quick pattering on the wind-tightened sail. For Martin there was grief and sorrow in the noise and feel of it. He sat, leaning forward on his stick, the rain trailing snail lines on his black hat, his face grim and motionless, and his eyes shut like a blind man. He yawned involuntarily, and when his son threw an empty potato sack across his shoulders, he never moved. In his mind he was reproaching himself for leaving his dead and the crumbling old church.

For Dermot the leave-taking was different. He looked at Mairéad as she arranged her shawl about her head and smiled at him with a gleam of white teeth. He pictured his sons to come growing up in a land where a spade sung with a soft sweet sound, instead of the ceaseless struggle against bog and rock that was the island. A shower of spray broke across the bow of the boat and made him pay heed to the tiller.

When they neared the mainland a cap-full of blue sky showed in the north. The rain ceased and the sun shone. The sea gleamed blue while vapor rose from the sail, the tarred sides of the boat, and the trousers of Martin and his son. The boat nosed its way into a narrow beak of water, high sheltering rocks at each side, around which the waves clopped before falling with a sigh on a small beach of shingle. Up the beach they hauled the boat, her keel grating on the stones. Dermot left them to the unloading while he walked a mile inland to the new house to fetch the donkey and cart.

When he returned, they loaded the cart with the bits of furniture. The old man was hoisted on, and with Dermot and Mairéad walking alongside they started off on their new life.

That evening Martin sat at the fireside in the new home. The red-tiled floor, where one could slip and break one's neck, the raised fireplace with the turf burning before iron bars, irritated him. And he thought yearningly of his island home with the fire on the hearth, where he could spit with ease, and the homely crickets chirping behind it.

"Sure we'll not know ourselves now in this grand house, Martin," said Mairéad brightly as she busied herself about the kitchen.

"Ah, maybe so," replied Martin listlessly.

"Come to the door, Father, and have a look at the great land that's in it, and it's all ours," said the son with enthusiasm.

The old man rose stiffly and went to the door. They looked out upon the untilled land, fenced in by new stakes joined by three parallel rows of bull wire. It formed part of a large tract of bog and hill and little homes. In the distance they could see where the better land began, the smoke from the farmhouses rising up from behind clumps of trees. But to them who knew only rock their own land was good.

"Aye, faith," said the old man, "it looks good — God bless it!" and with these words he turned in to the house.

At bedtime the three knelt for the rosary, their elbows resting on the seats of chairs. They prayed for their dead, good crops, good fishing, and the weather; and then Martin in a voice hoarse with emotion called for a prayer that they'd return to the island. The young people exchanged glances, but made no answer.

Weeks passed. Dermot went about his work with a singing hopefulness, farming early in the day and fishing in the evenings. Mairéad took pride in her home which, being one of the new houses in the neighborhood, had a slated roof. She got red geraniums for the windows, and whitewashed boulders for the path in front. At first old Martin took to sitting outside, but when they bought a goat he took it on himself to find fresh pastures for the animal. To keep the goat from wandering afar or going too quickly a slack rope spanceled a foreleg to a backleg. During the day they would be seen along the rough roads, the goat nibbling at this side and on that, and old Martin, sitting by the roadside with his stick, and a melancholy expression on his face. The young people were delighted with this friendship. They thought that it would dispel his lonesomeness, but always at night the cry came at the end of the rosary — "A Hail Mary that we'll return!"

One evening the goat strayed. For a long time Martin searched and at last he spied her white form clear against the green of a small hillside. He called to her. She looked up at him, gave a meh-eh-eh-ing of recognition, and went on eating. He called again, but she made no answer, her tail wagging with delight in her forbidden pasture. With difficulty he began crossing a hummocky field, stopping now and again to shake his stick at her. He reached the hill and sat down with his back to it to gather his breath.

His eyes brightened. From where he sat he could see over the cliffs of the mainland, and in front lay Inishleen. His heart thumped with wild joy. He arose and ascended the hill a bit more, the island rising with him. He saw it now more clearly. The sun was setting, tinting the clouds above the island red and purple like the color of bruised flesh. Its gray cliffs and blue sea reflected the glory of the sky, making the island look strangely near. For a long time he looked at it, his face quickening; then he turned and scanned the rough road he had ascended. Below him, whitewashed houses, like bits of smoldering paper, sent spirals of turf smoke into the evening air; and on the side of a hill the mainland churchyard looked like a field of mushrooms.

He turned again to Inishleen. The color had drained away from the clouds, leaving them as gray as turf-ashes. A cool breeze shivered the grasses beside him. He stood up facing the island. His eyes were alive with a strange emotion and his whole frame trembled with excitement. He raised his stick in the air and in the half-light he looked like the trunk of an old tree growing on the hillside. " 'Tis better to be with them and they dead than to be walkin' the roads here alone and me dead! I'll go back in God's name! Back I'll go in the name of God!," the strange eagerness in his voice shaking the lonely silence.

With great energy he descended the hill, the goat following at his heels. He moved quickly, one hand supporting the small of his back, his breath wheezing, his stick hitting the ground in short, crisp cracks, and he saying ironically, " 'Tis the good land that'd keep me from my dead! 'Tis the good land that'd keep me from my dead!"

Dermot and Mairéad who were just going to look for him, met him at the door. When they saw the great wildness that was on him, and the expression of happy determination on his face, they made no sign.

" 'Tis how he has found himself!" they whispered. Their hopes were strengthened when, at that night's rosary, no prayer was asked for the return; and when they went to bed they left the old man praying quietly before the dying fire.

In the morning Martin lay in bed, a smile on his face as he heard the bonnivs squealing and they going into sacks for the market. When the donkey cart was ready to go, he arose and stood in the doorway to see them off. Mairéad was seated on the cart, her eyes on the house, its slated roof, its rough stone front with its four little windows, and the outhouses, with their corrugated roofs. Dermot, with his eyes on the old man, stood at the donkey's head. Then he caught the reins and walking beside the donkey they set off.

"God be with you," shouted Martin.

"God and Mary be with you," they replied.

He stood watching the little morsel of a cart till it was swallowed in the jaws of the hills, and then he turned into the house.

He looked at the key of the island home where it had hung, since their arrival, on a nail in the embrasure of the kitchen window. He took it and put it in his pocket. He filled a can with food and after midday he set off on his journey to the coast. Large clouds hung low in the sky, blown seawards by the wind. The mission he was on filled him with new life and he walked the mile of rough road without resting. Presently he reached the top of the cliff and looked down its gray slopes to where the tarred boat lay on the white beach, its oars sticking out carelessly making it look like a large black snail. With difficulty he descended the steep path and reached the boat, part of her lying in the water and part on the stones.

It failed on him to launch her. But the tide was coming in fast, and meanwhile he busied himself bailing out the brackish water, hammering in the tholepins, and fixing the small mast in position. He cleared the small stones away from her keel, the incoming tide rushing over his boots, their brass tags shining up at him like herrings' eyes. The boat grunted at the stones, it swayed and floated. Martin undid the mooring ropes, and taking off his old hat he crossed himself before pushing her forward. Up through the beak of land and with its cool cliffs at each side, he rowed the boat, his feeble oars skidding the water into thin icelike flakes. Then he stopped to hoist the sail, but it was too heavy for his exhausted body: the gaff stopped halfway up the mast, swinging to and fro like a broken bough. The weight of the water hindered him from fixing the wooden tiller in its sockets, and he sat back in the flat stern steering with an oar placed in the sculling hole. Clear of the shelter of the cliffs, the boat caught the stiff breeze and moved out gurgling and clapping at the waves. There was great determination in his eyes and in the tilt of his short beard, as he saw the island with her gray arms of welcome. His heart filled with hope, and the desire of escape, of arrival, burned within him like a flame. Out and out he went, the boat slapping the Atlantic waves into light spray, and her shawl of a sail bellying in the wind.

While Martin was on the sea his boat nearing the island, Mairéad and Dermot were making home on the donkey cart. Dusk was falling and the two figures were seated blackly in front, their eyes on the white road twisting through the brown bog and over the soft folds of the darkening hills. The donkey's hoofs clinked on the hard road and the loose tailboard of the cart rattled cheerily. A strong wind blew around the hills, wrinkling the patches of lake by the roadside, tugging at Mairéad's shawl, and making dark ridges on the gray back of the donkey. Afar off a cart jolted, some one whistled impatiently to a barking dog, and then, like a speck of sound, a curlew cried once in the gathering darkness. As they drew nearer home dots of light shimmered on the hills from the little homes.

Dermot slapped the rope reins on the animal's back, and as it broke into a trot, his voice rose above the wind in joyous song. Mairéad's shawl was over her head, held out at the sides of her face like horse's blinkers. Now and again she'd steal a glance at her husband, looking at him softly, admiringly. When he had finished his song he turned to her. "Faith 'tis up in himself he'll be now with the new hat!" Stretching his arm to the back of the cart he groped among the parcels and pulled forward a black felt hat with a broad brim. He put it on his head, hunching his shoulders, and making a grimace at his wife.

"How does it look on me?"

She looked at the big hat falling over his ears.

"Sure it's worse looking than the old pig jobber you are," she said smilingly. They both laughed and he took it off immediately.

When they entered the house it was empty and still. The fire was dead out and the kitchen was filled with a red-wine glow from the little lamp that always burned before the picture of the Sacred Heart. They went about the house quietly for fear of wakening the old man, and on his chair by the fire they placed his new hat. Then they tiptoed up the bare wooden stairs to bed.

In the morning Martin who usually got up early was not abroad. The hat was still on the chair lying like a black cat curled in sleep. Martin's room was off the kitchen. Mairéad called him and there was no answer. She entered his room and found it empty and the bed unslept in. A panic seized her. She called up to Dermot who was just rising. In a flash he was in the kitchen, standing in his trousers and shirt. "'Tis to the island he's away," he said, his voice quavering. "He'd never make it with the wind that was in it." The key was gone!

Dermot, pulling on his blue jersey ran across the fields to his nearest neighbor, Christy King. Soon they were at the rock-heads launching Christy's boat and soon the sail was up, the wind blowing strongly islandwards. A wild terror possessed Dermot, a terror that made him impatient with the boat.

"He never could make it with the sea and the wind that's in it!" he breathed.

"Faith could he," said Christy, "I heard of an old man that rowed a curragh from Cleggan to Boffin and it's the rough channel of water."

"'Tis too old me father was: God be merciful to him! 'Tis

blamin' myself I am that I didn't stay on Inishleen. It broke his heart and he with the years on him."

As the boat drew near, both men's eyes scanned the rocks and the sea. There wasn't a soul to be seen, only the gulls diving and shrieking, and the waves racing along with smoking tops. Dermot felt a great fear on him when he saw the mad stir of island-water. Then a breath of hope arose within him as they passed into the bay, through the two guarding spears of rock, with the white waves roaring across them and not a bit of wreckage to be seen. They approached the rocky quay, Dermot catching sight of a black object cast up on the white stones of the beach. Nearer they came and he saw it was a boat, its tarred sides gleaming wetly in the light.

They ran over to it without speaking. The boat was lying on her side, her mast on the stones, and the sail heavy and dusted with sand. They lifted the cloth gently, and below it lay the old man. One arm lay outstretched on the stones, the other lay across his breast, clutching his beads, their wire-joins red with rust. His face with half-shut eyes was raised to the sky, a strange peace upon it. His black hat gray with sea salt slanted on his head, his fine white hair matted with sand and wet. His feet were in the boat, one leg tied to the seat with a rope.

" 'Tis a miracle how he made it," said Christy quietly, "and 'tis a blessing of God he tied himself for it's the Christian burial he can get now."

Dermot stood, his jaws tightening, his eyes full of his dead father, while the gulls screeched pitifully overhead and the sea crashed on the stones below.

" 'Tis the truth you're saying, Christy! 'Twill ease our suffering that he's here and we not searching every cove for his drowned body — God's will be done!"

The two men stood dark against the white stones, the black boat beside them with its cargo of dead, and behind them the empty houses with the gaunt face of Cnámh Mór looking grimly down.

In silence they joined Martin's cold hands, and lifted his feet out of the water, with its rusty bailer and tholepin floating on it.

In his pocket they found a key and a piece of well-smoothed slate stone. Placing him on a wooden beam they carried him to his island home, the water dripping from his body, leaving a wet track on the dry path.

The Storyteller

FRANK O'CONNOR

AFRIC and Nance went up the mountain, two little girls in shapeless, colorless smocks of coarse frieze. With them went the lamb. Afric had found it on the mountain, and it insisted on accompanying her everywhere. It was an idiotic, astonished animal which stopped dead and bucked and scampered entirely without reason. It was drawing on to dusk.

Shadow was creeping up the mountain. First light faded from the sea, then from the rocks, then from the roadway and the fields. Soon it would dwindle from the bog; everything there would fill with rich color and the long channels of dark bog-water would burn like mirrors between the purple walls of turf. Behind each of the channels was ranged a file of turf stacks, black sods heaped to dry and looking like great pine cones.

"And the priest came," continued Nance, pursuing a litany.

"And what did he say?"

"He said — he said Grandfather would die tonight."

"You said 'twas the doctor said that."

"The priest said it, too."

"Hike, you divil!" yelled Afric. The lamb had walked straight up to the edge of a bog pool, bent down in innocent rapture, and then tossed itself high into the air and off sideways like a crow.

"And Mom said you were to stop talking about the boat."

"What boat?"

"The boat you said would come for Grandfather. Mom said there was no boat."

"There is a boat. Grandfather said it. And lights."

From *Harper's Bazaar* (N. Y.), November, 1937. Printed by permission of the author and of *Harper's Bazaar*.

"Mom said there's no lights either."

"Mom doesn't know. Grandfather knows better."

"Mom said Grandfather didn't mean it."

"Ha!" said Afric scornfully.

" 'Tis true."

"And I suppose he didn't mean about Shaun O'Mullarkey and the Sprid either. Or about Con of the fairies and the Demon Hurler. Or about the Gillygooley. Or the Gawley Cullawney and his mother."

"Mom said," continued Nance in the tone of one reciting a lesson, "that 'twould be better for Grandfather now if he hadn't so much old stories and paid heed to his prayers when he had the chance."

"Grandfather always said his prayers. Grandfather knew more prayers than Mom."

"Mom said he told barbarous stories."

"But if they were true?"

"Mom says they weren't true, that they were all lies and that God punishes people for telling lies and that's why Grandfather is afraid to die. He's afraid of what God will do to him for telling lies."

"Ha!" sniffed Afric again, but with less confidence.

The mountain did not inspire confidence. The shadow, quickening its mighty motion, rose before them among the naked rocks. Two tiny stars came out, vibrating in the green sky. A pair of horses, head down before them, suddenly took fright and rushed away with a great snorting, their manes tossing and loose stones flying from their hoofs. To the right, a cliff, a pale veil dropped sheer to the edge of a dark lake, and from its foot the land went down in terraces of gray stone to the sea's edge, a ghost-pale city without lights or sound.

It was queer, Afric thought, the way Grandfather had stopped telling them stories all at once, the way he seemed to fix his eyes on the wall. Even when she had asked him about the boat he had only muttered, "Whisht, child, whisht!" But all the same Afric knew that Mom must be wrong. Grandfather had meant it all. There must be some other reason for his silence.

"Maybe death will come like a traveling man, like it came to some," she said thoughtfully. "A man with long, long legs and a bandage over his eyes. Maybe that's why Grandfather would be afraid — a big man the size of a mountain. I'd be afraid of him myself, I'm thinking."

It was almost dark when they reached the mountain top. There was a cold wind there, the grasses swayed and whistled, and their bare feet squelched calf-deep in the quaggy ground with its almost invisible hollows. Plunging on, they lost sight of the sea, the other side of the mountain came into view. A chain of lakes with edges like the edges of countries on the maps in school shone out of all the savage darkness, and beyond them, very far away, another inlet of the sea.

They almost failed to see the fire. It was in a deep natural hollow. It burned under a curiously shaped metal drum. On top of the drum was another metal container, narrow below and broad above like a bucket, and a jointed pipe led from this into a barrel with a tap on it. Under the tap was a mug covered by a strip of muslin. Four children were solemnly seated on the edge of the pit looking down on this queer contraption, their bare legs dangling in the firelight, their faces and heads in shadow. They were not speaking but looking with fascinated, solemn eyes at the still. Afric's father was standing before it, his hands in his trousers' pockets. He was a tall, handsome man, big shouldered, broad chested, with a wide gray kindly face and gray eyes, but now he seemed melancholy and withdrawn.

"What way is your grandfather?" he asked.

"Mom said to tell you there was no change," said Nance.

Nance and Afric sat within the hollow out of the wind so that the heads and shoulders of the other children rose up on every side against the starlit sky like idols grouped in a circle. The lamb seemed to take the greatest interest in the whole proceedings, sniffed at the turf, the tub, the barrel, backed away from them, staggered to the mouth of the hollow and scampered back as though horribly shocked by something, licked the legs of the little girls and gazed with blank eyes into the fire. Its antics caused a sudden diversion among the four other children; they laughed without restraint. Then, as though they had grown self-conscious, they fell silent. Two wiped their noses in the sleeves of their little frieze jackets. Then they rose and went off silently down the mountain. After a few moments the other two did exactly the same thing. It was growing very dark.

Then their Uncle Padraic came, and, standing against the sky, leaned on a turf-cutting spade. You nearly always saw Padraic leaning on something; a wall, a turf rick, the pillar of a gate — there always seemed to be something for Padraic to lean on. Whatever it was, his whole body fell lifelessly about it. He stood like that now against the sky, his hands resting in a crossed position on the handle, his chin resting on his hands. He was a tall, gaunt gentleman wearing a frieze vest without sleeves over a knitted gansey and very much patched frieze trousers. He didn't say anything, but seemed to breathe out an atmosphere of tranquillity. It looked as if he could go on leaning forever without opening his mouth.

"Himself is the same way," said their father.

Padraic spat sideways and rested his chin again upon his crossed hands.

"He is."

They fell silent again. Their father dipped a mug in the barrel of ale and passed it up to his brother-in-law. Padraic drank and carefully emptied the mug onto the ground before returning it.

"One of ye better go for more turf," said their father.

"I will," said Afric. "Keep a hold on the lamb, Nance."

She took the bag and began to run down the mountain. It was a high hollow starry night full of strange shadows. From behind her she heard Nance's cry of distress, and a few moments later something warm and white and woolly came between her flying feet and nearly threw her. She flung herself head foremost on the soft turf, rolling round and round downhill, while the lamb rolled idiotically on top of her, its warm nose seeking her face. There was a smell of earth and grass which made her drunk. She boxed the lamb's ears, caught it by the budding horns, pushed, shoved, wrestled, and rolled with it.

"Ah, lambeen, lambeen, lambeen! You foolish lambeen! I'm

going for turf and the fairies will catch you, the fairies will catch
you! Look, lambeen, they're searching for you with little lanterns!"

She filled her bag with turf. The bog was now wild and dark.
The channels of bogwater were shining with inky brightness; as
though the bog were all a-tremble they shook, but with a suave
oily motion that barely broke the reflected starlight. Below, very
far below, were a few lights along the shore.

She recognized her own house on the little spit of land that
pushed out into the bay. There was light only in the west window
in the room where her grandfather was lying. She could imagine
all the others in the kitchen in the firelight: her mother and the
baby, her mother's two sisters, old Brigid, their mother, sucking
her pipe, and Padraic's children. They would be talking in low
voices, and then her mother or old Brigid would go into the west
room to the old man who would tell no more stories, and they
would talk to him of the will of God, but still his face, pale as
the little beard about his chin, would be bitter because he did
not wish to die. Not wish to die and he eighty and more! And
up on the mountain were she and her father, making poteen
which would be drunk at the old man's wake, because he was a
famous and popular man and people would come from twenty
miles around on ponies and in traps to pray for his soul.

Maybe he was dying now! But Afric felt sure if he was dying
there would be some sign, as there always was in the stories he
told: along the road a huge man, dressed in rags, a bandage
about his eyes and his hands outstretched, feeling his way to
their house; all the air filled with strange lights while the spirits
waited; a shining boat making its way across the dark water
without a sail. Surely there would be signs like that! She looked
about her furtively, suddenly trembling and all attune for the
wonder. But there was nothing. Not a sound. In sudden panic
she repulsed the lamb and began to run, her bag of dry sods
knocking her shoulders.

It was all placid and homely up there. Padraic was sitting on
an upturned tub, smoking. It was so silent you could hear the
noise of the stream near by, loud in the darkness. Her father came
up from it, carrying a bucket.

"He had a long day," he said, as though continuing a conversation.

"He had a long day," agreed Padraic, not looking up. He spat and sucked his pipe again.

"He was a good man," said Afric's father.

"He was. He was a good father to you."

"He was so. 'Tis a pity he couldn't be more resigned."

" 'Twas what they were saying."

"He said a queer thing last night."

"Did he now?"

"He says a man sees the world when he comes into it and goes out of it; the rest is only foolishness — that's what he said."

" 'Tis a deep saying."

" 'Tis deep."

"But there's meaning in it," Padraic went on.

"I dare say."

"There is. He was always a deep man, a patient man."

Afric was astonished. She never remembered her uncle to have spoken as much.

"Do you remember," he continued, "on the boat? He never liked one of us to do a thing in a hurry. 'Mother was drowned a year ago,' he'd say, 'and she'd have been round the lake since then.' That's what he'd always say."

"He would so."

" 'Tis a pity he didn't do more with himself — a clever man."

" 'Tis. But he wouldn't stop in America."

"He wasn't sure."

"There was nothing he cared about, only the stories."

"No, then. And he was a wonder with them."

"He was. You wouldn't miss a day in a bog or a night in the boat with him. Often he'd keep you that way you wouldn't know you were hungry." Afric's father spat. It was not often he made such admissions. "And there were times we were hungry."

"You never took after him, Con."

"No, then. 'Twasn't in me, I suppose. But 'twasn't in our generation. I'd get great pleasure listening to him, but I could never tell a story myself."

"The place won't be the same without him," said Padraic rising.

"Ye'd better go home with yer uncle," said her father.

"I'll stop with you, Father," said Afric.

He thought for a moment.

"Do so," he said.

She knew then he was lonely.

When Padraic and Nance had gone, everything seemed lonelier than before, but she didn't mind because her father was with her. He wrapped his coat about her. The lamb snuggled up beside her. And now she let the mountain come alive with all its stories and its magic. Because she knew it was up here the spirits lived and planned their descents on the little cottages; at night you could often see them from the bay, moving across the mountain with their little lanterns. Sometimes the lights would be close together and you would know it was a fairy funeral. A man from the place, making poteen in the mountains at night, had come across just such a funeral, and the spirits had laid the coffin at his feet. He had opened it, and inside was a beautiful girl with long yellow hair. As he looked at her she had opened her eyes and he had brought her home with him. She had told him she was a girl from Tuam, and when inquiries were made it was found that a girl from Tuam had been buried that same day; but she wouldn't go back to her own people and remained always with the man who had saved her and married him.

Afric could see her father moving about in the smoky light, his legs seeming immense. Sometimes she saw his face when he bent to the fire. Then he sat on the upturned tub with his head between his hands. She went to sleep at last.

When she woke again the helmet of shadow had tilted. It was cold. The high hollow drum of the sky had half filled with low drifting vapors. Someone — she did not know who — was speaking to her father. Then he caught her in his arms, and the jolting and slithering of his feet in the long slopes wakened her completely. He stumbled on blindly as though he did not know she was in his arms. Even when she looked at him he did not seem to be aware of her.

There was a little crowd kneeling even at the door of the west room. The kitchen was in darkness only for the firelight, and this and the flickering of candles made the west room unusually bright and gay. The people kneeling there rose and made way for her father. He put her gently down on a stool by the fire and went in, taking off his hat. The low murmur of prayer went on again. Afric tiptoed to the room door. Yes, the west room was very bright. Her grandfather's great bearded head was lying, very pale and wasted, over the bowed heads under the light of two candles. Her father was kneeling awkwardly by the bedside, covering his face with his hands. Her grandmother, old Brigid, suddenly began to keen and sway from side to side.

Afric went out. She looked up and down the lane. She was looking with a sort of fascinated terror for the big man with the bandage over his eyes. There was no sign of him. The lane was quiet only for the whispering of the bushes and a blackbird's first bewildered, drowsy fluting. There were no lights, no voices. Frightened as she was, she ran down the lane to the little cove where her father's boat was drawn up among the slimy rocks and seaweed. Over it was a grassy knoll. She ran there and threw herself on her face and hands lest anyone should spy her and take fright. The light was breaking over the water. But no boat came shining to her out of the brightness. The blackbird, having tried his voice, threw it out in a sudden burst of song, and the lesser birds joined in with twitters and chuckles. In the little cove there was a ducking of water among the dried weeds, a vague pushing to and fro. She rose, her smock wet, and looked down into the cove. There was no farewell, no clatter of silver oars in rowlocks as magic took her child away. Nothing, nothing at all. With a strange choking in her throat she went slowly back to the house. She thought that maybe she knew now why her grandfather had been so sad.

The Hand of the Master

ALFRED NOYES

IT WAS on Christmas Day, 1914, that I received one of the strangest documents I had ever read. It was in the form of a letter from Jonathan Martin, who had made himself a torch of ambition and fear to many moths in London by painting portraits that were certain to be the pictures of the year, but also to reveal all the idiosyncrasies, good and bad, of their subjects. It was the fashion to call him cynical. In fact, he was an artist, and a great one.

His unusual power of eliciting unexpected meanings from apparently meaningless incidents and objects was not confined to his art. In private conversation, he would often startle you with a sentence that was like the striking of a match in a dark room. You didn't know that the room was dark until he spoke; and then, in a flash, mysterious relationships at which you had never guessed, were established. You caught a glimpse of an order and a meaning that you had not discerned before. The aimless thing over which you had barked your shin became a coal scuttle; the serried row of dark objects that irritated your left elbow became the works of Shakespeare; and, if you were lucky, you perhaps discovered the button by which you could switch on the electric light, and then sit down by the hearth and read of "beauty, making beautiful old rhyme."

But this is a very faint hint of the kind of illumination with which he would surprise you on all kinds of occasions. I shall never forget the way in which he brought into a queer juxtaposition "the Day" that Germany had been toasting for forty years

From *Walking Shadows,* by Alfred Noyes. Stokes, 1918. By permission.

and the final request for an answer before midnight, which was embodied in the British ultimatum. He would give you a patch of unexpected order in the chaos of politics, and another in the chaos of the creeds — patches that made you feel a maddening desire to widen them until they embraced the whole world. You felt sure that he himself had done this, that he lived in a re-integrated universe, and that — if only there were time enough — he could give you the whole scheme. In short, he saw the whole universe as a work of art; and he conceived it to be his business, in his own art, to take this or that apparently isolated subject and show you just the note it was meant to strike in the harmony of the whole. He was very fond of quoting the great lines of Dante, where he describes the function of the poet as that of one who goes through the world and where he sees the work of Love, records it. But, please to remember, this did not imply that the subject was necessarily a pleasant one. Beauty was always there, but the beauty was one of relationships, not of the thing itself. As he once said, "an old boot in the gutter will serve as a subject if you can make it significant, if you can set it in relation to the enduring things." It is necessary to make this tedious preface to his odd letter, or the point of it may be lost.

"I want to tell you about the most haunting and dramatic epi-sode I have encountered during these years of war," he wrote. "It was a thing so slight t' t I hardly know how to put it into words. It couldn't be pain.ed, because it includes two separate scenes, and also — in paint — it would be impossible to avoid the merely sentimental effect.

"It happened in London, during the very early days of the struggle. One afternoon, I was riding down Regent Street on the top of a bus. The pavements were crowded with the usual throng. Women in furs were peering into the windows of the shops. News-paper boys were bawling the latest lies. Once, I thought I saw a great scribble of the Hand that writes history, where a theater poster, displaying a serpentine woman, a kind of Aubrey-Beardsley vampire, was half obliterated by a strong diagonal bar of red, bearing the words, 'Kitchener wants a hundred thousand men.' My mind was running on symbols that afternoon, and I wondered if it did perhaps mean the regeneration of art and life in England at last.

"Then we overtook a strange figure, a blind man, tapping the edge of the pavement with a rough stick, cut out of some country hedgerow. He was carrying, in his left hand, a four-foot pole, at the top of which there was nailed a board, bannerwise, about three feet long and two feet wide. On the back of the board, as we overtook him, I read the French text in big red letters: 'Venez a Moi, vous tous qui êtes travailles et charges, et Je vous soulagerai.'

"On the other side of the board, as we halted by the curb a little in front of him, there was the English version of the same text, in big black letters: 'Come unto Me, all ye that labor and are heavy-laden, and I will give you rest.'

"The blind man was tall and lean-faced, and held himself very upright. He was poorly dressed, but very clean and neat. The tap of his stick was like the smart tap of a drum, and he marched more rapidly than any of those who were going in the same direction.

"There were several things about him that puzzled me. There was no advertisement of any sect, or any religious meeting, nothing but the two texts on his placard. He went past us like a soldier, and he carried it like the flag of his regiment. He did not look as if he were asking for alms. The pride on his face forbade the suggestion; and he never slackened his quick pace for a moment. He seemed entirely unrelated to the world around him.

"Possibly, I thought, he was one of those pathetic beings whose emotions had been so stirred by the international tragedy that, despite their physical helplessness, they were forced to find some outlet. Perhaps he was an old soldier, blinded in some earlier war. Perhaps he was merely a religious fanatic. In any case, in the great web of the world's events, he seemed to be a loose fantastic thread; and although he was carrying a more important message than anyone else, nobody paid any attention to him.

"In a few moments, the bus had carried my thoughts and myself into other regions, and, for the time, I forgot him. I occupied myself, as I often do, in composing a bit of doggerel to the rhythm of the wheels. Here it is. It is pretty bad, but the occasion may make it interesting:

> *Once, as in London buses,*
> *At dusk I used to ride,*
> *The faces Hogarth painted*
> *Would rock from side to side,*
> *All gross and sallow and greasy,*
> *And dull and leaden-eyed.*
> *They nodded there before me*
> *In such fantastic shape,*
> *The donkey and the gosling,*
> *The sheep, the whiskered ape,*
> *With so much empty chatter,*
> *So many and foolish lies,*
> *I lost the stars of heaven*
> *Through looking in their eyes.*

"Late in the afternoon, I was returning westward, along the Strand. I remember walking slowly to look at the beauty of the sunset sky, against which the Nelson column, in those first days of the fight, rose with a more spiritual significance than ever before. The little admiral stood like a watchman, looking out to sea, from the main mast of our Ship of State, against that dying glory. It was the symbol of the national soul, high and steadfast over the great dark lions, round which so many quarreling voices had risen, so many quarreling faces had surged and drifted away like foam in the past. This was the monument of the enduring spirit, a thing to still the heart and fill the eyes of all who speak our tongue today.

"I was so absorbed in it that I did not notice the thick crowd, choking the entrances to Charing Cross Station, until I was halted by it. But this was a very different crowd from those of peacetime. They were all very silent, and I did not understand what swarming instinct had drawn them together. Nor did they understand it themselves — yet. 'I think they are expecting something,' was the only reply I got to my inquiry.

"I made my way round to the front of the station, but the big iron gates were closed and guarded by police. Nobody was allowed to enter the station. Little groups of railway porters were clustered here and there, talking in low voices. I asked one of these men what was happening.

" 'They're expecting something, some train. But we don't know what it is bringing.'

"As he spoke, there was a movement in the crowd. A compact body of about forty ambulance men marched through, into the open space before the station. Some of them were carrying stretchers. They looked grave and anxious. Some of their faces were tense and white, as if they too were expecting something, something they almost dreaded to see. This was very early in the war, remember, before we knew what to expect from these trains.

"The gates of the station swung open. The ambulance men marched in. A stream of motor ambulances followed. Then the gates were closed again.

"I waited, with the waiting crowd, for half an hour. It was impossible now to make one's way through the dense crush. From where I stood, jammed back against the iron railings, in front of the station, I could see that all the traffic in the Strand was blocked. The buses were halted, and the passengers were standing up on the top, like spectators in some enormous crowded theater. The police had more and more difficulty in keeping the open space before the station. At last, the gates were swung apart again, and the strangest procession that London had ever seen began to come out.

"First, there were the sitting-up cases — four soldiers to a taxi-cab, many of them still bandaged about the brows with the first blood-stained field dressings. Most of them sat like princes, and many of them were smiling; but all had a new look in their faces. Officers went by, gray-faced; and the measure of their seriousness seemed to be the measure of their intelligence, rather than that of their wounds. Without the utterance of a word, the London crowd began to feel that here was a new thing. The army of Britain was making its great fighting retreat, before some gigantic force that had brought this new look into the faces of the soldiers. It was our first real news from the front. From the silent faces of these men who had met the first onset with their bodies, we got our first authentic account of the new guns and the new shells, and the new hell that had been loosed over Europe.

"But the crowd had not yet fully realized it. A lad in khaki came capering out of the station, waving his hands to the throng and shouting something that sounded like a music-hall jest. The crowd rose to what it thought was the old familiar occasion.

" 'Hello, Tommy! Good boy, Tommy! Shake hands, Tommy! Are we downhearted, Tommy?' The old vacuous roar began and, though all the faces near me seemed to have two eyes in them, every one began to look cheerful again.

"The capering soldier stopped and looked at them. Then he made a grotesque face and thrust his tongue out. He looked more like a gargoyle than a man.

"The shouts of 'Tommy, Tommy,' still continued, though a few of the shouters were evidently puzzled. Then a brother soldier, with his left arm in a sling, took the arm of the comedian and looked a little contemptuously at the crowd.

" 'Shell-shock,' he said quietly. And the crowd shouted no more that day. It was not a pleasant mistake; and it was followed by a procession of closed ambulances, containing the worst cases.

"Then came something newer even than wounded men, a motley stream of civilians, the Belgian refugees. They came out of the station like a flock of sheep, and the fear of the wolf was still in their eyes. The London crowd was confronted by this other crowd, so like itself, a crowd of men in bowler hats and black coats, of women with children clinging to their skirts; and it was one of the most dramatic meetings in history. The refugees were carrying their household goods with them, as much as could be tied in a bundle or shut in a handbag. Some of the women were weeping. One of them—I heard afterward—had started with four children but had been separated from the eldest in the confusion of their flight. It was doubtful whether they would ever be reunited.

"Now, as this new crowd streamed out of the gates of the station toward the vehicles that had been prepared for them, some of their faces lifted a little, and a light came into them that was more than the last radiance of the sunset. They looked as if they had seen a friend. It was a look of recognition; and though it was only a momentary gleam, it had a beauty so real and vivid that I turned my head to see what had caused it.

"And there, over the sea of faces that reached now to the foot of the Nelson column, I saw something that went through me like great music. Facing the gates of the station, and lifting out of the midst of the crowd like the banner of a mighty host, nay, like the banner of all humanity, there was a placard on a pole. The sunset light caught it and made it blaze like a star. It bore, in blood-red letters, the solemn inscription that I had seen in the earlier part of the day: '*Venez a Moi, vous tous qui êtes travailles et charges, et Je vous soulagerai.*'

"My blind man had found his niche in the universe. It was hardly possible that he was even conscious of what he was doing; hardly possible that he knew which side of his banner was turned toward the refugees, whether it was the English, that would mean nothing to them, or the French that would speak to them like a benediction. He had been swung to his place and held in it by external forces, held there, as I myself was jammed against the iron railings. But he had become, in one moment, the spokesman of mankind; and if he had done nothing else in all his life, it had been worth living for that one unconscious moment.

"You may be interested to hear the conclusion of the doggerel which came into my head as I went home:

> *Now, as I ride through London,*
> *The long wet vistas shine,*
> *Beneath the wheeling searchlights,*
> *As they were washed with wine,*
> *And every darkened window*
> *Is holy as a shrine.*
>
> *The deep-eyed men and women*
> *Are fair beyond belief,*
> *Ennobled by compassion,*
> *And exquisite with grief.*
> *Along the streets of sorrow*
> *A river of beauty rolls.*
> *The faces in the darkness*
> *Are like immortal souls.*"

Billy

JOHN CURRAN

BILLY closed the book and quietly sank back into the chair. His long, thin face seemed paler than ever and his black eyes burned, hot and dry, under a mop of hair. He wished the story hadn't ended. He wished it had been twice as long. Curling one leg under him he took the slim volume in his white hands and gazed at it for a moment before slowly laying it down again on the great library table. *The Awakening*, by John G-a-l-s-w-o-r-t-h-y.

He leaned his head against the tall back of his chair and gazed at the rows and rows of books against the wall. Little Jon Forsyte's mother! The rows of books seemed to dance. How perfectly wonderful to have a mother like her! He closed his eyes and imagined that Jon's mother was his own. She would be playing the piano in the evening, he thought, and the twilight would stream down through the high window and fall on one side of her face. He would go up to her on that side and sit next her. Still playing, she would look down at him, smile, and say, "Well, darling!"

Billy shivered and hugged himself. Her beautiful brown eyes, her mouth, her voice, would love him! He would say, easily, "It's almost dark, Mummy. Shan't we take a walk through the garden? There are three little red buds on one of the Bleeding Hearts, and one of the purple lilac bushes is all in bloom." She would smile and stop playing; he could see her beautiful hands putting the music away. Then she would throw her arm around his shoulder and he would put his around her waist and they would walk out through the kitchen into the garden. They wouldn't

From *The Catholic World*, October, 1938. By permission.

talk much. She would hum under her breath and perhaps stoop
to touch one of the buds of the Bleeding Hearts.

He opened his eyes wide and for a moment stared breathlessly at
the rows of books. Rising slowly, then, he wandered to the window and looked down upon the grounds. It was almost dark;
soon the bell would ring for dinner. Most of the snow was gone;
there was only a dirty white fringe at the bottom of the wall on
the avenue. Down there a long black roadster shot in through the
stone gateway and raced toward him. This was the first time
today he had seen Peggy — but after lunch, when he had been
in the back, going to the river, he had seen Jim back her car out
of the garage. He tapped on the window now as she left the car,
but she did not hear. Her tall figure hurried out of sight.

Propping his elbows on the window sill, he cupped his chin in
his hands. He *did* wish the dinner bell would ring! But then perhaps his mother wasn't home anyway. He couldn't remember, he
told himself anxiously, having seen her since luncheon. Some
friends had been there, he knew, for coming back from the river
at about three o'clock he had heard them talking; the hall had
been full of smoke, too, and there were a good many bottles in the
kitchen.

A bell above his head began to ring and he jumped nervously.
Then he hurried toward his own room to wash his hands and to
see if his face was clean. He *did* hope mother was at home.

His sister was alone at table. Billy's eyes rested upon her face
an instant and then flew over the room.

"Isn't Mother home, Peggy?"

"I don't know, Billy." She touched her lips with a napkin and
took another little sandwich.

Would he go to her room? But she would think it strange. He
wouldn't know what to say. He *could* ask to see a movie — but then
he'd have to go, and he didn't care to. He turned quickly and
pushed in the swinging door to the kitchen. Julia was at a table,
cutting a cake.

"Is my mother home, do you know, Julia?"

Her sharp eyes stared at him over her glasses, and she licked whipped cream from a bony finger. "I don't know, Billy; ask Kate. She went out this afternoon, I think."

The cook was boiling water in a frying pan at the stove. Billy went over to her.

"Is my mother home, Kate?"

"How? Home? She is that, Billy. 'Tis she told me not an hour ago to order more ginger ale for the night, and that she'd be here for dinner." She turned away and scraped the bottom of the frying pan with a pancake lifter.

Billy went back to the dining room and sat across from his sister. His black eyes fastened intently upon her face, but she did not become conscious of him. Peggy, he supposed, was very beautiful. In the same way that little Jon's mother was beautiful? No, he supposed not. For Jon's mother was beautiful because — well, principally because she loved Jon so much.

He took a sandwich, frowned upon it, glanced quickly over his shoulder at a sound he thought his mother might have made, and then poured coffee for himself. Of course, Jon's mother *did* have large brown eyes, perhaps something like Peg's. And she had a pretty mouth and soft cheeks. But then it was something — well, inside of her, that really made her beautiful. It was as if. . . .

"Billy, why are you frowning at me!"

He dropped his eyes quickly and took a drink of coffee. It was too strong; it would keep him awake tonight. The door to the kitchen swung open and he almost dropped the cup in his eagerness to see who it was. It was only Julia with cake or something. He did wish his mother would hurry.

Peggy was taking her salad. There was that faraway look in her eyes. He would bet she didn't know what she was eating. He would bet she couldn't even taste that awful old mayonnaise. She had been like that for a long time now, ever since she started to college three years ago. He guessed all grownups were like that. His mother was, even though she talked a lot; you could tell even while she was talking that she was thinking about something inside of her. His father had been like that, too, before he got a divorce and went away, although he *never* used to talk. And his face was always stiff and straight like a cement wall, but if you watched, you could tell there were thoughts running around behind his eyes.

He dropped his hands on his lap and looked at his sister. Somehow he had got used to her, but now she seemed like a stranger. It was months and months since he had talked with her. Not long ago, he remembered, he could almost tell what she was thinking and what she was going to say. But he couldn't tell anything now. She buttered her bread very patiently, as if it were very important, but he knew she didn't even see the bread.

"Peggy," he said, "do you remember five years ago when I was six and. . . ."

"Yes, Billy?"

"Do you remember you got some wild rosebushes down by the river and transplanted them out by the garage?"

"Yes, Billy?"

"Well, where did we find those bushes? Was it down by the birch tree, or was it farther down, near the cave?"

She wasn't listening. Just buttering her bread, as if it were very important. And her eyes were still, and yet they were moving very fast on the inside. It was as if they were running up and down streets somewhere, as he did at night when he had bad dreams.

"Peggy, did you ever read a story called *Awakening* by John Gallisworthy?"

"What *are* you saying, Billy?"

He leaned toward her and repeated his question.

"John *Gals*worthy, Billy. Yes, when I was a freshman in college. It was on my reading list."

"Yes, your name is in the back of the book. Well, do you remember when Jon is all painted up like an Indian and is hiding in the bushes to scare his Aunt June and the rest? Well, that made me think of the wild rosebushes that you and I found once down by the river. Do you remember? It was the same week that I was six and you were fifteen, because I. . . ."

"Yes, Billy?"

She wasn't listening to him. She hadn't heard a word he'd said. It was because all sorts of things were always running around inside her head as in his own. He poured himself another cup of coffee and stirred it slowly. Really, he felt very miserable. He felt as if he wanted to cry, but the tears were too heavy, and they were away, way down in the bottom of him and couldn't come up. He felt cold and hard inside like the big white rock outside the cave. He felt all tied up inside of himself. He *always* felt that way. Maybe everybody did. Maybe Peggy did, too?

He raised his eyes quickly. If they could only let each other come out again — if they could only look at each other, and *see* each other. . . .

"Peg," he said, softly, "do you ever. . . ."

But she had risen and dropped her napkin on the table. "I must hurry now, Billy."

Billy's mother met Peggy in the parlor and his face brightened hopefully when he saw her.

"Margaret," his mother said, "have you seen the evening paper?"

His sister patted a wave in her hair. Billy wished his mother would hurry.

"Dad's got married, you mean?" Peggy answered.

His mother came to the table and sat down; there was an expression on her face Billy had never seen there before. Peggy hung in the doorway. Billy could see she was waiting just to be polite; she was in a hurry to get away. He wished his mother would look at him. What did it matter if his father had got married? Ted Lawrence's dad had been married for five years.

Now the strange look was gone from his mother's face. It had been as if for a moment she had been *making* herself look as she always did, and now she was doing it without trying.

"Margaret, I wonder if you could stop at the florist's for me?"

"But we're going to the Country Club, Mother!" The florist's was at the other end of the city.

Billy's mother dropped a napkin on her lap. "Very well. I'll try to get down myself." Peggy hurried away.

Now he had her all to himself. What should he say? Should he ask her to play the piano for him? But she hadn't played for a long time, not since he was a very little boy. Maybe she wouldn't like to. And besides she had never played really for him. Perhaps she wouldn't even look at him while she played. And anyway he didn't *like* to ask her.

She was eating salad. Her eyes were fastened on the sugar bowl as always when there was no one to talk to. Her face looked very, very tired now; it always did when she was alone this way, her eyes holding on to the sugar bowl while her mind was away off somewhere. When there was company, her eyes were cold and bright and she sat very straight. She was just her "play self" then, Billy knew, but she was never tired as at times like these. He would have to hurry or she would be finished with her dinner.

"Mother, couldn't we take a walk tonight?"

There, she was looking at him now. He had been afraid she would look like that.

"Take a walk! What on earth, child!"

He ran his finger back and forth swiftly on his upper lip in a way he had. "Well, you see, it's really quite nice out. I thought," he dropped his eyes and touched a bit of lettuce on his plate, "thought that if we'd take a nice walk as far as the zoo and back, we'd — well, we'd get a good sleep tonight."

"A good sleep? Aren't you sleeping well, Billy? Nonsense! You're drinking too much coffee."

Her eyes were going back to the sugar bowl.

"Let's do, Mother, please!"

She was looking at him again, vacantly. He pushed his cup and saucer away.

"Darling," her voice was sort of vacant, too; she had forgotten what he asked. "Darling, do run up to Mother's room like a good boy and get the three letters on the desk. They are opened, Billy."

He walked silently away, his head hanging. When he returned with the letters and handed them to her, he said,

"Mother, did you ever read a book called *Awakening* by John Gallisworthy — I mean *Gals*worthy?"

"I don't think so," she said absently, and removed a letter from its envelope.

Billy stood at her side for a moment, looking into her face, and then turning slowly, walked away.

Bread and Soul

GEORGE CARVER

NEAR a side altar in St. Boniface's the statue of an angel looks down from a niche somewhat above eye level. It is by no means conspicuous; yet few who come upon it remain unmoved.

The figure is slim, fragile, almost ethereal in spite of its more than mortal proportions. The weight rests upon the right foot, the left knee being bent to break the monotonous line of conventional drapery. The color is that of antique ivory, and in the diffused light of the great aisle a gleam is imparted which seems to emanate from some inner source. Line and color are gentle, mellow, flowing together in utter harmony. It is position, however, which contributes perhaps most to the statue's effectiveness: its poised grace, its balanced stance. It inclines slightly forward, head a trifle bent and turned toward an archway leading into the nave, so that the wide eyes include both the arch and the main entrance — obliquely the length of the nave removed — and suggest expectancy, but expectancy certain of fulfillment, an effect stressed by half-parted lips and the graciousness of half-extended hands.

We who have formed the habit of pausing before it see an exquisite image; but always after a moment of contemplation we become aware of pure spirit: someone had glimpsed perfection and had all but grasped it. But one need not be a regular visitor to be affected; strangers are as readily stirred. We have not had it long, something less than a year. None the less the city has already come to know it as a thing of beauty; and almost every

From *The Sign*, October, 1935. By permission.

day one sees unfamiliar faces in the church, persons who would no doubt never enter St. Boniface's — now sadly in need of repair, for the most part unattractive, and not at all easy of access — except to view the statue. In fact, it was a group of such visitors standing before it during Holy Week from whom I caught the idea of writing about it; to tell, that is, as much of the story as I have come to understand.

The light was perfect that afternoon: raw, spring sunlight out of door but refined by the shadows within to a sustained glow, which lifted the darkness from obscure corners as if removing heavy shroudings. It brought out the image in fullest detail, lighting it almost to refulgence, more brightly than I had ever seen it. One of the group, an older woman, with the high-held head and the sharply etched eyelines of sensitive awareness, remarked across indrawn breath, "It is more than lovely; it is so beautiful that one forgets the existence of sin." Then her tone changed to that of ordinary conversation. "What a pity," she went on, "it bears no *sculpsit;* surely nothing short of genius created it!"

I could have told her who had created it and something about its creation; only, I doubt that she would have recognized the one or credited the other. That last I should not myself have done except that I had had the story from Father Paul Forrest, the assistant at St. Boniface's, to whom the statue had come by bequest of the dying artist, and who had heard, in the fevered accents of Dubroc himself, the account of what had occurred. And it was such a tale as five hundred years ago would have swept through the artists' quarters of Florence, Rome, even Paris on sibilant whispers, moving nervous fingers to cross agitated breasts with the sacred sign and perplexed lips to mutter breathless *Aves.* Father Forrest and I may look upon it in a manner less naïve perhaps, but by no means with less awe. He had known Dubroc, and I had seen many examples of his previous work. We both look at the statue and wonder; it could have been wrought only as Dubroc described — but I shall report the affair as nearly as I can in Father Forrest's version:

"Dubroc came to America soon after the war and went to work in the Stancati studios, down on Epiphany street," he began, one evening several months after the statue had been established in its niche. My curiosity would not be contained any longer, and I had asked almost point-blank for details. "Stancati, you know," he continued, "manufactures objects of religious art. You can find his products all over this section of the state, in churches, in schools, even in homes. Some of his statues and not a few of his pictures are very good indeed, but most of what he turns out is nothing more than the usual commercial crudity sometimes referred to by the derisive as the art of St. Suplice.

"At all events, Dubroc — I believe his first name was Etienne, although I never heard anyone use it — went to work turning out models for the images of saints, madonnas, angels, cherubim, and once in a long time a large crucifix. Stancati used to point with pride to a Pietà, the masterpiece of the establishment, which Dubroc had made soon after his arrival, but I notice that it is still on hand — after some twelve or fifteen years. And so it went. Dubroc, it seems, had learned his art in Paris. He had little to say, nothing at all about his previous life. One drew from his bearing, from his general attitude that he had served in the army, probably as a noncommissioned officer; but there was also about him more than a hint of inferiority of outlook, something connate with the hunted, and from his occasional remarks about America it was clear that his exile, if it was truly exile, was most unhappy.

"I came to know him first upon introduction by Stancati. I had gone down there about some matter of decoration for the school and was advised to consult Dubroc. I found him taciturn but not unpleasant, and we soon concluded our business. His little replica of a famous St. Scholastica, as a result, now stands on the first landing in the grade school — but there seems to have arisen no great demand for duplicates.

"I did not see him again for more than a year. He came to the rectory one night seeking information about the immigration quota. He said, I remember, 'I must not be sent back, mon père; you will explain to me, yes?' I would have encouraged him to tell me why he was so fearful of being deported, but his eyes, dark, somber, troubled as if by some overtension of the soul, did not make questioning easy. I contented myself, therefore, with assuring him that his being French and having lived here so long now rendered him safe enough; and he went away, it seemed to me, somewhat less overwrought.

"After that I met him rather frequently on the street, often stopping to talk with him, and almost every Sunday I noticed him at the communion rail, kneeling in all reverence as befitted one of his occupation. Sometimes I wish that these St. Suplice artists would allow more of their instinctive reverence to creep into their work — but, then, I should not say things like that after seeing what can happen and after learning something of what may be weighing on their souls.

"One evening, it was late in August, a dry, dusty, sultry August evening, I was called to the telephone by Stancati. 'Can you come to Dubroc?' he asked. 'He is ill and asked for you.'

"I found the man in a highly excited state. His temperature must have been close to 103 degrees. Stancati told me as I entered that the physician whom he called had only that moment left, extending small hope and advising that a priest be summoned. As soon as Dubroc recognized me — his eyes were slightly filmed and he seemed very ill — he motioned Stancati out of the room with a feeble yet imperious gesture: he who had formerly been meek almost to obsequiousness in Stancati's presence had become suddenly masterly in spirit. He had been stricken while at work, it seemed, and some of the workmen hearing him fall had run in — they had, I learned later, been forced to break in the door — and placed him upon an improvised couch there in his private studio. Now it was too late even to remove him to a hospital.

"He gestured in much the same imperious manner for me to bend closer. I hurriedly prepared to hear his confession, but he shook his head — and this evidence of strength together with the vitality of his voice as he spoke reassured me somewhat, although I was still doubtful about waiting to perform the rites. 'Remove the cloth from the figure there by the wall, *mon père*,' he said. I hesitated, but he raised his hand in insistence. A moment later the statue of the angel as we know it lighted up that dingy studio. Bare walls, only a dim light, floor littered with an indescribable mass of plaster, molds, wood, cement, paint brushes, cloth, all the paraphernalia of artists such as he; but there in the midst was revealed that figure of unimaginable beauty. Even in such surroundings it gleamed as if illumined from within. 'It is beautiful, yes?' whispered Dubroc when again I had bent over him.

" 'More than beautiful, Dubroc,' I said. 'I have never seen anything so nearly perfect.'

" 'It should be perfect. But it is not really mine. I was possessed by the angel. It dominated me.'

"I wish I could reproduce for you the effect of this extraordinary speech. Dubroc was unaware of imminent death, and for all his fevered condition he was not out of his head; he was quite in command of his faculties. The whole thing may sound commonplace now as I try to tell you about it. Yet it was anything but commonplace at the time. I felt as though he were a being utterly removed, completely remote from the ordinary scheme of illness and death. He had acquired a more or less grammatical English but spoke it with a suggestion as of translation, and his accent was very French indeed. In spite, however, of the handicap created by language, a difficulty accentuated by declining strength, prosaic and mundane as both these were, he communicated to me a sense of something added to mortality, something preternaturally aged, immeasurably wise, miserably weak, and yet overpoweringly courageous. I could not shake off the effect of him. The excited, exclamatory sentences, breathed against time and an encompassing atmosphere of death, became woven together in a pattern of exaltation. Dubroc had triumphed over all the obstacles that life had contrived against him; he was conscious of his triumph but unwilling to receive credit for it — as are always those whose triumph is authentic. As he spoke I receded further and further into a dream. Only the statue and Dubroc's voice were apparent to me and neither was real — yet at the time they were the only reality I knew. Actuality had become cushioned against the incomprehensible.

"It is only within the past few weeks, since you and I have been talking about the statue and so many persons have become interested in it, that I have been able to draw my impressions into some sharpness of focus. I know that I cannot make you feel

what I felt or understand what I understood; nevertheless I shall
do what I can.

" 'But, yes,' Dubroc continued, 'the angel itself opened my eyes,
guided my hand, commanded, and I obeyed. You do not understand? Attend. The summer, it has been hot, no? And the work,
it has piled up. Stancati ordered one hundred new models for
the Jubilee. They must be ready. My helpers hurry. Always they
interrupt to see when a fresh one is ready. I work my swiftest. A
little time — St. Catherine. A little more — a big St. Peter. Next
day — a Moses six feet tall. Do you remember the Moses of
Michelangelo, *mon père?* Saints, shepherds, madonnas, women of
Jerusalem, angels — everything, anything Stancati could think of
he ordered. It is all religious. All pious. He knows the people will
buy, that they will like what he shows them. I understand. They
will like it because it is religious — they do not know what it is
they are denied. And I have wanted to produce only beauty, not
just beauty of meaning, but of form, of color. You and I know
that there is beauty in significance, but it takes thought to bring
it out in full. And the people don't want to think; they want to
feel. Form, color, pattern, yes; but these in tune with spirit. To
lack spirit is to lack everything. But I must have bread. Then I
must work. Stancati knows best. I do what I can.

" The work is well started. I have fashioned many models. The
workmen are busy turning them out. I begin to make an angel,
a big one, more than life size. I finish it. Hideous. An angel only
because it had wings. No grace. No balance. No spirit. Just earth.
But the wings, they make the angel. It stands there and Stancati
can make fifty like it and sell them for money. He is a good man,
Stancati. He cheats no one. He makes what people want, statues,
pictures, medals. Nobody pays for something he does not receive.
But nobody seems to realize how ugly it all is; nobody misses
beauty the handmaid to religion and so loses so much unawares.
My angel is no such handmaid. It is ugly. It is awry. Its face is a
mask. Its hands push me away. Nothing can give it breath. Only
sin is expressed.

" 'The air is hot. Dust is thick everywhere. Motes dance in the
sunlight; then they run together. A time of blackness comes, and

I can see nothing.' Dubroc's voice vibrated with extraordinary vitality. I reached for his hand and managed to feel his pulse. It was strong, whether from excitement, I could not tell. He jerked away from me, resorting to gesture as he went on in his rapid, almost incoherent flutter of speech.

"'Everything disappeared. But only for a moment. A light went up, a soft, mellow light, and it washed the figure of the angel. But the figure had changed. It was no longer the angel that I had just completed. Look, *mon père*, it was exactly as it is now — all ivory and flowing line and inner fire, with the air of something living, as if endowed with speech. And it did speak. To me. It told me what I am. What I was, that is, for now I am different. Now I have known beauty and I have realized the absence of sin. Where that statue was there could be no thought of sin. But wait. It spoke.

"'Dubroc, it said, and I did not so much hear a voice as I knew that words came and I understood them. Dubroc, what have you done? Am I what you designed, what you want me to be? Can you say that I came from your hands? Much as you love beauty, did you make me as you see me now? No. But you might have done so. In the old days, before you gave in to suffering. An artist suffers. But he does not let it kill his soul. Suffering is his life; without it he never lives. You gave in to it; you failed.

"'You loved, Dubroc. Marie, remember? And the studios in Paris? Marie standing for hours as you struggled to fix in clay the dainty poise of her head, her gently sloping shoulders, her delicate arms and hands? And you loved her. Then the war, and the little village of Desprez. Marie back home. The fighting that swallowed up Desprez, and Marie was killed. Then you ran away. You could not remain and suffer, Dubroc. It was too much for you. Marie was beauty. But so was France. You loved Marie. Did you not love France? Yet you deserted. Something was taken from you, yes; but you threw the rest away. Did you escape suffering? No, denied beauty, you plunged into the ugliness of despair. Do you think that Marie does not live? Her beauty, was it all of the face, the poise of the head, the soft, round figure? The

soul, Dubroc, could you not see? And is it dead — it, that was
pure beauty?

" 'Yes, overwhelmed by despair, you thought only of yourself,
forgetting France and her enemies. You wandered, lost. You
crossed the sea at the first opportunity. You created ugliness because you were hungry, salving your tortured conscience with the
thought that what you wrought was pious. Now you have created
me. And what was I? Nothing more than a twisted mass. But
could you have created me as you see me now? You must, Dubroc.
I am what you might have made me. For your soul's sake you
must give me form. I cannot remain as you have made me. I
was hideous. I symbolized your sins. You must atone. You must
make reparation.

" 'You learned to work in beauty when you loved Marie. Marie
died, but she lives again. She was stainless; she cannot die. You
deserted France. But France still lives. France is beauty, Dubroc.
France cannot die. But you, Dubroc. You must some day die.
Will your soul endure? Can it survive with all this stain of ugliness
upon it? No, ugliness is sin. You must remove it. Just one work
of utter beauty, one work to wipe out all the memory of sin, and
you will have been fulfilled.

" 'The light dropped, *mon père*. Dark came and covered everything with a thickness like night. The angel was blotted out. Then
suddenly it reappeared as light returned. But it was not the same.
My statue was gone — the one I knew to be mine. The other, the
one I had made for Stancati, stood there against the wall. I saw
all its grossness, the whole hideous caricature. I stood up. Hastening to the door, I locked it. A hammer lay close at hand. Two
blows and the wretched thing I had made lay in fragments. I
went to work again. My mind blazed with remembrance. I brought
forth the image that was flaming there. I do not know how long
I worked. Sometimes I heard steps approach the door, and whispered speech. I did not stop. Then, suddenly, it was finished. My
angel was finished. It had come from my soul. It will live, *mon
père*. Shall I? Have I atoned for all the ugliness I have made?
All the ugliness that first stained my mind and then smirched
my soul? Marie. France. Marie was killed. I thought that France

had killed her. I ran away. I who could not suffer one agony have suffered a thousand. And now, have I suffered enough? Have I accomplished enough? Have I atoned?'

"His voice faded; his eyes closed. I knew by the labored breath that he had spent himself. His pulse was nothing more than a quiver. But again he roused himself. He opened his eyes and looked toward me. 'It is yours,' he said; 'my angel is yours, *mon père*. Tell Stancati I give it to you. He is a good man.' The last word was merely a sigh in his throat. Swiftly I worked. There was yet strength enough for the whispered answers, for a scarcely uttered Act of Contrition, for the Viaticum. The holy oils. The holy office. Dubroc was dead."

Lonely Lives

SEÁN O'FAOLÁIN

FROM between the little wayside platforms the railway shot two shining arrows off into the vast bogland where they vanished over a rise that might have been imperceptible without them. It was just before sunset in early spring, a soft evening of evaporating moisture and tentative bird song; for the birds seemed to be practicing rather than singing, twirling and stopping, and twirling and stopping, and when the bold thrush rolled out a whirl of sound he might have been mocking all the other eager, stupid little fellows like the bullfinch or the tits who had not yet learned their songs.

The three men, leaning on the wooden railing along the platform, looked at the blush of the sun on the last drifts of snow on the far-off mountains, and though every rail was cut into an A shape on top, uncomfortable for arm or elbow, they found it restful to lean and look over the bog, speaking hardly at all. They had been walking all day on the bogs and now were dog tired. They were waiting for the last train to take them into the country town where they all three taught in the Diocesan College.

The priest stood in the middle, a young man, too fat for his years, with drooping lids, puffed lips, and a red face as if he suffered from blood pressure. The same features on another man might have suggested a sensual nature but there was in his heavily lidded eyes a look that was sometimes whimsical and sometimes sad, and that look, with the gentle turn to his mouth when he smiled, gave him the appearance of a man who had gone through many struggles and finally solved his problems in a spirit of good-humored regret. So, now, as he pulled at his pipe and

From *Story*, October, 1936. By permission of the author.

looked down into a cold bog stream that flowed beneath them, his chin and his piggy jowls rested on his Roman collar, expanded around his little mouth as if he might at any moment break into a little, silent chuckle. Only, you might have felt, those tired eyes would not even then have changed: they would have mocked his own smile.

On his left, carrying the haversack, was a small dark man, with a slim small body and a button of a head and clipped dark mustaches. The main thing about him was that he did break occasionally into sudden talk, and when he did he banged the hard railings repeatedly or lifted his two fists in the air and slapped his forehead. He did all these things suddenly, when he cried out:

"Why on earth is this ten-thousand times accursed station three miles from the village? What's it here for at all? My God, what a country! What — is — it — for?"

"To take us home," said the third man, and the priest's belly shook a little, too tired to expel laughter.

There was nothing remarkable about this third man except that he had handle-bar mustaches and a long black coat and a black hat that came down low on his forehead and shaded his melancholy face; when he spoke, however, his face was gentle as the fluting of a dove. There was nothing resigned about him; his oblong face was blackberry colored where he shaved and delicate as a woman's where he did not. His eyes were lined with a myriad of fine wrinkles. They were cranky, tormented eyes, and his mouth was thin and cold and hard.

"I know," cried the small man. "It's some bloody Czar that did it. Some fool of an undersecretary long ago or some ass of a flaming lord lieutenant who took a ruler and drew a line across Ireland and said, 'That shall be the route of the new railway!' God, what a flaming country!"

"I wonder," said the sad man, Hanafan, in his slow voice, "do the common people ever admire scenery?"

"Now, that's very interesting, Hanafan," cried the small man across the priest's chest. "That's a most extraordinary thing. I often thought of that. Isn't that a coincidence?"

"Well," said the sad Hanafan, blushing modestly, "it's a common enough idea, you know."

"Of course they do," said the deep basso of the priest.

"But do they, do they, do they?" shouted the little man, hammering the railing.

The priest nodded, never taking his eyes from the stream or his pipe from his little mouth.

"How do you know?" demanded the small man, leaping backward and whirling his head left, right, and up in the air, as if the answer were a bird.

"Why wouldn't they?" grunted the priest.

"I know what you mean," interrupted the small man and he wagged his finger into the priest's face. "I know. I met men like that. Our gardener at home, for example. I'd say to him — he was an awful old drunkard — he'd be lying of a hot summer's afternoon under an apple tree — a lazy old ruffian. 'Grand day, Murphy,' I'd say. 'Oh, a grand day, God bless it,' he'd say, 'and isn't it good to be alive?' But, that's not admiring the scenery," went on the small man. "It's not being *conscious* of it. It isn't, if you understand me, projecting the idea of the beauty of the scene, into one's own consciousness. Is it, now, Hanafan? And that's what you mean by admiring the scenery."

"Well," said Hanafan, and his words were like prize pigeons that he released one by one from his hands, "I don't know. I'm not sure I mean that."

"Then what the hell *do* you mean?"

"If a man said to me," went on Hanafan, in his downy voice, " 'I do be sometimes sitting here, Mr. Hanafan, enjoying the cool of the evening,' I'd say that that man was enjoying the scenery even though he might not know he was doing so at all."

The priest nodded. The small man looked contemptuously at Hanafan who now began to quote from Gray's "Elegy" in his round, womanly voice, all the time looking sadly at the warmth of the sun fading from the distant grains of snow, and the mountains becoming black and cold:

The lowing herd winds slowly o'er the lea. . . .

"I know, I know," interrupted the other, but Hanafan went on quietly,

> The ploughman homeward plods his weary way;
> And leaves the world to darkness, and to me.

"You see I feel," he said, "that the ploughman responded to the sense of the end of the day, and the way the fields were all gentle, and dark, and quiet. Just like that bog there . . . is . . . all. . . ."

His voice died out.

"Ah, damn it," said the small man in disgust, "that has nothing to do with it."

"It has, Mr. Governey," murmured the priest. "In a sense it has."

"Every man," cried Hanafan, aroused with such vigor that the other two glanced at him, "lives out his own imagination of himself. And every imagination must have a background. I'll tell you a queer thing. It's about the station master in this station a few years ago."

The priest nodded and chuckled aloud.

"He was nearly sixty-five," said Hanafan. "And he was married, and had a grown-up son in New York, and a daughter, a nun in South America."

"I sent her there," said the priest. "A nice poor girl she was, God rest her."

"Did she die?" asked Hanafan, and when the priest said, "Yes," he fell silent and forgot his story until the other teacher reminded him crossly.

"Yes," said Hanafan. But, again, he stopped because the station porter came out with two oil lamps, one of which he put into the frame of the standard near them.

"It's a grand evening, father," he said as he turned up the wick.

"Is she late again?" asked the priest, and the porter looked up the line at the signal, and said:

"Aye, she's a trifle behindhand, I'm thinking."

He got down and drew a great silver watch from his corduroy vest and held it up to the setting sun, peering through the yellow celluloid guard.

"She's due, bedad. Ah, she'll be here in a quarter of an hour all right."

The small man groaned and said, "What a country!" The other two looked up at the lamp and then away, and Hanafan said,

"Isn't it dark!"

The porter had walked away.

"Well," resumed Hanafan suddenly, "this old stationmaster! His name was Boyhan. He thought he had a great voice for singing. He was stationed at N ——" (he mentioned the town where they all lived and taught in the college) "and he used to come and sing in the choir with us. That was before your time, Mr. Governey. And he sang in the parish choir. And he'd have sung in the Protestant choir and the Wesleyan choir and the tin-hut choir if they let him. There was not a concert in N —— that he wasn't the head and tail of it, and he always sang twice and three times and it was all they could do to keep him from giving encores all night long. For," sighed the teacher, "he had no sense and the people used to make a hare of him. He couldn't sing any more than I could. He had a small little voice, a small range too, but it had no strength or sweetness; there was no richness in it."

The teacher said these words, *strength, sweetness, richness,* with a luscious curl of his thin lips around the fruit of sound. His eyes widened. Clearly he was seeing nothing but the old stationmaster. Earnestly he went on, a small glow on each cheek:

"That was all right until they shifted poor Boyhan to this God-forsaken place. And if N —— is a lonely hole, this is the back of beyond. At the same time they started the new Broadcasting Station in Dublin and Boyhan conceived a great ambition to sing there. He formed the idea that some day or other a passenger would be on his way to Dublin, or from Dublin, and he would hear him singing and say, 'My heavens, who is that with the grand voice?' And he would make inquiries — some director or government official — and stop the train and seek out Boyhan and say to him, 'What's the meaning of this neglect? Why haven't you been asked to sing over the radio?' Then there would be paragraphs in the newspapers about, Discovery of Great Irish Baritone, and Romance of a Chance-heard Voice, and so on.

"The result of this was that whenever a train rolled in, Boyhan used always to come out of his office singing. He'd be singing little trills up and down the scale, or a bar of *The Moon Hath Raised Her Lamp Above*. He was known to all the passengers and, sure, they used to be looking out for him. And there he would always be, rubbing his hands and pretending he was doing his *Dohsohmedoh*, just for delight and jollity. And even if it was a miserable wet day he'd be at it, up and down the train.

"Well, one hard, moonlight night in December, I was here, like this, waiting for the last train back to N ——. The snow was white on the hills. It was blazing. There wasn't a sound but the wind in the telegraph wires. The clouds were in flitters, in bits. I well remember it. A rich night. A deep, rich night, and no harm in the winds but they puffing and blowing."

Again Hanafan's cold thin lips sucked the sound of those words, *rich*, *deep*, and his eyes dilated under his black hat with the image of his memory. His eyes were not cranky now, but soft and big.

"I was here with a- a-. I was here with a- a friend."

He stopped for a second. The small man's eyes pounced on him, observing at once his strange embarrassment. He glanced at the priest but he had lowered his face and his mouth was clamped. In that hesitant second he saw at once a piece of Hanafan's secret life revealed, a memory of something known also to the priest; the thought of a dead friend — or perhaps a woman — something or somebody that made the memory of that night so precious to Hanafan that he could not speak of it openly.

"Was this long ago?" probed the small man inquisitively.

"We walked up and down," said Hanafan, "looking at the snow under the moon and the clouds tumbling. Then Boyhan came out and he took us across the line. He had a fire and we sat around it. The smell of the peat, thick and slab, was struck into everything in the room."

"Was it only two of you?" prodded the small man, eager to know if it was a woman.

"He showed us photographs of his daughter, the nun, and of his son, Timsy, with, as he said, a lawn tennis in his hand. He had no wife. She was dead. And there he was living alone, in the station,

three miles from the village, and his only two children in the world
away in exile. I quoted Sir Thomas Browne for him, the passage
in *The Quincunx*. We all looked out the little window. "Think!"
said I. *"The quincunx of heaven runs low and 'tis time to close the
five ports of knowledge. . . . To keep our eyes open longer were to
act our Antipodes. The huntsmen are up in America and they are
already past their first sleep in Persia. But who can be drowsy at
that hour which freed us from everlasting sleep, or have slumbering thoughts at that time, when sleep itself must end, and as some
conjecture all must wake again?"*

"Then, by way of no harm, he began to talk about music and
singing and he gave us one song after another. He sang us, *Oft
in the Stilly Night* — and, you know, he sang it well. He sang, *The
Moon Hath Raised Her Lamp Above*. I heard the signal bell ring as
he was in the middle of it and far away the train began to purr. He
was singing it so heartily we didn't like to interrupt him and as
the train became a roar across the bog and the lights went flashing across the window, he rose and went out to the platform. By
heavens, that man saw the trainload as a vast audience whirled
before him. He stood out on the platform singing like mad to
them.

"We rushed for the bridge, we had no tickets, he gave us no
tickets, and as I ran I shouted back to him, 'Hold the train!' He
paid no heed and when we were up on the middle of the bridge
he got to the grand burst, the last crescendo, of —

I come! . . . My heart's delight

and waved the train on. We were left looking at it vanishing up
the line. I roared at him for a fool, and a vain fool, but he only
bowed to us, and he bowed to the porter, and he bowed his way
backward to the office like a Caruso. The train purred into the
distance and there we two were with the wind in the wires and
the white moon on mountains.

"I went back to abuse him — it was the last train — but he only
looked at me like a child you'd strike and said he couldn't hold
back a train for anyone. The porter paid no heed to us. He outed
the lamps and locked the place up. We left the old fellow alone in

the station. We had to walk home. It was a grand, bright night. A lovely, thick night. . . ."

Hanafan's voice broke. Just then a signal bell rang. It was dark over the bog where far away the train murmured and it could easily be heard because the birds had stopped singing. There was nothing but the deep scent of the night air, and below them in a marsh, still deep from the March rains, a prattling as of a thousand tiny frogs.

"This is a lonely place he lived in," whispered Hanafan. "A lonely life. No children. No wife."

The priest rose up and knocked out the ashes of his pipe as the train roared nearer.

"Yes," he agreed.

"But," cried Governey, "what has all that got to do with admiring the scenery?"

"He sang to the night," cried Hanafan passionately. "He sang to the whole night. The moon was up. The moon!"

His voice fell and they barely heard him over the rumbling train at the end of the platform.

"We saw the moon in the flags of the Liffey as we left the station. In the flags of the river, through the trees. So must he."

"Still and all," cried the small man, "he didn't form any intellectual concept. . . ."

The train drowned his voice and its lights flitted across their faces. When they climbed into a carriage the windows were speckled with rain and the three men inside, who leaned back to let them pass, had a cold, damp look. They had been talking when the train stopped but when they saw the priest they fell silent; looked at him under their brows; and shyly tipped their hats.

"Raining up the line?" asked the priest in a friendly voice.

"Oh, pouring in Dublin, father," said one of the three men — an elderly, soldierly looking man, probably a warder in the jail at M —.

The three teachers fell silent, sensing that they had interrupted a conversation. Then they were rolling through the night, looking at the lights racing along the little hedges beside the line. Suddenly the rain that had hit Dublin half an hour before swept down on them across the mountains, slapping the windows like a bucket of water. It kept trickling and shining on the windows.

"He died there last year," said Hanafan suddenly, looking at the trickle outside the pane.

"I once asked him," the priest leaned forward to say to the small man, "what his favorite song was. Do you know what he said? *Scenes That Are Brightest.*"

The priest leaned back and gave a merry little laugh.

"Still," cried the small man, thumping his knee, "I can't see what this has to do with the question we were discussing!"

The priest looked at him, and kept looking at him, as he swayed with the carriage, but he said nothing. Angrily the small man looked back, and then he looked angrily at Hanafan whose eyes had become cranky and tormented once more. He began to wonder why Hanafan was always so sour, and why he remained on in N — if he didn't like the place, and why he had never married. His eye lit up a bit at that and he determined to get it all out of the priest when they were next alone. He tapped Hanafan on the knee and he began to ask him some question, but when he saw that Hanafan's eyes were closed he leaned back again. The priest was still looking at him so he nodded toward Hanafan and winked. The priest's lidded eyes were as immovable as an owl's.

As they rolled on through the bog the small man kept looking around him restlessly, and at last he shifted over to the three countrymen, determined to find out if the common people really do admire the scenery. He started a conversation about turf cutting, but before he could lead up to the question the train halted at a small station and the strangers got out. Then the three friends were left alone in the cold, damp carriage, listening to the battering rain. Tired and sleepy, nobody noticed that, in his corner, Hanafan was weeping silently through his closed eyes.

The Paper Costume

RICHARD SULLIVAN

RICKABY, wearing a rain-spotted brown hat pulled over his eyes, walked into the dime store and stood uncertainly looking around. In the pocket of his flimsy brown topcoat his damp hands were clutching and reclutching a dirty handkerchief and a key ring with one key on it. He strode through a thick smell of peanuts and chocolate, then through a sharp smell of perfume, all the time listening to the babble of voices in the store, a brittle drumming sound like the cooing of the doves he had kept in the back yard fifteen years ago when he was a boy, and all the time glancing around with a hurried, anxious look at the counters and the red and yellow signs above them.

Ahead, he saw a shower of orange ribbons looping down from the ceiling; he headed for the counter beneath them: pumpkin heads and horns, masks and orange rattles, witches' hats and crepe-paper napkins and aprons and tablecloths and streamers, and a row of tiny hunched black cats with erected tails. Rickaby stopped and nervously unbuttoned his topcoat. A button caught in the frayed loop of cloth where the coat had worn through, but he did not seem to notice untangling it with his left hand as his right stretched hesitantly, eagerly, timidly out to pick up a paper horn and then to put it back, to pick up a little orange frying pan with two rattling wooden knobs attached to it and then to put it back. With fumbling haste he fingered the big leering twenty-cent pumpkin heads with the grinning red and white teeth. He looked carefully and hurriedly at everything on the counter. All the time he kept glancing anxiously at price cards; he kept frowning. At last he went back to the little frying pan and picked it up, shook it softly. It made a sudden tinny clatter. He put it down. The

From *Scribner's Magazine*, October, 1937. By permission.

dark-toothed smile of the girl behind the counter faded as she watched him and waited. Finally, with one of the small ten-cent pumpkins in his hand, he asked how much those little purple and yellow cheesecloth costumes cost. The girl said twenty cents for the cloth ones, ten cents for the others made of crepe paper. Rickaby hesitated. He picked up one of the folded crepe-paper costumes, examined it, set it down again, and kept looking at the cloth one hanging on the rack on the counter.

"I'll take this," he said then, handing the girl the pumpkin head. "And these." He picked up a couple of masks, two for a nickel, one a bright-green frog face, the other a glowing blue death's head. His eyes had been wandering back to the cloth suits on the rack. Now he picked up one of the paper costumes and thrust it abruptly at the girl. "And this."

Fishing in his vest pocket, which drooped enough at the edge to show a soiled lining, he drew out a dollar bill, damp and limp from the heat of his body.

As he held out the money he glanced along the counter; then hastily he picked up one of the little orange frying-pan rattles. "This too," he said quickly.

He chewed his thin dark lips as he waited for his change and his package. When the girl gave him the bag bulging with the pumpkin head there was a corner of the paper costume sticking out. He scowled almost in alarm, tucked the corner in, and covered it carefully with the flap of the bag. Then he hurried to the front door, still furtively fingering the package.

Striding down the street, he wore the stern preoccupied expression of a businessman immersed in thoughts of big deals, gigantic combinations. He stopped at the corner, stared idly into the jewelry-store window, and noted by the clock there that it was eleven minutes to twelve. Turning he saw his streetcar half a block away. He stood waiting at the curb; then climbed aboard.

Seven minutes later, in another part of town, he got off. On the corner there was a big red-brick house with an iron fence around it. He walked up the cross street, past white houses on deep evergreen-dotted lawns, past tan-brick bungalows with slanting red-slate roofs; he carried his package carelessly in the crook of

his arm, his head high, a lofty thoughtfulness on his lean face beneath the down-turned hat. As he passed one large high brown-
brick house set close to the sidewalk, he glanced amiably up at it,
with a casual familiarity, as if he half-expected to see someone at
the windows to whom he might nod. There was no one at the
windows. He walked on.

Beyond the large brown house, almost hidden by it, there was a
small frame bungalow; it looked shrunken and out of place between the big places on either side; looked embarrassed, as if it
knew it did not really belong in this neighborhood. Rickaby
turned into the sidewalk of this house. From the pocket of his
thin brown topcoat his hand brought up the key ring with one key
on it. He was sticking the key out toward the lock when the door
opened.

"Hello, Anna."

"I thought you were never coming," she said. The noon whistles,
cold-sounding and distant, blew as she spoke.

Rickaby kissed his wife on the cheek. She was willowy and
fragile; her white skin was lusterless; thin blue veins showed on
her eyelids; a coil of pale-yellow hair went tightly around her
head; she wore an old black skirt and a white sweater that was
too big for her.

"Did you get them?" she cried, reaching for the package.

"Wait! Is she here?" Rickaby looked hastily though the archway
that led to the back part of the house.

"She's out at the side playing." Anna was already opening the
bag. She smiled, her eyes crinkling, as she looked at the pumpkin
head. Then: "Oh, is this the costume, Eddie? But it looks so
small!"

He was hanging up his coat in the closet.

"It's folded up," he explained. "It'll fit her all right. It's marked
for kids from three to five. What's the matter? Don't you like it?"

Anna had unfolded the crepe-paper costume and was looking
at it. She said nothing.

"They had some others," Rickaby went on quickly, "but I liked
this one best. Is dinner ready, Anna? I got to get back. It took
me a long time at the dime store."

"It's all ready," said Anna. "You call Julie."

As she spoke she picked up the pumpkin head and the masks, the little frying pan and the costume, and put them all on the hat shelf in the closet.

"Jooooo-lie!" yelled Rickaby, his head out the front door.

A woman in a glistening black fur coat was walking across the front lawn toward the driveway. Rickaby bowed to her. The woman nodded. She had bright-red lips.

"I wish you could see her dressed up, Eddie," said Anna, shutting the closet door.

"Yeah. I wish I could too. Mrs. Martin just went by."

Anna hurried to the window.

"That's a new coat," she murmured, in a rather plaintive voice. "Eddie, we ought to charge them three dollars for our garage."

"Then they wouldn't rent it at all," said Rickaby. "Jooooo-lie!"

"It was nice of them to invite Julie to that party," said Anna. "I bet Mrs. Martin's going downtown now to get the ice cream."

"I don't know what to think," said Rickaby.

"What do you mean?"

"I don't know why they asked Julie to that party."

"Well, it was nice of them, Eddie!"

"Yeah, it was nice of them. I wish I could see her when she goes. You wouldn't want to give her just the pun'kin now?"

"No, Eddie. She'd get too excited to eat."

As he stepped to the door again he heard Mrs. Martin's car backing out of his driveway. He called: "Joolie!"

"I'm *here!*" said a child's voice in a tone of exasperated politeness. He looked behind the storm door and saw her standing there, a red-woolen midget with a peaked hood pointing up over the triangle of hair which slanted down to her frowning eyes. "Daddy! You keep callin' me when I'm here!" It was plain that she considered him a very stupid man.

"Ho-ho! That *is* a joke!" He turned to Anna and explained in loud and grave self-accusation: "Here I've been calling Julie and she was here all the time!"

Anna made a face like Julie's, half a frown, half a sniff.

"Did you bring me a mask?" demanded Julie, tugging at the zipper of her snowsuit.

Rickaby glanced at his wife, who shrugged her thin shoulders and nodded. She was standing with her arms folded, hugging herself as if she were cold; her long white fingers lay tightly clenched over the elbows of her white sweater. She smiled helplessly at Julie.

Rickaby went to the closet. Julie stopped wrestling with her waving red sleeves to watch him. He turned to her, holding something behind his back.

"Let's *see*, Daddy!"

He shoved the pumpkin head suddenly out at the child. Julie stared at it, began to smile, then frowned.

"I — want — a — mask!"

Rickaby looked apologetic. He thrust the pumpkin head forward hopefully; then, with another look at Anna, this time as if sheepishly begging her pardon, he stepped back to the closet and got the frog mask. At sight of it Julie whooped.

"Gimme it! *Gimme* it, Daddy!"

"She's so excited," murmured Anna.

"I wish I could see her when she gets dressed up," said Rickaby. "She'll be the best-looking kid at the party!"

Anna, smiling thoughtfully, seemed about to say something, but Julie cut in: "Take my snowsuit off, Daddy!" Anna went to the kitchen. Rickaby helped Julie get out of the snowsuit, and showed her how to hold the mask over her face. A couple of minutes later, while Julie was yelling, "Quack, quack, I'm a big frog," Anna called: "All right! Come on, everybody!" Rickaby and Julie followed the slippery strip of rag rug which led across the bare yellow floor of the dining room. It was sixteen minutes after twelve by the alarm clock on the kitchen window sill.

"My gosh! I got to hurry," said Rickaby. "It took me longer than I thought at that dime store!"

He ate the baked beans rapidly, and took only one cup of coffee. It was twenty-five after twelve when he rose.

"I better go," he said.

Anna scowled slightly as he kissed her.

"It's awful trying to get home and eat and everything in an hour," she said petulantly. "I wish you could get a new job, Eddie."

"You don't want to wish too hard," said Rickaby. "A guy got laid off this morning."

He kissed Julie on the forehead. "Goo'-by, honey. You have a good time at the party now, won't you? — You think she'll like that — that costume all right?" he asked suddenly, frowning at Anna.

"Sure."

"Do you like it?"

"I think it's real nice, Eddie. It looked sort of small — "

"Oh, I think it'll fit her all right," he said quickly. "If that's all . . . Here, Anna."

He took out of his pocket the seventy cents change he had got at the dime store and laid the coins in his wife's hand.

"Don't you need any?"

"I've got my streetcar pass," he said. "Bye!"

He ran all the way to the corner and just caught the streetcar that passed any time between twenty-eight and twenty-four minutes to the hour.

The same streetcar, coming this time from the opposite direction, brought him back to the corner about five and a half hours later. He got off wearily, and stood for a second at the curb, waiting for a string of cars with flashing headlights to whiz by before he crossed. In the early darkness, now when no one could notice him, he no longer walked with shoulders back and head high. He walked as if he were very tired. He did not swagger or make believe he was a big businessman lost in thought. He did not glance with lofty familiarity at any of the big houses along the street. He walked slowly, the wind pressing his light topcoat flat against him, his battered hat bent down over his eyes. When he came to the large brick house next to his own, he stopped and peered into the bright yellow windows. He caught a flash of children dancing around inside, children in red and purple and green and black and golden costumes, with masks on their faces and grotesque hats on their heads. He saw one little girl with a high witch's hat from which two thick braids of orange swung wildly as she skipped past the windows. Rickaby smiled, stood on his tiptoes in the darkness on the leaf-strewn sidewalk, staring into the windows. Then suddenly the front door of the house slammed; someone came whistling down the steps. Rickaby hastily bent to tie a shoestring which did not need tying. The whistler, a burly man, strode hurriedly down the sidewalk toward him.

"Hello . . ." In the greeting there was that curious incomplete note that comes with a half-recognition in the darkness.

"Hello, Mr. Martin," said Rickaby. Straightening up, he walked on; he turned hastily to cut across his own lawn.

When he opened the door, Anna was sitting in the big chair looking at the midsummer number of a fashion magazine. The radio, which for the past few weeks had been fading out and then bursting wildly on, was now scratchily, softly humming.

"She's not home yet," announced Anna as he kissed her.

"No. I saw the kids in the window just now when I went past."

"Did you see Julie?"

She put the question so quickly and in such a strange voice that Rickaby stared at her a moment before answering.

"No. I couldn't find her. How did she look?"

Anna hesitated. Her eyes flew around the little living room, and she seemed to be swallowing.

"What's the matter, Anna?"

"The other kids all had cloth costumes," she said.

For an instant Rickaby looked hard at the hook on which he was hanging his topcoat. The coat closet was dark, but the hook caught a queer metallic reflection of light.

"Why, I saw those cloth suits at the dime store," he began. "I — they looked cheesy, Anna. They looked cheap."

Suddenly the radio burst out in a fierce crash of music. Quivering, vibrant noise filled the room; the air tingled with noise. Rickaby jumped to the radio, glaring at it; but before he could twirl the knob the music softened to a scratch again.

"These were handmade costumes," said Anna. "They were wonderful, Eddie." She stopped to swallow and blink. "Danny across the street had a little pirate suit with a felt hat and a big feather in it. Shirley had a clown suit out of silk — "

"Silk?" muttered Rickaby. "Silk?" The muscles at the side of his jaw tightened, and a little lump began to wiggle across his dark sunken cheek.

"It made me feel bad," Anna murmured, bowing her head over her midsummer fashion magazine. "Maybe I shouldn't want so much for her. But when I saw those other kids — "

"This neighborhood!" burst out Rickaby. "They're all a lot of snobs with their silk suits for kids! Ha! Kids with silk suits!"

A tear fell — tap! — from Anna's eyes to the flat black-and-white page of the magazine.

"I'll go get her!" yelled Rickaby. "I'll tell old man Martin! I'll tell them all what the hell — !"

"No!" cried Anna. "No, Eddie!"

"They won't insult my kid with their silk suits!"

"Eddie! It isn't *their* fault! It was nice of them to invite Julie!"

The tears stood in big brimming drops on Anna's eyelids. Rickaby started toward the coat closet.

"What would they think if you came after her like that?" murmured Anna reproachfully.

"I wouldn't care what they thought," said Rickaby in a low voice as he swung around and seated himself on a stool with cheeks in palms, and glared at the worn spot on the rug.

"Eddie . . ."

He looked up.

"It made me feel bad, Eddie. She's cuter than any of them."

"Yeah! And she's just as smart as any of them! Hell!"

"Eddie . . . Eddie, don't look that way!"

"Oh, hell," he groaned. "She oughta have a silk costume. She's got it coming, that little honey! But I can't help it, Anna! I can't help it. They had those cloth suits at the dime store, and I wanted to get one of them, but they cost twenty cents. I saved a dime. A dime! God, and the rest of those kids have silk suits!"

He cried out at her frantically. Her eyes were very round and dark and on her clasped hands the bones showed bluish and smooth beneath the skin.

"Eddie . . ." She spoke in a low, sweet, sad voice, as one some-times speaks to a crying child; and before she went on she waited a moment, as if to let her silence soothe him. "Eddie, I know you can't help it. I know. I'm sorry I felt that way, Eddie."

"Aaaah! It's the only way you can feel!"

Just then there was a scraping and bumping on the front steps. Rickaby sat on the stool glaring at the rug while Anna hurried to the door. He didn't even glance up as Julie bounced proudly into the living room. The radio became a trifle louder when the door slammed.

"Well!" cried Anna. "Look who's here, Daddy! A little girl home from a party! Did you have a good time, honey?"

Without answering, Julie stared at Rickaby. She pulled away as Anna was helping her off with her snowsuit, and with one red sleeve on her arm and the other dangling she swaggered impor-tantly up to her father. She held the green frog mask up to her face. "Boooo!" she screamed, and giggled delightedly. Rickaby did not look up.

"Booo!" cried Julie at Anna.

"Oooh!" Anna backed away, her hands to her face. "Here's an old frog going to get me. Ooh! Help me, Daddy!"

Julie chuckled.

"It ain't a frog — it's me," she announced, giving Anna a con-temptuous but indulgent grin, as if after all the mistake had been natural. Then she drew a little cellophane bag of orange and black gumdrops from her pocket.

"Oh, candy!" exclaimed Anna. "No, no, don't eat it now, dear! Come here. I'll help you take your snowsuit off. Did you have a good time, honey?"

Julie stared at her mother, and began marching up and down the room in time with the radio. Her face was puckered up in an impudent smirk, her eyebrows raised, her lips pressed tight together. She swung the frog mask and the bag of candy wildly, her empty sleeve flapping.

"March, march!" she cried. "March, march, march!"

Anna looked anxiously at Rickaby. Then she pulled Julie to her and tugged at the snowsuit sleeves.

"What did you do, honey? Did you play games?"

Julie twisted her lips and arched her eyebrows.

"Did you have ice cream?"

"Yes — !"

"Cake?"

"Yes — !"

"Chocolate milk?"

Julie shook her head and squirmed out of Anna's grasp. Anna giggled and glanced again at Rickaby.

"But tell me what you had to eat, honey. What else?"

"On'y candy." She swung the bag of gumdrops and hit Anna in the forehead. Again Anna giggled. She lifted the child to her lap, rumpled Julie's hair playfully, and, seizing the snowsuit by the ankles, yanked it off.

"*Mamma!*" stormed Julie. "Be — careful — of — my — *costume!*"

She jumped off Anna's lap and fussily, indignantly, very carefully began to straighten the crumpled little crepe-paper costume across her chest. Rickaby looked up.

Julie stood in the middle of the room, frowning. Her little hands were patting the wrinkles in the paper costume. It was a yellow apron with orange dots; it went from her neck to her knees and tied at the back in a battered bow. She patted it and smoothed it, like a bird preening, and they could see her indignation gradually turning to concern, and then her concern to pride.

"There!" she said sternly. "Now you be careful, Mamma!" She fluffed up the skirt of the costume and pranced across the room swinging the bag of candy.

Rickaby looked at Anna. They looked at one another for the space of three breaths. Rickaby's eyes became gentle and a little ashamed. Over in the corner of the room, in front of the radio, Julie had all the orange and black gumdrops dumped out on the rug. When they glanced at her she was chewing juicily, her eyes closed, her eyebrows arched complacently, her head nodding from side to side to the tune of the music. In each hand, very daintily, she held a corner of the paper skirt.

Rickaby stood up, walked across the room to his daughter. He picked her up and snuggled his face into her little warm shoulder beside the neck. For a moment he stood there, holding Julie, sway-ing with her, rocking her a little, loving her. He was very careful not to disturb the folds of her paper costume.

Then Anna came across the room to them. She put her arms out.

"Be careful, Mamma!" warned Julie cautiously.

Anna smiled, very softly and a little pathetically. She stepped back.

"See?" murmured Rickaby to his wife. "She likes her costume! Don't you, honey, don't you?"

The Tempting of Michaeleen

THOMAS F. HEALY

MICHAELEEN was up with the dawn. He untethered Finn mac Cool, the brown-bearded billy-goat, behind the house and led him up the hill to graze and romp in his little field. Putting the hasp on the gate, he climbed one of its mossy, high stone pillars that rose above the adjoining wall of the field, and looked down the long, white ribbon of road toward the heathered slopes of the mighty mountain of Knockfierna. He sat on top carefully so as not to rip the new patch his mother had sewed on his breeches the night before. It was the second patch in a week.

It was an hour earlier than usual for him, but he did not feel sleepy. He kept looking off intently to where the road ran softly through the early-morning mist into the middle distance. Every morning with Finn mac Cool, Michaeleen had looked down that road, a long one, for it led away to the great city of Limerick where the big ships sailed outbound on the shining sea for America and for the ports of the great foreign world. And Michaeleen used to let his thoughts follow them. But this morning he looked at it a different way, for up that road was coming a part of the great world itself.

Suddenly he craned his neck and cupped his hands to his eyes as he saw a black spot afar off, and it was moving slowly toward him.

"That must be it surely now," he said to himself. "Arrah, they'll be here in no time."

The spot grew larger and larger. With fixed, steady gaze he watched it; his heart beat quicker. Now he could hear the clop-

From *Columbia,* June, 1938. By permission.

clippity-clop of the hoofs of many horses sounding sharp over the still morning air, and the black clod began to take form. He saw now first four great horses drawing a wagon, and behind it came many other horses and wagons.

The first wagon came abreast of him. Michaeleen got set to take it all in before it passed him. It was painted in many colors, and it was drawn by four horses, two black leaders with two bays behind. A tinkling of tiny bells came from them, and on the crown pieces of their bridles they wore high white plumes that tossed up and down with their heads. And on a high seat, the highest he had ever seen, there sat perched a big fat driver with a long-thonged whip in his hand, his face half-hidden in a long-flowing scarf and with a bottle-green bowler hat on his head. He looked as if he were half asleep, only when he came by the gate he suddenly opened his eyes and turned toward Michaeleen.

"Whoa, whoa!" he shouted to the horses in a voice that boomed and bumbled from his chest, and drew rein right before the gate, and all the other horses stopped behind him. With bated breath Michaeleen looked at him, knowing he was about to say something and wondering what it would be.

"Hey, laddie, where's the Fedamore circus field — how far now?"

"An even Irish mile from here, sir," shouted Michaeleen between his hands, for he saw that the driver's ears were covered with his muffler.

"Ho, ho, an Irish mile is it? Straight, or full of twists and turns?"

"Only two turns, sir. First to the right and you come to Fedamore, and then along the high street till you turn left, and you're in the Castle field."

"You know the way?"

"I do that, sir." Michaeleen took a deep breath for courage now, as a big and daring thought came into his head. "I can show you, sir," he said.

"Well, how'd you like to come aboard then?"

Michaeleen jumped down from the stone pillar. He paused a moment and looked at the driver with wide open eyes, wondering if he had heard aright, but the stranger, smiling kindly down at him, already was reaching way over with his whip hand, and taking it Michaeleen was lifted with a mighty pull into the seat beside him.

"Giddap!" said the driver with a grand flourish of his long-thonged whip, and they were off again. Michaeleen saw that Finn mac Cool had come to the gate and was looking up at him with doubtful eyes and wide nostrils. His horns were lowered like two black spears of battle and he was set on his hind legs as if he was going to buck through the gate itself, but then as if he thought better of it he tossed his head and backed away into his little field.

Michaeleen sat silent, gripping the edges of the seat tightly and looking down from his high place at the broad backs and quarters of the bays with their polished harness and its shining mountings. Then the stranger spoke to him.

"And what's your name, laddie?"

"Michaeleen O'Conaire, sir."

"Ha, a fine mouthful of an Irish name! And to put the English on it, wouldn't it be Young Michael O'Connor? — it would. Sure, amn't I from the North country myself, only to run away from school this many a year. And it must be the fine scholar you are."

"There's no school today, sir. 'Tis like the day of a fair or a fox hunt among the gentry itself, because of the circus."

"Well, you can count this the biggest day of all and it the first circus ever to come to Fedamore; aye, the greatest ever to visit these parts. Giddap!"

Michaeleen lost his nervousness. "Everybody's waiting for it, sir," he said. "We saw the signs and poster of it. And have you got real lions and tigers?"

"Ho, ho," laughed the driver. "A whole menagerie of them, no less. And lemme see now, two big elephants from Indiay, and nine clowns, and the great Indian chief, Rain-in-the-Face, as great as Tecumseh or Sitting Bull himself any day. . . ."

"A real Red Indian?"

"No less, and chief at that of the great tribe of the Sioux, and best of all we have the one and only original Wild Man from

Borneoho. Sure didn't I capture him myself, single-handed, in the dark jungles of Harlem — I mean of Zanzibar."

"And the tigers too?"

"Well, well, not exactly, but I drew up the directions for the expedition on how to do it, and I trained them till they'd eat out of my hand. And I used to go in the cage with them till I had to take over management of the circus, and then I trained our Captain Bosco to take my place. And did I tell you about the great Barnum himself when he heard of it all, if he didn't offer me fifty thousand dollars to go in with him, only I turned him down flat. My own boss I'd be, so . . ."

"It must be the great circus you have entirely," said Michaeleen.

"What?" broke forth the driver, as Michaeleen listened with head toward him. "What, what's that? 'Tis the world's most gigantic superspectacle, with desperately dangerous, death-defying displays, of the unrivaled acme of expert equitation and acrobatic horsemanship, of champion flying-trapeeze artists flirting with death. . . . And haven't I the eight Algerian aerial equilibrists, and the dancing dwarf from Coney Island . . . no, what's the matter with me? . . . from Lilliputia I mean. And a regiment of jugglers, contortionists, sword-swallowers, and, and, but what's the use of me telling you beforehand to spoil it all for you. Sure, 'tis splen —, splen —, splendobborous, splendifferous."

Tensely Michaeleen listened, trying to understand it all in his own mind and the grand words that rolled from the stranger's lips. "Sir," he said suddenly and simply, " 'tis myself would like to belong to a circus the like of this circus and go over the wide world itself."

Only now the stranger looked at him with wrinkles on his brow. "What's that now, laddie?" he said. "Ach, let you think that over. Isn't that what I did myself, to run away as a lad and follow the bright heel of glory everywhere, only to be wandering over the crooked ways of the world, and never long enough in one spot to see the new leaves come where I had seen the old leaves wither or the wheat harvested where I had seen it sown, and 'tis getting old I am now and wanting to settle down in a wee spot of earth, in the old land itself . . . only I suppose. Ach, 'tis lonely enough, it is."

And Michaeleen heard him talk to himself in a changed voice until he gave a big, sad sigh and was silent for a while. Michaeleen sat silent too, and he could not bring his tongue to say any more of the questions that were tumbling around in his head.

Now the church spire showed in the distance, and they came to the outskirts of the little town with its white, thatched cabins and cottages; the homes of Fedamore. And a rubious sun was going up the sky, making the air ruddy with light and turning the mist to gold dust all about them, touching the prickly gorse bushes in the fields until their tops were patches of golden fire and the little dandelions that fringed the white road with a blaze of dusty gold. And there was gold all over, gold on the lowliest outlying cabins, gold on the walls of the poor.

But now as they passed a clump of tall trees there came suddenly a great cawing of crows from a high rookery, and it was as a signal. Dogs began to bark, ducks to quack, hens to cackle and the cocks crowed again. And there rose up a great stir and pother from the feathered and the furry tribe of the countryside. A big gander leading his flock of geese craned his neck and made strange, oathful noises at the wagon. And in a field a bunch of sheep looked at them with a great wonder in their mild eyes while the little lambkins sidled up to their mothers on long legs much too big for them. A crowd of magpies gave them a scolding talk from the hawthorn bushes; there was a donkey put his head over a wall and after a moment's pondering about it all grinned at them and brayed forth a loud defiant note; and a red squirrel stood on the end of a fruity hazel branch with a nut between its paws, and sniffed down at them. And there was a cry from a near-by covert where the little red foxes seemed to join in from deep in their ferny lair. It was a whole chorus of protest against this strange invasion from the great foreign world.

"What a reception!" said the driver. "They don't seem to think much of my circus. And was that gander trying to swear at me?"

" 'Tis only the noise of your great circus disturbs them," said Michaeleen.

And now they had come to the main street. The little town had suddenly come to life. Housewives ran to their half doors and leaned out over them, and from everywhere at once came a crowd of boys. With mouths agape they stared at the wagon, but most of all at Michaeleen sitting on the high seat. And a great cry went up from them, "Hey, Michaeleen, hey, Michaeleen!" — until he blushed and his heart beat faster. But he sat up as straight and as dignified as he could beside the driver.

And thus Carpo's Super-Circus came to Fedamore and the Castle field, already showing with its green grass spotted everywhere with little buttercups and great golden king cups. And Michaeleen was allowed to wait in the field as the rest of the wagons lumbered through the wide gateway, and he watched each wagon that passed.

Other drivers he saw too, strange, foreign men with brown and with black and with yellow faces, and it was a wonder before him. He saw a cage with a lion in it, the King of Beasts, a tawny one with a shaggy mane, and one with a tiger with black and yellow stripes just like the pictures of them on the matchboxes. And there was a black panther walking in a cage with noiseless movements, quiet and soft as a kitten's paws, and his eyes shining like two sloes on a bush or two blackberries on the briar. There was an elephant tied to a post, with the end of his great trunk in a tub of water and then eating a whole loaf in one bite.

And suddenly he heard a great shouting of voices in foreign accents. Commands rang out. A man with a long stick mapped out the ring, and rolls of canvas were spread out like oceans over the field, and there were big poles and little poles. He became aware of someone standing near him, and he was a man with a headdress of feathers on his head. Michaeleen knew that he was looking at a real Red Indian, and a chief too. It was Chief Rain-in-the-Face. Only Michaeleen looked sidewise at him so as not to let him know. And lo and behold, if the chief didn't turn around and look straight at him with a smile.

There were other things he saw. A house that moved, a house with wheels under it and steps going up and steps going down, with little red-curtained windows. From one of them a woman

looked out at him, and she had large, golden earrings and eyes
blacker than glassy black marbles. There was a chimney on the
roof too, with smoke coming out of it. It was a house that could go
anywhere in the world. And leashed to a wheel lay a big dog
sleeping quietly through all the noise and commotion about him.

He saw his friend, the driver, pass with a bucket of water in
each hand. When he saw Michaeleen, he stopped, put the buckets
down and mopped his brow, all asweat.

"Well, laddie," he said, "thought I'd lend a hand to my men for
a bit. Tell your friends outside the wall there I said they could
come in after the parade is over. So long now. See you at the
circus."

When he went out the gate Michaeleen found himself amid a
crowd of his schoolmates. He cleared his throat, remembering the
words his friend had confided to him.

"You can all go in the field after the parade is over," he said, as
they gathered about him, all plying him with questions — Ulich
Considine, Andar McGillicuddy, Dermot Sheridan, Darby
O'Rourke, Phelim Cochrane, Rory O'Grady, Conal McNeil, and
the rest. "Yes, yes!" said Michaeleen. "Lions and tigers and everything. 'Tis the biggest circus ever."

But now up came Liam Mulcahy, saying with a gleam in his
eye: " 'Tis the way that's all rameish and lies. 'Tisn't the biggest
ever. Didn't my uncle write from Amerikay of how he was to a
big circus in Chicago, and they had a hundred elephants and fifty
tigers and clowns galore in it and . . ."

"Well, 'tis the biggest ever come to Ireland," broke in
Michaeleen, "and didn't the manager of it all tell me himself."

"Manager?" sneered Liam. "He isn't the manager, that fellow,
but only an old fool and omadhaun of a driver, with the lead
wagon today. Sure he works for the circus, and didn't I see him
carrying the water buckets myself."

"He had to give a bit of a hand to his men."

"Arrah, he's an old liar!" shouted Liam.

Michaeleen walked toward him. He never had liked him since
the day a few months before when he made a foul blow with his

hurley in a game, and now he liked him less than ever. Liam was a year and a half older too, but that didn't matter.

"Take that back, Liam Mulcahy," he said, "or I'll give you a good punch in the nose for it."

"Well, I meant that. . . ."

But here Darby O'Rourke spoke up, who was the fixer of fights and the referee accepted by all for any test to settle the violation of the schoolboy code. "Will you fight him, Liam?" he asked. "Well, I will then," said Liam, "if he . . ." But Darby broke in. "And will you, Michaeleen?" "I will surely and two like him for saying my friend was a liar," said Michaeleen.

Only a great and grave question rose amongst them, and it was that if they went down behind Farmer Hogan's barn, the accustomed place where they held their fights free from the prying eyes of their oldsters, they might miss the parade or the growl of a lion itself. So it was decided to hold the fight the next day after school.

Soon the high noon had come and gone, and there came suddenly a great burst and shower of music that brought everybody from the houses, as brasses roared, drums sounded and cymbals clashed, and the parade went out the Castle field and up the road into the little town. The letters on the big bass drum read:

The Blue Hungarian Band

— and the players all wore the selfsame blue coats with red braid and epaulets of gold, only they all had different trousers under the coats. There was the big elephant too, and on his head, sitting on a crimson pillow with a spear in his hand, was a dark foreign man with a turban, outlined against the sky.

Everything Michaeleen noted, only he missed his friend in it and it wasn't the same without him leading it. But he forgot that for a moment as his heart leaped up within him and a great surge went through him when the band stopped in the market-place and played "The Wearing of the Green." And after the parade was over Michaeleen ran all the way home.

Michaeleen sat in the house a long time after he heard the half door close behind his mother. He felt empty inside of him, and he had a pain in the pit of his stomach. Her words kept running through his head like a refrain, "Ach, no money in the house today, Michaeleen!" He gritted his teeth to keep down the tears that arose unbidden to his eyes, half-angry tears. He could not blame his mother. Kindly she had spoken to him. What would she know of the circus anyway, what with the great worry on her, trying to keep herself and himself and Finn mac Cool together, and the little house over their heads, with her sewing and mending for others!

And yet he felt a great anger now, against something he didn't know what, against everything. He was alone in the house, in the whole town, in the whole countryside, alone in the whole land of Ireland. He thought of Liam Mulcahy, who had two ponies of his own, a Shetland and a Connemara, and could follow by short cuts the hunts of the gentry itself, who had no patch on his breeches and had a brand-new knife from America with four blades and an amber haft to it. And Mulcahy would go to the afternoon performance and the evening one as well.

Michaeleen put on his cap. He could not eat the potatoes and sour milk on the table. He went quietly out the back way through the cabbage haggart, along the rambling boreen path, through the twisted whins and belled heather to the fields, until he came to a forestine place where there was a cromlech of stones over an old mound, where ancient heroes lay buried. It was a place he used to go with his father before he died six months before, where sitting close beside him he would listen to the stories of Cuhullain and Concobhar and Maeve and Deirdre of the Sorrows, tales of the kings and queens and heroes of the elder time, that used to make his thought run out to the edges of his flesh and remind the soles of his feet of swiftness. And he would sit and listen there, under the old brown thorn tree.

He had gone there sometimes himself since then, and he knew it was the best place to get rid of the lions and clowns and tigers tumbling around in the bottom of his mind. For he could lie on his back to look up at the heavens whence the skylarks would be showering down a great sunshine of sound, and listen to the music from the throats of the thrushes and other birds around him, with no sound save the stirring of the leaves or of the insects and the little earthy things, or save the quiet noises of the small wild things like the coney and the squirrel and the hare, God's furry creatures, sure who made no sounds at all running so happy and so busy in their grassy-green kingdoms, but using all their wits about them too against the cruel snare and the peril that might trap them until with little wrinkled-up faces they died alone in their pain.

So Michealeen used to listen. Only today he could not listen, could not even look up at the sky. He sat with his head between his hands and looked deep into the ground. It was the circus that was on him, and he could not get the feel of it out of his mind. He wouldn't see the dwarf from wherever it was, nor the real Red Indian, nor the Wild Man from Borneoho. And the circus would go to Croom, to Rathkeale, to Dingle and to Bantry Bay and over the wide-swelling ocean forever. What was worse, everybody would know he was not there. They would ask him how he liked it and he would have no answer, and they would be talking about it for days on top of days with him having nothing to say. He would be shamed, he would have to hide his head. Sneak in he could not, not now after coming in before the whole village in the high seat; and if he was caught it would be a disgrace he could never live down, and maybe to be brought before his friend, the manager himself. What could he say to him?

He thought of saying a prayer to St. Anthony now, the patron saint of finders of things, only he didn't feel like saying a prayer, any sort of prayer. And it would be twilight soon anyway and asking too much of any saint to lead him to a bit of money in the dark. Besides you only prayed to him when you lost something of your own and wanted it back again. That was why he prayed when Finn mac Cool got the notion once to roam off to Bruree, four miles away, and he found him there.

No saint could find him a sixpence in the fields anyway, the price of getting into the circus.

Sixpence! A sixpenny piece! Suddenly Michaeleen sat bolt upright. There came a great hush on his mind for the thought of it. There was a sixpenny bit right in his own house, in the top-and-

marble box under the black oak cupboard. It had been there for months and he had forgotten about it. Only it was a bad coin passed on his mother on a visit to the city of Limerick. It was a c-o-u-n-t-e-r-f-e-i-t, she called it.

It was no good. Still he kept thinking about it. He could use it for a loan maybe, not a real loan but a kind of a loan, just for the circus. He could borrow the equal on it, only the one who gave him the money would not have to know it was that sort of a loan until he was paid back. And there was one person he knew would take it, and she was Maura Mulholland who ran the little huckster shop at the end of the street.

Maura was near-sighted and her shop was dim of evenings, with only an oil lamp on the counter. She would take the six-pence. She had often given him pieces of liquorice and lozenges and cakes. Everybody liked her and felt sorry for her because she was an old maid now what with her sweetheart having gone to America many a year to make his fortune and send for her, only she never heard from him again. And she waited the years for him, they said, and never married nor had aught to do with another, though many's the man asked her hand, for she was more beautiful than the singing of birds or the leaves in summer, as old Malachi Michael, the storyteller, said it. And there was a quietness about her now, they said, the quietness that grows about old maids.

She was the only one in the whole village. He could pay her back later and say that he had made a mistake. It was the only way to get into the circus.

The sound of the Angelus bell came to his ears, tolling out its slow, sad tones over the countryside. Michaeleen stood up; he crossed himself and bent his head. As he prayed he kept thinking of the sixpence; and he knew then that he could not pass it on Maura Mulholland.

The sun was sinking in a ball of gold fire and already the dark was coming up hushing the grasses. Blue stars began to glimmer faintly in the sky, and a dim horned moon shone like a silver cap set on the head of mighty Knockfierna. And near by the homeward humming of a brown bee told him of evening twilight's fall. It was time to bring in Finn mac Cool.

Michaeleen went a long way around to get to the hill. He did not want to meet any of the people, but he heard them on the road coming from anear and afar to the circus field, ahorse, awheel, afoot, while he was going away from it. Quickly he went along the pheasant heatherways of the fields. He felt like running, running forty miles away, over the hills and drouns and grassy billows of the land, beyond Knockfierna itself. Only for his mother and Finn mac Cool he would run away.

When he came to the gate Finn heard him and gave his cry of greeting. Michaeleen bent down and put his head against Finn's head, while Finn rubbed his face with his whiskers as if he alone understood the situation and the power of grief that was in it. And when he had tied Finn up he went into the house. It was empty: his mother was still at Mrs. McGroarty's who was down with the lumbago. Michaeleen sat in his sugan chair. He looked at the potatoes and sour milk on the table, but he had no wish for them, though his stomach felt as bare as a sally tree in winter.

Now to his ears there came a mingled rumor of noises from the Castle field. Michaeleen could not listen to them, and he went out the back way again into the fields so as not to hear them. Only he could not stop his feet from leading him around toward the Castle, where he never went after dark for fear of disturbing the ghosts of the heroes walking its walls and ramparts, not to speak of the Little People too that would put a spell on you in the twinkle of an eye and whisk you off to Tirnanogue forever.

But now he stood right by it, under the big red yew tree, and he could see the field with hundreds of people there and all of them laughing with joy. The show was to begin soon. A big lump rose in his throat at the sight of it all. He did not feel like fighting the next day, and what was the use of fighting over a circus you never could see!

With the fall of darkness his ears were sharper and he heard everything. The lights were going on too, and he saw the lamps and the swinging lanterns. And there blew a little wind from the field toward him and it carried the odor of the oil lamps. Long and deeply Michaeleen sniffed the smell of them and thought of all the wonders they would shine on. It was too much for him. Suddenly he turned and ran through the gorse bushes, through briar and bracken, through the long grass, over loose stones and lichened boulders, clumps of whin, mole hills and rabbit burrows. He bumped his shin on a stump, fell down and got up again. He felt a rip on the patch in his breeches, but he didn't mind it, as he ran on and on through the hedgy night.

Maura Mulholland was sitting behind her counter, knitting a shawl, when Michaeleen softly and shyly opened the half door.

"Why, Michaeleen!" she said. "And aren't you going to the circus?"

"I am, Miss Mulholland, only I forgot till now about Finn mac Cool." He paused and looked around him. The light was dim, and there was a big jar on the counter that cast a shadow. There he would put the coin. "Only I came in, Miss Mulholland," he added, "to get the change for a sixpence."

"Surely, Michaeleen," she said, "and how would you want it? — all in pennies?"

"Well, five pennies, please, and two halfpennies," he said.

She went to her little till and began counting out the money. She held it out to him over the counter, but Michaeleen did not move. He kept his fist tightly closed over the sixpenny bit. He wanted suddenly to turn and make a bolt of it out the door, but he could not.

"Miss Mul . . . Miss Mulholland!" he said, and then a dryness came in his throat and a flush to his face. He took off his cap and twisted it in his hand. He stared straight at a spot in the worn carpet.

"What is it, Michaeleen? What trouble is on you?"

But he could not look up now for the great shame that came upon him. "Miss Mulholland," he said, "I can't take the pennies. 'Tis the sixpence I mean. I don't know if 'tis good or bad. . . ."

"And why shouldn't it be good, Michaeleen?"

"Ah, 'tis a lie I'm saying. 'Tis bad it is." And now he remembered in a rush all at once the cakes and the sweets and the extra tidbits she had given him whenever he used to buy anything there; and he blurted out with the whole story of the day since the proud morning of it.

"Why, Michaeleen, Michealeen O'Conaire!" She spoke in a whisper and her voice sounded full of hurt to him. He looked up and saw her face with a sad surprise on it. "God save us all!" she said. "And you knew it all the time! Sure, 'tis just like stealing, Michaeleen!"

"Yes, 'tis!" said Michaeleen, and there was a silence now between them broken only by the faint undersong of the teakettle on the hob and the music of the turf flames, as they nodded and gossiped on the hearthstone.

"Ach, Michaeleen!" She was speaking softly to him now. "You couldn't have taken them anyway! You wouldn't, would you?"

He heard the appeal in her voice. "I wouldn't, Miss Mulholland, I wouldn't surely," he said, "and 'tis sorry I am this minute!" And a big dimness came over his eyes so that he had to grit his teeth on it. " 'Twas the circus and. . . ." He bent his head now and he could say no more.

"Yes, I know, Michaeleen, and yourself sitting on the high seat like the King of Ireland himself and hobnobbing with Red Indian Chiefs and the dark foreign men from the great lands of the world, and your thoughts on white ships and black jungles, and all before the people of Fedamore itself. Only now you're Michaeleen, without a sixpence. But 'tis the good boy you are, I'm thinking. Sure, don't I understand! 'Twas but the excitement that was on you."

Michaeleen saw that she was smiling as she spoke. "Yes, Miss Mulholland!" he said. "And I think I'll be going now, and 'tis sorry I am. . . ."

"Michaeleen!" she said. "Will you go to the circus for Maura Mulholland, and tell me all about it tomorrow. Here is a sixpenny piece now, and an orange to eat there."

"Ah, no, I couldn't. I can't take it now." He slowly backed toward the half door as she came near him.

"But you can't miss the circus with everybody there but yourself, alanay. 'Twould be a shame. And besides, 'twill please me if

you go. Here now!" As she spoke she took his hand and thrust the
coin and the orange into it.

"Arrah, Miss Mul . . ." Michaeleen tried to say something but
he could not for the great gulp that came in his throat.

"Ach, Michaeleen, asthore!" she said in a strange and gentle
voice with a sob in it. And now suddenly she drew him closely to
her and put her arms around him; she pressed his head against
her shawled bosom and kissed him, and it was just like his own
mother would have done, almost the same. He looked up into her
face and saw that her eyes were filled with tears.

She turned her head away. "Run along now," she said, "or 'tis
late you'll be and the circus itself just beginning." As she watched
him go the music of a wistful smile played upon her face.

When he came to the Castle field Michaeleen saw that all the
people were inside. He hurried toward the booth where the ticket-
man sat, but suddenly he stopped before a figure sitting on an
upturned bucket and looking deep into the ground, with a pipe in
one hand and slowly stroking his chin with the other. It was his
friend. And Michaeleen heard him give a deep sigh like the sigh
he had heard him give that morning.

And for a moment now came the sudden flicker of a thought
that maybe Liam Mulcahy was right after all and his friend only
a driver and bucket carrier, but Michaeleen put it from him
quickly, knowing it was only the tiredness on him maybe, after
managing the circus all day that made him sit down now for a
rest, the way he would be thinking to himself. And his friend
became aware of him and looked up wearily, his face lighting to
a smile when he saw Michaeleen.

"Well, if it isn't the laddie himself!" he said. "Now lemme see,
lemme see, hum, hum. Come with me, and maybe we'll get you a
good seat for nothing."

"But I have a sixpence, sir. I . . ."

"Put it in your pocket for candy. You'll be my guest tonight."

Michaleen stood back a ways and he did not hear his friend's
words, which were muttered low. He saw the ticket man lift his
eyebrows to look right at himself for a long moment and then
shake his head. But his friend the while kept on talking and mak-

ing big, wide gestures with his hands. And the more the man in the booth shook his head the more his friend talked and made great gestures, until finally the ticket man looked away with knitted brows and up at the sky, then at Michaeleen again, and pursing his lips in a sour grin slowly nodded his head.

"I had to take time out to give him some special orders about tomorrow he forgot today," said his friend, as they walked on. "Managing a circus, you know, is a big job, and keeping an eye on them all. But we're just in time now for the start of the Big Spectacle, the Super-Gigantic, Death-Defying Panorama of . . . No thanks, laddie, I ate a lot of oranges myself today. And here we are now." And taking Michaeleen's hand in his big hand, together they went through the quiet mysterious passageway into the Big Tent.

And all about him now shone such a blaze of lights as Michaeleen had never seen and a great sea of faces, tier upon tier of them, and with a deep hush over all, for the circus was about to begin.

Michaeleen's heart went thumping within him as he walked before all the people. His face was flushed, but he held his head high and tried to feel just as cool and as dignified as he felt in the high seat that morning. He could imagine everybody looking down at him, walking side by side with the manager himself who he knew now must be the manager and the only person there to get anybody in free. He was his "guest" tonight.

Even Liam Mulcahy could see him now, and would keep quiet after this proof and him having said his friend was a liar. Michaeleen's hand tightened in the hand of his friend when he thought of what a good punch in the nose he had to give Liam tomorrow.

Alarm

BEATRICE BRADSHAW BROWN

THE neighborhood of Perkins Lane was in the throes of its yearly panic. Old Pa Perkins was gathering sticks.

Pa Perkins was a very small, a very old, and a very mild man; and gathering sticks is a very mild pursuit. Nevertheless, Pa and his sticks caused each fall a wave of excitement which, starting at Perkins Lane, spread to the outskirts of the village. This was due to the purpose rather than the act: Pa Perkins was gathering these sticks to burn them.

Still there would have been no excitement if Pa had intended to burn his sticks in stoves and fireplaces where they belonged. But he meant to burn them, a great pile of them, in his back yard. Clustered all about were the neighbors' woodsheds, tool sheds, chicken coops, to say nothing of the neighbors' homes. For some years now Pa had not actually lit his fire, and always before that he had kept it well within bounds; but these facts did not lessen the annual nervousness. Pa was gettin' on now, and not to be trusted; he might set it any time; and like as not there'd be a high wind; and the sparks would fall on Will Dyer's shed, which wa'n't no better than so much kindlin'; and then —

The village foresaw a conflagration surpassing the burning of Chicago, London, and Rome.

Nell Dyer, Maria Higgins, and the Perkins girls, all of whose windows gave on the garden plot where Pa's sticks accumulated, had evolved a system of alarm and escape. Each slept with a dinner bell beside her pillow. The first one to be awakened by a red glare was to ring her bell, loud and long enough to rouse the others. Whereupon they would collect their belongings in the

From *The Catholic World*, September, 1938. By permission.

order of importance, beginning with the several cats, and depart. They had not yet had occasion to test their system, but they did not relax their vigilance, being sure that sooner or later Pa would give them an opportunity to do so.

Pa was an enthusiastic gardener, and his yearly bonfire was the result of his unwillingness to spend money for fertilizer when woodash would do — the only matter, Ma Perkins used to wail, in which he had ever been known to manifest a bent for economy.

The frame houses of the village were built close together and blown over continually by high winds from the sea. The town elders had long ago decreed that no one should light a bonfire within the town limits except by permit. Pa had obtained a permit in the days of his reliable youth; and as there was no authority by which a permit once given could be revoked, he was still privileged to burn the village down if he wished.

But as the town remained standing, there was no actual proof that he was not still reliable. Indeed, in a certain sense, his reliability increased with the growing feebleness of his memory, for during the past few years he had neglected to light his fire altogether. He continued to collect his sticks until the pile grew to a sizeable height, then forgot all about it. But as no one could tell what tricks his memory might play, the danger still loomed.

Pa Perkins — gentle, gullible, inefficient, a chronic failure in everything but gardening — was the last male representative of a family who traced their descent from the first settlers on New England shores. He had married the daughter of another old family. Both families owned houses and land and Pa and Ma Perkins, at the time of their marriage, were very well off. But Pa taught school, and failed at that; kept a shop, and failed at that; kept another shop, and failed again; went into the bank, and failed miserably. The Perkins property shrank accordingly until it consisted now of only the large house and the small garden which Pa tended with such diligent care.

The Perkins' house had originally stood alone on a large plot of Perkins' land. Its only near neighbor was a small cottage with an outlying shed which belonged to a spinster cousin. Then bit by bit the Perkins' property disappeared, parceled into lots on which other houses sprang up. The Dunhams and Nickersons and Higginses and Atwoods who moved into these houses were considered good friends and neighbors by all the Perkinses except Ma, who regarded them with cold hostility and suspicion. She scented something not quite savory in the mere fact of their being there, although her suspicions were founded on nothing more certain than her own intuitions and her knowledge of Pa's business methods.

"How much did Si Higgins pay you for his land?" she would demand at intervals.

"I got a-plenty for it," Pa would answer cheerfully, and that was all she ever got out of him.

But this "plenty" was not enough, and Ma and the girls began to let rooms. They did not lose caste, however, as the position of a Perkins could not be altered, even by poverty, and Sue and Abbie Perkins continued to patronize Nell Dyer as they had always done.

Nell Dyer lived with her good-for-nothing father in the cottage which had formerly stood alone on the edge of the Perkins land. When in her forties, the spinster cousin had married Will Dyer, to everybody's horror. She soon realized her mistake and corrected it a year later by leaving Will and a baby daughter to look after themselves. The grief-stricken Will was totally unable to look after anything, either then or afterward; and on Ma Perkins devolved the responsibility of seeing that Mrs. Dyer was laid to rest decent, and her daughter brought up respectable. Will spent the days following his wife's death mourning with Pa in the latter's garden; and as far as Ma could make out, he intended thus to spend the rest of his life.

In possession of his wife's little property, Will lived anyhow until his daughter was old enough to support him. This she did by taking in sewing. She never made more than enough to support one, and there was no question as to which that one should be. The only question was how Nell managed to live at all. A possible answer lay in the frequent church and lodge suppers to which Nell was always invited and where she ate so ravenously as to silence any doubts as to her chief means of subsistence.

Will Dyer and Pa Perkins continued inseparable.

"You're a couple o' peas out o' the same pod," said Ma Perkins bitterly. "Only you've got decent blood in you, and he ain't. I sh'd think you'd be ashamed, Sam Perkins, considerin' who you be, to be settin' 'round from mornin' till night chewin' the rag with a worthless — "

"He ain't worthless," protested Pa mildly. "He's jest out o' luck. You can't blame a body for bein' out o' luck. And besides I wa'n't settin' 'round. I was plantin' peas."

Such time as Will Dyer could spare from Pa Perkins' society was devoted to the interior of his dilapidated shed where he pursued some occupation known only to himself. His daughter had been brought up to regard the shed as hallowed territory, to be entered only at the risk of immediate and terrible punishment; and even in mature womanhood she would as soon have thought of walking into a roaring fire as into the forbidden shack. It never occurred to her to wonder what had been at the basis of this solemn interdict or why the shed held such fascination for her father. Nothing Will did caused her the slightest curiosity, anxiety, or annoyance. She never questioned, worried, or rebelled. She merely accepted.

Once only had she detected him in actual villainy and taken measures to prevent its recurrence. When she first began to keep house for him, he offered to do the marketing; but whatever the sum she gave him for the purpose, he never brought back any change. She took his word that his purchases totaled to the penny the amount she had given him, until he stretched even her credulity too far by asking her to believe that a loaf of bread and a pound of tea had cost two dollars. Thenceforward she did the marketing herself. If she happened to leave any coins on a table they always disappeared and she soon learned to keep money out of sight. How Will spent his pilferings she never knew; certainly not in any visible improvements of property or person.

Thus for nearly forty years Nell Dyer sewed to support her father and ate ravenously at church suppers to support herself. In all that time she never made more than five dollars for any single piece of work, and she never ate enough to counteract a thinness that cut the very air as she walked through it. She was not unhappy because she had never been happy; she was not old because she had never been young. At fifteen and at fifty her life was exactly the same; and at fifty its one event of importance occurred.

A summer lodger of the Perkins' wanted a quilt made, in exact reproduction of a valued heirloom. For this work she would pay fifty dollars. Sue Perkins recommended Nell Dyer.

In the grip of excitement for the first time in her life, Nell stitched as fast as her conscientious exactness and trembling fingers would allow. As autumn drew near she became obsessed with the premonition that Pa would light his bonfire and burn down her house with the quilt in it. But the quilt escaped cremation and Nell at length found herself the incredulous owner of five clean ten-dollar bills. These the bank had paid her without question in exchange for a bit of paper on the back of which she had only to write her name. This was inexplicable mystery to Nell, and she walked slowly home, with the bills in her worn black bag, trying to fathom it.

As she reached her gate she became aware of a familiar disturbance in her back yard. "Oh, my goodness," she thought. "Tommy's after the Higgins' hens again." Tommy was her cat and even with fifty dollars she could not afford compensation money for dead hens. She dropped her bag on the kitchen table and fled to the rescue.

She was in time to avert casualties, but never had the life of a hen been bought so dear. Returning to the kitchen, she opened her bag to take out the money. It was gone.

She walked slowly upstairs and stood looking out of her window, the empty bag in her hand. She was devoid alike of feeling and thought. She almost believed that she had never received the money, that the whole affair of the quilt had been fiction, as indeed it had always seemed. But she knew that it must have happened, because her own imagination was quite unequal to the task of inventing such a tale.

As she stared from her window she saw her father leave his

shed and come toward the house. Slow as her mind was, little as she was given to rational or intuitive deduction, she was still a human being and a woman; and suddenly she knew all things. Her body stiffened and trembled, and she clenched her hands till the nails dug her palms.

That night after Will Dyer had gone to bed and inviolably to sleep, the interior of his shack was desecrated by an alien presence — a thin presence with straggling gray hair and a worn dressing gown clutched about her. She carried a candle whose light exposed to her view a pile of firewood and kindling, some old newspapers, refuse of various sorts, and, in a corner swept clean of rubbish, a small hair trunk. She ran to it and lifted the lid. It was full of money.

There were loose coins of all sorts, from pennies to silver dollars, neatly sorted and piled. There were rolls of bills secured with string or elastic. Some of these were wrapped in paper on which writing was visible. On top lay five new ten-dollar bills.

Taking out one of the rolls of bills, Nell examined the scribbled paper in which it had been wrapped. It read: "Here is $1,500 paid to me by Silas Higgins for land sold to him. Same was bought by me from Sam'l Perkins for $200. W. Dyer, 1890."

Other rolls of bills were docketed with papers bearing like inscriptions, bearing the whole story of the parceling of the Perkins' land. "Bought from Sam Perkins for $500, sold to Will Atwood for $2,000." "Bought from Sam Perkins for $300, sold to Dave Nickerson for $1,800." And the money here, all here, in this trunk. Not a penny missing, not a penny spent. And smaller piles of miscellaneous coins neatly sorted — the pilferings from Nell's marketing money — from other sources unknown to her. . . .

She took off her dressing gown, spread it out, and into it piled the money from the trunk. She clawed it up in her hands feverishly and transferred it in frantic haste but she missed not one penny. She tied the dressing gown into a bundle and carried it back to her room. Then she returned to the shed with a can of oil from the kitchen.

At one o'clock in the morning the neighborhood of Perkins

Lane was awakened by the frantic ringing of Maria Higgins' dinner bell. The emergency so long and faithfully awaited had come to pass: Pa Perkins had lit his fire at last.

For the rest of the winter the village speculated over its baked beans and brown bread as to what might have happened had the fire department failed to appear when it did. They had had to forego a conflagration, but were not to be deprived of a narrow escape.

"Land alive, it's a mercy we're here to tell the tale. Another foot, and Will Dyer's house would a' gone. Ain't it a caution the way Will took on? Why, you'd a' thought it was his house burnt up, and Nell too, instead o' just that crazy old shed. And speakin' o' Nell, look what that quilt money done for her. Had the house painted and bought herself a new dress. What do you reckon they paid her for that quilt, anyway? Oh, I ain't begrudgin' her, mind. It does a body good to see Nell Dyer settin' up to look smart for once in her life. And she's took to bossin' Will around, too, Land knows it's high time. He liked to kill Pa Perkins the mornin' after the fire. And Pa, he says he never done it — swears he slept all night through like a top. But then, a body can't set any store by Pa's memory. Try some o' that baked Indian, Hannah. It's real tasty."

Man Going Home

HARRY SYLVESTER

"SO YOU have determined that no one will longer mean anything to you?"

"That's right," Stone said.

"Not even Michael?" his mother went on.

"No. Not even Michael." Stone's face was sullen. The last
March sunlight coming through the half-drawn blinds splashed
in a dull pool at his feet. In belted trench coat he looked solid
and sure; as sure as a sullen man can look.

His mother stood quietly by the console table. She had dressed
early for dinner and in her black gown looked even taller than
she was, and regal.

"You have the other children," Stone said, as though in partial
apology for his going away. "In the summer you'll have all five of
them."

His mother nodded abstractedly. "Yes. And now, having decided
that you will care for no one, you are leaving us. . . . You have
money?"

"Yes, about four thousand dollars. I was going to get married.
Remember?"

"That remark was unnecessary."

"That's right." Stone nodded briefly. "I'm sorry. I'm kind of
nervous." Quickly, he seemed younger than his twenty-six years;
younger in his sudden uncertainty, but not in his face.

"No one should be able to affect you so," his mother said.

"That's it!" He seized upon the words. "That's it!" His face,
pale through the tan, became harassed, almost haggard. "That's
why I'm leaving. Only people that mean anything to you, that
you — like, can hurt you. So I'm going where I don't know anyone."

From *Pictorial Review*, July, 1935. By permission of the author.

"I see." A certain flicker, perhaps of humor, quirked at her lips. "You have decided to become a misanthrope."

"I didn't have to tell you," Stone said. "I could have gone and said nothing. But I told you — and now you stand there and wisecrack at me."

They looked at each other, conscious that this was the first time any altercation between them had ever gone deeper than words.

Stairs creaked rhythmically, swiftly; then a long-legged boy of thirteen dropped easily onto the landing near them. Nearly as tall as Stone, he had a long, smooth face and silky brown hair. His large mouth worried about a chunk of apple he had just bitten off, and his eyes opened more widely for a second as they saw Stone.

"Where you going, John?" the boy said. "Can I go?"

"Away," Stone told him. "You can't come. I won't be home for a while."

"Oh. Going to the office?"

"No." Stone tried to cover his uncertainty. "I'm going away. I'm not coming back."

"Not at all?" the boy's face was less bright.

"That's right."

"Going away for them again on another job?" the boy went on, hopefully.

"No, Mike. I've quit there. I'm just going away alone."

"Why? What's the matter? What'll they do at the office?"

Stone looked at his mother, but she offered no aid. Stone turned to the boy again. "Listen. Can't I go away if I want to without telling everyone about it?"

"I didn't mean anything. Only. . . ."

There was a moment of silence. "Well, that's about all," Stone said. He glanced around the room as though to fix it in memory, kissed his mother without embracing her, and, turning to his brother, held out a hand. "Good-by, Mike," he said.

Impulsively the boy flung an arm about him and kissed him. Stone pushed him away.

"You fool kid," he said, "don't do that! Didn't I tell you not to do that? You're grown up now."

The boy's eyes were luminous with tears. Stone picked up the two heavy bags at his feet and went out the door, not stopping to close it after him. He got into an old coupé and drove off.

Bill Manners had been Stone's friend at the University. They had roomed together for three years, played on the same teams. Upon occasion, Stone had even dated some of Bill Manners' innumerable girls. "There's safety in numbers," Bill Manners used to say, stretching and laughing, and Stone believed him.

It had happened two days before commencement, one day before the last track meet Bill Manners and Stone were to run in and in which they were relied upon for two first places. Stone saw it on the front page of the more sensational of the city's two newspapers:

UNIVERSITY ATHLETE
WEDS WEST-SIDE GIRL

After reading the story he became suddenly very sick. He wondered after a minute how a man could be both angry and sick — it had never happened to him before. Any girl, he thought, any girl but that one. Bill must have been drunk.

Back in their room there was a note from Bill: "Won't see you for a while. I just married Pearl Boden. Say ta-ta to Mahoney for me. — Bill."

But when Stone went over to the gym, he found that Piper Mahoney needed no telling. Whoever had ferreted it out of the marriage-license bureau had had it rushed into print inside of an hour, and not only Piper Mahoney knew of it, but most of the school.

"Couldn't you have done anything with him?" Piper said.

"I didn't know. I haven't even seen him since practice yesterday afternoon."

"We'll lose tomorrow," Mahoney said; "sure as you're born we'll lose."

"Maybe not. You were going to run me in the half with Bill,

as well as in the mile. Maybe I can take two firsts, like I did last year."

Piper nodded. "What was she like?" he said, more from a sense of duty than because of any real concern.

Stone looked at him. "I don't know," he said.

Piper nodded again and his lip corners curled in. "I hope you'll be all right for tomorrow."

But Stone wasn't, the next afternoon in the hot, bright sun. For all the previous afternoon people had talked to him about what Bill Manners had done, looking as though it were his fault. He had tossed in his bed all night. And early in the morning he had been roused from his dozing by Bill's father and half-hysterical mother. Hours later they left him, still in his bathrobe, sick for want of breakfast.

That afternoon, Stone did not run in the half as well as in the mile. On the last lap of the mile he dropped.

He never saw Bill Manners again, never heard of him — not even in the alumni magazine. But he remembered him.

Then there had been Pete Reilly. At school Stone had known him for the maddest, the most blustering, the wildest of the engineers. He had liked him, admiring his ability to do the things he bragged of doing.

When Stone was graduated and went to work for the engineering firm of Carteret, Forbes, and Company, he was pleased that Pete Reilly was to work with him. To an extent, Pete took Bill Manners' place. For one thing, Stone was convinced of Pete's greatness as an engineer. For another, the company's main office was in Stone's home city; and Pete Reilly, who came to the house for dinner, had begun to taken an interest in Stone's sister.

When they worked out of town, they slept in the same tent or shack. And when Pete Reilly got drunk, Stone would undress him and put him to bed. He blustered and swore and rolled in his walk, but he was a good engineer. So Stone liked him and knew him for his friend.

One day, stumbling on the spillway of a nearly completed dam, Pete Reilly fell a hundred and thirty feet onto rocks.

Finally there had been Linda Vaughn. Stone came back from

the completion of the dam, unconsciously looking for something. He found it, or thought he found it, in Linda Vaughn. Two months after he met her, he was engaged to her. Tall and very fair, she had come from many generations of beautiful women. Her ash-blond hair was drawn tightly back from her forehead, and her lips were usually faintly parted, giving her an appearance of breathless expectation. However childish this may have seemed to a few people, it was always apparent not more than a minute after you saw her that she was very much a woman.

She used to say: "John-ny . . ." and run her long fingers through Stone's brown hair.

Just before he left for Central America to work on a bridge, he asked her to marry him when he returned; and he thought her head had nodded against his mouth.

Stone was away nearly a year. He could remember her very easily in the still, blue nights of the tropics, when the stars were just over the mountains. He remembered her during the day as he cursed at Indians and peons in a broken Spanish patois. And at bedtime, when mosquitoes stung him and he could hear the tinklings of native lutes played by village girls in the hamlet below the hillside, he thought of Linda and her hands. Her hands were long and fine and very beautiful; he would go to sleep remembering their touch about his head and shoulder.

The building of that particular bridge was difficult. The native laborers were incredibly sluggish and dull, and they ran into quicksand on one side of the river. But they built the bridge, and Stone came back from its building lean and hard and feeling very much a man. Old Carteret raised his pay, told him bluntly that he was a good engineer, and to take a month off.

An hour after Stone reached home his mother told him that Linda Vaughn had eloped the week before.

So Stone had gone away. First, though, he spent three weeks at home, mainly to tell the youngest of his brothers, Michael, certain things that Stone felt he should know. Then Stone told himself and his mother that no one longer meant anything to him, not even Michael. And he strode from the house into the late March sunlight, got into his old coupé and drove off.

He went to a village in western Massachusetts, arriving with the spring, which was late that year and which he, being city bred, had never really seen. True, the university was near open country, but his eyes had been closed afternoons to all but a reaching gray stretch of cinder path. And as an engineer his interest in the seasons was wholly professional, as when he would note that the ground had begun to thaw, and they would have to be more careful. To him, nature was an enemy, subtle and powerful, to be overcome, circumvented, bound. Now, for the first time, he walked freely through the early spring.

Apple trees in a near-by orchard put forth tight, gray-green balls of leaf clusters. Robins, occasional at first, became ubiquitous. The green shoots of bulbs came out of the earth like knife blades. Forsythias, each day clearer and more golden, cried like bugles from terrace and lawn. Jonquils burned with a clear, still flame from corners of privet hedges, and always the ground was damp and lush. Brooks were fat now, roaring in their renewed strength and power; and Stone, lying on the ground to drink from one, communed deeply with the earth.

He lived in two rooms in the back part of an old house owned by two elderly sisters, Martha and Sylvia Morley. From his bedroom window Stone could watch the ever changing blueness of the hills.

"There are some fine young people in this town," Miss Martha Morley told Stone one day. "I must see to it that you meet some of them."

"I'm pretty busy," Stone said. He read a great deal when in the house and sometimes drew plans idly, so they would think he had work to do.

"But you ought to see people sometimes," Miss Martha Morley persisted. "Loren Hardesty and his sister are fine young people. He teaches in the school." There was, Stone had noted indifferently, a preparatory school near by.

"Yes," Stone said politely. Three days later Miss Martha Morley asked him to dinner, where he met a tall young man, a year or so his elder, and the young man's sister, Deborah Hardesty, a girl of twenty-one or two. Stone did not think her in any way beautiful. For a moment he was oddly angry at her, for her hair, though unparted, was a shaded blond like Linda Vaughn's and drawn as tightly back into a hard knot. Later he admired the clearness of her eyes and skin and her frank, nearly childlike gaze.

"You walk a good deal in the hills?" Loren Hardesty was asking. He had a longer face than his sister, but the same clarity of eye and skin. "Deborah and I do often. Have you been as far as the Leaping Water?"

"No, I've not taken many long walks; I'm still afraid of getting lost. But I've heard it is very beautiful there."

"It is," Deborah said. "We walk there often."

"We're going the day after tomorrow," her brother said. "Come with us, if you care to."

The pleased faces of the sisters Morley and the warmth of their elderberry wine prompted Stone to acquiesce, though he was vexed with himself later on.

April rain swept under the maple trees where he waited for the Hardestys on the small, triangular green in front of the white Congregational Church. Stone saw the girl coming along the flagged sidewalk, alone.

She wore a light belted raincoat, trim overshoes, and a felt hat whose wide brim was pulled low. She didn't look up until she was near him. Then she was laughing without sound.

"Hello," she said. "Loren couldn't come this afternoon. He had to stay at the school."

"You're sure it isn't too wet for you?" Stone said.

"No. I like the rain. I'd have gone alone, if neither of you could come."

"Let's go," he said. They struck off down a side road that led past the white church, dipped into a meadow, and was lost.

Stone saw the rain billow and fold like gray curtains. The road, now a thin path, straggled out ahead of them, a paler marking in the dun and dull yellow of the fields. Low stone walls divided the land into great squares. Brambles grew near some of the walls, and in spots the loosened stones afforded only an uncertain footing. Nevertheless, the girl walked surely, almost swiftly along the wet path, and climbed the walls unaided. But she was at all times a woman, never losing poise, never making an ungraceful movement. He saw these things.

She pointed once, almost without pausing, to a patch of quick yellow. "Crocuses were on time this year. Almost everything else was late."

The rain fell steadily, without force. The meadows had started to slope upward, and there was a scattering of still-bare trees and undergrowth. Abruptly the path began to climb, and when they reached the hilltop they turned sharply and went south along the ridge.

They had been walking over an hour when the girl stopped: "Listen." For some time there had been a roaring like the sound of wind; he could hear it now more strongly, through the whisper of the rain.

"The Leaping Water," she said. They continued upward with the ridge. The trees were thicker, the angles of the ground more sharp. Suddenly, through the moss-green tree trunks, Stone saw a flash of dull white silver. The roaring was louder. Their pace had quickened when, without warning, a narrow, steep gorge opened at Stone's feet.

Between the sheer walls its rocky bed fell rapidly to the east in a series of large, irregular steps. It was cool looking and green with its heavy blanketing of moss. From the step just to Stone's right and on a level with his head, swift water leaped in a thin, bright arc, almost clearing the succeeding step. Mist and spray filled the gorge, fountaining up and falling slowly back; and across the steps that stretched away and down the hillside, the shallow, swift stream of water ran, shooting from them in small cascades – miniatures of the glorious one above Stone's head that gave the fall its name.

Stone did not move. It was like nothing he had seen before. He had seen streams bigger and more turbulent, had helped to harness them. But always they had been his enemies. This stream he could like; it was small enough to be friendly and his eyes and ears drank in its beauty.

As they neared the village the sun broke redly through the clouds before setting behind the hills. And on a high terrace about a house on the edge of the village, forsythia, fresh from the rain, was more yellow than gold.

"That's our house," Deborah Hardesty said. Then: "Why don't you come for dinner?"

"I'm pretty dirty."

"Go home and wash." She laughed. "If you're cramped in the Morley's bathtub — why, we have a shower."

Stone remembered, caught himself. "No. I'd better not. I've some work to do."

She nodded. "I'm sorry. Some other time, then. Loren will probably see you around the village."

Stone avoided both the Hardestys for a week. Then, at the post office, he and Loren Hardesty met. "I'm sorry I couldn't go along with you and Deb last week," the latter said. "I hear you saw the Leaping Water."

"Yes. I'd never seen anything like it."

"We're going again tomorrow, if you'd like to come."

"All right. I'd like to see it in the sun."

Stone wondered later why he had said he would go. He told himself that what he liked about Hardesty was the man's impersonality. Neither he nor his sister had asked why Stone had come to the village, what he did, or even where he was from. That night, reading, Stone was curiously annoyed that he should wonder whether Deborah Hardesty would really be with her brother the next day.

Walking with them, Stone was happier than he had been in weeks. He did not see Deborah Hardesty look at him, once when he laughed throatily, with suddenly wider eyes. In this mood, without thought, he agreed to come to the Hardesty home for dinner the next evening.

There were other days in the hills, sometimes with the two, more often just with the sister. It was warmer. Jays squawked in the pines and maples, and a flash of orange flame proved to be an oriole. Stone told himself he had come to consider Deborah Hardesty casually, without comparing her to any other girl.

Stone stood watching her near a pool one day. Sunlight, filtered through the leaves, mottled her face strangely, making it beautiful but unreal. She was across the little pool from him, and her eyes were closed as she leaned against a birch. She opened her eyes, and they were like he thought another girl's had been.

Stone moved swiftly around the pool and kissed her. For a minute the spring was a bright cloud that enveloped him. Slowly it whirled back into its component parts of sunlight through leaves and the sound a brook makes, the noise of birds at a distance and the silver of birches. Stone remembered Bill Manners and Linda Vaughn and his reason for leaving the city. He released the girl and looked at her as she leaned against the birch, her head back and her eyes closed.

Stone wanted to make his voice harsh, but it was only sullen when he spoke. "Why did you do that?" Then he remembered that she had done nothing, merely looked at him.

He could not see her face clearly because sunlight was in his eyes, but he heard her voice, slow: "The . . . usual reason, I suppose."

Stone moved back into the shadow of a slanted trunk. He saw that her face was quite calm, even the eyes, now. He felt slightly callow.

"It's getting late," he heard her say. "We'd best go back."

"Listen," he said, looking straight ahead of him as they walked, side by side. "Listen. You probably think I'm a prig. Listen," he said. "If you don't love — or like — anyone, then no one can hurt you."

He told her the whole story, then, about Bill Manners and Linda Vaughn and Pete Reilly and how he had come to leave the city. She did not speak the whole time he talked, and Stone did not look at her. They were nearing the village by now.

"And so," he finished, "I don't want to . . . like anyone. I don't — "

"I see." She spoke thoughtfully. "Well — I'll try not to trouble you again."

There was an odd note to her voice; possibly of sarcasm, he thought, and he turned to her. But she was walking up the steps set in the terrace about her home.

When Stone got back to his rooms there were two letters on

his desk. One from his mother, the second from Carteret. This second letter told Stone with some bluntness that he was a fool; but, since they were going to throw a bridge across the river near Stone's home, they wanted him back. Construction would begin in September. "You've sulked long enough," old man Carteret finished; "come out of the sticks and start work."

Stone tore the letter up. But the next day he answered it, telling Carteret he was not ever going back to the city if he could help it.

His mother's letter was phrased as a request, but it more or less politely told him that Michael was coming to live with him for the summer. She wrote: "I could take him to Canada with us but he is at a strange age now, and since you have been so close to him, given him most of his ideas and ideals, I thought it best that he be with you this summer. Then you can complete the work you have begun with him.

"Of course, he wants to go. And I have little fear that his naturally cheerful disposition will be affected by your misanthropy."

Stone swore but without fervor. Somehow he did not feel displeased at the prospect of his brother's visit.

It was an older-seeming Michael he met at the train, a Michael who shook hands firmly. There was a baseball bat strapped to the single large bag he needed both hands to carry.

"Didn't you get enough ball playing this spring?"

"Mother said I wasn't to bother you too much," Michael said.

He was no burden to Stone. He played with the Hardestys' younger brother and his friends, whooping off to one of the several swimming holes near by or playing baseball in the morning. After the first week, Stone found himself able to resume, almost without interruption, the new and simple pattern of his life.

If Loren Hardesty knew of what his sister and Stone had said that day by the pool, and on the journey home, it was not apparent in his manner. He and Stone played tennis and occasionally walked in the now familiar hills.

Deborah Hardesty never went with them; but Stone saw her in many places. Mornings at the post office she would stop for a casual word, or lift her hand to him from her roadster fleeing by. He met her when he walked the hills alone, and when she sought the shadows on the Green at evening.

He saw her on his makeshift drawing board, sometimes she took form in the gray lines from his pencil. She stood in the shadows by his bookcase. She walked beside him in the long garden by the Morleys' house at twilight, moving like a mocking ghost through the hollyhocks and larkspur. At night he could see her in white under the drooping, dark leaves of the catalpas. And at times Stone was very bitter.

She never avoided him, and always they spoke when they met; usually it was Stone who broke off the conversation. He did not know that he looked forward to seeing her at the post office in the early morning until one day Loren was there and not she.

"Deborah's gone down to Maine for a while," Loren Hardesty said to Stone's too casual question. Then: "Why don't you come to the house for dinner tonight?"

Stone told himself he was glad her disturbing presence had gone, and that if it were not for Michael, he would leave this place, too, as he had left the city. Deborah was with him that evening — while fireflies moved slowly in the still air he saw her again under the catalpas. He felt then that she would always be with him. When Michael went home, Stone vowed he, too, would go away; not home, though.

Now it was August. Stone stood with Loren Hardesty near Long Pond, largest of the swimming holes near by, and watched Michael splash through the shallows, avoiding deep water. Once, when a plunge had carried him over his head, he swam back almost frantically toward shore.

"Still afraid of the water?" Stone said.

The boy's eyes changed tone and depth as he nodded once, stiffly. None of the Stones had ever liked to swim. In them, as in others, abided a deep, almost primordial fear of the water.

"I want you," Stone said, "to go and swim back and forth in the shallow water, edge out a little more until you're over your head, and then swim between the ropes twice."

"Yes," Michael said. There was still no depth to his eyes. He walked toward the water without haste.

"There's not a duck in our family," Stone said to Loren Hardesty. "Not even you? You swim better than anyone around here."

"No. I life-guarded every summer I was home from school, but I never liked it. I used to make myself fetch eighteen feet to bottom and stay there hunting for a shell, although I wanted to come up; and I used to swim sometimes for a mile or two in the ocean alone, just to prove it could be done. I gained self-confidence, but I never lost my fear. Even now, every so often I become panic stricken in the water for no good reason; then I swim fast until I can touch bottom with my toes." Stone laughed.

Hardesty nodded. "It's something born in one. I'm afraid of height, I know. Some are afraid in a crowd."

They watched Michael go into gradually deeper water, swim in it for a few seconds, then turn sharply and head for shore.

"See?" Stone said. But to Michael he said nothing.

In the days remaining he was with Michael more, taking him into the hills, showing him the things which had been so new to himself that spring. He swam with Michael, trying to give the boy assurance. When they took a long drive to the ocean and salt water, Michael did rather well; but the less buoyant, flat-tasting water of the ponds with their mud bottoms was disheartening.

Once, in late August, Michael took his brother's arm as they walked home and held his own head against it. "Don't do that, you fool kid!" Stone said. He drew his arm away.

Three days before Michael was to leave — and Stone had promised himself he, too, would go away — Stone saw Deborah Hardesty near the Green; and he went another way. That night, walking late in the Morleys' garden, he saw the gray beginnings of dawn before he tried to sleep.

He could not avoid her the next day at Long Pond, where he had gone for a last swim with Michael. Michael saw her first and called to her where she stood by the water with her brother.

"Hello, Michael." She came a few steps closer. "And John — how have you been?"

"Good," he heard himself say, keeping his voice steady. "You look well. I didn't think I'd see you again. Michael's going home day after tomorrow, and I'm leaving too."

"Home?"

"No. I'm not going home."

"Oh . . . Michael seems to have grown bigger in the month I've been gone."

"But he's still not much of a swimmer. Are you going in?"

"No. The water's too warm. I would have gone to the ocean today, but my car's being repaired."

Stone went into the warmish water with Michael following him. Michael shivered; Stone did not himself like the feel of the bottom as the coarse sand near shore changed to oozy mud. He began to swim, turning on his back to watch Michael. The boy hesitated a moment in patent distaste, then plunged awkwardly into his brother's wake.

Stone used a slow backstroke. "Relax," he told his brother; "take it easy. Put your head in the water and only take it out to breathe." But Michael swam clumsily, his head high, obvious distaste on his countenance. Gradually, talking to him, Stone led him into deeper water. Michael swam more surely as he saw how easily his brother moved in the water.

"Now you're all right," Stone said, "even though it's way over your head."

Michael nodded, unsmiling, swimming with comparative smoothness but still awkwardly. Stone paused and flattened forward until his head was close to Michael's. "Now follow me in," he said. He swam slowly past the boy, aware that Michael was turning stiffly in the water. Stone now swam a casual, easy, free style, not looking back.

He paused once and saw that they were nearly fifty yards offshore. On the small beach farther away and diagonally ahead of him, Stone thought he spied Deborah's green bathing suit. Then a hand clutched his shoulder and a strained, quickly choked-off voice said: "John — "

The fingernails on Stone's shoulder furrowed his flesh, but he didn't feel them. His head had gone under and his mouth, opened to breathe, suddenly filled with water.

At first, as Stone floundered, there was no thought surging in his skull: only a haze, as brownish and dimly translucent as the water. Then, very clearly, the truth came to him — it was Michael who was drowning.

With that realization, Stone's stomach seemed to turn over, and he was left suspended, weak, and all but helpless, in eight feet of pond water.

As his bodily strength went from him, comparative clarity of thought returned. Stone should get behind Michael; this much he knew. But as he turned, Michael's free hand caught his hair. Stone sank, touched mud-bottom with his toes. Even the feel of it made him shudder. He pushed against it and bobbed into the air. Stone found himself behind his brother. And as he began again to try to handle the struggling, choking boy, Stone found he was too weak to do so.

He knew, instinctively, he still had strength enough to reach shallow water — if he went alone. But towing Michael, no.

Their heads were above water at the moment, and he heard Michael's strangled breathing. He had Michael's wrist in his own left hand. And, as best he could see, no one was coming to help them. Stone's remaining strength was ebbing fast, then: Let go of Michael — that thought took possession of his mind.

After all, why not? He had segregated himself from people; no one, not even Michael, meant anything to him. Why not let go of Michael?

This thought persisted, and a great roaring was set up in his ears. But Stone continued to grip his brother's bony wrist as they bobbed feebly up and down, first one, then the other, in the water. And all the time, made one by Stone's tense grip, their two arms stretched between them like an umbilical cord of brotherhood. Stone would not let go, even when he thought it was the end.

Shorter, harder noises broke through the roaring in his ears — the sound of rowlocks, and the shoutings and splashings of men. Then, around a welter of spray, Stone saw Loren Hardesty's face, the level eyes now wild and a trifle bloodshot . . . and Hardesty had taken Michael. A boat rubbed against Stone; and even as he raised an arm to its gunwale, someone seized his hair.

Stone lay on the grass, feeling very sick. It did not seem to matter greatly whether life remained in him or not; all he wanted was for the hard, hot ball in his stomach to go away.

Hands touched him, and there was the sound of voices. Stone raised his head once and saw the vague outline of a group of people. "Why — the devil — don't you — go away?" Stone said. And his head fell again to the grass.

He lay still for what seemed a long time. The voices which spoke to him at intervals had a familiar resonance, and there was the touch of familiar hands. But when an attempt was made to move him, he cursed brokenly and asked to be left alone. For now Stone was thinking of how he had yearned to let go of Michael; and he did not want to look at anyone. . . .

Stone became aware that it was cooler and almost entirely quiet; that the fever had gone from him and some of his vigor had returned. With movements made ponderous by his lack of strength, he rolled over and sat up, shaking his head clear. He saw that it was early evening and the hills were blue. There were three people near him, Loren and Deborah Hardesty and Michael. Michael was crying without sound, but seemed otherwise all right.

"God," Stone said, from some great urge to tell his secret and have its horror diminished by confession. "God," he said, "I wanted to let go of him."

He closed his eyes, and the cool evening air felt good on his face. He heard Loren Hardesty's voice, level like his eyes, say: "But you didn't." Stone's eyes opened, then opened wide.

Michael, kneeling, buried his head in Stone's shoulder and wept without shame. "Listen," Stone said huskily. "Listen, you fool kid — "

But the boy looked up, suddenly, fiercely, "You must like some-one!" he said. "You must like me! Else you would have let go." Then: "John, you must like someone. Come on home." It was a natural, an inevitable corollary.

"Yes, why don't you go home?" he heard Deborah Hardesty say. But her voice had lost its normal coolness. Turning, Stone saw that her eyes were wet. And he wanted to laugh, for all of them, himself included, were crying; all except Loren Hardesty.

But Stone knew he was beaten.

The hills were bluer, and suddenly he was hungry. He was going home, and he was going to build a bridge. He looked up at Deborah Hardesty again.

"Sure," he said, "I'll go home. Will you come with me?"

Biographical Notes

Belloc

Hilaire Belloc, historian, essayist, poet, and novelist, was born in France in 1870 of French parentage; studied at the Oratory School under Cardinal Newman; served two years in the French army; spent two years in study at Oxford; in 1902 became a British subject and from 1906 to 1910 served as a Member of Parliament; in 1896 married an American wife, who died in 1914. With G. K. Chesterton he has been one of the most vital forces of the Catholic Revival. His publications have been numerous and varied. Among those best known are his *Verses and Sonnets*, 1895 and 1924; *New Canterbury Tales*, 1930; essays: *The Path to Rome*, 1902; *On Nothing*, 1908; *On Everything*, 1909; *On Anything*, 1910; histories and biographies: *Danton*, 1899; *Robespierre*, 1901; *History of England* (4 volumes) 1925, 1928, 1931; *Richelieu*, 1930; *Wolsey*, 1930; *Milton*, 1935; politics: *The Servile State*, 1912; *The Free Press*, 1917; fiction: *Mr. Emanuel Burden*, 1904; *Mr. Clutterbuck's Election*, 1908.

Brom

Teresa Brom (Mrs. Arnold Rhiel) was born in 1914 at Winona, Minnesota; attended the St. John Bohemian Grade School, the Cathedral High School, and the College of St. Teresa in Winona, from which she was graduated in 1936; in 1930 spent a summer abroad, visiting Austria and Czechoslovakia; has contributed stories and articles to *The Teresan Censer*, *The Catholic Girl Magazine*, and *The Sign*. Formerly an instructor in English and librarian at Slayton, Minnesota, she is now married and living in Austin, Texas.

Brown

Beatrice Bradshaw Brown, artist, musician, and writer, began her education at the University of Chicago; studied music in New York City and painting in Provincetown; has taught piano at the Pius X School of Liturgical Music, where she also studied the Gregorian Chant. She is a member of the Third Order of Carmel.

Byrns

Ruth Byrns, associate professor and director of teacher training at Fordham University, contributing editor of *The Commonweal,* and reviewer for *America,* was born on a farm near Lodi, Wisconsin; from 1926 to 1932 served on the staff of the University of Wisconsin Bureau of Guidance and Records; from 1932 to 1934 held a research appointment in the Psychology Department; has written a number of short stories and essays, as well as many technical and research articles for professional and scholarly journals, notably *The Journal of Educational Psychology, The Journal of Social Psychology,* and *School and Society.* She is the wife of William O'Meara, professor of philosophy at Fordham University Graduate School, and the mother of the late Ellen O'Meara and of Felicity O'Meara.

Callaghan

Morley Callaghan, born in Toronto, Ontario, educated at St. Michael's College, the University of Toronto, and Osgoods Hall Law School, has been seriously engaged in writing since 1926. He is the author of five novels: *Strange Fugitive,* 1928; *It's Never Over,* 1930; *Such Is My Beloved,* 1934; *They Shall Inherit the Earth,* 1935; *My Joy in Heaven,* 1936; two volumes of short stories: *A Native Argosy,* 1929; *Now That April's Here,* 1936. His work has appeared in many American periodicals. He is married and, with his wife and two sons, makes his home in Toronto.

Carver

George Carver, professor of English at the University of Pittsburgh, was born in Cincinnati, Ohio; educated at the University of Alabama, the University of Chicago, and Miami University. He served in the world war with the A.E.F. in 1918–19; became an instructor in English at the University of Iowa in 1919, assistant professor in 1924, associate professor in 1928, and professor in 1931. A convert to Catholicism, he has contributed widely to Catholic periodicals. He has edited several anthologies: *Representative Catholic Essays* (edited with Ellen M. Geyer), 1926; *Catholic Tradition in English Literature,* 1926; *The Stream of English Literature* (edited with Sister Eleanor and K. M. Bregy), 1931; *Periodical Essays of the Eighteenth Century;* and textbooks: *Points of Style, Index to Sentence Essentials,* and (with Ellen M. Geyer) *Communicating Experience.*

Chesterton

Gilbert Keith Chesterton, central figure of the Catholic Revival in England, was born in London in 1874; received his education at St. Paul's School, Slade School of Art, and King's College; during his life distinguished himself as essayist, satirist, novelist, artist, illustrator, controversialist, and lecturer; in 1925 founded the *G. K. Weekly*, which he edited until his death in 1926. He became a Catholic in 1922. His works include studies on *Browning*, 1903; *Dickens*, 1906; *G. B. Shaw*, 1909; *The Victorian Age in Literature*, 1913; novels: *The Napoleon of Notting Hill*, 1904; *The Man Who Was Thursday*, 1908; *The Ball and the Cross*, 1910; *Manalive*, 1912; philosophical and critical discussions: *Heretics*, 1905; *Orthodoxy*, 1908; *What's Wrong With the World?*, 1910; short stories: *The Innnocence of Father Brown*, 1911; *The Flying Inn*, 1914; *The Wisdom of Father Brown*, 1914; *The Incredulity of Father Brown*, 1926; *The Secret of Father Brown*, 1927; *The Scandal of Father Brown*, 1935; *Poems*, 1915.

Claudel

Paul Claudel, born in Champagne, France, in 1868, for many years a member of the French Consular service, lived at different times in New York, Boston, Pekin, Prague, Frankfurt, Hamburg, and Washington; served as Minister to Brazil, Denmark, and Japan; in 1927 became Ambassador to the United States, a post which he held until 1933. While rising to high diplomatic rank, he achieved similar distinction as one of the leading French writers of his generation as a poet and as a dramatist. Among his many works which have been translated into English are *Satin Slipper* or *The Worst Is Not the Surest*, translated by John O'Connor, 1931; *Three Poems of the War*, translated by Edward J. O'Brien; *Ways and Crossways*, translated by John O'Connor, 1935; *Bitter Leaven*; *Collected Essays*; *Book of Christopher Columbus* (a lyrical drama in two parts), translated by John S. Newberry; *East I Know*, translated by William Rose Benet, 1914; *Hostage* (a drama); *Letters to a Doubter*, translated by Henry L. Stuart, 1929.

Colum

Mary Colum, wife of Padraic Colum, was born in Dublin; educated at the National University of Dublin, the Dominican College, Dublin, and Pensionnat Sacré Coeur of Vaals, Holland. In 1914 she came with her husband to the United States; became literary critic of *Forum*, later of *Century Magazine*. A number of her stories and articles have appeared in *Dial, Scribner's Magazine, The New Republic, The Catholic World, The Yale Review, The Saturday Review of Literature,* and currently in *The New York Times Book Review.* In 1930 she was awarded a Guggenheim Fellowship in literary criticism; in 1934 the John Ryder Randall gold medal by Georgetown University for distinction in literature.

Colum

Padraic Colum was born in Langford, Ireland, in 1881; became editor of *The Irish Review* and one of the founders of the Irish National Theatre; since coming to the United States in 1914 has devoted his time chiefly to writing and lecturing. He is President of the Catholic Poetry Society of America. His writings — stories, plays, and poems — center chiefly about fairy tales or legends of Ireland. They include *Wild Earth* (poems), 1907; *My Irish Year,* 1912; *A Boy in Eirinn,* 1913; *Three Plays,* 1916; *The King of Ireland's Son,* 1916; *Mogu, the Wanderer* (play), 1917; *The Adventures of Odysseus and the Tale of Troy; The Boy Who Knew What the Birds Said,* 1918; *The Girl Who Sat By the Ashes,* 1919; *The Golden Fleece,* 1921; *The Road Round Ireland,* 1926; *The Fountain of Youth,* 1927; *The Legend of St. Columba;* and other plays, poems, and stories.

Curran

John Curran was born in Pittsburgh, Pennsylvania, in 1905; attended high school and freshman college at Duquesne University, Pittsburgh; received his A.B. and M.A. degrees from the University of Notre Dame. After teaching for twelve years in Catholic schools, he became a member of the faculty of the Florida Military Academy in St. Petersburg, Florida. In the past fifteen years he has published twenty-five short stories, two plays, one novel, and six poems. At present he is on active duty with the United States armed forces.

Derleth

August Derleth was born in Sauk City, Wisconsin, in 1909, began to write at the age of thirteen; at fifteen wrote his first play, which he presented to his home town as a Junior Class Play. In 1930 he was graduated from the University of Wisconsin; the following autumn accepted a position as associate editor with Fawcett Publications; five months later returned to Sauk City to devote all his time to writing. By 1933 he had received recognition from E. J. O'Brien, who triple-starred his novelette, *Five*

Alone; had begun writing poetry; had published a mystery novel; and had contributed to scores of magazines here and abroad. To date he has contributed over 1000 titles to over 200 markets. In 1938 he received a Guggenheim Fellowship to carry on his *Sac Prairie Saga,* his most ambitious literary undertaking, which, when finished, will consist of fifty books — novels, poems, short stories, and journals — depicting the growth and development of his home area, the Sauk Prairie Country, from about 1820 to 1950. Of the fifty books in the complete plan, eighteen have already been published. In addition to writing, Mr. Derleth serves as special lecturer in American Regional Literature at the University of Wisconsin and as director of his local board of education.

Dinnis

Enid Dinnis (Mrs. William Cassell), born in England in 1873, daughter of an Anglican minister, became a convert to Catholicism at an Ursuline convent in Belgium in 1897. Best known for her tales of the supernatural in everyday life, she has written biographies and short stories which have appeared in many Catholic periodicals in America, and which have subsequently been published in book form. Her short stories include *Once Upon Eternity,* 1922; *Out of Everywhere,* 1931; *By Fancy's Foot-Path,* 1932; *Curtain Rises and Other Stories,* 1937; *In Merlac's Mirror and Other Stories,* 1934; *God's Fairy Tales,* 1916. Her two best biographies are *Emily Hickey, Poet, Essayist, and Pilgrim,* 1927; and *Pauline Marie Jaricot,* 1922. She has also published novels: *Mr. Coleman, Gent.,* 1930; *Bess of Cobb's Hall,* 1940; and poems: *Meadowsweet and Thyme,* 1923. She died in 1942.

Eisele

Albert Eisele, born in Iowa in 1896, educated in the little red school house and a parish school, interrupted his studies to help his father plow corn; has remained ever since on a farm; began writing in 1913 and wrote for twenty-four years before his first magazine story was published in *The Catholic World* in 1937; later had stories and poems accepted by *Commonweal, Ave Maria,* etc. At present, in addition to running his farm in Blue Earth, Minnesota, he is writing a novel and, with his wife, contributes a joint weekly column on farm life to the *Sioux City Sunday Journal* and other syndicated Iowa and Minnesota papers. The Eiseles have three sons, all of whom live with their parents on the farm in Blue Earth.

Fante

John Fante was born in Denver, Colorado, in 1909; received his early education in Catholic Schools in Boulder, Colorado; later spent four years at Regis College in Denver, one at Long Beach Junior College in California; and two at the University of Colorado. He has published three books: *Ask the Dust; Wait Until Spring, Bandini;* and *Dago Red.* In addition he has worked for Orson Welles and Paramount; has contributed numerous short stories to American periodicals. He is married and lives in Roseville, California, where at present he is engaged in writing a play about Italians and a novel about the Filipino. His work has often been compared with that of his good friend, William Saroyan. He writes chiefly of his childhood and of the Italian-American people who were a part of it.

Greene

Graham Greene, born in 1904 at Berkhamstead, England, where his father was headmaster of the Berkhamstead School, was educated at Balliol College, Oxford; published his first book, a volume of verse, in 1925; turned then to fiction and wrote *The Name of Action,* 1930; *Rumor at Nightfall,* 1931; *Stamboul Train,* 1932; *The Basement Room* (short stories); and *Labyrinthine Ways.* In 1936 he published *Journey Without Maps,* and in 1939 *The Lawless Roads: A Mexican Journey.* He has worked as subeditor on the *Nottingham Journal* and on the editorial staff in London of *The Times.* His latest novel, *The Ministry of Fear,* has just been published, 1943.

Hammett

John Hammett, born in Buffalo in 1910, did most of his literary work while attending Canisius College, Buffalo, from which he was graduated in 1932 with a bachelor of arts degree; with C. A. Brady edited a Book of Canisius Verse in 1932; is at present working in the Real Estate and Mortgage Department of The Bowery Savings Bank in New York.

Healy

Thomas Healy was born in Limerick of Munster in Eire; emigrated to America and became a newspaper man, writing for small town and metropolitan papers in various parts of the United States; did publicity work and wrote advertising copy; returned to Eire to identify himself with the renaissance of his homeland

and decided to give up business in favor of writing about his own people and interpreting them to America. The author of the Irish section of the recent book, *Dictators and Democrats*, he has contributed articles and stories to *American Mercury, Commonweal, The Saturday Evening Post, America, Esquire, The Catholic World, Coronet,* and *Forum.*

Horgan

Paul Horgan, born in Buffalo in 1903, was educated at the New Mexico Military Institute; served on the production staff of the Eastman Theatre, Rochester, New York, from 1923 to 1926; since 1926 has been librarian at the New Mexico Military Institute, Roswell, New Mexico. In 1933 he won the *Harper's* prize novel competition with *The Fault of Angels,* which was also the Catholic Book Club choice for September, 1933. A number of his short stories have appeared in *Harper's Bazaar, The Atlantic Monthly, Harper's,* and *The Yale Review.* His story "The Surgeon and the Nun" from *Harper's Bazaar,* 1936, was reprinted by E. J. O'Brien in *The Best Stories of 1937.* His latest novel, *Figures in Landscape,* was published in 1940. Other publications by him include *Men of Arms,* 1931; *No Quarter Given,* 1935; *Main Line West,* 1936; *The Return of the Weed,* 1936; *A Lump on the Plains,* 1937; *New Mexico's Own Chronicle* (with Maurice Garland Fulton), 1937; *Far From Cibola,* 1938. He is at present serving as a captain in the United States armed forces.

Jordan

Elizabeth Jordan, born in Milwaukee in 1867 and educated at the Convent of Notre Dame in Milwaukee and at St. Mary's College, Milwaukee, was on the editorial staff of *The New York World* for ten years; served as assistant editor of *The Sunday World* for three years; from 1900 to 1913 was the editor of *Harper's Bazaar* and from 1913 to 1918 literary adviser to Harper and Brothers; has contributed widely to such Catholic magazines as *Extension Magazine, The Sign,* and *The Catholic World,* as well as to *The Saturday Evening Post* and *Scribner's Magazine.* Among her best known publications are *Tales of the Cloister,* 1901; *May Iverson, Her Book,* 1908; *The Blue Circle,* 1920; *The Lady of Pentlands,* 1923; *Page Mr. Pomeroy,* 1933. She has also written plays: *The Lady From Oklahoma, Beauty is Skin Deep,* etc. Her autobiography, *Three Rousing Cheers,* appeared in 1938. Her most recent book is a novel, *Herself.* She is at present dramatic critic of *America.*

Kaye-Smith

Sheila Kaye-Smith was born at St. Leonard's-on-Sea in Sussex, England; educated at Hastings and St. Leonard's College; married in 1924 to T. Penrose Fry, with whom she was received into the Church in 1929. A resident of Northian, Sussex, she has used her native countryside as background in her novels: *Joanna Godden*, 1921; *The End of the House of Allard*, 1923; *Iron and Smoke*, 1928; *Gallybird*, 1934; *Susan Spray*, 1931; *Superstition Corner*, 1934; *Rose Deeprose*, 1936; and in her short stories: *Joanna Godden Married and Other Stories,* 1926; *Faithful Stranger and Other Stories,* 1938. Her latest novel, *Secret Son,* was published in 1942.

McLaverty

Michael McLaverty, an Irish school teacher in Belfast and a regular contributor to *The Irish Monthly,* has written two novels. The second one, *Lost Fields,* was published by Longmans, Green and Company in 1941. Most of his short stories have appeared in *The Irish Monthly,* one of them having been included in O'Brien's *Best Short Stories* of 1933.

Noyes

Alfred Noyes, English poet and man of letters, was born in 1880; educated at Exeter College, Oxford. He received an honorary LL.D. from Glasgow University in 1927, an honorary Litt.D. from Yale University in 1913; gave the Lowell Lectures in America on "The Sea in English Poetry" in 1913; from 1914 to 1923 was visiting professor of English literature at Princeton University. He became a convert to Catholicism in 1928. His only book of short stories, *Walking Shadows,* was published in 1918. Primarily a poet, he has written numerous volumes of poetry: *Drake (An English Epic)*, 1908; *The Torchbearers (An Epic of Scientific Discovery)*: Vol. 1. *The Watchers of the Sky,* 1922; Vol. 2. *The Book of Earth,* 1925; *The Last Voyage,* 1930. In 1936 he published a biography of *Voltaire.* His collected poems were published in 1910; 1920; 1927; and 1941, *Shadows on the Dawn* being the most recent volume.

O'Connor

Frank O'Connor is the pseudonym of Michael O'Donovan, writer, journalist, and librarian. Born in 1903, educated by the Christian Brothers in Cork, he was until 1939 director of the Abbey Theatre. His publications include works of fiction: *Guests of the Nation,* 1931; *The Saint and Mary Kate,* 1932; *The Wild Bird's Nest,* 1932; *The Big Fellow,* 1937; *Lords and Commons,* 1938; *Three Brothers,* 1937; *Fountain of Magic,* 1939; *Dutch Interior,* 1940; and plays (in collaboration): *In the Train,* 1937; *The Invincible,* 1937; *Moses' Rock,* 1938; and other plays: *Time's Pocket,* 1939; *The Statue's Daughter,* 1940. His stories and poems have appeared in *The Yale Review, Fortnightly Review, Harper's Bazaar, The Atlantic Monthly,* and *Commonweal.*

O'Faoláin

Seán O'Faoláin was born in Cork in 1900. Graduated from the National University of Ireland, he became a Commonwealth Fellow in Harvard in 1926 and a John Harvard Fellow in 1928. He is the author of two novels: *A Nest of Simple Folk,* 1935; *Bird Alone,* 1936; two volumes of short stories: *Born Genius; Purse of Coppers,* 1938; *The Life Story of Eamon De Valera,* 1933, and *King of Beggars — Life of Daniel O'Connell,* 1938. He is a member of the Irish Academy of Letters.

Sullivan

Richard Sullivan was born in Kenosha, Wisconsin, in 1908; graduated from the University of Notre Dame in 1930; attended the Art Institute of Chicago and the Goodman School of the Drama. Since the fall of 1936 he has been on the faculty of English at the University of Notre Dame. He is married and has two daughters. In addition to radio plays and children's books, he has written numerous stories which have appeared in *Scribner's Magazine, The Atlantic Monthly, The Midland, The New Republic, Columbia, Mademoiselle, American Prefaces, Commonweal,* and other magazines. *Summer After Summer,* his first novel, was published recently by Doubleday Doran.

Sylvester

Harry Sylvester, born in Brooklyn in 1908, received his education at the University of Notre Dame, from which he was graduated in 1930. He has published approximately ninety short stories in various magazines, chiefly *Collier's* and *The Commonweal;* has also worked as a newspaperman for *The Brooklyn Eagle, The Herald Tribune,* and *The New York Evening Post.* Married, the father of three children, he lives in Orleans, Massachusetts. His first novel, *Dearly Beloved,* was published in 1942 by Duell, Sloan and Pearse.

Ward

Rev. Leo. L. Ward, head of the department of English at the University of Notre Dame, was born on a farm near Otterbein, Indiana, in 1898; received his elementary and high school education in public schools, his college education at the University of Notre Dame, and his theological training at Holy Cross College, Washington, D. C.; was ordained to the priesthood as a member of the Congregation of Holy Cross in 1927; and regularly since then, except for a year's leave of absence for study at Oxford, has been teaching in the department of English at Notre Dame. His short stories have appeared in various magazines; two of them were reprinted in the annual volumes of *Best Short Stories*.